SHADOWING THE SUN

LILY DUNN is a graduate of the Creative Writing MA course at Sheffield Hallam University. She has worked as a freelance journalist for *Time Out* and lives in London with her husband and daughter. This is her first novel.

Shadowing the Sun

LILY DUNN

Portobello
BOOKS

Published by Portobello Books Ltd 2008

Portobello Books Ltd
Eardley House
4 Uxbridge Street
Notting Hill Gate
London w8 7sy, UK

A CIP catalogue record is available from the British Library

9 8 7 6 5 4 3 2 1

ISBN 978 1 84627 117 5

www.portobellobooks.com

Designed by Richard Marston

Typeset in Garamond MT by
Avon DataSet Ltd, Bidford on Avon, Warwickshire

Printed in Great Britain by MPG Books Ltd, Bodmin, Cornwall

To Philip, 1946–2007, with love always.

Everyone chases after happiness,
not noticing that happiness is at their heels.
Bertolt Brecht (1898–1956)

PART ONE

Dad did photograph me that summer, I'm sure of it. There we were, just the two of us: a staged moment, deliberate. I am sitting on a chair in the downstairs study, the room next to the grand hall with its stone floor and uneven walls. He is opposite me, his big body propped on the edge of the table where the telephone is, a fax machine and a fan. There is little else in the room. The door to outside is open. I can hear the crackle of cicadas; feel the three o'clock sun as it floods into the room from behind me, burning my calves and my neck. My hair is tied back in a ponytail, the loose strands sticking to my skin in sweat. My hair was long then, long and blonde. I liked my hair.

Dad is changing the film. He is winding the crank and it's taking time. I am hot, so hot that I'm finding it hard to breathe, but I won't tell Dad that. Sweat is trickling down my sides, my bare legs are stuck to the chair; it's as if every part of my skin is prickling, but I won't scratch. I am staring at the floor tiles, they are brown and square, and some of them are broken. I am staring at them because I don't want to look up until he's looking through the viewfinder, until he is ready.

This is how I remember it, that summer in Italy. It's strange that I should remember Dad photographing me.

It's not that I'm fabricating it, or dreaming up some kind of fantasy. It did happen, I'm sure of it. I know because of the way the image visits me, always unexpectedly, bubbling into my quiet moments, late at night when I'm touching on sleep, drifting beside Jack; or that point of weightlessness at the end of a run, when my breathing settles and my head is buzzing. It's the unconscious moments when you have no control.

I see myself as Dad might have seen me: bleached out, my body and features blended into light, only my eyes remaining, dark and direct with that clarity that is so particular to children; or perhaps the sun throws me into shadow and it's hard to see my face. Sometimes I'm wearing Alanka's clothes, either a flowery skirt, a sari wrap of bright Indian silk, or the sexy black party dress, and other times I'm just in my scruffy shorts and vest. Sam is always there. He kicks a football against the side of the house: I can see his face as it appears through the window, serious and concentrating as I hear the gravel beneath his feet and the dull thud thud thud. I don't know where Max and Josie are. They seem irrelevant in this scene, almost as if they were never there.

Sometimes there's a presence of something else, a darkness where I don't want to go, a sad and lonely space. The distortion of a girl, smiling self-consciously, caught in a moment of pretence, uncomfortable in her lipstick, grown-up shoes and revealing dress; or Dad getting ready for a party, false eyelashes and a wig, always the joker, the performer. Or maybe it's just simply me: a twelve-year-old who's eager to please, desperate to have something of his to keep, impatient to grow up and turn thirteen. But my thirteenth birthday came and went without me even noticing it, as I was lost by then.

Where is that girl now? I abandoned her years ago. Raced her to the finish line, every part of me bigger, stronger, faster. Jack would say I've beaten her into insignificance along with any womanly charms. I rarely wear make-up, never wear skirts; dresses are out of the question. My hair is short, no longer blonde; it became mousy with the years and I won't dye it. I don't like hairdressers; hate being locked to the mirror, staring at my reflection, caught in a state of impatience. Jack cuts my hair now, methodically washing it, combing it out, trimming the fringe with a seriousness of the insane. 'Leave it and you'll look like an abandoned bird,' he says, but he won't let me cut it myself: he thinks I might hack away at it, make myself look worse. But I'm made of far simpler things. I like life to be practical, that's all: it's jeans and trainers, a T-shirt or sweater, neutral colours, nothing fussy. Now it's me who's behind the camera, no-one has to see me. I'm the one taking the picture now.

I open my eyes to the landscape as it curves past the train window, patches of yellow turning to green, the late afternoon sun still high in the sky. A young woman reads the paper. A child sits beside her father. Nothing has changed. Only now the child is asleep, her head on the headrest and his large hand resting on her shoulder. He reads but is always aware of her; whenever she moves, his eyes flick towards her. I sigh and rub my face. I wonder if age has mellowed my dad. In my imagination, we always meet in a park. He is standing on a path or sitting on a bench and he waves at me as I approach him. He looks happy to see me. Up close, he is still handsome: his floppy hair and creased smile. He says something silly to me, like – 'How's my noodle?' something like that. That's how I imagine it. I will ask him if he took the picture. I will see him and I will know. He may have kept it, framed it and put it near his bed, he may have.

I glance at my bag, bulging with a week's worth of clothing, my portfolio, the scrapbook at the top, dusty and speckled with damp. I press down on it. If I had the photograph I might have put it into my book, on the pages where I'd stuck the tarot card, the scraps of paper he left around the house – loving notes to Alanka, ideas on his latest book – the slice of towelling I cut from his dressing gown, flattened and frayed from weeks of rubbing it above my lip where it is soft and comforting, and I can smell him: vanilla pipe smoke and cigarettes, sometimes mint.

The train shakes as we speed into a tunnel. There's a sudden sound like a quick inhalation. It surprises me. I hold my chest, my heartbeat quickening. The light changes and the reflection of the carriage projects from the darkness. I search for my face in the glass. Now I am here: at the end of my twenties, on my way to London, the end of the line. Engaged, but running away. Always running, Jack tells me. I squint at myself, but there's nothing there. It's blurred, splintered, a broken shape caught in the double-glazing. I squeeze my eyes closed and see the watery imprint of my reflection, vague and indistinct.

'One, two… three, four,' Josie's breath smells of crisps. 'Five… six.' As she counts she smears her sticky fingers on my dad's brochure.

'Stop it,' I shove her, and the movement of the train almost throws her off the seat.

'*Mamma mia, whata ya doing?*' she slaps her forehead and Sam and Max laugh. An Italian man sitting nearby gives us a funny look.

'Seven – there's seven – look they've all got them.' Josie hangs over my shoulder and a piece of soggy crisp lands on the photograph of Dad and his friends, it almost covers the whole of Yogi's head.

'What are you talking about?' I flick it off.

'Beards,' she says. 'Look,' and tries to grab it back.

I struggle with her.

It's my dad's company brochure; he sent it to me a couple of months ago. It shows all the books that they're going to publish: names like *Aspiring for Balance* and *Beautiful Magic*, a book on angels. And on the back there's a photograph of everyone who lives in his house. I've had it on my bedroom wall next to my bed so it's the first thing I see when I wake up in the morning.

I hold it on my lap with both hands, stroking the creases out of it: *One, two, three* – they do all seem to have beards. 'So what if they have beards?' I mumble.

My dad has his arm around Alanka and he's holding his thumb

up to the camera. There's Paritosh, who sent me postcards telling me about spiritual sex and Kundalini; he also told me he's a homosexual. They're standing beneath the weeping tree, the Tuscan sun warming their faces.

Josie leans into me – 'My mum says men with beards have something to hide.'

'That's bollocks,' I say, covering the photograph so she can't see. My dad's had a beard ever since he left my mum. 'You don't know that.'

'Yeah, but don't you reckon it's a bit weird? Every single one of those men has a beard, it's like a beard disease, like the plague or something.'

'It's not weird,' I say.

Josie sits back and nods as if she knows more than I do, which is absolute rubbish because she's much more immature than me.

Max leans forward and grabs the brochure from my knee.

'*Oi,*' I shout as he rips it away from me.

He sits back and grins at it. 'Bloody weirdos,' he says. He nudges Sam and laughs. He's got such a freaky way of laughing. I reckon he's a bit psycho. 'They probably think they're Jesus,' he says. 'What do you reckon? They think they're on their way to sainthood or something.'

'Enlightenment,' I say, trying to grab it. I eye Sam – *Help me, won't you?*

'There's a kid at my dad's school who belongs to that lot,' Max says. 'His parents make him wear these hippy clothes, apparently he looks like a gypsy, and all the kids take the piss out of him. He can only wear shades of red, the colours of the sunset or something. I reckon he's brainwashed by that guru guy, what's his name?'

'Parameshvar,' I say, sitting up.

'We'd better be careful, eh?' he nudges Sam. 'If we don't watch out they might make us go all spiritual,' and he does this funny thing with his hands.

8

'Yeah, but who wants to listen to your dad?' I say. 'Who wants to listen to a headmaster?' Max sits back and squints at me, his freaky eyes that never look in the same direction. He is *so* ugly I can't even look at him, sitting there in his ripped T-shirt and scabby fingerless gloves. 'They don't wear weird clothes any more anyway,' I say. 'Do they, Sam?' Sam shrugs. 'They were over that a long time ago.' I grab at the brochure again. 'It's mine, give it back.' And then out of frustration I kick my brother. '*Sam!*' I shout.

Sam scowls at me, grabbing his shin. 'You'd better give it back, mate,' he says. 'She's a stroppy cow when she doesn't get what she wants.'

Max lets go of the brochure and I tuck it away in my bag.

I look out of the window. My face is burning. Max has his earphones on again, listening to his weird psychobilly music. I can see him in the window, rocking to and fro as he sucks on a Mars bar. I hate him. I can't believe that Sam has invited him to Italy. A whole month, it's going to be a total nightmare. Josie sinks into the seat next to me and puts her thumb in her mouth. 'Beardy weirdy weirdy,' she says under her breath and grins at me.

I press my forehead to the glass. It's cold, but I want to see through the blackness to the train track and the only sign that we're in Italy. I wonder where Dad is: I've been praying he'll be there to meet us, squeezing my fingers on both hands to be sure. But from here all I can see is darkness and the reflection of the carriage. Sam and Max rocking their heads to music and Josie's toy dog squeezed between her knees.

I close my eyes and try to see Dad's face. The last time I saw him was a year ago when he hugged me goodbye at Pisa Airport and I was crying so much that he went blurry. But I kept him in my mind for months, closing my eyes when I was at school or helping Mum make supper, wishing up his image and imagining him watching me, being a part of everything I do, until one day I realized I couldn't see him any more; however hard I

9

concentrated I couldn't see his face – his stretchy expressions that can look happy one minute and then really sad for no reason. His funny scarred eye. This year I'm going to do lots of drawings of him, so I can put them on my wall when I get home. Mum says that drawing is better than taking photographs because it captures an essence of someone, like a feeling that maybe a photograph can't see. Mrs Tomlin says I'm really good at drawing, particularly portraits. I can't wait to tell Dad. I put my hand on my bag and have a terrible thought: my sketchbook – I left it on Josie's kitchen table. Her mum reminded me when we were in the car.

'Did you bring my sketchbook?' I ask Sam.

He looks at me. 'No.'

'But I asked you to when we were in the car.'

He shrugs and goes back to his comic.

'Oh, bloody hell,' I hug myself to the window.

'*Oi* grumpy,' Sam laughs. 'It's only a sketchbook, I'm sure Dad will buy you a new one.'

But it wasn't only a sketchbook. It was a special sketchbook. Mum brought it back from Russia when she came home at Easter. It has pictures of dancing girls on the front and can be a sketchbook or a diary as the pages are thin and blank. I use it for both: writing how I feel, like Mum always tells me to, and drawing sketches when I'm pretending to watch telly, or waiting to be picked up from school. Josie's mum has been picking me up since me and Sam have been staying with her, and she's got a problem with her punctuality.

It's not a long journey from Pisa to Florence, Sam and I did the same trip last year and it only took about an hour. But today the train seems to stop and start and doesn't know what it wants to do. It's making me feel funny as I'm thinking: What if Dad is waiting and he doesn't know that we're late? He might turn around and go back home. We should have phoned him from the airport: I check my pocket where I've put his telephone number. But, of course, he may not be there at all. Like last year.

It was different then. It was the first time we'd been to Italy and it was the first time we'd travelled without an adult. A nice lady directed us to the train station at Pisa and Sam led the way, his face all serious. But when we got to Florence there was no-one there to meet us. It was OK at first as there were lots of people around, but it was late and slowly everyone started to go home, except for the tramps and the gypsies who tried to talk to us. When we told Dad about it later, he said that gypsies distract you by asking you the time while their children steal your bags.

The train slows and my stomach turns and my hands are hot and sticky in my lap. I check my watch because I think we might be there, but I can't tell any more as we were supposed to be there ten minutes ago and it doesn't feel like we're stopping at a station. Sam is staring out of the window, at blackness, at nothing. I wonder if he's thinking what I'm thinking. I pull on my cardigan and put my book and purse back in my rucksack, zipping it closed and pulling it onto my lap. I put my hand into my pocket and turn the plane ticket between my fingers; I've got all four train tickets as well, I managed to keep them as the train inspector never asked for them – Dad said we needn't bother buying a ticket, but I was worried we might get arrested.

Sam pulls his bag off the floor and puts away his comic. He looks at me. 'Have you got everything?' he asks quietly. I nod, leaning into my rucksack.

'Are we nearly there?' Josie asks excitedly.

The train stops and the carriage is quiet. I squint out of the window.

'What kind of car does your dad drive?' Josie puts her chin on my shoulder. Last year it was a big car, a jeep or something, but he never keeps the same car for long. I look at Sam and I can tell that he heard Josie's question, but he doesn't say anything. 'I don't know,' I say.

The train lurches and slowly rolls forward, my stomach rolls with it.

'Will he come to the station on his own or with…' She never remembers their names. 'Alain… A—'

'Alanka,' I say, annoyed.

'Alanka, *sorry*,' she says. 'I can't help it if they all have weird names.' She looks at Max who laughs again. 'Will he come to the station on his own or with Alanka?' she asks, and I glance at Sam and this time he catches my eye – a funny scratchy expression.

'I don't know,' I say, and squeeze my fingers tightly in my lap looking away from Josie and back to the darkness outside, black as black. *He won't be there, he won't be there, he definitely won't be there.* I whisper it into the window and the steam from my breath makes the glass foggy. I look at Sam again – Are you thinking the same thing? Remember last year when we waited for almost an hour with that horrible sinking feeling, not knowing where to go or what we would do if no-one came to meet us? We didn't have his telephone number, and I didn't want to phone Mum because it was late: it was after midnight and we couldn't remember if it was an hour earlier or later in England.

'I can't believe we've travelled all this way on our own,' Josie says. 'We were in London this morning and now we're in Italy and it's only taken a day. It's amazing. Do you think your dad will be worried about us? My mum says I have to phone her when we get to the house. What's your dad's house like? Is it far from the station?' she asks. 'It's funny. I haven't seen your dad since that Christmas we went walking in the snow – do you remember? There was so much of it that it went inside our boots and our toes nearly froze.'

I was the first to see Yogi that summer. We were sitting on our bags, preparing ourselves for a night in the station, when he came lolloping across the concourse, not towards us but in our direction, and I immediately knew he was one of Dad's friends. He had grey fuzzy hair like an afro, a long beard, big Indian nappy trousers and a mala strung around his neck. I nudged Sam as I watched this weird man walk really fast as if he knew where he was going, but he still wasn't heading for us. Then he suddenly stopped, turned and squinted at us. He didn't tell us where Dad was, he just held up his palm and said Hi, like a Red Indian – *How!* And he took our bags and we followed him out of the station. On the way to the house he lost control of the car and drove us into a ditch. One minute we were on the road and the next we were head first in a ditch and my neck pinged and there was a tick tick tick from the engine as cars sped past really fast behind us. Yogi groaned and got out and tried to push the car, and of course it was too heavy for him. He then stood on the road with his hand out, but no-one stopped for us. Sam and I didn't say a word. Sam just sat silently looking at me, then the ditch and the road sign that was full of words we didn't understand. Finally a man stopped and helped us. Back in the car, Yogi told us that he couldn't see very well because he'd left his glasses at home.

The train pulls into Florence station and Sam hangs back to help us with our rucksacks, but Josie gets tangled in her coat. I'm trying to help her but I'm worried that the train is going to pull out of the station and I can't hear what she's saying because my heart is beating loud and fast in my ears. On the platform, I try to catch up with Sam, but Josie drops something and I'm desperate for her to hurry up – *Hurry up Hurry up Hurry up.*

And then I know.

Sam's the first one to see him. I know he's seen him because he stretches to double his height as he picks up his pace and almost skips along the platform. I close my eyes and breathe deeply, waiting to feel what it is: a spin in my chest that's lighter than before because my insides are singing. When I open my eyes, there he is: his big hairy forearms wrapped around the back of Sam's neck, people moving to get around them, and I let that feeling flush through me, all soft and spongy like lying back into a hot frothy bath.

'Toots,' he says, and I melt into his arms. Soft cotton on my cheek, his firm and solid tummy, the smell of wood and sweet smoke. He looks at me: his large hands warm on my cheeks, and he is smiling so much that the scarred skin around his eye closes it to almost nothing. 'You've grown,' he says. And I wonder how much.

By the time I've travelled east from Paddington, it's almost dark. I enter the block of flats through the car park, stopping to tell the security guard my name and my uncle's apartment number before travelling to the top floor in the small flickering lift. As I turn the key, I realize I didn't buy milk and bread, and the nearest shop is a way away. I'll be feeding off reserves during my early morning run.

The flat is illuminated from the light outside the balcony doors, sparking off a large mirror in the living room, making the space seem vast and empty. I drop my bags on the floor. It smells stale, of somebody else's heat seeping through the walls. I pull open the doors and let in the thick city air.

I stand on the balcony: concrete curved around me like a cocoon, softened only by squares of glowing light and flourishes of geraniums, windows into other people's lives. I take a deep breath. This is where I am, back in London at last; the past week of waiting seemed like an eternity. I was desperate to close the door on our beautiful country home.

It's not that I'm bored – that would appear spoilt – but time seems to have slowed since we moved away. I had fantasies of a new life: a pale stone house with wisteria dropping from the walls and an allotment growing large cabbages and rhubarb, with wrens chattering in the ivy, woodpeckers knocking out a drum-like beat; in this dream I'm cleaning lettuces for lunch, with the back doors open and Jack outside, crafting furniture while I feed him; I see myself touch my stomach, feeling for a life that's growing within. We have talked about having a family, for our own reasons, not to be part of a thirty-something nappy happy crowd; not just to copy our friends. I can't say I'm sure about it, but it's definitely on Jack's agenda. And, of course, he's silently manoeuvred things so that there's no excuse but to embrace the family life: we have the house, the garden, the tools to make furniture, the bed to make love, the spare room to fill with a cot and toys. But it's not as simple as that. I thought the country would lighten me, fill me with energy like bright sunflowers and a clean crisp sky after rain, but instead it's made me tired. I might take my bike along the canal, go running, springing up hills and through valleys, small lanes and shady trees, but I'm left feeling constricted, bound up and dull-footed as I make my way home. I'm not complaining, how could I? On the face of it, everything is fine: I'm twenty-nine, still in my twenties. I'm young. I'm fit and healthy, happy, busy with a job in wedding photography; I wonder how we'd have time for a child. But it's not just that: I have a restlessness that takes me away, a hunger for the extraordinary, an obsession for something else. I like photographing troubled kids, their broken skin and cuts revisited again and again. I like to capture their scars. The girl at the swimming pool, every part of her skin marked, the welts on her body like tattoos. Or that night in a London club, early in the morning when my vision was askew. We met again after so many years. He showed me his arms, he asked me to photograph him. Perhaps that's where the obsession began.

A large crane cuts through the sky, the trail of an aeroplane: the sky is too pale to see stars. I am in the centre of London and yet there is so little sound: a regular trickle from the fountain in the central garden, the tap tap tap of hard-soled shoes in the concrete walkways, the twitter of birds, a different type of bird. I wonder if they see this as their oasis. I breathe in, the smell of dust and dirt. It's nothing like home: from Jack's and my bedroom window there's a valley and the distant spire of our local church. It's a beautiful church, medieval. We're thinking of getting married there.

Jack says I'm always trying to escape – never confronting problems or facing life's challenges – he prides himself on bringing me back, helping me ground my feet again, but sometimes I wonder if he is as much to blame. One morning he questioned our life, blamed it on his work: 'We should leave the city, start afresh. There's a much better market in restoration outside town. We could get a house with a studio where you could do your photography. So much more for our money.' He didn't mention the fact we'd been arguing, suffering from too many nights out at the pub, dinner with friends and another bottle of wine when we get home, the next day a dull ache, the London landscape foggy and oblique. He didn't mention that things hadn't been good between us. But the country doesn't work for me; it doesn't stimulate me. This is where the energy lives, in this flat, in time on my own. In London, my London, my home. I'm not running away: I have a meeting with a gallery, a wedding at the weekend. I'm here to see my father.

I fill the watering can, feed the shrivelled succulents and tip the water over the flowers on the balcony, humming to myself. A Joni Mitchell song has been running through my mind about painted ponies and the circle of life. I want to play it loud on the stereo, dance across the floor, smoke a cigarette even though I haven't smoked in years.

I stop and watch a plane in the sky, its taillight lit up as it flies overhead. It's on its way into London, probably City Airport, so it won't be a flight from California. I wonder if Dad has arrived yet. He'll be staying in a smart hotel on his own; Sam said he is single at the moment. I can imagine him lying on his hotel bed, bloated from the flight, his head propped up by a pillow, a plate of half-eaten food crooked on his lap and his bare feet falling to the sides, his socks rolled into a ball in the corner of the room. Sam says he has put on weight. He'll be heavier and his face will be sad.

I can't see him, but I can imagine him.

Apparently he's here about some inheritance: he still thinks he can make money for nothing, become a millionaire, there's no change on that front. Do I really want to see him?

In the kitchen I look in the cupboards, but there's nothing to eat except rice cakes and tins of sardines. The kettle is upside-down and dry on the drainer. I fill it and place it on its base, switching the power on at the wall.

How long has it been since I last saw him – thirteen years? Has it really been that long?

I was sixteen. He was staying in London for a couple of weeks, but he didn't tell me he was coming. I bumped into him on the street. I was in Hampstead with a friend and there he was, walking towards me, wearing a tan leather jacket with a camera bag over his shoulder, his hair long and unkempt. He looked like he belonged, like he was living in London again. I stopped and gripped my friend's arm, 'Is that him?' I said.

She turned to me and laughed – 'Who?'

'My dad,' I said. He was walking slowly, looking over his shoulder as if he were waiting for someone, Alanka; she must have been in one of the shops. My stomach turned. A vague, drifting expression on his face, he nearly bumped into someone, it annoyed me. My friend laughed: 'How can you not know if that's your dad, stupid! Are you all right?' She came right in front of me to see my face; I must have been white, from either shock or fury.

'It *is* him,' I said, and walked towards him.

Dad lived in various parts of Hampstead before he moved to Italy, mostly in a small commune in a terraced house near South End Green. Sam's and my school was just a ten-minute walk away, so we often spent our weekends with him or sometimes a night during the week. But he was never around for long. He would go on trips to India or America, leaving everything for months at a time. Sam and I would take a long route to school from the station, passing his old Citroën. It had broken down and was discarded on the road, sinking, the rust slowly spreading. One day we passed and its rear window was smashed: I glimpsed my old school shoes in the back, wet and sodden from the rain, and then one day the car was gone. When Dad finally decided to move to Italy, he got rid of everything, he sold all his possessions and he started again. Just like he did when he left our mum. But I always thought he might come back. I would wait for Sam on the wall outside our school, wishing Dad into my mind, imagining him walking up the road, his dog Hamlet at his feet, coming towards me to pull me onto his shoulders and take me home. So when I saw him walking up the High Street, just moments away, I didn't really believe it.

'Dad?' I said, and he opened his arms as if he'd been expecting me. There was no emotion, no surprise. I held myself against his chest. 'What are you doing here?' I asked. He lived in Italy; another place, far away. Why was he in London? Why hadn't he phoned to tell me he was coming?

We talked for a few minutes, I can't remember what about. But I do remember saying goodbye. I walked down the hill and he walked up. He told me to call, but I didn't. Why should I? He was the one who had come back; he was on my territory. I often hung around in Hampstead with my friends. I didn't want to feel that I might bump into him, so casually, as if everything that had gone before had meant nothing, had had no effect on my life. How can he have not understood that?

The years passed. We spoke on the phone, at birthdays, Christmas, but soon even the phone calls stopped. He never invited me to visit him, and why would I have asked? And now I'm here, thirteen years on. How do I tell him how I've been? Will he even ask me? Or can it be simple like before: a meeting in the street, a hug, a brief goodbye? I'm not sure I even want to see him. I don't have to phone him. He doesn't have to give me away at my wedding.

In the bedroom I sit on the bed and unzip my bag, pulling out my portfolio. I have an appointment at the Photographers' Gallery in a couple of days. Perhaps this time I'll be lucky. It only takes one person believing in you, giving you a chance. I lean against the headboard and flick through the sheaves of photographs, settling on my favourite. It's of an arm and really only an arm as the face is obscured, but for a wisp of ginger hair, his strong jaw line and the window of clear light in his dark eye. I worked hard to capture the life in his eyes. It was something I never noticed that summer when his eyes spooked me, the way one seems to wander as if it's loose on a string, but somehow age has made him more interesting to me; his quirks defining him rather than making him weird. And then there's the bandage and the cotton wool saturated with blood. He'd had a relapse, he hadn't done it since that summer and he let me photograph it. He showed me his weakness, escaping as it does through his skin. It was like having a glimpse of his soul. It took me back to that holiday in Italy, sitting on my father's lap, his scar.

I wanted to tell Dad something, something important.

My face was so close to him that I could see the hundreds of roots of his hairs as they sprouted from his neck. I leaned my head on his shoulder and gazed at his face, the little raised scar around his eye, pink and curved like a wrinkly worm. I touched it, running my finger along its ridge.

'Does it hurt?' I asked.

He smiled down at me, 'No,' he said. 'The skin is dead, the nerves died a long time ago.'

He was in hospital for two months, the injuries were so bad. He was only ten. He was brave — so much braver than I could ever be.

'What was it like in hospital?' I asked.

'I loved being in hospital.'

'How can you love being in hospital?'

'The nurses adored me,' he said. 'They told me I was the best patient in the ward. They'd secretly give me biscuits when we weren't supposed to have any.'

'Did you have the worst injuries in the ward?'

He nodded enthusiastically. 'One doctor said he'd never seen anything so bad. He said I should have won an award for the amount of glass they found in my face.'

I closed my eyes and tried to picture what he must have looked like: sleepwalking through a plate-glass window with blood all over his face. Maybe it was like skin that's been turned inside out. He used to sleepwalk all the time, through windows, doors, anything that was glass. His parents had to lock him in his bedroom. But I loved the fact the doctors didn't fix his eye because the scar is what makes him special, different from every other stupid and boring dad in the world.

'My mother blamed me,' he said quietly. 'She thought I did it so I didn't have to go back to school. She thought I did it to punish her for sending me to boarding school.'

'Did you hate school?'

'I despised it,' he said. 'It's for stupid people – people who don't think. There are many stupid people in this world.'

I shifted in his lap and curled into him like a cat. 'I don't like school either,' I said, the space around us suddenly closing in.

He cleared his throat and pushed his hand through his hair and I sat up relieved by the movement. 'Enough of the past,' he said. 'What was it that you wanted to tell me?'

I straightened my T-shirt, wiped the creases from my shorts, breathed in and sat straight. I opened my mouth but nothing came out. He shifted in the chair and I thought I must be getting heavy; maybe I'm getting too big to sit on his lap.

I catch my reflection in the mirror: a spark, something new, something alive in my eyes. I know what I wanted to say – I was sorry for crying at his wedding, for clinging onto him in all the photographs. But I couldn't say it. I couldn't say anything important like that. I didn't give it a chance, or perhaps he just didn't listen. I wonder if he would listen now.

Jack seems to think that seeing my father will change everything, give me direction and resolve my restlessness – as if it's just me that needs curing. How can it be that simple? A lifetime of fuck-up put to bed in one meeting. And what about him? Not all things can be turned around so tidily, packed away and sealed in a neat cardboard box. Like last week, he vacuumed and cleaned as if he could sweep up the words that I had spilled the night before. I was so angry. I pushed and pushed him to try to make him break: and for the first time since we met he buckled. He cried like a child and it was suddenly too much for me. I couldn't comfort him. I couldn't even be in the same room.

I take off my engagement ring and slip it into a small pink pouch, tucking it away in my bag. Maybe this is the answer: the brightness in my eyes, the hunger, the scent of freedom. Jack picked me from the single pool, he dragged me out of my contentment; perhaps I can drop myself back in again. I look prettier when I'm single. I take off my T-shirt, my trainers, kick off my jeans and stand in my bra and knickers. I'm slimmer, fitter than I have ever been, the solid curve of my thighs, my small firm bum, the tightness of my stomach.

The last time I was here, Jack was with me; we slept over after a gig at the Royal Festival Hall. We lay in bed and stared into the blue light and listened to how quiet the city becomes at night. He tried to kiss me, but I didn't want him to. I told him this would be the perfect place for an affair. He laughed at me; he thought I was joking. I stood in the mirror then, naked that time, and he watched me from the bed, his head propped on his hand, his eyes twinkling, a smile on his face, admiring. 'You'll never do it, you know, Sylvie,' he said. 'However muscly you get, you'll never cease to be sexy.' I looked at myself and thought, But I know I'm sexy. I don't need you to tell me that.

From the mirror I can see the scrapbook I found at Mum's. It was a surprise to find it again, rummaging around in the boxes in the basement, most of the books I found were too damaged by damp to retrieve, but this one I had wrapped in a jumper – a small red cashmere cardigan that was once Alanka's. I pull it out of the bag and open the front page.

This book belongs to Sylvie Morton it reads. *It is strictly private and if you dare to go any further I will hunt you down, and that means you, Sam.* It is signed, *Sylvie* in sharp italic writing, *Italy.*

I go to the next page. A plane ticket stub, Gatwick to Pisa, 25th July 1986, aisle B, seat 3 – I argued with Josie to get the window seat – and four train tickets from Pisa to Firenze.

The book falls open where a number of pages have been ripped out. They must have been Jeet's pages: a button from his shirt, a poem, a note ripped from his cigarette packet, and all the photographs that he took of me and he helped me take of him – his thin body bent like a bow, his small black swimming trunks.

A collection of loose photographs falls onto my lap. Josie and I are looking at each other and laughing beneath the magic tree in the orchard. Jeet told me that he took it to show her how pretty she could be, but I read it completely differently. Me at the beach: my legs hugged to my chest and my hair covering my face. I'd looked away by the time he'd taken the picture. And months later back at home: I'm standing in front of the Christmas tree and I look terrible. I had only just turned thirteen, but I don't look like a child. I am frightened, burdened by those images, things I should never have seen.

And here's the photograph of me at the party. It was a couple of weeks into the holiday, it was a new moon – Deeva had told me. I'm laughing. I look happy. My stark white hair like a halo. I don't know who took the picture, but it was taken with my snappy camera; it was before the photography and Jeet's equipment. I've got that smooth thick skin of youth, long slim limbs, the curve of my new breasts just noticeable beneath the black dress. My arm is outstretched to someone – is it Jeet, or Dad? Did I dance with him? Or perhaps he has spun me around, leaving me to find my balance again. This is where it all began. I tried to be so grown-up that night, wearing that dress, pretending to be that girl. Divine Leela, playing on the stage with no boundaries. I didn't know it, but perhaps that's what he saw, perhaps that's why he stopped, captured me in that moment. Did I have a choice?

I open my eyes and the room is blue, the morning light glowing through the slats in the shutters. I get out of bed quietly, so as not to wake Josie. I push open the window and squint against the light, pulling my sleeves down so I can lean on my elbows to look out. It must be early, as the sky is still pale, the air thin and chilly. From here I have a view from the side of the house to the big gate at the end of the drive.

I didn't stay in this room last year. Sam and I were next to Dad's room, with a view of the courtyard. I would sit on the window ledge and watch people as they arrived in their cars and parked beneath the weeping tree, pulling bags out of the boot and singing greetings to one another. I got to know everyone's routines: at about four o'clock every afternoon, Nim drank herbal tea, sitting at the table beneath the tree and smoking bidis; Paritosh would call out from the window of the study and soon he would be there too, and they'd be chatting about the day, making each other laugh (Paritosh laughs like an aristocrat, Dad says, while Nim sounds like a yackety dog). Every morning, Soma would get up before everyone else. I often heard the clunk of the front door below our room and her heavy steps as she walked across the gravel. She liked to sunbathe for an hour as the sun came up because that way she didn't have to wear suntan cream. Alanka was also often up early; she'd walk to the belvedere in her floaty dress and sandals where she'd look out over the hills, barely moving, for what seemed like ages, and she sometimes looked really sad.

A woman called Rumi slept in this room last year. She'd been living at the commune for only a week when we arrived, and she's not here any more. She was young and Italian and was having an affair with a married man. We always knew when he was here because her door would be closed and his shoes on the step outside, dark brown leather that seemed too hot for the summer. Sometimes they had noisy sex; Sam and I would whistle every time we passed her room so we didn't have to hear them.

From this side of the house I can see the caretaker's home and the knobbly olive trees on either side of the drive. That means that from here I can see people arrive *before* they get to the courtyard and park beneath the weeping tree.

I slip on my tube skirt and beetle crushers, with my favourite pink vest over my bra, and I quietly close the door behind me. The corridor is dark and empty, soft fluty music coming from one of the bedrooms. I look towards Dad's room but there is no light seeping from beneath the door. He did seem tired last night. He told me Alanka had been at a meditation weekend at a commune near Siena and he had done so much driving that day, picking her up and taking her home and then going straight out to pick us up. I was sorry that the drive to meet us made him more tired. I cross my arms and shiver, as it feels cold in the dark of the corridor. I forget that sometimes the house can feel cold.

It was winter when Dad first came here: they moved in a snow-storm and it took them two weeks to connect the telephone. I only spoke to him once, when he phoned from a hotel and told me that there was no central heating and that Alanka was sleeping in her furs. I imagined the house rising out of the snow, cracks in the windows and the doors falling off their hinges, and Dad wading through the wind and the snow in a heavy jacket and wellies. Of course it was nothing like that. When I arrived for the first time last summer, it was all colour and light: a gravel path with a huge house at the end of it, green shutters and flowering plants climbing up the walls. A dusty looking cat sitting on the bonnet of a car, bright blue eyes rimmed with black, and scabs on his head. 'What's his name?' I asked Yogi as he took our bags from the boot. He looked at me. 'You know what?' he said in his creepy soft voice. 'I don't know the answer to that question.' We later named him Calvin Klein after the adverts on the telly, and his mother (Alanka said she was his mum) Ralph Lauren, even though it's a man's name.

From the kitchen, I lean out of the window to look for the cats, but the courtyard is empty. There are three cars parked in the drive and a few small footprints on the bonnet, but no cats. I find a plate and knife and open the food cupboard but there is no bread. The cupboard is empty: there's nothing in the plastic containers that usually hold muesli, pasta and rice; there's no jam or honey, no crackers or dried fruit; there are only boxes of herbal tea, and a few sachets of English Breakfast. I go to the fridge, but there's no milk, no butter, no yoghurt, just a sign on the door, saying *Think before you fill, we do not eat meat. Beware of cat food!* followed by a heart and the word *Love*.

Dad's friends are so in to their little notes; just like the last place where Dad lived with Deeva, crazy Kusum and her hairy boyfriend. Kusum used to leave notes on everything, saying Our guru this, Our guru that: *Parameshvar would wash up these dishes; Parameshvar doesn't leave the light on when he leaves the bathroom.* Dad would write messages in response saying *Bet he fucking does*.

That was when Dad first met Alanka. She was doing a degree at London University and moved into a room on the landing, while Dad and Deeva slept in the big room upstairs. But then Dad realized he'd fallen in love with Alanka, so she and Deeva swapped rooms. I always thought it was weird how Deeva and Alanka became best friends. They used to sit on Dad's bed and talk in Italian so I couldn't understand; they made out that they knew each other in a previous life when they were both witches. About a month later, Dad and Alanka got married and I cried through the whole ceremony, and two days later Deeva moved out. Mum says I was upset because Alanka was so young: she was eighteen, only eight years older than me. But I like Alanka. She's beautiful and generous and we get on really well. I love sitting on her bed and talking about life. I don't think it's weird that she's young; I think it means we get on better. It's my fault that I used to be a crybaby.

On the kitchen table there is another note, it's written on the back of a brown paper bag in big messy handwriting:

Beloved Soma,
Perhaps some words were said but, my beloved, no-one is pissed at you.
You may be wanting to be silent right now, but talk to us before you fall
into aloneness. Please tell me when you are home, I will be in the garden
picking pomodori. I would like to see you, even if you don't feel the need
to share. I need to see your beautiful smile.
Love Nim.

Nim's funny. She's small and looks like a child even though she's nearly forty. She takes on different identities to stop herself from getting bored with life. Dad told us in the car last night that she's recently become a whiz at t'ai chi and she eats her meals with chopsticks even though she's not Chinese.

From the belvedere I look out towards the hills that lead to Florence, and the little houses on the side of the road that we passed last night as Dad drove around corners: they were so close I tried to touch them. A trail of ants runs out of a hole in the wood column and onto the wall where it forms a line down to the floor. I push a stone into the trail to obstruct them. If I had a cigarette I could smoke them out, their tiny twitchy bodies running in circles as if they're tripping.

Leaning over the wall of the belvedere, I imagine falling into the allotment below me, landing in among the tomato plants and lettuces, and stacks of terracotta pots. I wonder if I would hurt myself. I stretch onto my toes and look towards the orchard beyond. I notice something: a flash of pink among the green. I lean out further. A pink shirt and an arm, a black knee, there is someone in the orchard. There's still no movement from the house, so I walk towards the gate that leads to the lower part of the garden. I move through the lines of vegetables and netting, and lose the figure before finding it again, to the orchard beyond and in among the trees avoiding the over-ripe apples and plums on the ground. It's someone beneath a tree. A woman with her back to me: she has long dark hair and a silky shirt the colour of shells. Maybe it's Nim with her *pomodori* or maybe it's Soma, maybe this is where she's hiding. I walk to my left a little, hoping to get a better view, but her face is obscured by the tree, her arm leaning on her knee, her palm facing upwards, and her forefinger and thumb touching as if she's meditating.

It's Alanka.

I pick up my pace, and call her name, and then stop. I should have thought she might be busy. She may not want to see me. She swings a look around the tree and her face looks shadowy, and for a minute it doesn't look like her. She looks angry. I'm such a plank. But then she smiles. 'Hey,' she calls, and raises her arms. 'Look who it is.' And I'm with her, on my knees with my head against her silky blouse.

Alanka *is* meditating. She tells me that she does it every morning to set her up for the day. It's soothing, she says. It helps her think more clearly. She pats the ground beside her and I sit against the tree watching the sky get bluer, feeling the sun as it warms my face.

We sit like this for a while. My eyes are closed and I'm following the swirly sun patterns as they curl behind my eyelids while Alanka tells me about the house and everything that has changed in the past year. 'Your father has some exciting new projects,' she says. 'One that might involve you while you are here.'

'What?' I ask, sitting up.

'It is a beautiful book about children,' she says, and I smile hiding my annoyance that she thinks I'm still a child.

I watch her as she talks to me, her long neck and her delicate hands linked together in her lap, the gold and pearly rings glistening against her brown skin. Her dangly earrings jingling each time she moves. She has four piercings in one of her ears, with silver and turquoise hoops running down like decorations. I wish I had more than one piercing in each ear, but Mum won't let me. Alanka says now that my mum is working abroad, I should get my ears pierced – do it secretly. She asks if Josie's mum would mind. I tell her that Carol's really nice: she often lets me stay out late and I can tell her loads more things than I can tell anybody else in the world.

'So, Josie is like a sister to you?' Alanka says.

'I guess so,' I say. 'I've known her since before we were born. We used to talk to each other through our mums' tummies, and then we went to the same school, until a year ago when her mum and dad put her into private school.'

'Private school, what is that?'

'A posh school, where everyone wears uniform. My mum threatens to send me to one when I bunk off.'

'*Ah*. So, not a good school.'

'No, it *is* a good school, but it's not the same. I think everyone at Josie's school is weird or something, because she's changed since she's been there, it's like she doesn't get it any more. Like she thinks she's better than us just because she goes to a more expensive school.'

'But, Sylvie,' Alanka strokes my face. 'You are different from other girls your age. You have always been different since you were a little girl. I remember your father saying that when you were born you had a bubble in your mouth that seemed to encompass the world, as if you were born to be knowing.'

'But Dad wasn't there when I was born,' I say. He was running down the motorway because his car had broken down. He ran all the way from Reading.

'You cannot expect other people to be like you. You are blessed with wisdom,' she says.

'Yeah, and Josie is just immature.'

'You see, you have to remember that you will always be wiser than your friends. You have that way about you, but that doesn't make them worse than you, it just makes them different.'

'But Josie just annoys me sometimes. Some of the things she says, and she thinks Sam is God. He can't do any wrong. I reckon she fancies him she goes on about him so much.'

'And Sam, is he happy?'

'Sam is always happy,' I say, crossing my arms.

'And Sam's friend, Mac?'

'Max,' I correct her.

'Max, do you like him, do you fancy him?'

'God, no way, have you seen him? He's ginger and he looks like a punk. And he smells.'

She laughs and recrosses her legs, her skirt slipping off her knee, her brown silky skin shining in the sunlight. 'And a boyfriend? Do you have a boyfriend?'

I shake my head.

'Why is that? You are such a beautiful girl.'

I blush; does she think I'm beautiful?

She smiles her soft melting smile that makes me want to tell her things.

'I dunno,' I shrug. 'None of the boys at school think I'm pretty. They all go for small girls. They think I'm too tall, I hate being tall.'

'But they are boys,' she says. 'I never went out with boys my age at school. It is a waste of time. Boys your age might as well be two years younger than you, they don't develop as quickly.'

I nod, because that's just what I've been thinking. Sam and Max are two years older than me and even they act like they're younger.

'Many boys are frightened,' she takes my chin and brings my face level with hers. 'They are frightened to grow up, frightened to be honest. Whereas you, you are honest. You are just like your father. Continue to be yourself and listen to what's inside. It'll help release the knot that is up here.' She holds her palm against my forehead. 'I can feel it is tight. We need to try to undo it. Think of this holiday as a retreat, a chance to shake off all the confusion of back home. I will help you,' she says. I nod and smile and feel lucky that she always knows how I feel even when I don't know it myself.

We walk back to the house hand in hand and Alanka continues to tell me about how hard her love life was at my age; how she spent so much time wondering whether this boy loved her or that boy cared for her, and that, really, there is no knowing until you take your life into your hands. I imagine making the first move with a boy and I reckon I could do it; my mum always tells me that I'm brave.

As we get closer to the house, I can hear shouting. Through the kitchen window there is a fuzz of colour and movement. A man swears. Alanka drops my hand and rushes towards the house. I follow her and stand behind her in the kitchen doorway. Soma is doubled up against the cooker with her hands over her face, crying, while Paritosh struts around the room, his shirt off and his face sweaty and red. Nim stands between them with her arms outstretched, one warding off Paritosh, the other Soma. Paritosh turns around and paces the other way. I wonder if he sees me.

'You need to listen to this, yes?' he says to Soma in his funny Dutch accent. 'Are you going to listen?'

Soma glares at him.

'Get out of your own way,' he says, and flicks his arm at her.

Soma scrapes her hair back: 'What you mean exactly?'

'Think about it woman,' he says. 'GET OUT OF YOUR OWN WAY – you are creating your own trouble.'

'*You* get out of your own way you, you... *sapientone*!'

'Watch it,' Paritosh points at her.

She ignores him. 'It is you – don't you see what I have done? Isn't it clear in your face? You are all pathetic. You can't survive without me, you stupid people all of you.'

Paritosh suddenly lurches at Soma.

'*Bejeesus*,' Nim shouts. 'Will you guys calm down?'

'Ha!' Paritosh says. 'Why don't you give in Soma? What will you gain even by *winning* all the arguments you have going at the same time? You just have to be different don't you? You have to wind me up like a broken clock?'

Soma laughs. 'A broken clock? Come on. Your English is really stupid.'

Paritosh turns his back to her. I look at Alanka; her eyes are wide, she looks scared.

'All I do is go away for a couple of days. It is *your* problem. *Che cosa c'è?*' Soma shouts.

'Why don't you grow up, eh, why don't you go call your mommy?'

'*You* are a child,' she throws back at Paritosh. 'Just one week and you are having trouble. Do you have a car? Do you know your way into town? Do you have any money? No – because you are all stupid. There is a *taverna* up the road. But, no – we have to wait for Soma to return. We cannot do anything without Soma who runs this fucking house.' She picks up a tin and throws it at him. It hits the wall, the lid flips open, and coins bounce and roll across the floor.

'Hey,' Nim interrupts. 'Hey,' she strokes the air with her hands. 'Why don't we sit down and work this through? You both need to lose the battle, eh? Gain freedom from compulsion, remember what Parameshvar says.'

'I don't give a fuck what Parameshvar says,' Soma shouts.

They stop and look at her. I look at my feet.

'Power freak,' I hear Paritosh say. 'Your ego is too big for you to carry. It will weigh you down if you are not careful.'

'*Vaffanculo!*'

Suddenly there is a really loud scream and at first I think it's Soma, but she looks at me, stunned. Then I realize it's Alanka. She is standing beside me shaking: 'Will you stop it!' she shouts, and, grasping her skirt, runs up the stairs.

Paritosh smacks his hand on the table and storms towards me, letting out a hissing sound as he pushes past. In the living room he slams the door. I look down, and then at Soma and Nim who are staring at me. I quickly back away. As I run up the stairs I hear Nim say, 'Phew, this hunger shit is heavy. I might go shout at some clouds.'

The row was about food. Dad fills me in later when I'm sitting with him and Alanka in their bedroom. Apparently, Soma occasionally throws a fit when she thinks that everyone is taking her for granted and she disappears for a few days just when all the food has run out. People get more and more angry with hunger until the likes of Paritosh suddenly freak out. Dad tells me this as I lie on his bed in the dark. He and Alanka have just had a siesta and I can see that Alanka has been crying. Dad says she's fine, but he thinks she should take up a more dynamic form of meditation. 'She has too much energy,' he says. 'She worries too much.'

But I'm confused about the food situation. 'Why don't they go out and buy their own food?' I ask, and Dad nods and smiles and says: 'Precisely. Exactly my point.' Dad says that some of the members of the commune find it frightening going into town: they don't speak Italian and they're not used to having to buy their own food and deal with the real world. 'But what have they done all their lives?' I ask.

'They've lived in communes,' he says. 'Places where they haven't had to think for themselves.'

'But you're not like that,' I say.

'Yes, but I'm not as entrenched as others. They rely on me as their leader.'

'So, do you buy food when the food has run out?'

'No, your father just secretly stuffs himself on prosciutto sandwiches from the *taverna* up the road,' says Alanka as she blows her nose. 'That is why he is getting so fat,' and she squeezes his side.

By dinner time, everyone seems to be getting on again. Soma and Nim are cooking together, and people mill around the kitchen sniffing the air and asking what we are having for dinner. Josie and I had a peek and saw lasagne: two big dishes with layers of creamy sauce and mushrooms, tomato and pasta. I pass Paritosh in the corridor and am so happy when he wraps his arms around me and kisses my head apologizing for the row. 'Did you hear me shout?' he asks, and I nod enthusiastically. 'Was it a good one? How loud did I go? Did I sound frightening?' Last year he jumped up in the air and hit his head on the doorframe and shouted so loud I heard it all the way from the belvedere. For days afterwards he sat in bed and relived the experience, wanting to hear from everyone what a loud noise he'd made and had it surprised people? Dad says it's because he is uptight and spent most of his childhood in a strict regime. Apparently he's been told to scream and shout as much as he can.

We all sit at the table in the garden beneath the weeping tree as the light gradually fades. Someone praises Soma and she stands up and takes a bow and when I hear the word *pomodoro* I listen carefully and work out that it means tomato. Josie sits next to me and eats as if she has been starving. She excitedly tells me about an idea that Sam and Max have about making a video. Apparently, Dad has a video camera, but I reckon they must be lying.

When Soma brings out the salad she tells everyone she is sorry for disappearing and that she hopes they understand that she sometimes goes a little crazy, and she starts to cry as she says it.

'We have decided what we are going to do for you my beloved,' says Nim. 'We are going to have a big party and we are going to invite some handsome men and you are going to release some of this ugly energy, what do you think?' Soma is laughing and crying at the same time and her face is all red and wet from the tears.

'Excellent, *woah, yeah*,' cries Paritosh, clapping his hands.

Josie stares at him, and I nudge her because she's eating with her mouth open.

Dad sits at the head of the table with his arm around the back of Alanka's chair smiling as he looks from person to person. Then I notice Sam and Max whispering. They are bending down as if they can hide beneath the table. Paritosh glances over his shoulder and I look away so he doesn't think they have anything to do with me. Then I can see what they're planning: Sam dips a piece of bread into his glass of water and lobs it at Yogi. I gasp, closing my eyes, but luckily the bread bomb misses because when I open them again, Yogi is still chattering to Nim. Only the boys are laughing hysterically: Max breathing in loudly as he throws his head back and spits food from his train-track braces. When Sam catches my eye I give him my most evil look.

Later, after salad, Dad raises his voice above the chatter and says, 'I have some news.' Everyone stops talking. He puts his hand to the back of Alanka's neck and she closes her eyes. 'It is very exciting news,' he says, and someone claps and someone else sighs. 'I know that everyone has been wondering what Lanks and I have been doing for the past couple of weeks, and I know we have been secretive and some of you have been unhappy about that, but there is a very good reason for it. And it's not that we have been arranging some kind of bank robbery,' he says, pointing to a blond man sitting next to Nim. He is the new man, Peter, and Dad says his family owns the biggest bank in Germany. 'Although, much like a bank robbery, what we are doing is going to bring us lots of money.'

'But honest money, I hope,' says Nim, and everyone laughs.

Dad lights a cigarette. 'We are doing a new book, and it is going to make us very rich. It is called *Alpha Child*.'

'*Alpha Child*?' murmurings, and I think that must be the book that Alanka was talking about.

'It is a very important book,' he says. 'It is going to revolutionize the way people think about children.'

'Revolutionize?' says Paritosh. 'Hari, I like this.'

'It is going to help us get in touch with our more raw childlike qualities, showing that it is only conditioning that separates us from the children that surround us.'

'But, surely it's also our minds, our experience and awareness?' says Paritosh.

'Yes, of course, all those things,' Dad says. 'But the book will help us learn from children to get back in touch with our more primitive, feeling being. The Alpha Child is the child who feels and does not think.'

'But that is not about our children, that is about ourselves,' says Soma.

'Yes, Soma, my beloved, always questioning,' he smiles down at her. She puts her hands together and bows. 'But we are all fundamentally children, and by getting in touch with that part of ourselves we will understand ourselves better, and we all strive to understand ourselves, no? Anyway, more to the point,' he says, 'the publishers in Europe and America are very excited about it. We have a contract and the book is going ahead and it's going to make its author...' he elaborately points to himself, 'very very famous.'

I smile at him because he has always wanted to be famous.

'So,' he sits back. 'We begin. It will be hard work and I am relying on everyone to offer support to make the project go as smoothly as possible. It's a collaboration, yes, as always?' he puts his hand on Alanka's knee. 'This is the book that we have all been waiting for,' he says, and Nim rushes to him, flings her arms around his neck, and kisses his cheek repeatedly.

The sound of a phone ringing knocks me out of sleep. I reach for the light beside the bed but my hand hits air. I open my eyes. Where am I? An illuminated darkness, the muslin curtains, the pattern the streetlights make on the ceiling. I'm at my uncle's flat. I'm in London. I jump out of bed, almost falling through the hall.

I scramble for my phone and find it in the front pocket of my bag. The word 'Home' flashes on the screen. I stop, and hesitate before answering.

'Did I wake you?' his deep familiar voice.

I rub my eyes and fold onto the floor. A sudden image of being in Italy: smoking bidis with the window open; that song again. Was I dreaming? I didn't want to wake up.

'Is it late?' he says. 'You didn't phone, I wanted to check—'

'I know,' I yawn, slowly coming round. I let my head relax on the wall, close my eyes.

'Did you get there all right? The train.'

'Yeah, fine. And you, are you all right?'

'Yeah, I'm good,' he says. 'That building I saw today. It was a real find. They're making it into flats and getting rid of all their doors, beautiful thick Georgian things. Ollie came with me. He took me for a drink with some of his mates. He told me I was looking miserable, like I needed cheering up.'

Ollie's mates? Who are his mates? I switch the light on in the corner, catching my reflection in the window: my messy hair, naked legs tucked into my body. 'Where did you go?' I sit up. Since we moved, we hardly ever go out.

'Oh, just the Griffin, there was some band, some two-man acoustic thing. This guy belting it out, like he was trying to prove something, it was terrible. Ollie kept telling me I should get up there, show them how it's really done.'

I laugh, 'You should have done.'

'Yeah, I probably would have cleared the floor.'

I shift my position, put the phone to the other ear. 'Did you have a good night?'

'It was funny. I met some new people.' He sounds happy, energized.

'Who was there?'

'Just some people, no-one you know.'

'Oh,' I say: that's strange, why doesn't he want to tell me? 'Have you been out all evening?'

'Most of it.'

'Are you drunk?'

'A little,' he says. 'But it got me thinking. The thing that Ollie said—'

Something rises in me: I don't want to talk about this.

'I don't know Sylve. It's been weird, hasn't it? That row the other day and then this and you're there on your own. I know you want to do it alone, but it's a big deal seeing your dad after all this time, and… well, I've been thinking, and—'

'It's all right,' I say. 'Honestly.'

'— I could be there too,' he says. 'I could come down, I haven't got much on this week, we could do this together—' He pauses, and I put my head back on the wall, the phone almost slipping from my fingers. 'That's how it's supposed to be, isn't it?' he says.

Supposed to be? I sit up. 'What do you mean that's how it's supposed to be? What's supposed to be?'

'Me and you,' he says. 'I just thought—'

'I don't understand what you're saying Jack. It's not just that. I have to work, I have a wedding to do.'

'Oh, yes, a wedding,' he laughs.

'Why are you laughing?'

He doesn't say anything.

'What do you mean?'

'Oh, forget it,' he says. 'I'm tired. I'm talking shit, forget it.'

'No, what is it? Are you annoyed with me? Did I do something?'

'Sylvie, it's all right, don't worry.'

We're silent for a while. I stare past my reflection to outside, at the balcony and window boxes level with my eyes.

'There was this guy there tonight,' he says. 'He and his mates go fell running most weekends.'

'Oh, yeah?'

'Crazy guy, fit as hell. He suggested I go along some time, meet some new people. I'd like to give it a go.'

'Fell running?' I say. 'Since when have you been interested in fell running?' He doesn't answer me. 'I'm the runner, aren't I?' I laugh, flexing my quads. 'I didn't know you were interested in fell running.'

'I wasn't until he told me about it.'

'But I've talked to you about it before.'

'So?'

'Well—' I stop myself. I'm being stupid. 'Well, maybe I'll come with you.'

'OK.'

'That's all right, isn't it?'

'*Sylvie*,' he laughs.

I get to my feet and walk to the window. Many of the flats are still lit up: it can't be late. I pull open the door and step outside. It's hot and clammy. Silence hangs in the air.

'So, what have you been doing?' Jack asks. I can hear him move around the kitchen, he's humming: something familiar. He's probably making himself a cup of tea. I never understand why he wants to drink caffeine before he goes to bed. 'Has your dad arrived yet?'

'I don't know,' I say.

He pauses, hums some more. I can hear the whistle of the kettle, the spoon as he adds one sugar. 'You don't know?' he says.

I move to the end of the balcony where a pigeon sits in one of the window boxes, it's been there since I arrived.

'What do you mean, you don't know?'

I pause, it's giving me the stare as if to say, Don't come too close, stay right where you are.

'I thought you were going to ring him when you arrived. I thought Sam wanted to talk to you about something, haven't you spoken to him?'

'No.'

'*And*?' he asks impatiently.

'I don't know,' I say. 'I've been thinking about it, Dad and everything, and I don't know if I want to see him.'

There's silence. I kneel down and cock my head at the bird.

Jack sighs. 'Right,' he says. 'You don't know if you want to see him,' he repeats slowly. 'I thought that was the whole point of you going there. You told me that our relationship relies on it.'

I swap the phone to the other ear and sit on the ground. 'I never said that.'

'You did. You said you had to sort things out with your dad before we get married. He needs to give you away. Why else would you be sitting there in that flat on your own? Away from home, from me?'

'Jack—'

'What about Sam? He wants to talk to you, what if it's something important?'

'I've only been away for a day, Jack—'

'You're just chickening out,' he says steadily.

A heat builds up inside me.

'You're just scared—'

'I am not scared,' I say firmly. 'It's a big deal Jack. It's not like I can just pick up the phone – *Hi Dad, how are you doing? We haven't spoken in thirteen years, but do you fancy a cup of tea?*'

He's silent.

'Fucking hell, Jack. Lay off will you, give me a fucking break.'

I can hear the TV twitter in the background, a presenter's ramble, canned laughter. He's in the living room: the low-beamed ceiling; the leather sofa we reupholstered, his muddy walking boots outside the door. 'You're running away,' he murmurs. 'You're doing it again – it's all you ever do.'

I lose myself in the flicker of the bird's eye: a small bead anxiously watching. Sparks of light against the darkness, as if there's something living inside, there's something alive and beating. It shifts its bottom and raises its tail.

'There's a pigeon here,' I say, almost to myself.

'Hmm?'

'A pigeon,' I say. It splays its wings: a bright fan of white and grey. 'It's been here since I arrived, sitting in a window box. I thought it was dying, but it seems pretty healthy.' It looks up at me again, its plump body pert and protective. 'Do you think it's nesting?'

'Probably,' he sighs.

'But how does it eat?'

'There won't just be one,' he says. 'It'll have a mate who'll take over when the other one needs a break. Like shift work, they'll share the load.'

I thought as much. I'm sure the pigeon I saw this morning was smaller: perhaps that was the female, if it works like that.

'But he's so calm,' I say.

Jack pauses, 'I guess he's just doing what feels right.'

Dad does have a video camera: he bought it in America. The boys are acting as if they've never seen one before.

'It's just like the one in *Back to the Future*,' Josie gasps as Sam holds it in both hands.

'It's even better than that.' Max takes it from him and studies it as if it's something rare, holding it like gold.

'It's only a video camera,' I say, leaning against the tree. I've seen loads before in Mum's magazines and at her work.

'It's not a video camera,' Sam feeds Max's hand through the strap. 'It's a camcorder.' He presses the eject button and they both stare down at it as the cassette holder slowly opens.

'What's the difference?' Josie asks.

'This,' Sam holds the mini-cassette between his thumb and forefinger. 'Do you reckon it fits into a video recorder?'

'It can't,' I say. 'How could it?'

'It's magic,' he says. 'You'll see.' He lifts the camera to eye level, looking through the viewfinder and pretending to film.

Max puts his hands in his pockets and leans against the tree. He sticks the toe of his boot into the gravel, his big DM boots that must make him really hot in this heat, especially with those weird fingerless gloves. He hasn't taken them off since we arrived, ratty around the fingers and reaching right up to his elbows.

'Don't you get hot in those?' I ask, stepping towards him. He doesn't answer, just looks at me and creases his brow as if

43

I'm stupid, so I step back and look at the ground.

'Does that mean we can watch what we've filmed?' Josie asks.

'You can either watch it on the telly,' says Sam. 'Or you can see it through the viewfinder as you're going along. Brilliant, isn't it?'

'I'd like to watch it on telly,' Josie says. 'That way we can pretend to be famous actors.' And she twirls around like a clumsy fat ballet dancer.

We are trying to agree on what to film. I want to film the life and times of Marilyn Monroe with a suicide scene where she jumps from an upstairs window and we cut to her lying on the gravel outside. But Sam and Max aren't interested. All Sam wants to do is prance around like a cameraman and Max has this stupid idea about species and communities that sounds as if it's been stolen from a science book.

'It's a wicked idea,' Max jumps about excitedly. 'We can do a study on communities, like this one here. All these people have come together for a common good, to praise this guru guy, what's his name, Pardonmefarty?'

Sam slaps his thighs and laughs.

'Parameshvar,' I say.

'Pardonmefarty,' Max nods and continues: 'The community is brought together for the sake of religion, it could be interesting. We can ask questions: *So, how do you feel about living in a bearded community?*' A pretend microphone to his mouth and a silly posh accent. He then swaps places as if he's answering his own question. '*Wow, man,*' he says holding his fingers in a peace sign. '*It's absolutely amazing. When we're not dancing the beard dance, we get to groom each other, and things can get quite steamy, you know what I mean?*'

Josie yelps into her hand and glares at me. 'That's funny,' she says.

'We can't ask them questions like that,' I say.

'Well, obviously,' says Sam.

'Why not?' Max looks at us innocently.

Josie pipes up: 'We could ask them about how they joined the religion, what they think of God—'

'How long they intend to grow their beards,' Max interrupts.

'You're just being stupid,' I say. 'Josie, I thought you liked the Marilyn Monroe idea. You can be Marilyn, I don't mind.'

Josie shrugs. 'Yeah, I guess so.'

I step towards her. 'Come on,' I say. 'It's a much better idea.'

'Yeah,' she says. She looks at me, and then at Sam. 'But maybe Max's is a bit more fun.'

I nudge her.

'It's just that,' she whines. 'It's maybe better for all of us to play his idea, whereas what characters would Max and Sam play in a Marilyn Monroe drama?'

'Her husband? Her dog? I would have found something,' I say.

'Anyway, I think a study of communities might be interesting,' Josie says.

I raise my eyebrows: 'Right.'

'Or we could look at species,' Max says. 'Gorillas – they're quiet, gentle creatures, vegetarians.'

'That's intelligent,' I say.

Max ignores me: 'Funny,' he flicks his fingers together. 'Sam, what about it – maybe your dad and all his mates are really gorillas.'

Dad comes out of the house and puts a bowl of cat food on the ground, looks at us and then goes back into the kitchen.

Sam points at him: 'There goes the silverback.'

Max laughs: 'He's got long arms. He's hairy, you know, all over his body.'

'No, he's not,' I laugh.

'Well, it would explain the beards,' Josie says. '*Ug ug ug ug.*' She sticks her fists into her armpits, hunches her back and walks around in circles.

'Stupid,' I whack her.

'Look, there they are,' Max says pointing to the kitchen window from where we can see Dad talking to Yogi and Nim. Yogi is waving his arms around as though he's annoyed about something. He's probably still going on about the wild boar incident up in the hills: apparently Peter was desperate for a pooh and he was a long way from home so he stopped and did one in the undergrowth and a wild boar came up from behind him and ate it. We think it's a hilarious story, but Yogi's got it into his head that if he leaves the house he too might be eaten. *But you're not a pooh?* Sam and Max chanted to one another when we overheard the conversation over dinner last night.

Max peers into the kitchen from the open window: 'Things are pretty quiet in the band at the moment, but wait until it gets heated, they might start beating their chests and barking.'

'Gorillas don't bark,' Josie says.

Sam leans against the tree and lets out a humongous yawn; it is so big it nearly covers his whole face.

Max does an impression of an overexcited monkey, and Yogi looks out of the window and frowns.

'Forget it,' I say. 'You're all being stupid.'

I walk off and sit at the table with my back to them. I dig my fingernails into the wax that's melted onto the plastic tablecloth, while Calvin Klein wraps his body around my legs. I lean down to stroke him. 'It's unbelievable, isn't it?' I say, looking over at Josie who is practising her twirly jumps. Calvin Klein purrs loudly so I can hear him. He looks up at me. 'It's unbelievable how completely and utterly embarrassing it is,' I tell him.

Josie runs up from behind me, simulating swimming with her arms. 'Film me,' she calls as she throws herself around the court-yard, running to the belvedere and enthusiastically kicking her legs in the air. Sam follows, filming her, and they sit together on the wall replaying the film through the little viewfinder. Sam's skinny pin-sticks next to Josie's chubsters.

There's a really tasty bit of thick wax that I want to get off the table. It's shaped like a flower. It unsticks and I hold it in my palm, denting my fingernails into its surface, making it mine. I put it in my pocket.

Josie rushes over to me. 'Come on,' she says. 'We're going in now. We're going in for the kill.'

Sam and Max are setting up the scene, the video camera on Sam's shoulder with Max beside him. I slowly walk over to them. They're talking in hushed voices, pretending to be professional, Sam using his potted knowledge from when we've watched Mum filming. I hang back, I'm not sure I want to be part of this. Sam is pretending to be David Bellamy – 'And now,' he says in a lispy whisper. 'After weeks of study of these strange bearded creatures with overproductive tear glands, Max has decided to infiltrate the band.' I slowly follow them as they enter the kitchen.

'*Ssh*,' I say. 'They're busy, they might be talking about work.'

They ignore me, Sam filming and Max beside him. Josie hangs in from outside the window, grinning. Max moves in front of Sam and takes a banana from the fruit bowl. 'There's the silverback,' Sam says pointing the camera at Dad. Dad stops talking. 'The leader of the pack.'

Dad raises his eyebrows. 'What's this?' he asks.

'Can we see the evidence of his silverback? – Dad, turn around,' Sam says, and Dad turns his back to us. 'Yes, just a faint sign of greying at the back.'

'Hey,' Dad strokes his hair.

I slip back out of the door to join Josie by the window.

'If we're lucky, they might bare their teeth,' continues Sam, and Dad gnashes his teeth. 'Yes, as we suspected, very large molars for chewing all the vegetables they find in the forest.'

Dad does a gorilla impression, pulling a face and letting his arms hang down from his shoulders. Josie is giggling, and it does look funny so I start laughing as well. He suddenly lurches forward and roars like a lion making Sam and Max jump and Josie and me scream.

'All right, all right,' he holds up his hands. 'Watch the noise.'

Max nudges Sam and then holds out the banana. 'We would like to offer presents,' Sam says. 'The banana is their favourite food as it is rich in sugar.' Max moves forward and offers it to Yogi. 'It is given to the most bearded one of them all – Yogi bear monkey with the most hairy features.'

Yogi raises an eyebrow.

'Would you like to share your thoughts about the banana?' Sam asks. 'Or maybe with the banana?' he says, and he and Max crack up laughing. Yogi's smile fades.

'Come on guys, enough now,' Dad says firmly.

I wave at the boys to try to make them stop, but Sam is already tugging on Max's sleeve to pull him outside. 'Sorry,' he mumbles to Dad. But Max doesn't let him. He grabs the camera. 'They are not violent creatures,' he directs it back at Dad. 'The gorillas are surprisingly placid, known for their meditation and beardy—'

'Hey,' Dad says. 'The joke is over.' He holds out his hand for the camera.

'But if pushed, it's a different matter. The silverback can attack and he can kill.' Dad shakes his head. I eye Sam – *Come on*, I mime.

'The warning signs are lips pressed tightly—'

'*Basta!*' Dad shouts suddenly, his voice sharp. It makes me jump. I've never heard Dad shout like that before.

Sam grabs Max's arm and pulls him out of the kitchen. Max is still laughing.

'Dad,' I lean in from the window reaching my arm out to him. 'Sorry Dad, it wasn't my idea, honestly,' I say, but he doesn't seem to hear me as he turns away.

Max twists his stupid long body as if he knows he's been an idiot. Sam bites his lip, kicking his feet into the gravel.

'*What?*' Max says. 'It was brilliant,' he smacks his fingers together. He skips backwards towards the side of the house. 'Come on *man*, let's see what we've got.'

Sam hesitates before following his friend; Josie twitters something and goes after them.

My heart beats fast as I look in through the window. Yogi has placed the banana back in the fruit bowl and Nim is laughing – is she laughing at us? I glance at Dad. Is he angry? But I can't see his face because he still has his back to me as he takes the coffee pot off the stove.

It's Mum on the phone.

'I was worried about you darling, is everything OK?'

I've got the cable twisted around my finger and it's making it go blue.

'Yeah, it's fine Mum,' I say.

'Why didn't you call? Did you forget to take my number?' Her voice sounds distant and small.

'No, I've just been busy that's all. We arrived late and all this stuff has been happening.'

'Sam says that Dad met you at the station this time.'

'Yeah.'

'Was it good to see him?'

'Yeah,' I say.

'Did you talk to him like you said you wanted to?'

I have a flash of him being angry in the kitchen – 'No.'

'Oh, well, you've got plenty of time. I'm just glad he came to meet you.'

'I always knew he would,' I say.

There's a pause. The line is crackly. Mum says something I can't quite hear.

'What?' I say.

'Have you all been getting along?'

'Yeah.'

I'm pushing the chair forwards and backwards on its wheeled feet.

'Good,' she says. 'And the other people in the house? Are they nice?'

'They're all right.' I can hear excited noises downstairs as Soma and Nim are washing up and Peter is drying; they're listening to music and singing.

'Well, things are good here,' Mum says. 'I've been very busy. Some days we shoot late into the night and it's tiring, but I'm enjoying it. I've probably learned more in the past couple of months than I ever learned on any course. Matthew, the lead cameraman, says he'd like me to come along on his next film. It's a love story based in Montenegro—'

'Where's Montenegro?'

'Yugoslavia. It's very beautiful.'

Where's Yugoslavia?

'But it won't be immediately,' she says. 'These things always take a while to get off the ground. It might not happen at all, you never know. Hey, I'm thinking when you get home, you could come out here, have a week or so before you go back to school. What do you think?'

'I dunno,' I push my legs and the chair bangs into the desk behind me.

'You'd like it here. My assistant's daughter came out and she's about your age. I'll ask if she's likely to come again. Maybe you could be here at the same time – give you someone to hang out with when I'm working. That would be nice.'

I don't really want to think about it now. I'm in Italy, why would I want to think about being in Russia on some film shoot?

'I showed a photograph of you to the guys here,' she says. 'They'd all love to meet you.' She pauses. 'Are you OK?'

'Yeah, I'm OK.'

'Sam says that your dad is looking good. How is he?'

'He's fine,' I say. 'He's writing this new book, it's going to make him famous.'

'Oh, yes?'

'Yeah, it's going to change the way people think about children.'

'Really?'

'Yeah, it's all about getting in touch with your feelings.'

'*Ah.*'

'It's like the idea is that all adults are really children and it's just the expectations of society that make them adults. So they need to learn from children about getting in touch with their feelings again.'

'Sounds like another excuse to talk about themselves,' she says.

'No. It's all about conditioning and he's writing it with a scientist this time – he says it's going to make him really rich.'

'I see.'

'Don't you believe me?'

'Darling, your father always thinks he's going to be rich. He's always got some scam or other on the go and it'll never happen, it's just poor souls like us who fall for it all the time.'

'Well, this time it sounds different. This time I think he's going to make it. They all seem really excited about it and he said that I can help him with the book. I'm going to be one of the models.'

'Good darling, I'm pleased,' she says.

I hear laughing. I want to go downstairs to see what's happening, so I tell Mum I have to go, that Josie will be wondering where I am, but she quickly asks me about Sam. 'Carol told me about the nightmares back home, it sounds like he's having them again, did you know?'

'Yeah.' I try to unravel the phone cord.

'I didn't realize,' she says. 'I asked him if he's all right and he didn't say much. Do you know how bad they were? Carol didn't know, she just said she woke up to noises and found him shivering in bed with the window open. I didn't want to alarm her and tell her about the ghost episode, but if it means putting bars on the windows, then it'll have to be done. Did he tell you anything?' she asks. I see an image of him standing by the window, his palms against the pane. He often saw Dad in the months when nobody knew where he was. Dad started visiting him at night, floating outside his window, and we thought it was his ghost; we thought he must be dead.

'He only told me he was having the waking dreams again,' I say quietly. 'But I don't know if he has had any since we arrived,' I add, thinking of his pale face, the yawns.

'Oh God, why is he having them?' she asks. 'What's happening? What's he seeing?' One day when Sam saw Dad floating outside, he opened his window and tried to throw himself out. Mum put bars up after that. And Dad's ghost revisited him only a few more times. I often stood in the dark when Sam slept to see if I could see him, but I never did.

'I don't think he's seen Dad's ghost since we've known he's alive.' That was six years ago. Sam was eight and I was six. He disappeared out of our lives and it was six months before he phoned: I remember hearing music and voices in the background, laughing and singing, and every time I answered his questions he was asking me the next one because he was so far away there was a delay on the line. He was in India. He had joined a religious cult and had changed his name. When we saw him again he was wearing a shiny maroon bomber jacket and faded orange jeans.

'I want you to keep an eye on him, Sylvie. I feel terrible about it. He hasn't had the dreams for years and I don't know why he should have them again now. Maybe you should tell your dad. No, he'll come out with some mumbo jumbo. Keep an eye on him and phone me if he behaves strangely.'

'But, Mum, he always behaves strangely.'

'I'm serious, Sylvie,' she says. 'And tell that father of yours to behave like a father. I don't want him making out you can do whatever you want. Sam told me he's hiring mopeds and I'm not happy about it. I don't want you coming home in a wheelchair again.'

'It wasn't that bad,' I say. 'It was only the scabs that made it so bad.'

'Well, you remember who was there for you last year and it certainly wasn't your father.'

It was weird that accident. I was on a dirt track in the middle of nowhere, miles away from the house and yet Sam seemed to find me. An old man sat me on the side of the road and squirted antiseptic all over my cuts and it made me cry it hurt so much, and there was Sam driving towards us on his moped as if he had sensed his way to me. I still can't work out how he managed to do that. Dad was having a siesta when we got back to the house. When Sam woke him up and told him about finding me, Dad said it had to be some kind of miracle.

I watch a woman as she waters her plants in the flat opposite, a verdant forest of geraniums that bursts from her balcony – she has by far the best display. I'm holding my mobile phone. Jack says I'm running away. What does he know? I flick open the phone and scroll through the contacts: Kai, Kiera, Liam, Lucy... Mark...

I catch sight of the pigeon. It's nesting: it makes sense now. It twitches and its eye darts towards me. It probably feels vulnerable now that I'm here; it would have thought it was safe when the flat was unoccupied. My uncle only stays every couple of months.

'Don't worry,' I say. 'I won't hurt you.' I clear my throat and my voice sounds loud and awkward in my ears.

I slip my phone into my pocket, go back to the living room and pull closed the door. I switch off the light and the room looms large around me. I tiptoe across the floor, holding myself in as if it's too quiet to even breathe. I stop at the table, put down my phone. I'll call Sam tomorrow. I'll find out where Dad is; see what Sam has to say: he's probably just checking up on me like everyone else seems to be. I catch my reflection in the mirror, dark shadows beneath my eyes. I should sleep. I tap my fingers on the table. But it's hardly late, not too late for Jack to have called. Not too late for some people.

Jack will be smoking a joint: his treat at the end of the day. He'll be turning the pages of a book, not really engaging. He'll slowly take off his socks as he reads, unbutton his trousers, stand up to let them slip down his legs, before stretching through his T-shirt, slipping off his underpants with one hand. He loves to walk around the house naked. He never closes the curtains even though the neighbours could easily be passing after their lonely half-pint in the pub at the end of the road. After his joint he'll drift to the bathroom. Eyes bloodshot, he'll be moving slowly in the mirror, spending too much time with the dental floss, before brushing his teeth. He'll curl his body into bed forgetting about the covers, and within moments he'll be sleeping, breathing deeply, his naked bottom white and soft in the darkness. I wonder whether he'll think of me, I wonder whether the bed will seem big and empty. Will he be wondering what I'm doing here all alone, imagining that I'm lonely? He doesn't know that I'm thinking of someone else.

It's someone who likes the night. Not like Jack. He likes to be out, on the streets, seeing London expand into its space, emptying its lungs, the tarmac stretching and popping back into place. He likes to be awake as the rest of London sleeps. He once told me this and I asked if I could join him on a walk exploring the backstreets of Stockwell and Brixton where he lives, at three or four in the morning, when only the homeless are around, the drunks and the junkies, the clubbing stragglers and the taxi drivers taking their last fare home. I asked if I could come with him, and he winked at me and said, Of course.

I wonder if he is still awake. I wonder if I can call him.

I scroll back to my contacts, past Lucy and then Mark, and I find his name. I could phone: there's no harm in that. He might answer and then he'll be there, on the other end of the line, listening to me, taking in my words. We'll be together at that moment, just me and him, phone to phone, mouth to ear. But what if he doesn't answer? He might see my name flashing on the screen and decide to ignore it. How would I cope with that?

Something catches my eye in the mirror: a light reflected from a flat opposite. It flickers at me before going out, like a candle flame smothered. The room shimmers blue, the silence and still-ness suddenly stifling me.

I'll leave it. I told myself I wouldn't phone him, that's not why I'm here. I can't do it to Jack; imagine how I'd feel if he did it to me.

I stand in the doorway. I wait.

But we're only friends, there's nothing wrong with that.

I turn to face the phone. Just a friendly hello.

I hold the phone in my hand.

Doing a job in London, I write. *Are you around?* Casual. A question so he'll reply, nothing too demanding. I could be out with mates, in a bar, impulsive, unaware of the time. My thumb touches the send key. Don't run away, you always do. I press it, throw the phone onto the sofa, and walk away. As I leave the living room, I hear a beep that tells me that the message has been sent.

Even though it's in the attic, the office is the coolest part of the house during the day because Dad always insists on having three fans blowing air around in all directions, otherwise he gets flustered and sweats a lot.

Dad is sitting at his desk typing really fast and smoking cigarettes. I'm drawing him on an old pad he has given me. It's quite easy, as he tends to stay in one position for long periods of time while he's thinking. I reckon Dad is writing his book. He was talking to Paritosh about a quote from the *Prophet*. Something about children not belonging to you and having their own thoughts.

From here I can see the side of his face. I'm drawing his profile: making his nose slightly smaller than it is, his lips a bit more frilly, but I'm having difficulty with his eye. I can barely see his eye from this angle, for the tight knitted skin around it.

'Dad,' I say. 'Just stay there a minute, I need to capture something.' He sits still, his mouth twitching like it always does. 'No, look at your work. Like you were, but be still, that's it. Thanks Dad.' I move until I can see a little more of his eye and I sketch and then move back to the position I was in. I've seen pictures of Dad before the accident, and his eyes were exactly like mine. I like to think that we look similar.

Nim comes into the office and wraps her arms around Dad's neck and she calls him Shining One. Dad leans back with his head on her chest, so I have to put my pad down for a minute and wait for them to stop talking.

'What does she mean by Shining One?' I ask when Nim has gone.

'It's my name,' he says. 'Harideva, it means God, Shining God.'

'Oh,' I say, going back to my drawing. It's funny that all their disciple names have such big meanings, like Enlightenment and Beloved and Love. I don't think English names have the same meanings. 'Did you ask to have that name?' I ask.

Dad stops for a minute, thinking about what he just wrote. 'Did I?' he asks looking at me. He frowns. 'I didn't need to,' he says. 'Parameshvar gives the names that his disciples will be able to carry. For some people the name God would be too much.' He takes a long drag of his cigarette and blows smoke into the fan.

I can see what he means. I can't imagine someone like Peter being named after a God; he looks too much like a boy for that. 'Like Peter,' I say, laughing, which makes me think: 'Is he a disciple?'

'Everyone here is a disciple.'

'Then why is his name Peter?' I reach for one of Dad's cigarettes. They are filterless Camels. I like smoking them and picking the tobacco from my tongue like Dad does even though they make my throat sore.

Dad stops and looks at me. 'What was that, noodle?'

'Peter,' I say. 'It's hardly an Indian name is it?'

He smiles. 'Ah, I see what you mean.' He lights my cigarette for me with his shiny silver lighter. 'I never thought of that.'

'And it's not German either,' I say, blowing smoke into the fan like Dad did.

'Well, maybe his family are English,' Dad says, and goes back to his typing.

'Maybe he changed it because he didn't like the name Parameshvar gave him,' I say. Like Yogi. I'm surprised he doesn't use his real name. But then I remember you're not supposed to call it a 'real' name. Yogi would give me a dismissive look if he heard me say that, as if he doesn't expect me to understand because I'm not on the path to enlightenment like they are. 'I mean, "birth" name,' I say.

Dad nods.

'I know it's not the "real" name,' I say. 'It's the "birth" name.'

'Yes,' Dad squints at the page.

Dad says that when people become disciples they give up their past because it no longer belongs to them, therefore any name they had doesn't exist any more, and their previous life isn't theirs either. Apparently it's all about detachment, not being attached to things. He says that he was reborn when he became a disciple, which makes me feel weird because Sam and I are part of his old life.

I take a drag of my cigarette and look at Dad. His birth name is David Morton. David is what everyone called him when he lived with us, before he became a disciple. It's the name my grandparents still use. Sometimes he looks like David, and other times he looks like Hari. I quite like the name Hari – it sounds mysterious.

Dad does a flurry of typing and I lean in to look at what he's writing. *About five or six years ago*, it reads. *We became friends.*

'What are you writing about?'

'About fatherhood.'

'What about it?' I move closer.

'About honesty – how a father should be honest about everything that he feels.'

'That's true,' I say. Dad always prides himself on being honest, even though Mum calls him a compulsive liar. Dad says honesty is really important in the quest to being enlightened.

'Dad,' I say. 'Are you enlightened?'

He stops and thinks for a minute. 'No,' he shakes his head. 'I'm not enlightened.'

'Do you hope to become enlightened?'

He looks at me. 'You can't *become* enlightened,' he says. 'You can become unenlightened, but you can't become enlightened. To be enlightened is just to be.' He's talking in a way I imagine he might write in his book.

'What do you mean?' I ask.

'It's peace,' Dad says, looking at me. 'It's freedom. You stop striving because you are already there.'

'Like living in the present?' I ask.

He nods. 'Like living in the present.'

'But how will you know when you are enlightened?'

'You'll just know,' he says. 'It happened to Parameshvar when he had renounced all religion, when he had given up trying. Things often happen when you're not looking for them.'

Parameshvar is Indian and has big eyes and a wispy beard. He wears long robes and holds his hands together in a triangle in all the photographs. 'Can you tell when someone is enlightened?' I ask.

Dad leans back. 'They have a peace about them,' he says. 'The peace that comes with emptiness.'

Parameshvar seems quite peaceful; I've seen a video of him. He takes ages over his words and sentences, and, apparently, he doesn't blink, although I've never been able to keep my eyes open long enough to see.

'And they don't blink,' I say.

Dad smiles, 'Yes, Parameshvar doesn't blink.'

'But how does he clean his eyes?'

'Perhaps he doesn't need to,' Dad says. 'Perhaps he is beyond that.'

Dad sits back and reads what he has written.

'What does it say?' I ask, moving closer.

'You want to know?' He looks at me.

'Yes,' I nod. 'Yes, please.'

'*I have a son and a daughter,*' he reads. '*Or I did biologically speaking at some time, but I don't any more. About five or six years ago we became friends instead. Sometimes when addressing me they use the word Father, or Papa, and I don't know who they are speaking to...'* He looks at me and says, 'What do you think? Do you think we are friends?'

'Yes,' I nod. But what about the Father bit? And I've never called him Papa.

Dad puts his arm around me and pulls me to him. 'I love you, you know that?' he says kissing me with his twitchy beard. 'You're the best friend any father could have.'

'Where's Max?' Sam calls from the living-room door.

'Don't know,' I shrug, staring at the telly. 'Probably lying underneath a car.' Last time I saw him he was beneath the Cinquecento; maybe he was trying to work out how it could possibly be so small.

'There's some mad conversations going on,' Sam is beside me. 'Outside, now – we've got to go and film them. Are you sure you haven't seen Max?'

'Yeah.'

'Shit,' Sam shifts from foot to foot, glancing outside.

'Why do you need him so badly?' I ask, annoyed. 'Can't you film whatever it is on your own?'

Sam pauses for a moment. 'Come on, come outside,' he says. 'If we stand by the tree we should be able to pick up their voices without them knowing we're filming.'

'Who?' I sit up.

'Paritosh and the others: he's telling them about his passion for trees – he's mad – he gives them names and thinks they're more important to him than his friends.'

I laugh. 'I love Paritosh,' I say.

'Weirdo,' Sam flits to the window, twitching like a nervous animal. Mum always says he looks like a deer, sensitive and serious. 'Come on,' he waves me over. 'Come and help me before it's too late.'

It is so bright outside after the darkness of the living room that my eyes take a moment to adjust. Paritosh is at the table beneath the tree, sitting with Soma, Nim and Peter. Nim is wearing a really long skirt that makes pools on the gravel, and she's got pretty white flowers in her hair. Soma's scraping beans from their pods into a big pot.

'Pretend that you haven't noticed them,' Sam says holding the video camera close to his body as we walk towards the gate that leads to the orchard.

I push into him, whispering: 'I can't pretend I haven't—'

'Hey, you guys,' it's Peter. 'What are you doing?' He's leaning back in his chair, his white shirt rolled up at the sleeves. He grabs hold of the back of my T-shirt. 'Have you been out filming today?' He pulls me towards him. He puts his arm around my waist and squeezes my flesh. 'We've got to watch out for these kids,' he says. 'They are armed and dangerous with that machine, they may see things that other people never see.' He tucks his hand beneath my T-shirt and strokes my back. It tickles, making goosepimples on my skin.

Soma whispers something to Paritosh while looking towards the house.

'Sit down,' Peter says. 'Have some wine.' I glance at Sam, and we both pull up a chair, sitting side by side next to Peter and opposite Paritosh, who has a naked chest, the dapples of sunlight from the tree like patterns of hair. Sam positions the video camera in the centre of the table.

'He's got neurosis,' Soma tells Paritosh in a hushed voice. 'As if we've got to worry about the wild boar.'

Nim leans over and breaks apart some bread, dipping it in oil, while Sam fumbles with the recording switch on the video camera. He gives me a secret look and I smile.

'There are plenty more things to be worried about.' Soma frowns at Paritosh as he looks at her, amused. 'But it is a problem.

He has a delusion – no? Sometimes I think he is crazy. What is the problem with wild boar? Wild boar is for food. If we all ate meat I would be laying it on the table and then he could see how small it is, how unfrightening when it is sliced up into little bits on the table.' She takes the bottle of wine and sloshes some into her glass. She almost finishes it in one gulp. 'These animals, they are a tradition here, they are our… what do you call it? Our prey. We kill them.'

Paritosh smiles and fiddles with his lighter. 'Yes, Soma,' he says. 'But Yogi is sensitive, you know that.'

'I know, Tosh, but come on.'

Peter fills two tumblers with wine, deep red drops spilling on the table. He notices me watching him, flicky light hair that covers his eyes, a long nose, a dimple on his chin. 'It is good for you, red wine,' he says as he passes me a glass.

'Yes.' I put it to my lips. 'I like it,' I say, even though I've only tried it once before. When he sees me look at him he winks and I immediately look away.

'There are far more important things to worry about in this world,' says Soma.

'Name a few things more important than Yogi's wild boar and my delightful pooh,' Peter raises his glass and Sam sniggers.

'Scorpions,' Soma says. 'Killer spiders, the Florence Monster.'

I glance at Sam.

'The Florence what?' I hear Nim say.

'Hey,' Paritosh says. 'Hold that – when did we last see a scorpion, when did we last see a killer spider?'

'When did you ever see the Florence Monster?' Nim asks, leaning forward. Did she say *monster*?

'I saw a scorpion within the first weeks of living here,' Soma says. 'It was lying in my bed, right beside my pillow when I went to go to sleep, and it was warning me – I tell you – it was making me stop and think before climbing into bed, just as I had to stop and think before taking that man to my bed, what was his name?'

Paritosh laughs. 'Saananda, come on, he wasn't so bad.'

'He wasn't so bad then, but Rumi told me he has gonorrhoea – he got it from those young girls in India. Imagine gonorrhoea coming into this house, how bad would that have been?' Soma stares into space, shaking her head as she chews on a bean.

'There's been a lot going around, we have to be careful, no?' Paritosh says.

'Careful? No, we have to stop fucking,' say Soma.

Fucking? My face burns and I look away.

'Fucking. Scorpions – it all adds spice to our lives,' says Paritosh.

'Yes, that delicious Bombay spice,' Peter says, pretending to be an Indian.

I nudge Sam. Scorpions. I want to ask him: don't they kill you with their long tails?

Paritosh sighs and focuses on the weeping tree. 'You see,' he breaks the silence. 'All you can hear is the sound of the tree in the wind, he is speaking to us.'

'Tsk,' says Soma.

There's a mewing from beneath the table: my friend has come back.

'What's this about a Florence Monster? Have I heard of this guy before?' Nim asks.

Calvin Klein wraps himself around me, tickling me. I reach down to scratch my leg, keeping my eyes on the table.

'The Florence Monster – the local murderer,' Peter says casually.

'Really?' Nim looks from Paritosh to Soma, her eyes wide. 'We have a local murderer?'

Soma solemnly nods. 'Yes we do,' she says.

Sam nudges me. *A murderer*, he mimes.

I know, I mime back.

'We are in these majestic hills, this peaceful place and we have our very own murderer,' Nim laughs. 'Bejeesus!'

'Oh, it is just tradition,' Paritosh says. 'It has been going for years, and mysteriously, no-one has ever been caught. It is an Italian myth: the oldies want to frighten the kids who go fuck up in the hills. It's called fear. Parameshvar would raise his hands in knowingness. It's the stupid Catholic parents' ploy to control their fuck-starved kids.'

A myth? I nudge Sam.

'That's bullshit, *sciocchezze*!' says Soma.

'Language, my friends,' says Peter. 'We have children in the vicinity.'

Soma flaps her hands and Nim and Paritosh look over at us. Sam leans forward to try to disguise his camera, and I fiddle with my fingers.

'So, it isn't true?' Nim asks, looking back at Soma.

'Of course it is true. It is as true as this chair beneath my backside. The newspapers are obsessed with it, the people who live here don't want to go out at night. He is a murderer that can't be caught, of course it is very frightening for everyone.'

'My god,' Nim clamps her mouth, and Sam presses his foot on mine.

'And he is not just a normal murderer,' says Soma. 'He kills like an animal,' she says.

Is he an animal? I don't understand. And what about the killer spiders?

I look at Sam, who is peeling a sticker off the camera. I kick him. '*Listen*,' I whisper.

'It's crazy,' says Nim.

'But wonderful gore,' Peter says, lighting a cigarette. He holds his arm above his head, the cigarette smoking from his fingers, as he balances on the back legs of his chair. 'It's like the lepers in India – you don't really live in a country until you feel some element of fear. Here, we are in the most beautiful place, but how can we appreciate beauty without knowing fear? You have the hills, yes, you have this stunning countryside, but that is why you have scorpions and murderers.'

'Oh,' Nim sighs, reaching for Peter's hand and pulling it to her chest. 'Why can't life just be beautiful?'

Soma laughs. 'You are so naive Nim, you are like a little girl.'

'I am not so naive. I just want happiness, that's all.'

Peter strokes her hand. 'It is not naive to want happiness, only naive to expect to find it everywhere. Anyway,' he says to me and Sam, 'what do you think of all this nonsense? I hope we haven't frightened you too much not to want to go out. You might be rooted to the spot like poor old Yogi and his obsession with pooh.'

I shrug and look at Sam. I want to ask questions, but I don't want to seem stupid.

'Oh, there is no real concern,' Soma says, as she stands with her bowl of beans. 'Just don't go out after dark, and don't the two of you go on those mopeds. He might think you are a couple, and these are the people he likes to kill.'

Sam laughs nervously.

'I'm serious,' Soma says. 'Sylvie, you are the girl, you are the sensible one.'

I blush and smile, repeating to myself: Don't go out after dark, and don't share a moped with Max or Sam, he might have a gun, he might kill us and then we will be dead.

Paritosh stretches his arms over his head to reveal a mat of sticky underarm hair. 'Anyway,' he says, 'I much preferred my conversation about trees.'

'If only life could be so simple,' Peter says.

Paritosh nods and laughs.

I lean towards Sam: 'Did you understand?' I whisper. 'They said it was a murderer, but it's a monster – is it an animal or a person?'

'*Ssh*,' Sam says, ducking behind the video camera. 'I'm recording.'

'So, turn it off,' I say, looking back at the table. Paritosh and Peter are still talking about trees. 'Tell me Sam, I'm confused. Why do they call it a monster?'

'It's not really a monster, stupid.'

'And what about the killer spiders, what are we supposed to do about them?'

'You know what?' It's Soma, back from the house. 'Jeet takes some beautiful photographs of trees. He is a wonderful photographer, perfect for *Alpha Child*.' Calvin Klein rubs his soft fur against my toes.

'Jeet,' Nim says, tapping her head. 'I'm sure I know him. Perhaps we met in a commune in Cologne. Yes, I remember,' she says. 'He has a beautiful girlfriend, Uta.'

Soma nods, 'Yes, Uta – a favourite of Parameshvar. He once talked about her long limbs in discourse.'

Peter and Paritosh laugh. 'So typical of Parameshvar.'

Someone whistles and Sam looks around. Max is hanging out of the kitchen doorway. He beckons to Sam, and Sam presses the stop button on the camera and stands. I grab his arm. 'Don't leave me here,' I whisper, and then realize the table is quiet. Did they hear me? Sam scrunches his face and pushes me away. 'Can't I come with you?' I whisper. He rushes off towards the house. I watch him. I shift to get up when Peter puts his hand on my thigh, a heavy weight. He looks on: 'Jeet and Uta are coming?' he asks Soma. His hand is warm. I hold my breath and try to keep my leg really still.

'I don't know,' Soma waves her arms. 'I never know who is coming and who is not coming. Nobody ever tells me.' She stands behind Paritosh and starts to massage his neck. Paritosh closes his eyes, humming, groaning, as though he's having sex. I shift in my seat. Peter winks at me and takes his hand away. 'Another mouth to feed,' Soma says. 'Always another mouth.'

I look towards the house: maybe Dad has finished work, maybe he is having a break and I could ask him about the Florence Monster; or maybe I'll find Alanka sitting on their bed, she'll tell me the whole story. I look around the table: everyone's eyes are closed, contented smiles. I'll make such a noise if I get up now, so I lean down and stroke Calvin under the table. He looks at me and closes his eyes. *A monster*, I say in my head. *What about the killer spiders, Calvin? Are they like those tarantulas I saw on TV that came out of crates of oranges and killed people?* I tuck my fingers around the side of his cheeks and he lifts his head, guiding me to stroke beneath his chin, purring. *You're my friend*, I say. *I protect you, you protect me, you'll see.* His ears suddenly shoot back to some invisible sound, and he jumps to his feet, his tail in the air exposing his backside as he saunters off.

'Look at the size of those balls,' Peter says, eyeing the cat as it walks away.

It starts to rain – little drops.

'Come quick,' Soma calls grabbing a handful of cups and glasses. 'When it comes, it comes with force.'

I look up and all I see is grey. The raindrops are getting bigger, wetness in my eyes. Soma runs to the house, while Peter nearly falls over, pushing his dusty feet into his shoes, still smoking and carrying a bottle of wine.

I'm left here, looking up at Dad's room as the rain makes stains on my T-shirt.

I run inside, up the stairs and down the corridor. I stop outside his bedroom. The door is open slightly and someone's there. I wait to hear who it is before I go in.

Even though the corridor is dark, I can still see the details. If I look into the corners, I can see that there is nothing there, even if I have to bend down and get close, because that is where they'll be hiding, in the corners of the walls where the dust gathers.

I hear Dad clear his throat. He is there. I peek through the gap in the door and see that he's alone. He's sitting on his bed. He is concentrating on something; I think he might be reading his tarot cards.

The air feels thick, a yellowy grey soup. The rain patters against the leaves and the gravel outside, far louder than any breathing or movement of the cards on the bed. He doesn't know I'm here. Maybe I could stay for a whole hour and he wouldn't know. Would he sense me? Would he look up to see me standing here?

My dad is alone. I love it when he is alone.

A slash of light fills the room, lighting the grey to white to pink, and then thunder so close that it could be right here, above our heads. I don't know if I scream but Dad is on his feet and he is shouting as the rain throws itself from the balcony, through the open doors. A gusty wind and I'm there too, struggling with the balcony doors as the rain drenches us. '*Woohoo*,' the noise like the wind as we finally close them and the quick ratatat-tat on the doors' windowpanes.

'Bloody hell!' Dad stands in the middle of the room, his eyes wide. I look down at my T-shirt; it is soaked. He wipes the wet from his face. His smile, his skin glistening. 'It's like having a shower with all your clothes on,' he says, and flaps his T-shirt. We both laugh.

He goes to the bathroom and I stand here, my clothes sticking to me, no part of me dry enough to wipe my face.

He has a white fluffy towel: he rubs his hair, the back of his neck. He whistles. He strips off his T-shirt and throws it into the corner of the room and he wipes his arms and his chest and his underarms and then he throws the towel at me. I put it to my face. I inhale. He puts on his dressing gown. The faint smell of his body, sweet and sour. I sit beside him on the bed where it is warm and dry.

'What does it say?' I ask, pointing at the cards. There's a woman on a throne, and a hooded man with an axe: the one you never want to choose. 'Oh no, Dad, you've got that one.'

'Oh, it's nothing,' he picks it up and flicks it, and it twirls and falls onto the bed like a feather. 'It's not death,' he says. 'Your poor old dad isn't going to die just yet.'

I look up at him. The rain is slowing; the room is brightening again. His floppy blond hair, his laughing eyes. He won't die. He won't let himself die.

I close my eyes while he shuffles the cards. What am I going to ask? *Can I live with you? What's the Florence Monster? Do you love me?* But I'm trying to focus on just one thing.

'Think about your question, repeat it in your head,' Dad says.

I know you love me, you must do. But will you say yes to me if I ask you things? Will you be there for me?

'Now, take ten cards, holding the question in your mind.' He opens the cards like a fan. I pick one after letting my hand hover for a moment, trying to feel its energy as if it is speaking to me.

I pick ten cards and pass them to Dad.

Dad lays them on the bed, one at a time, making a cross in the middle and a strip down the side. I scan them. There's one of a person wearing a blindfold with two swords crossed in front of him, and another of a big hand holding a yellow globe like a sun: I like this one best.

'What does it say?' I ask.

'Hmm,' Dad shifts to make himself comfortable. 'This one here,' he says pointing to the blindfolded card, 'is a good card, it's about freedom.'

'Really?' I say. 'I thought it was a scary card.'

'None of them are scary,' he says. 'This one is about being yourself. Not being held back by fear.'

'Like being scared?' I say. 'Not being scared?'

Dad smiles, 'Yes, I guess it could mean that.'

I smile and sit back. The rain has stopped and the clouds are parting again, brightness, a clarity, the deep blue sky. 'Look,' I say pointing outside.

'That was quick,' Dad says and peels himself off the bed. He goes to the balcony doors and opens them. His feet pad on the wet carpet.

I sit back, taking a deep breath as new air fills the room: it smells sweet and green.

Dad sits down again. I cross my legs and lean towards him. 'And that one,' I say, looking at another card. 'What does that mean?' It's a dark image of a woman and a child on a boat with lots of knives stuck in front of them.

'Hmm,' he says. 'This one is about pain.'

'Pain?'

'But not all pain is bad. Sometimes pain is necessary to help you get what you want.'

'Oh,' I say.

'And here, the Knight of Cups tells me of change, like moving house, living somewhere else?' He looks at me.

'Really?' I say, the blood rushing to my face.

'Yes,' he smiles. 'You are a strong person, and you have a strong desire for change.'

My eyes widen. Maybe this is about moving here. Dad giving me what I want.

'So,' he says, looking at all the cards. 'Is this change going to happen?'

I lean forward hugging my chest, squeezing the fingers together on both hands. I do want to live here, be here, with you, for ever. Please let it happen.

'Something *will* happen,' he says. 'But it may not be what you intended it to be. See here,' he says, pointing to a picture of a little man sitting beneath lots of gold cups. 'This card is in an important position, and the cups are a sign of emotion, the nine of cups is one of the most emotional cards in the deck.'

'What does it mean?'

'It means you'll have some big emotional upheavals. Some big event going on in your life.'

71

'Like what?' I ask. Moving house, that's emotional.

'Perhaps you will row with your brother, or your mother, or take a lover? Or maybe it's just a state of mind, an imbalance inside—'

'Or something that will happen in the future? Some big event?'

'Perhaps. But it's very hard to predict the future: even the most advanced psychics can't always get that right. Although I do, sometimes. See this one,' he shows me a picture of a couple dancing beneath four wands. 'This is the ultimate outcome. Your first response will be to run away from these situations – either your internal confusion or whatever is going on around you – but this card says that you must face them, you must not be swayed by other people, you must be yourself. You see?'

'Yes,' I say, nodding. I think I see.

Dad pushes up his sleeves.

'But, what does it mean?' I ask, shifting forwards. I don't want the reading to end. I don't want him to go. 'Do I get what I want?' I ask.

'You're so funny,' he laughs. 'You're just like your mother. You want results and you want them now, eh?' He punches my knee. 'As I said, sweetie, I can't predict your future with these cards. You should only be concerned with the now. The past and future don't matter.'

'But doesn't it say just a little bit?'

He looks at the pattern before him and nods. 'You'll get what you want,' he smiles. 'You'll most definitely get what you want.'

'Really?' I ask looking at him, trying to see deep into his eyes. Is he lying? Is he making it up?

'Yeah,' he sighs. 'But it may not happen in an obvious way. You may not get it while you're looking for it.' He gets up from the bed. 'It's the same as with life, sweetie,' he says. 'You have to sit back and let life take care of itself – it will all make sense in the end.' He undoes the sash of his dressing gown. 'Hey, you know what?' he says. 'I have to go. Can you put those back in the silk scarf when you're finished, and back in the drawer?'

But I don't understand. Does it mean I'll get to move here or not?

Dad takes off his dressing gown and opens the wardrobe.

'Where are you going?' I ask.

'Into town,' he says, slipping on a shirt.

'Can I come?'

'No, lovey,' he says. 'I'm literally in and then out. I'll take you there soon, I promise. Alanka wants to take you shopping.'

'To Benetton?' I ask, sitting up. 'To get something for the party?'

'You can go wherever you like.'

He sits on the edge of the bed and pulls on his shoes.

'Dad,' I say.

'Yes, lovey.'

'Can I ask you something?'

'You can ask me anything, lovey.' He stands in front of the mirror, tidies his hair.

'Who is the Florence Monster?'

He turns to me, surprised for a minute, then he laughs. 'Oh, that nonsense,' he says. 'Who's been telling you stories?'

'No-one, just Soma and Peter were talking about it.'

'That bloody Peter, don't listen to him, he's a nincompoop.'

I laugh. 'He didn't say anything,' I say. 'They just mentioned the monster, and they didn't say anything else. They were talking about killer spiders and scorpions.'

Dad comes over and sits down. He strokes my hair, smiles at me. 'Toots,' he says. 'Some of the people in the house talk silliness, OK? Don't believe what they say. Yes, there are scorpions in the area, there are scorpions everywhere but they won't kill you and no-one has seen one since we moved into the house—'

'Soma said—'

'And, as for the Florence Monster, it's just the crazy Italians, they always have to have a drama.'

'But, what is he? Is he actually a monster?' I don't know what a monster looks like: maybe a werewolf or the yeti from Sam's Tintin book.

'No, he's not a monster. He's just a man who apparently murdered couples up in the hills for about ten years. They call him the Florence Monster because he is a serial killer and did some pretty gruesome things to his victims.'

'Like what?'

'It doesn't matter. None of it matters because the *carabinieri* have caught him.'

'When did they catch him?'

'Earlier this month.' He stands up. 'It was in the paper.'

'Oh,' I say.

'Silly thing!' He ruffles my hair. 'You have a vivid imagination, huh?'

'So, he's been caught?' I ask as he walks away.

'Yeah,' Dad tucks in his shirt in the mirror.

'So, Soma and Peter were wrong?'

Dad puts his wallet and keys in his pocket and turns to me. 'That is not the only thing that Soma and Peter are wrong about.'

'Soma said that we shouldn't go out after dark and we shouldn't go on our mopeds.'

'Soma is Italian. You'll get to know what they are like my sweetheart, you'll see.'

'So there's nothing to worry about.'

'There is only something to worry about if you believe there is something to worry about. Remember that.'

Dad pats his pockets and looks as though he is ready to leave. I sit forward, there's something I want to ask him; I've been meaning to ask since we arrived. 'Dad,' I say.

'Mmm?'

'You know how I should be drawing and writing things every day?'

'Mmm.'

'Well, Sam left my sketchbook at home and I've got all these things I want to keep and I wondered if you could buy me something to put them in. When you go into town, this afternoon, could you buy me a sketchbook?'

He pulls a funny face. 'I've got loads of books upstairs. Have you had a look there?'

'Yes, but I wanted something special. I had one and I left it at home. I'd really like one, more than a dress from Benetton or anything else. Will you buy me one?' I say it quickly. I can feel my heart flutter in my chest: I hate asking him for things.

'Yes, I guess I could,' he says. 'I'll look out for one. Remember to put those cards away,' he says. 'They're precious.' And he kisses me goodbye before leaving the room.

I sit back on the bed and push my hand through the pattern of tarot cards. I hope he didn't mind me asking for my own book. I know exactly the one I want. I saw them last year when we went to Florence: they are big and the pages are thick and the cover has swirly patterns on it like oil. I hope he doesn't think I'm bad asking. Then I can stick in the train tickets, the leaves I found in the garden, the flower wax from the table, the sunflower petal that lay wilting on the side of the road. It can be a record of my time here, from start to end. I want to prepare myself for the fact that I probably will have to go home. Mum would never let me stay. She'd rather I lived with Carol than my own dad, even though we're not related.

I look down at the cards and the Knight of Cups looks up at me. I turn it over in my hand. He looks strong, like a warrior. He's dressed in armour and he's carrying a yellow cup like he wants to give it to someone. This card told me things were going to change. I might find a new home: that's what Dad said, as if he was reading

75

my mind. Maybe if I don't say anything, it'll happen anyway. Sit back and let life take care of itself, like Dad said.

I look up to check that no-one is coming before I slip the card into my pocket.

I have decided exactly what I want to wear for the photographs that Dad's photographer friend is going to take of me. Dad says that I'm going to be the main model for the book, *Alpha Child*.

'*Alpha Child* – it sounds like a superhero,' Josie says. 'Wouldn't it be funny if you had to wear blue starry pants?' Her arms are wrapped around her ankles as she tries to squeeze her whole body onto the chair so that the ants can't crawl up her legs. She's decided she hates all insects: the flies dying on the sticky strip in the kitchen, the mosquitoes whining in her ear when she tries to sleep.

Then I told her about the killer spiders and the scorpions.

Last night I awoke to find her sitting up in bed, her knees to her chest and her eyes scrunched closed. She was chanting – *It's all right, it's all right, it's all right.* When she saw me awake she jumped out of bed. I had to check it three times. I told her that Dad says there's nothing to worry about; I told her it's her mad imagination. But Sam had been telling stories about the Florence Monster: that he could kill any time now. So I put her right on that fact as well.

I'm sitting on the floor of the belvedere with my legs out-stretched around the photography books that Dad gave me to mark up for ideas for his book. My legs are bare against the concrete, and the ants must think they're mountains as they crawl up and over them, running down the insides of my thighs and circling my knees. It really tickles so I flick them off.

'It sounds just like *Wonder Woman* or something,' Josie says, still going on about the *Alpha Child* book. 'Maybe the next book your dad writes will be called *Bat Baby*,' she laughs. 'Imagine, a little baby in a batman suit, flying through the air.' She stands up and holds her arms out like she's flying.

'Yeah, or *Spider Granny*, a little old lady who climbs walls,' I say, and Josie thinks this is hilarious, doing her funny breathing-in laugh that makes her sound like she's hyperventilating.

I go back to my books. My favourite is open on my lap to a photograph of a pretty girl in a swimming costume. It's a book of photographs of girls aged twelve and thirteen. Some look young, as though they aren't developed yet, while others look as old as sixteen. I look more like the sixteen-year-olds as I've got boobs like them and I've started my periods – much earlier than most of the girls at school. Josie hasn't started hers yet. The swimming girl sits with her legs over a chair, her wet hair around her face as she looks sulkily at the camera. Her swimming costume has spots on it, which sparkle like diamonds. She's so pretty I could look at her for hours.

'I'm going to look natural,' I say, sitting back. 'Alanka said that I can borrow any of her clothes, but I'll probably just wear mine, because that way I'll look my age and Dad says he wants photographs of children, not grown-ups.'

'Why would you want to look like a grown-up anyway?' Josie asks.

I pick up my lighter, staring at the flame.

It's not that I want to look like a grown-up. It's just that I watch Alanka sometimes when she's ironing or tidying, and she has this way that she does things, dressed in soft loose trousers turned up at the bottom, her small ankles and feet, her perfect pearly toenails: the way she leans over and touches the floor without bending her legs, or gently moves the hair away from her face with the back of her hand.

I hold my finger in the flame until it goes black.

'Don't do that, silly,' Josie says. 'You'll hurt yourself.'

'It doesn't hurt,' I tell her.

Looking through the rest of the books, I mark the pictures that I like with little stickers. One is of a girl sitting on her dad's knee, looking back at the camera as if she is surprised that it is there; her dad is holding the outside of her body like a cradle. Another is of a girl with long brushed hair and plimsolls; she stands between two boys as if she could choose one of them if she wanted to.

'Listen,' Josie calls. It's the sound of shouting and the whine of motorbikes coming up the hill. 'Is that them?' She jumps up and leans out of the belvedere. 'It's Sam and Max coming back with the mopeds. Come on, let's meet them at the top of the drive, see if we can get there before them.'

'Are they back already?' I join her at the wall. 'Did you see them?' I lean out, but I can't see anything.

'No, but listen,' she says. But it could be anyone: the boys that drive up the road, their Italian sounds coming and going as they turn corners.

'Look,' Josie points. 'It's them.' And then I see it, a fuzz of ginger then blond, their heads rising with the curves of the road. They've got their own mopeds; Max was desperate to get one – apparently he's a bike freak.

The boys stop at the top of the drive. By the time we get there we are hot and out of breath.

Josie hops about. 'Can I get on?' Sam gets off his moped and holds it for her while she slips onto the seat. 'Oh my God, it's so exciting,' she beams. 'Did you have fun in town? What did you do? We've been waiting for you.'

'We just looked around,' Max shrugs and squints in the sunlight.

'How did you find your way back?'

'Sam knows the way, and he knows some Italian. Enough to get us a – what is it? *Prosciutto panini*?'

'*Un panino al prosciutto*,' Sam says in a silly Italian accent.

Josie squeals and claps her hands. 'Where did you learn that?'

He shrugs, trying to hold back a smile.

'Oh, yeah, we got this—' Max goes into his bag.

'Did you get one for us?' I ask. I'm hungry.

'No,' Max says pulling out a newspaper. 'But look at this.' He thrusts it at me. 'Read it and weep baby.'

I try to read it, shading my eyes from the sun. *Il Mostro di Firenze* says the headline above a photograph of a body lying in front of a car; the body looks as though it is dead. 'What does that mean?' I ask.

'What do you think it means?' Sam asks. '*Il Mostro* – the Monster – of—'

'*Florence*,' we all chant.

'Oh my God,' Josie inhales.

'But—' I say.

'Another killing,' says Max.

'But Dad says—'

'Up in the hills just north of here,' says Max, his eyes glistening.

'How do you know?'

'Cause we asked the man in the shop.'

'So, he hasn't been caught?' I say. 'But how did you understand him? Did he speak English?'

'We just guessed—'

'So you could be wrong?'

'Let's find out. Where's that crazy cook, what's her name?' Max pushes his bike and rolls down the hill before the engine kicks in.

'Soma,' I shout after him. 'Ask Soma.'

Max is in the kitchen with Soma before we've even got there. She is reading the newspaper; she mimes the words that she reads.

'*Porca Madonna.*'

'What?'

'It is not good,' she shakes her head.

'Was it him?' I ask. 'Has there been another murder?'

'No,' she says.

'Not him?'

'Yes,' she says.

'What?'

'Yes it is him but this time he didn't kill.'

'And they caught him?'

'No, they didn't caught him.' She continues to read: 'Poor poor people,' she says. 'He had a gun.'

'Where?' Max asks.

'Near here,' she says looking up. '*Mamma mia*, it was Vicchio de Mugello, just to the north. We have had picnics there.'

Josie looks at me.

'*Che stronzo!*' Soma says.

'What? Tell us what happened,' I say.

'A young couple, always a young couple,' she shakes her head. 'They are sitting in their car – probably kissing or something, you know? – and they see this man. He comes out from some trees, *portando un revolver* – he is carrying a gun and he is about to shoot and something happens like a noise and he stops enough time for the young boy Niccoló to start the car and get away—'

'So they didn't get killed?' I ask.

'No,' she shakes her head and reads on. 'But how scared they must have been. Here,' she says, pointing to the photograph. 'This was the last attack, it was last year, it was again a couple and the young girl was found lying on the ground, naked and, I think, if I am right, that her – you know,' she says pointing downwards, 'her area down here, it was removed. They found this strange thing: *un pampino sporgente*,' she reads. 'What it is? A leaf, a branch or something it is sticking out of her.'

'Out of her where?' I ask.

'Her... Her pussy,' Soma says.

'*Urgh.*' Josie has her eyes closed and her hands over her ears.

'Blimey,' says Sam.

'And this man,' Max says. 'What does he look like?'

'Mmm,' she says, retracing the words. '*Alto, di mezza età, con capelli grigiastri.*' She translates, 'He is tall, yes, he is tall, middle-aged, with hair that is grey.'

'Is that all, is that all it says?' Josie asks.

'The last girl,' she continues. 'The one last year, she was stabbed many times.'

'How many times?' Max asks.

'A hundred or more,' Soma says.

'Oh no!' Josie hugs my arm.

'You see why you have to be careful, yes?' Soma passes the newspaper back to us. 'You be careful,' she says, and goes back to the sink where she is rinsing dishes.

The adults are playing a house game, which means that there won't be any sit-down meals for the whole weekend: we just have to help ourselves to food whenever we're hungry. It's a game that is going to be in Dad's book, and it's about timelessness and being a child. I asked Dad if we can play, but he said no because we are children so we don't have to pretend. Sam and Max have a better idea anyway. They have decided to make a film about the Florence Monster.

Dad says we should stay away from the house because everyone is going to be in a constant state of meditation. So we hang around on the belvedere planning our film.

'It's perfect,' Max paces from wall to wall. 'We're right in the middle of it. We're staying here, in this house and moments up the road there's this man and he's trying to kill people. He could be walking just up there,' he says, pointing to the road. 'He might drive past the house. I wonder what car he drives.'

'Oh, don't,' Josie waves her arms.

'But, honestly, we should make a documentary. This is part of history. We should ask people what they think, people in the street. Normal people who have to live with it every day. Sam, you can talk Italian.'

'Not that well, I can't,' he says.

'All right, well even if we just speak to these hippies here, we might get something good.'

'No way,' I shake my head. 'They're all in meditation, Dad said we should leave them alone.'

'Bollocks to that,' Max says. 'They need a smack in the face, meditation.'

'What about a drama?' says Josie. 'We could make up our own story, you could be the monster Max, and me and Sam, we could be one of the couples—'

'Yeah, a drama,' says Max. 'That's a better idea.' He paces the other way and Josie smiles, looking pleased with herself.

'Only because you want to pretend to have sex with Sam,' I say under my breath. I pat my pockets. I want to light my cigarette, but can't find my lighter.

'No I don't,' Josie blushes and looks towards Sam who is sitting with his feet tucked up on the wall. 'I only meant on the motorbikes,' she says. 'Do you think he shoots you down first and then stabs you when you're already dead?'

'I reckon,' I say.

Josie pulls a lighter from her pocket and lights my cigarette for me. I frown at her: 'Hey that's mine,' I say, as she slips it back into her pocket. What's she doing with my lighter? She doesn't even smoke.

'Does the monster scare you?' Max paces back again, looking straight at me.

'No. It doesn't scare me.'

'It scares me,' says Sam, and we all laugh.

'It scares me as well,' says Josie. 'I find it really scary thinking of him roaming around when we're sleeping.'

'That's why we should make a film about it,' Sam says, jumping off the wall. 'We make it into fiction, then it's not so scary.'

Josie looks at him and smiles.

'OK,' says Max. 'Let's set up a scene. Maybe we could have a camping scene in the garden. Josie, you said you want to be a victim, you and Sam could be sleeping in a tent. I'll be the murderer.'

I raise my eyebrows at Josie. 'The victims, eh? Couples?'

Josie jumps forward, 'No,' she says. 'I'll film.'

'I thought you wanted to be the victim? *Chick-chick-chick-chicken.*' I flap my arms like a chicken.

She waves the smell of smoke away as it wafts from my cigarette. 'I've changed my mind,' she says, trying not to look at Sam. 'I'll film.'

'You'd better have a lesson first,' I say. 'Sam won't let you touch that thing before you know what you're doing, will you Sam?'

'She's all right,' Sam says and passes Josie the video camera.

I pull a face at him. 'I was only joking,' I say.

'OK. Sam, you be the murderer,' Max says.

'Why can't I be the murderer?' I ask.

'Because you're going to be the victim,' he says. 'You're the female and I'm the male, and we'll be in the car. That one there,' he says, pointing to Dad's car. 'We'll be asleep in the car, and Sam, you come along and scare us and we get on our moped and try to escape, but you shoot us down with a gun.'

'Brilliant,' Josie says. 'And you've got to pretend to have sex.'

'No fucking way,' I say.

We black out the car windows with felt that we find in Dad's office to make it seem like night time. Max and I climb in. Sam works out that the best way to film is from outside, under the black felt. They insist that Max and I have to pretend to kiss. I tell them, if they're lucky. The passenger door closes with a clunk. It's dark in here, dark and quiet. I try not to breathe. I'm sure he smells of BO.

'OK, sis,' he says. I look up at him, the outline of his face. Is he smiling?

'I'm not your sister.'

'Doesn't it make it easier that way?'

I sit as far away from him as I can, looking towards the windscreen for Josie, but she's not there. It's hot in here, hot and dark, dark and smelly.

'Here,' he says, and lifts his arm, putting it around me. 'If you put your head on my shoulder like this, it'll seem like we're kissing.' I do as he says but I hold my breath. I close my eyes, listening to his breathing, in, out, in, out. What is taking them so long? I cough and open my eyes. I shift myself and knock into him, the scratch of his fingerless gloves.

'Why do you wear those gloves?' I ask. I can see them in the shadows, dark and long, a slice of skin between the gloves and his T-shirt.

Silence – in and out, in and out: is his heartbeat quickening? He clears his throat. 'Why do you wear those silly beetle crushers?' he asks. I'm so close to him I can feel his voice moving from inside of him.

'Why not?' I sit up.

'Yeah,' he says. 'Why not?'

I look at him sideways before putting my head back on his shoulder, a warm musty smell. 'It seems like you're hiding something,' I say. I gently move my hand to the end of the glove, right into the crook of his elbow. He doesn't flinch, so I ease my fingers around the rim. It slowly releases from his elbow, and eases down his arm. He lets me. His skin against my knuckle, soft, rough to ridged. There's something there – something raised and rough on his skin. If I pull it further, I'll be able to see. He doesn't stop me.

'Ready,' Josie calls. A stream of light floods into the car; Josie's beneath the felt. She laughs. 'Come on, you've got to do better than that.' I pull my hand away and suddenly Max's face is on mine. He's gripping the back of my head and his mouth is on my face, kissing me full on the lips. I struggle, pulling my head back, pushing him away. He follows me, groping me with his mouth. I can hear cackling laughter and imagine Josie's face pressed against the windscreen.

'What the fuck,' I say, my head banging against the window. I

84

imagine his tongue lolling from his mouth, the flash of his train-track braces. He's laughing. I lift my knees and kick him really hard, and he falls back, knocking against the steering wheel. '*Argh*, fuck,' he grips his chest.

I reach for the door lever and push myself out of the car, wiping my face, trying not to breathe his stench, it's so disgusting.

'What happened?' Sam asks half laughing.

I run towards the house, the tears stinging my eyes. He was laughing at me, so was Josie. I can't believe it. He was doing it to make me look stupid.

In the hall everything suddenly goes black. I stop. I hold the wall. It's dark, a calm as if my brain has stopped. I wait. I count to three.

'Sylvie,' it's Josie. 'Are you OK?' I try to focus, but I can't see. There's colour rushing past my eyes, colour shot with needles. I'm dizzy. She grabs my arm. 'What did he do?' she asks. A waver in her voice: she thinks it's funny.

I push past her and rush up the stairs. My head spins. *You're OK. You're OK. You're OK.* But it makes me think of Josie last night, too scared to go to sleep. I laughed at her; I didn't care about how scared she was. I open the door and see her bed next to mine. I throw myself down. *You'll be OK*, I say, burying my head into the pillow, and no-one, not even Josie, follows me.

Later that evening I knock on Dad's door and he and Alanka are sitting up in bed. I've been saying to myself, over and over, that I mustn't cry, taking deep breaths, but the minute I walk into their room I burst into tears. Dad puts his arms out and I collapse onto the bed. I lie down with my head in his lap and his large rough fingers stroke the tears from my face while Alanka holds my hand. 'Things are never as bad as they seem,' she says but that doesn't help right now because the tears just keep on coming and I feel like I want to die.

Alanka goes downstairs to make me a cup of camomile tea and I tell Dad that I don't know why I'm upset, but I'm sorry that we called him a gorilla and that we didn't stop when he asked us to. Dad smiles and strokes my face. 'I wasn't really angry. I don't get angry,' he says. I tell him that I tried to get the others to shut up and that it was Max and he is so horrible that I hate him and I wish he wasn't here, and I cry again thinking of that kiss and the smell, and my eyes hurt and I don't know why I feel so sad. Dad gently strokes my hair.

'Sometimes it helps to feel the pain you have, and to own it,' he says softly. 'Because then you realize that it is your pain, and therefore if you own your pain, you can control it: you can switch it on if you choose to, just as you can turn it off if that is what you decide.' I look up at him and wipe my face with my sleeve. Dad reaches over and gives me a tissue. 'Do you understand?' he says. 'Now you feel pain, but you also have the capacity to be happy. If you close your eyes,' he holds his palm over my eyes. 'Close your eyes,' he says and I close them, his flesh blocking out the light. 'Where is your happiness?' he asks gently. 'Can you see it?'

I hiccup, 'No.'

'OK, visualize your happiness. When were you last happy?'

I stop for a minute, trying to remember. That sense of warmth when Dad met us at the station: seeing him for the first time, the comfort of his smell. The touch of his hand on my face. 'When we got off the train,' I say.

'Visualize it,' he says. And I take myself there, to that feeling of immersion, disappearing into a deep soft piece of sponge. 'Now, does that feel good?'

I nod. 'Yes.'

'And where did that come from?' he asks, taking his hand away from my face.

'Me?'

'Exactly,' he says. 'You see? You have all the power. You needn't be frightened of anything. Your happiness is in your hands.'

As I leave their room I remember about the sketchbook: I forgot to ask if Dad bought me one in town. I stop to turn around to ask him, but I remember what he said: my happiness is in my hands. I want to cling onto that now, not let anything ruin it.

It feels good to be running on pavement again. I love the shock through my joints as my feet hit the ground, the hard impenetrable surface. I love exploring the tangle of the city's streets.

This morning, I woke up early to the rumble of rush hour, angry horns outside my window and the roll of courier motorbikes. I lay in bed and my mind filled with possibilities. I opened my eyes and watched as daylight moved with the curtains, and I thought – this could be my life.

I checked my phone. No messages.

I turn the corner and almost hit a woman, smaller than me in her smart blue jacket and skirt. I call out, 'Sorry,' and she curses – 'Fuck off,' she says under her breath, she doesn't even look at me. I turn on my toes, skipping, and wave at her, calling – 'You mustn't be late for work!'

Jack came into my dreams last night: a fragile face, shady in tones of blue. He was telling me I had to do the washing up. Looking at me intently, he tried to see deep into my eyes, as if he could recognize what I was hiding from him. All I could do was cry. I was sobbing, gasping for breath, my body thick and heavy; such a deep sense of sorrow that it shook me awake. I had only been asleep an hour. I kept my eyes open, curled in a ball with the duvet right over my head in case something touched me out there in the dark.

Jack loves me more than anyone he has ever loved, that's what he tells me. He wants to marry me, to spend the rest of his life with me, the two of us equal – always loving, supporting, always trusting.

The red pedestrian says stop, but I don't. I scan the traffic as I run but fail to see a motorbike as it rushes up the inside lane, missing me by millimetres. He hits his horn and shouts at me. I jump onto the pavement, my heart beating fast, but I continue to run. Sometimes I feel invincible, as if I could crash into vehicles and I would survive.

Is he right for me? No, he's not. Jack Dawson is not right for me: how easy it is to say. He is too calm; too passive; he doesn't challenge me. It's as simple as that.

I take a corner and look up, searching for a street sign. I don't know where I am. I stop and jog on the spot, looking this way and that: so many suits, black, grey, blue, coffee in their hands, talking into their mobile phones; I don't want to ask the way, I don't want to stop. I close my eyes and turn around – this way, I sense it. However lost I get, I always find my way.

He's always there for me. If I asked him to, he would drop his pen, turn away from his work, leave a room that's filled with his friends. I know he would, if I asked. Everyone tells me what we have is perfect, a normal relationship: my friends laughing – but it's normal, welcome to the normal world. Who wants normal? Me loving him, him loving me, no pedestal, all equal. Can it really be that simple?

I speed around the corner, dodging a lamppost and a woman with her young child. I keep my head straight, my eyes dead ahead. Comfort versus risk; safety versus fear. Is that all it is: the excitement and the thrill of the unknown? I didn't expect this to happen. I didn't ask for it.

My breath feels short. I wish I'd brought my pedometer to measure my speed.

I suppose I fed off it, the unusual, the unknown, after Jeet and the mess and the ensuing relationships with older men. The unattainable, never really knowing someone: it's easier that way; it's easier to leave.

Three men take up the pavement with their navy shoulders and briefcases. They are talking about serious things, walking slowly, one of them on his mobile phone. 'Excuse me,' I puff. Their heads nod, their conversation continues. 'Excuse me,' I say a little louder. 'Excuse me,' I shout and press the toe of my trainer into the back of his shiny shoe. They stop and look at me as I push past them, faster than any of them could smack a squash ball.

He likes dogs; I like cats.

He's got no sense of time.

He'd go fishing if only I'd let him.

He likes to walk; I like to run.

He would be a marathon runner; I would be a sprinter, faster and faster.

I run along the riverbank; I can see another bridge. I count with my footfalls. The world seems to shake, my breathing tight in my chest. I can't think about how slowly he walks, how it makes me feel heavy, it makes me feel as if I have to slow down. He tells me I can't relax, he tells me I don't let myself think, and it might drive him crazy, but it doesn't stop him loving me. Nothing stops him loving me.

Southwark Bridge, my breathing is shallow, I need to loosen it, lower it, breathe from the gut. I'll take the roads again. Perhaps I'll slow, a little. I'll head north: it should get me back to where I came from.

He loves me so much that he asked me to marry him. It was a year ago. We were up in the hills. His face was serious. I guessed it, didn't I? 'We've been together three years,' he said, 'and I want to have kids.' How practical is that? 'I think we should get married.' I told him he should have got on one knee, given me a ring, so he did it the next day. But it was a band he'd made from copper piping and it made my finger go green. It was funny, so typical of him, so unaffected. About a month later, I got a proper ring: it was his grandmother's. It was – it *is* – beautiful: three one-carat diamonds in a platinum setting; it's worth a fortune. I touch my finger and get a sudden shock that it's gone. Of course, I took it off: I was practising life without him.

A sharp pain shoots up my leg and I've stopped suddenly, clamped my hand onto my thigh, massaging, trying to rub it away. The pain eases and I attempt to run again, one foot in front of the other, but the pain has shot right the way up my leg, catching me in the groin, almost paralysing me. I stop. I don't know where I am. I feel off balance, dizzy and – something strange happens – tears start to well up in my eyes. A man walks past and looks at me, up and down, his lips turned up at the edges. I feel exposed, naked. I pat my sides, no pockets in these blasted shorts, no money, no phone. I didn't want to bring my phone. I hobble to a wall and sit down, rubbing my leg. It's just cramp; it'll pass. I close my eyes, regaining my breath, settling. How strange just to cry like that, for no apparent reason. I breathe in and out, sitting back. I was running. I'm happy. There's nothing wrong. People's bodies move fast above me, but no-one stops, no-one asks me if I'm all right. If I'd brought my phone, I'd be able to call Jack.

'Excuse me,' I say softly. 'Excuse me.'

A woman looks down at me.

'Can you direct me to St Paul's?' She pauses as if she doesn't understand me – 'St Paul's,' I say again.

She nods, 'Yes, I heard what you said.' She points straight up the road, and there in front of me is the handsome dome rising above the buildings and I wonder why I didn't see it.

As I walk towards the cathedral, a tune comes into my mind. I'm humming, but I can't find the words. It's something important, what is it? '*I would never leave you when the sun is shining.*' Jack was humming it on the phone last night. It's a silly song that he made up one morning when we were both in bed. We had just made love and it had left me feeling strange, as if he'd filled me with an intensity that took me away from myself. I'd lost control. I looked up at him, and the light was so bright, his face so alive, as if he was enjoying every drop of me, and I was overwhelmed. I didn't know how to handle this thing we had created: my world felt unsteady, everything spilling. I reached out to him and he told me to shush and took my face in his hands, kissing away the tears. He didn't ask me what was wrong but he whispered to me, '*Nothing will take me away, nothing,*' and as I closed my eyes and held my face against the warmth of his chest, it felt as if he had been given to me, like a gift.

We lay side by side, our arms in the air above us as if we were flying. We were laughing, and he started to sing: '*Even if it was raining, I wouldn't go.*' And I believed him at that moment, as if everything suddenly fell into place. We got up and made breakfast; we sat together in the kitchen, the back doors open, the cool air chilling our bare feet, and I looked at him and saw what I needed to see, his open face, his clarity. I took his hand and whispered: '*If you ever leave me, can I come too?*' He winked at me and said I could follow him anywhere.

I see a couple sitting together on a patch of grass surrounded by flowers. They are talking and laughing and looking at the sky. I sit down on a bench. I rub my thigh: the pain eases when I sit down. I continue to hum, it helps, but I can't remember all the words; I should have asked Jack to sing it to me last night. The man guides the girl to the ground and lies beside her. He is stroking her face and talking to her. I squint at them. They look as though they're in love. Picnics, I like picnics in the summer. The man climbs on top of her. Are they kissing? I stretch my leg and flex. Perhaps I *was* running too fast. Jack always tells me I overdo it: 'You'll fuck up your knees,' he says. 'Why do you always have to be the best? Why push yourself so hard?' The man has both of the girl's hands pinned behind her head and he is trying to kiss her, but she's turning away. I sit forward and shade my eyes. She looks distracted, as though she doesn't want his attention, but he hasn't noticed or doesn't seem to care. She struggles with him, but he doesn't listen. She is pushing him away, turning her head, but he won't stop kissing. He won't stop kissing.

Peter told me I'm good at playing cards. He called me a natural. He said that when I'm thinking about what move to make, I frown and twist my mouth in concentration. He told me it looks cute.

I open my eyes to the bright morning light. Josie has opened the shutters already. I can hear her breathing, slow and measured as if she's reading. He likes the way I rub my nose with the palm of my hand. He says it looks funny.

I turn over. Josie is sitting up in bed, her glasses halfway down her nose as she reads her book. I clear my throat to show her I'm awake, but she doesn't seem to notice, her eyes flicking over the words, line by line, absent-mindedly tucking her hair behind her ear when it falls onto the page. She's such a bookworm; aren't there more important things in life than reading books? I groan and move around so that the sheets rustle; she puts her finger on the page and looks at me.

'Hiya,' she says.

'Hi,' I yawn, showing her I'm tired because I stayed up late. She goes back to her book. I stare at the ceiling. I don't know what time it was when I went to bed, as there are no clocks in the house because of the timelessness game, but it must have been late. I yawn. '*Oh*, I'm tired,' I say.

'Yeah,' she says. 'You must be, you came to bed really late.'

'How do you know?' I turn towards her.

'I saw you come in. I was awake, I couldn't sleep.'

'Oh,' I say. She doesn't say anything. 'I was hanging out with Peter in the kitchen,' I say. 'He and Soma and Nim were still playing the timelessness game and they were awake because they were pretending it was daytime even though it was dark outside, it was really funny. Soma cooked a big pasta dish and we ate it even though it must have been after midnight.'

Josie gazes at me as if she's looking straight through me.

'I don't know what time I came to bed, but I reckon it was about three,' I say.

'It was later than that,' she says. 'More like three-thirty. I looked at my watch just before you came in. I was awake for about an hour—'

'Were you frightened of the invisible scorpion again?' I laugh.

'No,' she says. 'I had a really horrid dream.'

'God, three-thirty,' I say. 'I don't think I've ever stayed awake that late. And I wasn't even tired.' Although I did have a yawning fit at one point and Peter threw a tea towel at me because every time I yawned he yawned as well. Then everything felt really weird as if I were living in some kind of dream and my arms were too heavy to lift off the table. 'Peter is trying not to sleep at all,' I say. 'He said he was going to stay up and play patience all night and try to stay awake during the day as well. I wonder if he is still awake.' I pull the covers back and get out of bed. I go to the wardrobe and think about what to wear.

'I might phone my mum today,' Josie says. 'Do you think that's all right, for me to phone my mum?'

'Yeah, why not?' I find my shorts.

'Then maybe we could go for a walk, or a drive on the moped, buy some food and have a picnic. The boys have found this great place that sells crisps and Yop and packets of ham. What do you think?'

'Yeah, maybe,' I say, turning away from her as I take off my vest. I slip on my bra and fasten it at the back. Josie is sucking her thumb and twirling her hair, looking at me.

'It might be fun if we do something on our own today,' she says. 'We could take the video camera, do some filming.'

I put on my shorts and slip a T-shirt over my head.

'Or maybe your dad could take us somewhere. For a trip. He said he'd take us to Florence, didn't he? Why don't we ask him? He's probably upstairs in his office. I'll come with you.' She flips the covers back and goes to get out of bed.

'No, it's all right,' I say. 'I'll ask him. He's probably working anyway.'

'Why can't I come with you?'

''Cause he'll be working, he doesn't like being disturbed.'

'Oh,' she says and shrugs. She sits down again and picks up her book. I look at myself in the mirror.

'I bet you any money he'll say he's too busy to take us to Florence, anyway,' she says.

I turn around. 'No, he won't.'

'He will,' she says, looking up. 'He doesn't want to do anything with you. We've been here a week already and he hasn't suggested anything. It's true.'

I blush hot. 'What do you mean?'

'It's just weird,' she says. 'He's your dad and you haven't seen him in a year and he doesn't want to do anything with you. If it was my dad—'

'He does want to do things with me,' I say. 'I was in his room just the other day. He was reading my tarot cards. I asked him to buy me a sketchbook.'

'Yeah, but proper things. You know, going places, seeing things. Things you do when you're on holiday. Much better than sitting in the house all the time.'

I frown at her.

'Sam thinks he should be doing more stuff with us, he told me himself. Sam says that sometimes he gets nightmares where people are trying to kill people he loves, he thinks it's because your dad left. He says he feels sad sometimes.'

'Well, that's not my problem,' I say and grab my shoes. I open the door. The chill of the corridor. 'I'll see you later, OK?' I look back at her. She puts her thumb in her mouth and shrugs. I close the door.

I stand in the hallway. What was she talking about? When did Sam say those things to her? He was in the living room late last night, curled up on the sofa watching MTV. He'd come into the kitchen earlier, so quietly, like a ghost: it gave us a shock. It was almost as though he was sleepwalking, like Dad used to.

I walk down the stairs.

It's her problem not mine. Just because I'm making friends with the adults; she's just jealous, that's all.

I hear a voice. I stop just before I get to the bottom of the stairs. There's laughter that's different and yet familiar: a woman, Italian, with a hint of American, it sounds exactly like Deeva. I jump the last two steps and swing around the door and there she is – my dad's ex-girlfriend is standing in the kitchen, she's behind Peter and she has both her hands down the front of his shorts.

'My little Sylvie,' she says pulling her hands away. Peter looks at me and his eyes twinkle.

Deeva hugs me, and her body is soft and fleshy like I remember, her smell like a warm unmade bed. 'How many years?' she holds my face, her hands are clammy. 'Since London,' she says. 'Your dad and Alanka's wedding, you only this high.' She holds her hand below her breasts. 'Your little pigtails and your pretty dress, you were crying,' she says, and I blush. 'You looked so beautiful,' and she pulls me towards her and hugs me again. I can't believe she is here. Where did she come from? From over her shoulder I see Peter rearranging his shorts.

Deeva makes me a delicious milky coffee that tastes like hot chocolate, and she tells me that she arrived early that morning and found Peter in the kitchen buzzing from too many espressos. I nod and tell her we were playing cards, but she doesn't seem to hear me.

She has been living in Alaska and has gone back to stripping. She's married to a man called Glenn. 'Oh,' I say, looking at Peter. But then she goes on to say that she didn't realize when she married him that he is a wife beater, so she decided to leave him and asked Dad if she could come and stay here. Dad has an idea for a new book that he wants her to write – it's called *Love Magic*.

Deeva and Peter have only just met, but they're all over each other. Deeva is talking about Glenn and how he stole her heart and then broke it, while Peter strokes her arm, kisses her shoulder, plays with her hair and laughs at her jokes even though they're not funny. She also tells us that she is pregnant. She found out just before she left Alaska, and at least it means she will have a part of Glenn, who she loves but never wants to see again. Even this doesn't seem to bother Peter.

Deeva asks me about Dad and Alanka, and if they seem happy. I tell her that Alanka has been meditating a lot and Deeva nods as if she understands.

She puts her hand on Peter's lap and kisses him on the lips and I wonder what has gone on between them in the hours between me sitting with Peter playing cards, and waking up this morning. 'Excuse me a minute, my sweetheart,' she says, and he smiles like a soppy dog as she stands and helps herself to more coffee.

'Your father is not the easiest person to live with,' she says, turning to me. 'He used to drive me mad. Totally crazy. He doesn't commit you know. He makes out that he is the best lover, but he expects his women to fit around him. And he is not an easy man. He has a lot going on up here,' she taps her head. 'He is all brain and no feeling. It is like someone has pushed a plug into his heart. Even though he is a genius, he is a complicated man,' she says. 'I could never be with him again, even if he asked me. Even if he was the last person on this earth, I would say no.' She pours herself more coffee and fills a pan with milk. I watch her as she moves around the kitchen. She is totally different to Alanka. She is dark like her, but she is much bigger – big boned, says Mum – her hair, her nose, her mouth, her bum, her boobs, and I suppose her personality. She has always been really nice to me, always made me feel comfortable, as if I can say anything to her and she would magic my problems away. Maybe she is a witch, and she'll have a little witch or wizard baby.

'Even when I met him, he was crazy,' she says, sitting down. 'He had been roaming around looking for something, and I was so surprised when he turned to me. I was so happy that I could give him what he wanted. I was just a foreigner, stripping for money in a strange club,' she says, laughing. 'You know what I mean?'

I smile and nod as she pours milk into her coffee.

'He waited for me outside the club. And it was funny because even though I didn't know him, I knew that night that I was performing for someone special.' She holds her mug with both hands. 'I gave it all I had that night because I sensed someone was there, someone different from all the dirty old men with their greasy hair and their tissues.' She looks at me. 'And I was right,' she says. 'There, after the show, he was leaning against the wall waiting for me. He was an odd-looking man. His trousers were too short and he had this strange haircut, like a pudding bowl. Do you remember that haircut?'

I shake my head. I was only six. It was when he left and we didn't know where he was. When he went to India for six months, before coming back and telling us he was moving house. Deeva was in the car outside. We were in the hall.

She clears her throat. 'Oh, the past,' she smiles. 'I am looking forward to seeing your father, handsome old Harideva.'

Deeva starts talking about Glenn again. Peter leans into her, his face serious as he strokes her hand and she tells us how Glenn promised her a horse. She pats her tummy – 'But he gave me a smaller version of himself instead.'

I'm thinking about that day when Dad came home from India.

He looked different: taller because he was so thin, his hair white from the sun, his skin dark and foreign looking. He had a beard, and a mala strung around his neck with a photograph of Parameshvar in a little oval frame. The first time we saw him again, he came to the door with Deeva, and Mum invited them in. We hadn't seen him for six months. All three of them sat in the living room: Dad in the middle and Mum and Deeva on either side. Sam and I stood in the hall and tried to listen to what they were saying. Mum kept on getting up and walking to the kitchen, standing silently with her back to them. I think she was crying. Then Deeva left to wait in the car, and Dad went upstairs to the bedroom and opened the wardrobe and took out a bag and started throwing things into it, not thinking, just ripping his shirts from the rail, his trousers; taking his pants from the drawer, his socks, and stuffing them all into his small bag as if he might not stay away for long. I stood at the door and watched him. As he walked past me on the landing he knelt on the floor and ruffled my hair and said – 'I have to say goodbye.'

In the hall we were all crying. It was dark outside and the hall light was a horrible yellow colour. He hugged me goodbye; I said I was worried he wouldn't be able to see through his tears and that he might crash his car on the way to his new home. I didn't think that maybe Deeva would be driving.

Peter keeps staring at me while he strokes Deeva's hand, smiling and looking at my face as though he wants to see all of it, not just my eyes. He then says, 'She is beautiful, no?' and I think he is talking about Deeva, so I nod and he laughs and says, 'No, you, silly, I am talking about you,' and it makes me blush.

'No,' Deeva says looking at him. 'I'm beautiful,' she says. 'Repeat after me, *I'm beautiful.*'

'*I'm* beautiful,' Peter says, and Deeva whacks him.

That evening, after dinner, Nim moves around the table lighting lots of little candles that flicker in the breeze. She slides her fingers through Dad's hair as she passes, and says: 'So Harideva. Tell us about *Alpha Child*.'

Dad sits up, and puts his arm around Alanka's chair. He takes a cigarette from its packet and taps it on the table. He smiles to himself. He passes his cigarette to Alanka. 'That sociologist, what's his name?' he clicks his fingers.

'Doherty,' Alanka says. She leans forward and lights the cigarette from a candle, barely inhaling and delicately holding it between her fingers. She passes it back to Dad.

'Doherty,' Dad says. 'He's helping me do the book.' He picks tobacco from his tongue. 'A genius. The best in his field. He has studied families and birthing techniques, and he is a fountain of knowledge. We were on the phone today for an hour and a half, discussing. He thinks we're going to hit the big time with this book. It's going to make us millionaires.'

'*Wow*,' Nim beams and claps her hands. 'Tell us about your ideas, share it with us.'

Dad flicks his fringe and sits back. It is getting dark. It is difficult to see the whole of his face. 'Well,' he says. 'I guess it's a kind of utopia. A utopia where communes rule, the family is dead.'

'Of course,' Paritosh says.

'It's simple,' Dad says. 'The child is no longer raised by his parents; he is raised by everyone. Everyone in the commune is an uncle and an aunt, a grandmother, a grandfather.'

'Hold that thought,' Soma interrupts. 'We need more wine.' And she rushes into the house.

'This way a child will be more fulfilled, a child will have a bigger soul.' Dad takes another drag of his cigarette. 'It's like this. In normal life, a child, he becomes obsessed, you know? Obsessed with his mother because she is the only woman that he knows.'

I look at Sam. His face is in shadow.

'Then he will start to search the world for a replica of her. And it is not healthy for a man to marry a carbon copy of his mother.'

'Not natural, either,' Peter says, and everyone laughs.

'But if a mother or father is a friend, that is different.' Dad looks at me and winks. My mouth breaks into a smile and I have to rub my face to try to get rid of it. 'If parents don't possess their children, don't tell them what to do, the child will be relaxed with the parent, and they will be able to let go.'

'I know what you mean,' says Nim. 'I always fall for men like my father, and I don't even like my father.' She whacks her forehead. 'How crazy is that?'

'Exactly,' says Dad. 'It is compulsive. We can't do anything about it.'

'It's frightening,' says Nim. 'It's a crazy sort of attachment.'

'We don't want to feel obliged,' says Dad. 'We don't want to feel we have to do things that are expected of us, because then we won't want to do anything at all. All the joy will be gone.'

'But surely we need some discipline,' says Paritosh.

'No,' Dad shakes his head. 'What is discipline?'

'Some sort of structure—'

'I know, I know,' Dad interrupts.

'Come on,' Soma is back from the house. She is standing at the end of the table. 'Children need to be guided or there is the risk they will go wild, I have seen it happen many times.'

'Children,' Dad continues, 'are like plants. You see? You can't "bring them up" – "*I brought my children up*" – it sounds like you built them with bricks and mortar.'

Everyone laughs.

'They are plants, not buildings.'

'Uh-huh,' Nim says.

'So, let them grow.'

Soma twists her mouth at him. She waves the kitty tin at Deeva and it jangles with coins. She puts it on the table. It has a picture of Parameshvar on it, he is sitting in a shiny silver car and he is waving.

'Like a plant, you can feed a child, fertilize it, water it, and you can watch it grow, but then you have to let it be. If you constantly check it, pull up its roots, it will retreat from you and you will cease to know it. It will not trust you.'

'A very good analogy, Harideva,' says Yogi.

Josie fiddles with one of the candles.

'The moment you put pressure on your children – do this, do that – you imprison them, and they will hate you for it, they will never forgive you.'

Soma sighs. 'I am not sure it is so simple.'

Dad nods. 'It is simple,' he says. 'Life is simple if you let it be, Soma. It really is.'

'Hey,' Paritosh says. 'We've got them here, the Alpha Children. What do you guys think of this theory? Is it true?'

I look around. Josie sits up. Everyone is looking at us.

'What do you feel when your dad tells you what to do?' Paritosh asks.

'I dunno,' I say. 'I can't remember.'

They all laugh. I meant, I can't remember him ever telling me what to do.

'But Dad,' Sam's voice comes out of the shadows, small but clear. 'You never seem to care what we do.'

'*Ooooh,*' says Peter. 'Big words from a little man. Hari, perhaps you need to start paying more attention to these kids.'

'Come on, lovey,' Dad says. 'Of course I care. It's only your mind that equates discipline with care. I care silently.' And he puts his arm around Alanka and pulls her towards him.

I look at Sam, a match flicking between his fingers.

'Can I interrupt?' Soma says, clearing her throat. 'Something important for our new member, Deeva. Welcome my beloved—'

Deeva bows, says '*Namaste.*'

'—to show you that this is the kitty,' she waves the tin. 'We put money in it weekly, whatever. If you are working for the house and you don't have the money, then ask Harideva, perhaps he can give you money until you have some. If Harideva has nothing for you to do, you can help in the kitchen, or help in the garden, hmm?'

Deeva nods again, smiles.

There's something going on beside me: Dad whispering and Nim giggling. I look around. She is hugging my dad while stroking her lips with a scarf. 'Oh Hari, it is beautiful,' she says holding it to the light.

'This is part of what I will do for you,' Dad addresses the table. 'I will buy you each a present to celebrate our new future. I don't want anything in return. I just want everyone to be happy. So, we will all be happy.'

I frown at him. He's giving everyone a present. Is he addressing just the housemates, or does he mean me as well?

People shout and laugh, clapping their hands, and I watch Nim move from person to person as she shows them her scarf.

'So generous,' I hear someone say.

Something rushes up inside me: a sick feeling, and my throat constricts. He won't look at me. It's as if he's pretending I'm not here. Tears spring into my eyes. He bought Nim a present. I push my chair back and run into the house. I can't believe it. When I reach the living room, I let the tears fall.

I throw myself on the sofa. I hug my knees to my chest, bury my head in my hands, and hide in the dark so no-one can see me. There is laughter outside, an excitable chatter. I can hear Dad's voice. No-one has noticed I've gone. Why didn't he buy me a sketchbook? Why did I ask him to? *I shouldn't ask, I shouldn't ask, I shouldn't ask.* But I needed that sketchbook. It's not like wanting a stupid scarf. Why did he buy her a present when I am his daughter?

The light comes on. Sam stands at the door. 'They're all going mad out there,' he laughs. 'Just over a stupid present.'

I hold my head to my knees.

'Shall we play ping—' it's Josie. 'Sylvie,' she says. 'Are you crying?' She rushes over to me, puts her hand on my back, lightly rubs up and down. 'What happened?' she asks.

'Nothing,' I say into my knees. 'Nothing happened.'

I can see Sam's feet. He's standing in front of me.

'Obviously something happened,' she says. 'Otherwise you wouldn't be crying.'

'Nothing, it's nothing,' I say, sniffing.

I wipe the snot from my nose. I rub my eyes because they sting. I look at Josie and she smiles. I smile back. I want to say something.

'I know what happened,' says Sam.

I look at him.

'You're pissed off with Dad,' he says.

I pause. 'No I'm not.'

'Yes you are, you're pissed off because he gave Nim a present and not you.'

'No I'm not,' I laugh.

'Yes you are,' he says.

I close my eyes, looking away, stroking my forehead.

'Go on, Sylvie, I know you are.'

I sigh. 'It's just that I asked him to buy me a sketchbook.' I trace my fingers along the ridge of the sofa. 'I wanted to use it as a scrapbook, to keep all the things I've found since I've been here, and he said he'd buy it for me, but he didn't and he bought something for her instead and who is she? She's not even his girlfriend.' I look back at Sam. 'And he's my dad, and I'm his daughter,' I say, and the thought makes me cry again. Josie sits beside me and tries to hug me but I don't want a hug. I look up at Sam. 'It just hurts,' I tell him.

He looks down at me and nods. He pushes my leg with his knee. 'But he's an idiot, isn't he?' he says. 'Isn't he?'

'He's not an idiot.'

'What? He *is* an idiot?' he says, imitating me but getting it wrong.

'No, he's *not* an idiot.' I say it a little louder.

'He *is* an idiot?' he says, and it makes me laugh.

I nod. 'He *is* an idiot,' and I'm laughing now, laughing and crying at the same time. Josie is laughing as well, looking out from her funny curly hair.

'He's just a big fat idiot,' Sam says.

He's an idiot. Dad's an idiot, I say to myself, but I don't really mean it.

'Do you want a glass of water, or a tissue?' Josie asks.

'No,' I shake my head. 'But you could get me a cigarette.'

'*Urgh*, you don't want one of those,' she says.

'Yes I do.'

'But where will I get it from?'

'My dad, he'll give you one.'

''Cause he's an idiot,' Sam says and it makes me laugh again.

'Go on,' I say to Josie, who hesitates before leaving the room.

Sam kicks the bottom of the sofa. 'Are you all right?' he asks quietly.

'Yeah, I'm all right,' I sniff. I sit up. 'I don't know what's wrong with me. It's nothing really.'

Josie comes back with one of Dad's cigarettes. She passes it to me. 'They're all talking about gurus now,' she says. She reaches into her pocket and takes out a box of matches. 'Your dad's talking about a man who can make gold watches appear out of nowhere and Nim said that stupid word again, *bejeesus*.' She strikes a match, the kind that's made of wax.

'Where'd you get those?' I ask as she lights my cigarette.

She shrugs. 'Just found them.'

I take a drag, deep and rough on my throat. 'What does *bejeesus* mean anyway?' I ask.

'I don't know – The Beegees are Jesus?' Sam says.

I laugh again. Swirls curl past my eyes. My head spins. I feel heavy and tired. I lean back on the sofa. It feels nice to smoke after crying, it's different, more satisfying. I must remember:

cigarettes are good after tears. It makes me laugh again.

'Or big Jesus,' Josie says, laughing, falling onto me.

'What's so funny?' It's Max. He's standing in the doorway. He looks strange, his body crooked. An itch on his left arm, he's been scratching it all evening.

'Nothing,' I say. 'We're just being stupid.'

'Not as stupid as that conversation out there – it's like they really believe that crap, men with long beards, con artists more like,' he says.

'Hmm,' I sort of agree.

Max shuffles around before letting out a big yawn. 'I'm going upstairs,' he says, 'to listen to my Walkman. I'll see you later.'

Listen to his Walkman?

Sam turns on the telly and Josie touches my arm. 'Are you OK?' she asks.

'Yeah,' I say. 'I'm fine.' Really I am.

'I understand why you were upset,' she says. 'I think it was mean of him to buy a present for Nim and not one for you.'

'Oh, it's all right,' I say. 'It's fine. They're his friends, aren't they? I was just being stupid.' I lean forwards and stub out my cigarette.

'Do you want to watch some telly?' she asks, grabbing a cushion.

I shrug. 'Maybe,' I say. But then I remember Max. 'In a minute,' I say, and leave the living room.

As I get to the top of the stairs I stop to see if I can hear anything: the sigh of movement, the sound of a door closing. I walk towards my room, and put my hand on the handle. Looking around I see Max heading for the bathroom, his wash bag under his arm.

'Hiya,' I say, and he nods at me. 'Just getting a tissue.'

He closes the bathroom door behind him and I go to my room, get a tissue and blow my nose. I wait in the doorway, half hiding behind the door.

Max takes ages in the bathroom. The longer he takes, the more I want to wait, the more I want to see what he does to himself in there, under those gloves, when he is alone. I lean against the wall. I don't put the light on.

Finally I hear the bathroom door unlock.

I walk into the corridor.

He stops when he sees me. He looks different, smaller somehow.

He grips his arm to his chest and his wash bag falls on the floor. I walk towards him. As I get closer, I see blood seeping through his sleeve.

'Did you cut yourself? Here, take this?' I hold out the tissue. My heart is beating fast.

He shakes his head. 'No,' he says, and squats to pick up his bag. I squat down and reach his bag before him. He looks at me; his eyelashes catch the light, his creamy skin mottled with freckles. He looks away.

'You did, I can see,' I say. 'You've cut yourself, you're bleeding.' I try to bring his arm down to show me.

'Don't,' he says, a flash of aggression, warning. He backs away almost losing his balance. I pick up his bag and stand up before him, holding out my hand to help him up, but he twists his body away from me. He slides up the wall. The blood is not only on his sleeve but also on his T-shirt, red splodges the shape of slugs.

He leans against the wall. 'Give it here,' he says wearily.

'Does it hurt?' I ask. He looks at me and his eye twitches. 'What does it feel like?' I ask.

'Come on man,' he says. 'Give me the bag.'

I don't move, my body feels locked, my eyes to his.

'Give me the fucking bag,' he says.

I pass it to him and he moves his shoulder to reach it without letting go of his wrist.

'I won't tell anyone,' I say, and he backs away before turning around and rushing into his and Sam's room. I open my hand that was holding his bag and there is a small patch of blood on my palm.

Back in my room I pace up and down thinking about the marks, the scars on his arm, the pain. I stop in front of the mirror, 'Does it hurt?' I ask myself. 'Does it hurt?' looking at my lips, wondering what he might have seen when I was so close to him. I move nearer to the mirror, my face, my lips, my eyes, and I kiss my reflection. 'What does it feel like?' I ask. I take off my T-shirt slowly, my bra, my skirt, to my knickers, looking at myself, my body. I've never looked at myself like this before. I push a chair against the door.

Lying on the bed I touch myself, opening my legs to the breeze from the window, the images in my mind, imagining what it feels like to cut yourself. I see Max's pale freckly skin, the welts of pain. I touched his arm. I felt the marks beneath my fingers. How many times has he done it? How many times has he cut through his skin? I curl into a ball, my hand sandwiched between my legs. I don't know if I could ever do that to myself, however much things hurt inside.

'Yee-ha!' I scream, as I try to overtake the boys on their moped. They are tired after spending all day filming by the lake, and I'm determined to try to catch them out, speed faster than them. 'Catch me if you can,' I shout, twisting the accelerator. Josie is gripping my waist so hard it hurts.

Sam comes up from behind me. 'You can't keep it up, Sylvie,' he calls. 'You're both too heavy – *lard arse.*' He speeds past us and up the hill. That's total bullshit, look at Max squeezed onto the back: there's no way he's lighter than Josie, even if she is shaped like a pudding.

'Dipsticks,' I call after them as they disappear over the hill. I want to get them, show them up.

Today felt like the hottest day ever and all day we've been in the sun. It was my idea to come up into the hills because we're running out of things to film in the house, and the housemates are getting annoyed with Max sneaking around trying to catch them arguing or having sex. But it took a bit of persuasion: Josie is totally convinced that we're going to be killed by the Florence Monster, and Sam and Max just grunted around, avoiding me. I suggested Josie and I go on one moped, and Sam and Max on the other, so we don't get mistaken for couples. And even so, Sam hasn't let us out of his sight – *Don't do this... Don't do that* – it's enough to drive you crazy.

Luckily, it's been my turn to film today, not that anyone has been listening to me. I told Sam and Josie to pretend to drown in the lake and they played dead beside a tree instead, and Max has been avoiding me all day. I don't like this stupid film anyway. Deeva is preparing potions and asked me to get some rosemary. I'd much rather help her with her magic instead.

I hang back, slowing the moped to let the boys go off ahead. Deeva says that rosemary is the perfect herb for *Alpha Child*, because it opens your heart to your innocent and childlike self. Josie eases her grip on me.

'Phew,' she says. 'You were going really fast. Are we nearly there?'

There's a dirt track that goes off to the right and leads to the forest: maybe I'll find some rosemary there. 'Nearly,' I say. I check that the boys are far ahead and I take the bike off the main road. 'I just want to do something first.'

The sun has dipped behind the trees and it's much cooler here. The light a bluey grey, the air crisp and damp, shadows cast along the road.

'Where are we going?' Josie asks.

'I just need to get something.'

'But Sam says we should stick together.'

The forest looks dark, dark and dense, the big fir trees sitting silently, their branches still with the windless air. I slow down,

letting my feet scrape against the gravel. It is difficult to drive when
the ground is so stony – this was the kind of surface I fell onto last
year when I hurt my leg. Did Deeva tell me rosemary grows in the
woods? I stop and let Josie get off the moped.

'What are you doing?' she asks. Her face is burnt from the sun.
She goes red, whereas I go a deep nutty brown.

'I'm just going to look for something. Deeva's rosemary, I won't
be long.' I lay the moped on the ground.

'But I don't want to stay here,' she says.

'I'll be a minute,' I say, and look towards the forest. It suddenly
feels cold, like a sharpness that runs through the skin and leaves
goosepimples. I hold my arms and shiver. The only thing to do is
run. 'I won't be long,' I say, and head towards the trees.

'Wait,' Josie says. 'I'm coming with you.'

Josie follows me through the field. I try to run faster than her,
so she can't keep up. The blood is rushing through my body, the
warmth coming back. She calls after me, she has lost her flip-flop.
'Wait for me,' she calls, but there's something under my skin,
something that's making me want to go on.

Josie catches up with me. She's having trouble running, she
looks awkward, funny.

'Do you remember what Soma said?' I call between breaths.
'About the Florence Monster?'

'What?'

'That he is tall, old, grey hair. We have to keep an eye out for
him, make sure he isn't following us,' I say.

Josie looks behind us as she runs.

'Why do you think he's called a monster?' I ask.

'I don't know,' she says.

'I reckon it's because he's a werewolf. He's a man, but, come the
full moon, he turns into an animal. Do you think he tears his
victims' limbs off with his teeth?' I shout. 'What do you think he
looks like? Do you reckon he's handsome?'

'I don't know,' she's out of breath. 'What do you mean?'

'Do you think he's Italian? Maybe he's really wrinkly with yellow teeth – teeth that are stained with blood.' I know I'm scaring her, but it makes my heart beat faster, a tingling feeling running up and down my body. I catch her looking at me, her face fraught. 'Do you think he's got small hands? Small hands, small willy. Do you think he cuts off women's bits because he can't get sex? No-one wants to have sex with a small willy. *Small wrinkly willy*,' I say curling my little finger, it makes me laugh. 'How do you think he gets the genitals?' my voice is getting louder. 'Do you think he cuts them off while his victims are still alive, screaming with pain, or does he kill them first?'

'Soma said he kills them. He shoots them first,' she says.

'But I once heard of this murderer who skins his victims alive and they watch him doing it – every little bit of skin – until they die of shock.'

A sharp pain shoots through my side, a stitch. I stop, trying to catch my breath. I lean forward, pressing into my side and breathing into my stomach. I catch her looking at me, her eyes wide. She looks scared, unsure of me; her face red and shiny, her hair stuck to her forehead. I lean forward again, laughing, breathing – it's making me laugh. I throw my head back and my laughter carries off into the sky, rising to a scream. There's a piercing scream.

I stop dead and look at Josie.

She stares back at me.

A scream so high it punctures our ears, cuts through us, a pained scream, it sounds like death. It's coming from the woods. We stand still. There's a thrashing deep in the trees, something large panicking. A man runs. I grab Josie's arm. He has a gun and all the while the screaming continues in waves, rising, falling, the woods shaking with sound. Black birds like bullets swoop through the air. There are voices, chattering and shouting, speaking fast, too fast to hear. More men emerge from the woods, they run around in circles, around the object thrashing. Is it a person? An animal. But there's something about it that sounds human.

Suddenly everything stills, and then a shot as clear as glass. I grab my ears and release them to hear it echoing into the sky, *boom, boom, boom*, among the crying birds.

There's another, and a third.

The ground shakes to silence.

The shouting rises up again and Josie grips my arm and mimes, *RUN!* but there is no sound.

Somehow Josie knows how to drive the moped. She manages to get on it, push the pedals to start it, and drive in a straight line along the dirt track, and back onto the road and to our house without me saying a word. I don't know if I'm in shock, but all I want to do is hold on to her and try to block out the sound of that scream.

Now we are home and it's almost dark. Emily excitedly tells the boys what happened. I'm hearing wild boar, dead, death, shot, killed and it's making me feel dizzy and I think I need a glass of water, or maybe I need my dad.

My body feels floopy, my head numb, tiredness, something. I walk down the corridor towards Dad's room. The door is closed. *Knock, knock*. No sound, I put my ear to the door. 'Dad,' I hear a rustle, someone, a duvet. 'Dad,' a little louder, silence again. The air vibrates. I can still hear the scream and the silence that came after it. I head back to my room.

I sit on the bed. I don't know what to do. I pick up my pad and start to doodle, thoughts of death and pain and the idea of never seeing someone again, someone that you love. Why did they kill it? Are they going to eat it? It sounded so horrible. I think of animals being killed in slaughterhouses, of birds lying dead on the side of the road, of foxes, their bodies squashed, blood staining the tarmac, badgers, and I decide that from today I'm going to be a vegetarian. I draw little circles that go round and round, until there is no more space on the paper, just blackness.

I look up to the open window and the darkness outside. It's not a full moon. Deeva would have told me if it was. I get up to close the window and look outside: it's completely black except for a square of light from my room, and the hazy imprint of my dark shadow. I lean out and reach for the shutters. There's a noise, a rustling in the bushes. I grip hold of the shutters, pull them towards me and don't look down. I don't want to be seen by something out there in the dark. I lock them closed.

There are voices in the hall. The door opens, Josie. She stands in the doorway.

'That funny programme's on with the stripping housewives,' she says. 'There's this really fat woman with bumpy skin and she's only wearing a bra and a pair of stockings. They're making her dance on a podium and she looks really embarrassed. Come downstairs – it's really funny. We can make some hot chocolate.'

'No, it's all right,' I sit back on to the bed and lean against the wall.

'Come on,' she says. 'It's much better than being in here on your own. It'll make you laugh.'

'No,' I pick up my pad. I can hear Deeva in the corridor. I look up: she walks past the open door.

Josie stands there a minute. 'But it's miserable being on your own.'

'No it's not,' I say. 'I like being on my own.'

'But what are you doing?' She steps into the room.

'Nothing,' I hold the pad to my chest so she can't see.

She pauses. 'I don't mind if you want me to sit here with—'

'It's all right, honestly,' I say annoyed. 'You don't need to follow me around everywhere, you know. Do what you want – I don't care.'

'All right.' She looks hurt. She pauses a minute, as if she wants to say something else. I don't look up to see her expression as she closes the door.

Deeva's bedroom light is on. It glows through the glass panel of the door. I knock, once, and a voice calls out. '*Pronto,*' it says. It is a man's voice. I think it's Peter's.

I open the door and he's lying on the bed, completely naked.

Candles flicker all around him. He's lying on his side, facing me as if he is waiting for me: his thin body, his bare legs, arms, chest, face. He looks at me. He looks shocked.

'My God,' he says, and moves his leg to cover his bits. I'm really glad because I was trying not to look at them. 'Why the fuck didn't you knock?'

'I *did*,' I say. I *did* knock.

'Get out, will you?' he shouts, and the blood rushes to my face. I back away and quickly close the door, running back to my room and pulling the sheets over me. I did knock. He was waiting for Deeva – of course it wasn't me – he looked as though he was ready for sex, he was waiting for sex and was horrible to me because I wasn't her. I press my hands to my face. I will never ever be able to look at him again.

I lie like this under the covers for what seems like ages, my breath warming as I listen to the sounds of people in the kitchen downstairs, preparing food, music and laughter. But I don't want to go down. I'm not hungry and I don't want to see anyone. I don't even want to see my dad.

I don't know whether I fall asleep, but suddenly there is a knock at the door. It is dark. I turn my back to the door as it opens and light floods the room.

'Sylvie,' it's Sam. 'Are you there?'

'Yeah,' I say.

He turns on the light and I pull the sheet up to cover my eyes.

'It's your turn to wash up, what are you doing?'

I don't say anything.

'Why weren't you at dinner?'

Nothing again.

'Don't try and get out of it, pretending you're ill.'

'I'm not pretending.'

'What?'

'I'm not pretending,' I shout, and turn over to face him.

He looks at me, 'Are you crying?' he says, softer. He takes a step into the room.

'No,' I say, sniffing and wiping the tears from my nose. I don't want him to see me like this again: always crying. He moves further into the room, goes to close the door behind him.

'I didn't say you could come in,' I shout.

He backs away.

'*Go away!*'

'You're such a fucking crybaby,' he says. 'Who's supposed to do the washing up now? Me? You always turn the waterworks on to get out of things. You've got to grow up, Sylvie. When are you going to see that? We've both got to grow up.' He slams the door behind him. I jump out of bed, open the door and shout – '*Bastard!*' really loudly as he runs down the stairs. I slam it closed. I *am* grown-up. I can push away the tears. I won't dwell on the sad things, because I have a choice, just like Dad said. I have a choice.

Sometimes when I wake up in the morning I can barely move. I flip onto my back and lie still, my eyes twitching with the weight, my breathing slow, my chest constricted. I lie there bound, stitched to the sheets, the duvet pressing down on me. I am so full of weight that I can't even move my arms to push it away. I sometimes wonder if it's the daylight, the birds, the ticking of the central heating, the day, that I can't face.

Jack always knows what to do when it happens. He doesn't need to ask if I'm all right, he can tell from the length of my breath that something is wrong. He'll touch my back with his fingertips and quietly step out of bed, gently closing the door behind him. He'll return what seems like seconds later with a cup of tea, his mouth miming words like, 'I'm off now. I'll be back later,' so quiet they are barely there, as if he knows his words aren't strong enough to soothe me.

I can make it to the loo. I can make it to the computer to switch it on and send an email to a freelance job I might be doing. I can make it to the phone to unplug it. But there's little else I can do.

It's like a waiting game. Waiting for things to return to normal, sometimes I think they never will.

Jack and I rarely talk about it. I think he's just accepted that it's something that I do. I know he thinks it's depression. That's what the doctor tells me, but I won't take pills. Sometimes I wonder if there's a part of me that likes the emptiness, the deadness, no more thinking, no more analysing, because that way you have no choice but to stop.

Jack says I'm always on the run. He teases me for going out every day even if it's just a jog up the lane. And it's not just about being fit: it's bigger than that, it's more of a search, the need for some form of recognition, someone quietly putting their hands on my shoulders and saying: *I had something to do with it too; it wasn't just you.*

And, of course, Jack has me worked out like one of his handsome houses. He knows my dimensions, what lurks in my dark corners. That solid calm. He'll bring my attention to my fiery moods, but he won't try and change me. It's as if he has always known me. I sensed it the first time we met. We hardly spoke, but there was something about him that stayed with me. And then he phoned: he set me up and knew exactly how to handle me when I misread the signs. He rang, totally out of the blue. I wasn't prepared.

'You photographed my sister's wedding, in May.' His voice was faint. I was standing outside Marks & Spencer, above Liverpool Street Station. It was hard to hear him. 'Jack,' he said again. 'Rose's brother.'

Rose's brother. The man who picked me up from the side of the M4 after my car broke down the morning of the wedding. He and his friend asked if I had a pair of tights to fix the fan belt. It was a hot summer day; of course I didn't have tights.

'Jack,' I said. 'My helper.' We had joked about the fact that he kept finding bits of my equipment around the house: a camera lens on the mantelpiece, a roll of film in a flowerbed. He'd catch up with me and slip it into my bag. He was tall, dark-haired and clear-eyed. He appeared to be ludicrously organized, but then he surprised me.

'The singer,' I said, remembering.

He laughed.

At the reception he stood up and sang. It seemed unplanned. A baritone voice, but not trained. I thought he must be joking at first, but everyone was caught by it. It was beautiful. What a show-off, I thought, but he's not really, he's just unashamedly himself.

'I'll spare you that,' he said on the other end of the phone.

I found myself giggling.

I remembered liking him. During the reception I kept looking for him, searching through a busy room, catching sight of him on the dance floor. When I developed the photographs, I had so many pictures of him I had to edit them down. He danced like a fool but it tickled me. Someone spilled red wine down my blouse; he lent me a T-shirt.

'Your T-shirt.' A funny face on it like a lollipop; I'd been wearing it in bed.

'Oh, don't worry,' he said. 'You can have it.'

There was a pause. I suddenly thought – why are you ringing?

'I just wondered if—' he said something else, but an announcement was made, I was waiting for a train. I pushed the phone to my ear.

'I'm available? You want a booking?' I said, I thought he must be getting married to that small blonde girl with bubblegum nails. She was wearing Jimmy Choos; I photographed her feet against a handsome terracotta urn.

'Yes, I guess,' he laughed. 'But probably not—'

'Have you got a date yet?' I held the phone in the crook of my neck and dug around in my bag for my diary. 'I get pretty booked up, but I've got a few weekends left in the summer. When are you planning it for?'

'Well, I was thinking a little sooner than that. More like this weekend.' He sounded amused.

'This weekend?' I grabbed the phone before it slipped from my shoulder, and my bag and its contents fell on the floor. 'Did you say this weekend?'

'Yep,' he said.

'That's a bit short notice isn't it?' I thought he must be joking. He was a bit of a joker, his loud voice carrying through the hall. I pushed everything back into my bag, my wallet, lipstick, rolls of film. 'Wait,' I said. 'Sorry, I've just dropped something—'

'I would like to take you on a date,' he said.

'You would like to…'

'I would like to take you on a date.' He said it so patiently, confidently.

'Oh,' I said. 'But I'm always busy, I don't really have any time.'

'Everyone has time for a cup of tea,' he said.

He is never swayed. He's like a rock. I've never known anyone like him.

I open my eyes. It is dark. Did I hear a noise? There it is again: a slow long banging downstairs. I lie completely still. Josie groans and turns in her sleep. A bang, and then another. I sit up in bed. Is it someone trying to get in? My heart beats fast and I try to calm myself so I can hear properly. I imagine a man outside the front door, bashing it with his fist, pushing it with his shoulder, the door gives way and he looks up the dark long stairway straight to our room.

But then there's a different sound: the scrape of a chair in the kitchen. My body relaxes; it could be anyone. It could be Dad helping himself to bread and butter or a glass of milk, or maybe Sam after a bad dream. I quietly lie down again and concentrate on going back to sleep.

The boys are already on the mopeds when we get downstairs. Josie rushes out: 'We're coming,' she calls. There's a camper van in the drive. It's big and yellow and has a British numberplate. 'Come on Sylvie, let's go,' Josie calls excitedly, climbing onto the back of Sam's bike.

We're going to Florence. The boys want to buy frankfurters and Babybels from the Co-op, and I want to find something to wear to the party tonight. Dad's given me some money. I stop at the kitchen window: there are voices. I remember the banging I heard last night, the scrape of a chair. I turn to look in. There's a man standing beside the kitchen table, he's talking to Dad. He is dressed in white – white hat, white shirt, white trousers.

'*My bag, my bag,*' Josie chants as she rushes past me. 'I forgot my bag. *Wait for me.*' She runs into the house. I look back at the boys, their small mopeds rumbling between their legs.

I walk into the kitchen. Dad is standing at the stove. The man is sitting down. He is fiddling with a box of matches so I can't see his face. I have to pass him to get to Dad. A waft of perfume, strong and sweet.

'Dad,' I say, tugging on his sleeve while he makes coffee. I want to say something. 'What time does the party start?' I glimpse the man: he is smoking, inhaling deep into his lungs; brown fingers and big white nails.

'I don't know, lovey, some time this evening, not late.'

'Can I help set things up?' I ask. It's hot in here, sweat is trickling down the back of my legs. 'Tonight,' I say. I can feel the man look at me. 'Do you think I can help?'

'I'm sure you can. You should ask Soma, she'll know what needs to be done.'

I can hear the boys outside, revving their engines.

'You must come tonight,' Dad says to the man. He looks up. A tanned, lined face, his eyes in shadow. 'We're having a party. It's been planned for weeks. Something about the women in the house needing to release some energy, whatever that means.'

The man laughs. A flash of white teeth. He coughs. He looks at me. I look at his feet. They are bare, brown against the white stone floor, long toes like fingers. 'Have you met my daughter?' I feel myself blush.

The man holds out his hand. I move towards him. 'Hello,' he says gently, he is English. He looks straight at me. He has nice eyes: bright milky blue.

'Where the hell did she go?' Sam swings around the kitchen door. '*Josie,*' he shouts up the stairs.

'And the noisy boys,' Dad says. 'Of course, you've met them already.'

I stand near the bikes, leaning against the wall, looking at my hand.

'Did you meet that weird man?' Max says. 'Hello my name is *Jee Jee Jee Jeet*.'

'What are you talking about?' I ask.

'He couldn't say his name,' Sam says, 'without *straining*. His eyes looked like they were going to pop out.'

'What do you mean?' I ask.

'That man,' Sam says. 'He's got something wrong with his voice.'

'*H h h h hi, I c c c c can't t t t taaalllk pr pr pr properly*,' Max imitates him.

'*Ssh*,' I say, looking towards the house. 'He'll hear you.'

'And, look, he's got the Florence Monster Mobile,' says Sam. 'A camper van – didn't Soma say some couple was killed in one? Some German boys? He thought one of them was a girl. He must have been well disappointed when he took off their trousers. Not one dick, but two,' he shouts. Max slaps his hand, both of them laughing.

'*W w w would y y y you l l l like a drive in my c c c car l l l little girl?*'

'Shut up,' I whisper.

Sam and Max skid around singing 'Thriller', trying to do monster moves on their bikes. I wish they'd fall off.

'What did you say his name was?' I ask Sam quietly as he comes near me.

'Jeet,' he says, as he accelerates away.

Jeet. My stomach turns. He's the photographer; he's going to photograph me.

I slowly walk back towards the kitchen. Maybe I don't need to go into town; maybe I can borrow one of Alanka's dresses for the party instead.

'Sylvie,' Sam calls after me. 'Go and get Josie off the toilet or wherever she is, or else we're going without you.'

'Just go,' I say, waving at him. He looks at me. 'Go on, I don't want to go into town anyway.'

'What, and miss out on all that food?'

'What, cold frankfurters?' I say. 'Why would I want them when I'm a vegetarian?'

'Ooh, sorry miss fussy,' he says. He pauses: 'What about Josie?'

I shrug. 'I don't reckon she wants to go either. Dad said he'd take us tomorrow.' Perhaps he will, if I ask him.

'Come on *man*,' says Max, revving his engine. 'Fuck it, let's just *gooo*.' And he pulls on the accelerator, speeding off.

Sam looks at me. 'Should I wait?' he asks.

'No, just go,' I wave. I want them to go away.

He shrugs and pulls on the power, following his friend as they shout over the whine of the engines. I hover around the kitchen door. The man is talking. He sounds funny, as if there's something stuck in his throat.

Josie runs down the stairs and outside. 'It was in the wardrobe!' she shouts. 'I swear I never put it in there.' She's red-faced and out of breath. I look over at the boys just as they turn from the drive onto the road. 'Where are they going?' she asks.

'To Florence, I guess.'

'But what about us?' She drops her bag. 'Why didn't they wait? I said I was looking for my bag.' Her redness spreads to her neck, her chest, her arms. I bend my flip-flop into the gravel. 'Sylvie,' she says. 'Why didn't they wait?'

'I don't know,' I say. 'What are you asking me for?' and I go into the house.

Alanka has the most beautiful selection of dresses I've ever seen. Her wardrobe is full of them. There are red ones, blues and greens, and every kind of fabric, from Indian silk to cotton to wool. She says I can choose whatever I want to wear to the party. She's even given me a special pair of sandals embroidered with little sparkly jewels. I take out a long yellow silk dress and hold it against me.

'Come on,' she says. 'We can be a little more daring than that. This one is like a tent. Let's get you into something that has a little bit of shape, no?' I pass the dress back to her and stand away from the mirror so I don't have to see my gangly body. I'm not sure if I want to wear something shapely; I'm not sure if I like my shape. She pulls out a red dress with a scooped neck. 'Try this,' she says, and I take off my T-shirt and step out of my shorts. She slips it over my head. 'See,' she stands behind me in he mirror. 'You are beautiful,' and I look at myself and then away because it seems so strange to wear a dress.

'Maybe we want contrast,' she goes back to the wardrobe. 'Something striking with your baby-white hair. I think you could wear black.'

I see a glimpse of a dress I recognize: I've seen Alanka wear it before; I think it's one of her favourites. 'What about that one?' I ask.

'You want to wear that?' she raises an eyebrow. 'You will look sexy,' she says, pulling it out of the wardrobe. I slip the dress on and it falls over me like water.

I spend all afternoon with Alanka. She washes my hair and I sit with a towel around my head. We do a face pack that itches when it dries and she tells me how I should only ever wash the roots of my hair as the ends get washed when you rinse it, and I should only use conditioner on the ends or else the roots will get greasy. I stand in my pants as she covers me with cream that smells of grapefruits. It makes me feel shy to be so naked in front of her, but she tells me I have a lovely body, and even that I have beautiful breasts, which makes me look at them in a different way when I catch sight of myself in the mirror. When I'm feeling clean and smelling nice, I sit in the bedroom in her dressing gown and she dries my hair with a hairdryer, and then she starts to crimp it. Dad comes in at one point and throws his jacket on the bed, kissing Alanka on the back of her neck. She closes her eyes. He sits down and takes off his shoes, rolling his socks into a ball and throwing them into the corner. I look at him from the mirror, willing him to notice me with my new hair. When he leaves the room, Alanka watches him.

Back in our room, I ask Josie if she likes my dress. She stands beside me and picks up the skirt, so it fans out from my body. 'You can wear my tube skirt if you want,' I say. She looks at me and our eyes meet in the mirror. Her hair is hanging over her face. 'Maybe you should wash your hair,' I say, and step away from her.

'I don't know if I can be bothered to dress up,' she says, falling onto the bed. 'Sam and Max don't want to go to the party. They said they think everyone is going to be weird, doing freaky dancing and stuff. They were talking about having a ping-pong tournament. I think I might just play with them instead.'

I swish the dress around and tuck my hair behind my ears. Having it crimped makes it look even blonder. I can't wait for Alanka to do my make-up. I want to wear red lipstick.

Josie shuffles against the wall, pulls the cover over her knees and puts her thumb in her mouth. I've noticed that she sucks her thumb when she's homesick.

'What did they do in town?' I ask.

'Walked around, I think. They brought back lots of really nice food.'

'Did you have some?' I ask, sitting on the bed beside her.

'Yeah, Sam gave me a whole packet of frankfurters. I'd almost forgotten what meat tastes like,' she says, and I laugh to show her that I do still like her – I'm sorry for being a crap friend.

I notice a package on the floor in between our beds. 'What's that?' I ask. It's a large package, wrapped neatly in brown paper.

'Oh, yeah, look.' She kneels and reaches for it. 'It's for you – open it.'

I hold it in my lap. It has my name on it: *Sylvie* in black marker pen. It's square and heavy like a book. I look up at Josie who is smiling.

'Go on,' she says.

I turn it over and slide my finger under the edge of the paper. The tape unsticks and the corners open. I turn it on its side. I know what it is. It slips out of the paper and lands on my lap. A Florentine book. It has swirls of blues, greens and gold, and is bigger than I imagined, with lots of pages of thick crêpey paper for sticking in all my precious things. My tummy fills with butterflies.

'Wow, look at that,' Josie says, tracing her finger along its cover. 'Your dad must have bought it for you after all.'

I can't believe it. I hold it to my chest. It's one of the most beautiful books I've ever seen.

Dad is standing on a chair wearing a yellow dress, and Alanka is sitting on the floor beside him. It's the dress I nearly tried on this morning. It looks funny. It's far too small for him: it clings onto all his fat bits and makes him look hairy, like a big oversized gorilla.

I stand in the doorway. Alanka is holding the hem, telling Dad to stop moving as she has scissors in her hand. 'I will cut you,' she says. I clear my throat.

Dad looks over his shoulder. 'You're ruining my surprise,' he says.

'Shall I go?'

'No, sweets, it's fine. What do you think of your crazy dad?'

'You look really funny,' I say. 'But pretty,' I add quickly.

'He does not look pretty,' Alanka laughs. 'He looks like an ugly hairy man. We have a lot of work to do,' and she starts to unpick the hem.

'Are you going to wear one of your wigs?' I ask.

'Well, of course, madam,' Dad says in a silly French accent.

Dad and Alanka start arguing about what length the dress should be, so I don't say anything about the book. I hold it to me and walk over to the mirror, looking at myself in the light. It's still weird to see myself like this. I've never worn something so revealing before. I hope I don't feel too embarrassed to go outside. I look out to the courtyard and see Deeva and Nim decorating the belvedere with candles and flowers. Peter is laying the table. People will be arriving soon: I feel excited; it is almost time. Jeet's van is still in the drive.

I look at Dad from the mirror. Alanka is fussing over him. Maybe that's why he likes to dress up as a woman, so he can be fussed over. He's always the star of a party. He once took over from the fire-eater at my birthday and nearly scorched his lips. I look at myself again. He hasn't said anything about *my* hair and dress.

Alanka goes into the bathroom and I stand beside him, the book in my hands.

'Which wig are you wearing?' I ask. I've seen him wear a scarlet one before, and a black one that made his skin look green.

'I was thinking of something blonde,' he says, 'something dramatic. Then I can have false eyelashes, too, Alanka has bought a new pair, extra long.' He bats his eyes at me. He looks like a rock star with make-up on – his features are too big – like how I imagine Mick Jagger might look.

'But won't a blonde wig look a bit funny with your beard?' I ask.

'Probably,' he says. 'But who cares, hey? It's all a bit of fun.' He makes a farty sound with his lips. It makes me laugh. Shall I show him that I found the book in my room? He doesn't seem to have noticed it.

Alanka sits on the floor and tips out her make-up bag.

'Are we going special?' she asks.

'What do you think?' Dad turns to me. 'Red lipstick, or is that too obvious?'

I nod, 'I think red could be nice,' I say. I wanted to wear red lipstick.

Alanka passes it to him.

'No, you have to do it,' he says to her. 'Get the wig, let's do the whole thing.'

'Come on, Sylvie,' Alanka says. 'Put that book down and help us with the wig.'

I walk over to the window and carefully place the book on the dresser.

When we have finished arranging Dad's wig and applying his make-up, Alanka rushes to the wardrobe and pulls out some dresses, stripping off her clothes and trying them on in front of the mirror. The music has started on the belvedere and Soma knocks on the door to ask for help as she is running late. Dad looks at me because he knows I wanted to help, so I rush over to my book while Dad stands in front of the mirror adjusting his dress and I cling on to it and wait for a moment looking at him, wondering whether I should say thank you or whether I should say nothing. And it's then, as I watch him concentrate on his legs and the way the dress falls when he points his toe, that it suddenly doesn't matter that Alanka didn't have time to do my make-up, as the sound of music and laughter from outside hits me. It flushes through me and makes my stomach leap to my chest and I look at Dad and I think maybe it's easier having him as a friend, like he said. Maybe I should call him Hari from now on, I think he'll like that.

Soma is swearing over the burnt crust on the quiche and I'm standing at the window watching as people arrive. Lots of long hair and flowing dresses, men with silky shirts and open-toe sandals, sunset colours and brown skin. I clutch my camera. I want to take photographs tonight.

'*Porco dio*, this is supposed to be my party, *my* party,' Soma shouts, and I rush to help her by taking bread and napkins outside and putting them on the table.

The guests that have arrived are talking and laughing, and drinking the bright green drinks that Nim has been making all afternoon. I lean against a chair, fiddling with my camera, wondering whether someone will talk to me, when I see Dad. I head straight for him. He is talking to a woman and he is making her laugh, she is laughing so much she has tears in her eyes. '*Aaah*,' she says, 'that story is so beautiful, you must tell it to the others,' and she hugs him, her head on his chest and her arms linked around his back. 'Hari,' she says, looking up at him. 'You make me laugh like a child. You free me.'

'It's not me,' my dad says. 'You have made yourself free.'

She puts her head back on his chest and closes her eyes.

I reach out for his arm. 'Dad,' I say. 'I mean *Hari*. Hari,' I say, and he looks down at me. 'Can I stand with you for a while?'

The woman laughs: 'Who's this?' Her eyes stretch open.

'My daughter,' Dad says.

'I thought for a moment—' she stops. She shakes her head. 'Of course she is your daughter,' she says. 'And I never knew you had a daughter.'

'Yes, and I had a wife and a house and a mortgage,' he laughs.

'I don't believe it, Hari, I never had you down as the conforming type.'

'Times have changed,' he says and narrows his eyes, giving her a strange smile.

She holds her arms out to me: 'You want to hug?' I tentatively move towards her and let her hold me. Her bony back, her pointy boobs pressed into me. 'So sweet,' she says, but she is squeezing me too tightly.

When the lady finally leaves us, Dad lets me come close. He holds my shoulders with his big warm hands, and moves me so I'm standing in front of him. He lets me lean back on his chest and I imagine that my body has melted into his, as if I'm watching and listening without anyone knowing. People have already started to dance. They fling their arms in the air and let their hair fall over their faces. I watch as Paritosh lifts his face to the sky, his palms turned out and his eyes closed. Dad's friends look funny when they dance. It makes me feel embarrassed to watch them.

'Hey, maybe we could have a dance later,' Dad says. I look up at him and nod. He wants to dance with me. I'd feel OK if I did it with him.

We stand together for a while. The weight of Dad's hands on my shoulders as we watch the dancing figures turn to shadows in the fading light. Dad doesn't need to speak. He just stands and lets others flap around him, stroking his arm, picking up his dress and making stupid comments about his wig. I don't find it so easy: I keep looking over my shoulder, thinking someone will take him away from me.

Hari, Hari Hari, I could say it like a mantra, again and again.

'Hari,' I say to test it. 'Do you like my dress?'

He looks down at me, his funny long eyelashes almost obscuring his eyes. 'Let me see,' he says. 'Hey, it's Alanka's.'

I nod.

'It's a beautiful dress,' he says. 'One of my favourites.'

But do I look beautiful? I want to ask him.

'Look at my daughter,' he suddenly calls. 'She looks like a woman.'

I press my face to his chest, trying to hide. From here I can see Jeet. He is sitting at the table smoking a cigarette, his leg up on one knee, his stark white trousers and open shirt, bare ankles, white shoes. He's no longer wearing his hat; his hair is thin and sandy. He's smoking and watching. I wonder what he's thinking.

Crickets spark at each other in the shadows and the music tinkles with flutes and triangles, and the rushing sound of waterfalls, repetitive drumbeats, pounding, like music from some other land. Deeva stands with us. She sways her hips as she watches the dancing. I link my arms around her waist and press my face against her soft back. Her hands feel warm as they cup mine. Her hips go up and down as she pulls me with her, humming to the tune. It feels comfortable here, with Deeva, with Dad. I could stay like this for ever.

I try a green drink and it tastes like mint, so I have another. I find myself swaying to the music. I help myself to some food, a wedge of bread and aubergine dip. I casually sit opposite Jeet.

It is dark here under the tree, lit mainly by candlelight. I know why it's dark: it's because tonight is a new moon. Deeva told me. She says the new moon makes you do things with feeling.

Jeet sits with his back to the house and half of his face is totally black, while I'm facing the light. I feel as though I'm lit up, glowing like a beacon, every part of me exposed. He clears his throat and I fiddle with my camera. He takes another drag of his cigarette, and I quietly put a lump of bread in my mouth, chewing slowly.

There is something fluttering on the table and it's hard to see what it is, so I move the candle. It's a moth. Its little wings are crashing against the surface as if it is gasping for life. I look up to see whether Jeet has noticed, but he doesn't look at me. I prod it with my finger and it jumps and stills, before fluttering again, the frenzy of its wings making it flit around the table. Maybe it got burnt in the candle flame, maybe it's in shock and will calm down and be able to fly off again. Moths only have small brains; I don't think it can feel pain.

'Sometimes it is better to let them die,' Jeet says, and I'm surprised to hear his voice, all his words said perfectly.

He opens another packet of cigarettes, takes one and lights it.

I take a sip of my drink and it makes me feel warm inside.

I look at the cigarette packet on the table. Can I ask him for one?

I push my chest out, my arms on the armrest. I let my sandal fall to the ground, and I roll my ankle. I put my head back and sigh, flicking the hair from my shoulders. But he doesn't look at me. Instead he twists around and looks towards the house, and at one point I think he might get up and walk away.

I uncross my legs and slip my foot back into my sandal. I slouch and fiddle with my hair, weaving long thin plaits. I look up to the attic window: I've been hearing the occasional shout or laugh and the sound of bats and light plastic balls bouncing on the table, Hall and Oates from the mini stereo. Does being grown-up mean you have to give up having fun with your friends? Or can I just do it sometimes when it suits me? Like Dad wearing false eyelashes and a wig.

There are laughs coming from the belvedere as people dance. It's as if they're meditating. Parameshvar tells them to meditate in everything they do, when they're eating, washing, singing, dancing – 'Lose your head in it, open your heart, lose connection with the ground, shake the blood from your veins'. Dad's there as well, flopping around in his undersized dress, his mascara smudged under his eyes.

Alanka steps out of the house, delicate like a fawn, her naked feet, and her long flirty dress skimming the ground. She smiles as she comes over and I ask if her feet hurt on the gravel and she shakes her head and tinkles as if it's a silly thing to ask, but I don't think it's silly – I had to run out in my socks the other day, when Sam threw my shoes into the allotment, and even that hurt.

She stands behind me and touches my hair, making little shivers run down my spine. I gaze at the candle mesmerized. The moth is no longer moving. It is lying still on the table; it must be dead. The tips of Alanka's fingers touch the back of my neck and they are small and cold.

She and Jeet are talking. He is smiling, one side of his face lit up by the glow of the house, the other in blackness. He has a wide smile, crooked teeth, and deep long lines that run from his eyes, cutting through his cheeks like scars. He tries to say something, but stammers, and the veins in his neck pop out.

'Sensitive,' Alanka says for him, and he shakes his head. I wonder whether it annoys him when people finish what he is trying to say.

'I'm sorry,' he says. '*Sommme sommme sometimes* I have to find different words.' His eyes glint in the light.

Then they are laughing. They are laughing about dancing and my dad and how he can't dance. He just bounces up and down on the same spot – *boing boing boing*. But that's rubbish, the only time Dad bounced was when we were at a disco and Alanka was outside talking to her ex-boyfriend and he was worried she was going to leave him.

'I've seen him dance and he's good,' I say, and it just pops out, I don't mean to say it. Jeet looks at me.

'He *I I I is*?'

'Yes… he is… he's better than…' I'm about to say all the other people here, but I don't want to be rude. 'Lots of other people, who… don't know how to dance,' I say, my face reddening. I look down and all I can see are my boobs, so I cross my arms over my chest. Alanka laughs and hugs me from behind, her long silky hair covering my shoulders. 'And you, Sylvie? When are we going to see you dance?' she asks.

'With Dad, I mean Hari,' I say turning around. 'Hari said he was going to dance with me.'

'So, you are calling him Hari?' she laughs, and then she calls over to him: 'Hari, your daughter is calling you by your name, have you been ignoring your responsibilities so much that she has forgotten you are her father?' It annoys me her saying that. That's not why I'm calling him Hari.

Dad strolls over in his dress like flames. I want him to stick up for me, but he puts his arm around his wife. She leans back to look at his face, laughing at the make-up smudged under his eyes, peeling away his eyelashes. She picks up my camera and takes a picture of him. He pouts and tilts his hips towards her.

'We were talking about dancing,' Alanka says. I sit forward, showing him that I am ready to dance; all he has to do is ask. He kisses Alanka's forehead and says something into her hair.

'Come on then,' she says. 'Are you going to show us how good you are?'

I stare at him.

'Anybody's got to be good compared to these fruitcakes,' Dad says.

The tempo of the music changes and Alanka rolls her hips into my Dad's leg.

'Dad,' I say.

He wrestles Alanka under his arm.

'*Dad*,' I say again, sitting forward.

He doesn't hear me.

He drags her to the belvedere.

I slouch back. I called him Dad. I wanted to call him Hari. I watch as he spins her around and her body gives in to him like plasticine.

Jeet stubs out his cigarette and moments later he goes to light another and I think he might offer me one or maybe a drink, but he stands up, straightens his trousers and shakes his leg as if it's gone numb, and he walks away, towards the house, without even looking at me.

I look up at the illuminated attic room.

A ball pings from the hard floor, and I see Max's ginger hair flash there and then gone, and a shout, *Oi, you big tosser!* Josie laughing. I get up and run to the house grabbing my skirt into a ball as I climb the stairs two at a time.

The music has got louder. We all stand and watch from the window. We are smoking cigarettes and drinking wine. We are staying up really late. Peter is playing a guitar; Nim is singing, her voice high and thin. I can see Dad sitting at the table, slumped, his face deflated like a tired old clown. Suddenly Soma runs up the drive wearing nothing but sandals and a mala, with her large boobs violently swaying.

And then all four of us are outside. Sam and Max jump around the belvedere like nutters, head-banging the air, their skinny legs flailing, as Dad's friends stagger out of the way, clenching their teeth behind their smiles. I can't believe it, so I just stand against the wall, beckoning to Josie to stand with me so I don't look like a total plank.

Suddenly, Dad runs towards us and literally pulls Sam off the dance floor. He drops him on the gravel beneath the weeping tree and they roll around as Dad tries to pin him down; it must hurt with the stones digging into their backs and knees, particularly Dad in his thin silk dress. And of course, Sam doesn't stand a chance. Dad soon has him on his back and he sits on him, dress and all, and everyone is clapping and screaming. They are all on Dad's side, so I start hitting Dad, trying to get him off Sam who is trying to shout through his laughs, and Dad turns around and, next thing, my feet are off the ground as he carries me away under his arm.

We all crowd in – thumping his big body and picking up his dress, trying to see if he's wearing women's knickers. He flaps his arms and we duck and hide behind the tree, but he gets me again, grabbing hold of my dress until I struggle free and run towards the house. He grabs hold of my hand and pulls me towards him and he has such a huge grin as he swings me around until I nearly trip over my feet. He spins me, before letting me go. I carry on spinning, my arms outstretched helping me stay upright, as I slow, and the world is blurry, but my face is aching I'm smiling so much … and it's then… that, somewhere between the blur, I see the flash of light just once, startling my eyes, a bright white blot that takes all night to fade.

When I finally stop there are people laughing all around me and I press my hands on my thighs and I'm catching my breath and trying to see straight. I rub my eyes and there's Dad talking to someone, and behind him is Alanka and she's standing on a chair and I don't know why she's standing on a chair until I see her lift Dad's dress and put it over his head and tie a knot in it. He struggles and shouts, pushing with his arms, making monster shapes in the silk, and down my eyes go: past his big hairy chest and his tummy large and round and the dark pool of a tummy button, to a triangle of shiny pink hardly covering his bits, surrounded by a forest of hair. A silky pair of knickers, with blue ribbon stitched through. Another white flash, someone is taking pictures. And I don't know whether it's my dad or the spin, but my head feels light and I start to laugh, and everyone is laughing, and I just can't stop. And my cheeks are aching and people are pointing and Dad rips his hands through the dress, tearing it off his body and standing there in just his knickers, and still everyone laughs and it is then that I see Jeet. He is looking at me and he is not laughing. His eyes are narrow as if he's thinking, looking, thinking, and his mouth is slightly open. I laugh less and less and stand up and straighten my hair and my dress and I look away and then back again and his eyes follow me, looking at my body, slowly up and down, and he knows I can see him looking at me in this way, but it doesn't stop him. When he meets my face again he smiles a soft friendly smile, and my heart beats so fast that I feel it might explode. I've got him, I think, as I smile to the ground, I don't know how I got him, but I did. I'm shaking, the feeling somewhere between sickness and ecstatic crazy joy.

PART TWO

I wish I were a liar like my father. I wish I could morph into another state, another human being, for an hour, a day. I could do with a bit of dishonesty, a bit of bullshit.

'It's not that I'm trying to make some kind of social comment about self-harm,' I say, leaning forward. 'I'm more interested in scars. All of us have flawed skin, and it's that that I'm primarily interested in. The question is, is there any such thing as being perfect, untouched? The self-injury is just a step further. Many self-harmers injure themselves because they find it hard to communicate their emotions. I want to show their inability to express themselves, as it is here, etched into their skin, almost like a map of what goes on inside.'

Laura Davies looks at me from over her glasses, her pale eyes, pinched nose, as a naked woman with welted arms stares up at her from the pages of my portfolio.

'This is one of the smaller photographs,' I say. 'You'll see that most of them are much bigger.' I lift the edge of one of the sheaths and help her turn it over. 'So, I've included photographs of some of the larger images hanging in my studio, and with others I've shown just a fragment. But you should get the gist of what I'm trying to do.'

She nods and lets out a dry cough.

There he is: an early picture. I took it soon after we bumped into each other at the nightclub; it must have been one of the first times he sat for me. He's in a café, looking out of the window. He seems peaceful. He's leaning on his hand, and his sleeve is rolled up to reveal a strip of scars like needle punctures down his arm.

'I like this one,' I say. 'Because it's spontaneous and captures him at a vulnerable moment when he thinks no-one is looking. The thing about a lot of self-harm victims is that they are secretive about what they do: they wear long sleeves or gloves to hide themselves. But here his sleeve is rolled up, it's like he's been caught off guard. I'm proud of this one,' I say, smiling. 'Because even though it looks spontaneous, the picture actually took most of the day to get right: I had full on lighting, props, and I've shot it on a slow film to get the depth of colour, so he had to sit really still.'

She nods and turns the page.

'That's Maria,' I say about a close-up photograph of a scar. 'She cut into this particular scar again and again. It was the first place she ever made an incision, she was only eleven when she started. She was abused by her uncle and found relief only when she started cutting herself. So it's as if this scar is significant, as it's the start of her feeling better about herself. I wanted to photograph it up close to get the textures. You see here,' I say, stroking the ridged patterns, 'it could be a piece of fabric, woven wool: I wanted to make it beautiful.'

Laura nods, cocking her head. She spends a little longer on this photograph. Does she like it?

A couple come into the café to look at the exhibition on the walls behind us. Coming close, I notice the girl sneak a look at my work. I sit forward. I don't want her to see it. She notices me stare at her and they both start to move towards the canteen. I relax back again, take a gulp from my bottle of water. Laura looks at me and then over her shoulder as the couple lean into each other – are they talking about me? Laura twitches her head, so slightly that for a moment I think she's nodding.

On the next page he's there again. It was a couple of months later. He'd started a new job as a care worker, and he seemed more comfortable in his body, less ashamed of his arms. He always said he had to be a good role model for the kids he looks after, most of them the age he was when it all started.

'The same model,' says Laura.

'He's not exactly a model,' I laugh.

She looks at me with a half-smile.

The next photograph is of one of my largest works hanging from the wall in my studio. Again, it is a close-up of a scar, a burn mark on a hand that's been blown up to the size of a head. You can see the creases of the scar tissue, the white thickness of the dead skin. 'The burn was so bad,' I say, 'that he had to have skin grafts.' My voice wavers: I'm losing confidence. I take a deep breath and sit straight. Don't let it slip, Sylvie.

She smiles weakly at me. 'Must have been terrible,' she says, and without looking down turns the page again. She's not into this. She's hardly spending more than a couple of seconds on each photograph. It's making me feel sick.

She stops at another portrait of him; his serious face, the dark shadows, the detachment. I look towards the door. I bet she doesn't see what I see.

'Who is he?' she asks. 'You photograph him a lot.'

I look at her. A question, she's asking me a question.

'He's a friend,' I say.

'A good friend?' she asks. 'There's a sort of intimacy.'

She does see it. Maybe she likes them after all. Maybe she's just trying to intimidate me.

'This photograph reminds me a bit of a photographer called Birkin, do you know him?'

I nod, wracking my brain, Birkin – an actress?

'He always made a point of having his models sit for him many times, building up a relationship with them, an intimacy. More like the relationship between an artist and his sitter, you know?'

She sees it.

'He painted women. Often had passionate relationships with them, the series of photographs going on as long as the affair, and when he started to lose interest, he moved on to the next one and so a new relationship would begin.' She looks down at my work again. 'Is he a boyfriend?'

'No,' I jump, much too fast. 'He's a friend.'

But are we friends? Without either of us noticing something has changed, everything has become more intense. When we met that night he showed me his scars – 'Do you remember?' he said. 'You always wanted to touch them.' I told him I was a photographer and he asked if I would photograph him. I started to phone him when I was in London. He'd sit for me, we'd have a drink, but nothing more. Until the last time. I don't think either of us expected anything like that to happen. It wasn't planned, but it felt so comforting, so familiar.

But he hasn't responded to my text. Perhaps it meant nothing to him.

'He's someone I met a long time ago,' I say. 'His name is Max. We spent a summer together and I discovered he was a self-harmer. I didn't see him again until about a year ago, at a nightclub, totally out of the blue.' I smile, remembering how different he looked, the same scruffy clothes, but a confidence to him, a self-possession. 'I was interested to see how his scars might have changed over the years. He used to cut himself when he was a teenager and then he stopped, until recently – he had a relapse. His mother died when he was really young and…' she smiles at me and turns the page.

I twist in my seat, trying not to catch a glimpse of the photographs as she flicks through them. I focus on the display on the wall behind us. It's hard to see much from here, but they're black-and-white photographs and they don't look contemporary. They are all in strange asymmetric frames, the kind that demand attention when the piece of work doesn't.

I thought she'd ask me questions. I usually prepare myself for that favourite: who are your influences, your favourite photographers? But no names immediately come to mind. All I can think about is that artist whose work I saw recently. I must go back to the gallery to make a note of her name. Her paintings are ethereal, her children like angels, their sweet worlds, and their knowing eyes as if they belong in a secret place, somewhere we could never go. They reminded me of Bria, that summer. They made me want to sketch again.

Looking down at my portfolio, I catch a glimpse of Emma. A pretty girl, one of Max's kids at the centre; she's particularly attached to him. He would talk about her as if she were his child, protective, loving, and I had to stop myself thinking nasty thoughts about her. It's a portrait of her, but half of her face is in shadow, the half where she has a huge scar from her eye down to her lip. 'That's Emma,' I say leaning forward. 'She asked her brother to cut her with a broken bottle—'

'You know an awful lot about these people,' she interrupts me.

I sit back, the blood rushing to my face. But you compared me to Birkin, what was his name? You made out that that was a good thing.

She flicks through the remaining photographs nonchalantly. She clears her throat. 'Well, thank you,' she says closing the portfolio and standing it on its end. 'I think I've seen enough.' She passes it to me and goes to stand. That can't be it. What about the pictures you liked? I must ask her. I always keep quiet, too afraid of criticism, and then I kick myself for days afterwards. 'Do you think you might be interested in any of them?'

She holds my gaze for what seems like minutes. 'They are a little too...' she pauses, 'big,' she says. 'I don't know where we'd put them,' and she waves at the walls around us. But this is only the café, there's a whole gallery out there. 'Big is not always good in the photography world,' she says, pushing a smile. She gets up holding her hand out to me.

Is that it? Is that all you're going to say?

'What if they weren't so big?' I ask.

'Why? Have you got smaller ones?'

'Well, no. I mean, they're big for a reason.'

She nods expectantly.

'I don't want people to be able to get away. I want the photographs to reach every part of their vision.'

'Yes, but in my experience, small generally says more,' she says, directing me towards the exit. I put the portfolio to my chest and something falls onto the table. Some watercolour sketches, the ones I did after seeing the paintings: Bria, standing at the top of the drive, weightless, like a sprite. I pick one up and look at it.

'That's small,' she says. 'Can I see?'

I'm not sure I want her to see. It's experimental, not complete, something personal. Her face questions, her cold eyes. I pass it to her. The closest I could get to Bria was copying a photograph of my niece, Isabelle, whose auburn hair I coloured white, whose open innocent face I deadened with a knowing frown; her clear, trusting expression just like her mother's. She drifts against the hills, a lush landscape of winding roads and Cyprus trees.

'Is it yours?' she asks.

'Yes, but it's nothing really,' I look at my feet. I clear my throat. 'It came from an image of a girl I met when I was a child and I never really knew her, but her face has stayed with me. Anyway, I thought she was an angel – you know kids' minds, imagination,' I laugh. 'And I suppose I wanted to try to capture the image of her here – something pure and perfect.'

'Do you have more?' she asks, eyeing the other bits of paper that fell out alongside it.

I pass them to her. 'They're just sketches,' I say.

It's so clear. I'm right back there in the orchard, watching as Bria and Anya are photographed. Neither of them was innocent or untouched by life, but there was something about Bria that made walk into the living room and Jeet is there. He is sitting on the sofa reading, half in, half out of the shadow. He is wearing a vest and shorts. I hold my breath and carry on walking. Has he seen me? Shall I stop and say hello?

'Hey – *h h h* hi,' he says.

I stop. I blush.

He puts down his book and shades his eyes. I look at the floor: the cold tiles, my bare feet, pink toenails. I painted them for the party last night.

'Hey,' he sits forward, pats the seat of the chair in front of him. 'Come here.' His voice is croaky. It's Dad's chair. It's caught in a stream of light, dust glittering the air. 'Come and tell me about yourself, talk to me.'

Talk to you? Tell you about myself?

I walk towards him. My body feels funny, too big. I sit on the chair.

'Sylvie,' he says.

He looks different in the light: his skin is smooth and thin with long lines to his cheeks and marks like spot scars. His bright eyes flick across my face, it makes my stomach turn. Big eyes with spidery veins: Sam says he looks like a frog; the thought of it makes me want to laugh. A frog – *croak croak croak.*

His hand rests on my leg.

'*La la – last,*' he strains, and I try not to look at him. What should

me think that given the chance perhaps s

years I heard stories of what happened to t

lost in India, addicted to drugs, died of A

about Bria.

Laura squints at me. Smiling, she passes

me. 'Photography,' she says, 'how did you get i

I blush. There we are: Josie and me, sitting

tree. I was upset about something. What was it?

our bare feet in the grass. I was wearing Alanka

would never have dressed like that at home. Jeet

took photographs of us: an image of two young gir

by wild flowers, their heads bright in the evenin

dreamily gazes into the distance, while I look straight i

Another image of us looking into each other's eyes, lau

we are best friends, as if everything was as it should have

had a way of making the impossible seem real.

'I was taught by a friend of my dad's,' I say. I remember

was upset about the girls being photographed for the book. N

chose them over me.

'And drawing?' she says, pointing to the sketch of Isabelle.

'Drawing,' I say. 'Drawing is something different.'

me think that given the chance perhaps she might have been. For years I heard stories of what happened to the disciple kids: they got lost in India, addicted to drugs, died of AIDS, and I often asked about Bria.

Laura squints at me. Smiling, she passes the sketches back to me. 'Photography,' she says, 'how did you get into it?'

I blush. There we are: Josie and me, sitting beneath the magic tree. I was upset about something. What was it? Our tanned legs; our bare feet in the grass. I was wearing Alanka's green skirt; I would never have dressed like that at home. Jeet approached us, took photographs of us: an image of two young girls surrounded by wild flowers, their heads bright in the evening sun. Josie dreamily gazes into the distance, while I look straight into the lens. Another image of us looking into each other's eyes, laughing as if we are best friends, as if everything was as it should have been. He had a way of making the impossible seem real.

'I was taught by a friend of my dad's,' I say. I remember now. I was upset about the girls being photographed for the book. My dad chose them over me.

'And drawing?' she says, pointing to the sketch of Isabelle.

'Drawing,' I say. 'Drawing is something different.'

I walk into the living room and Jeet is there. He is sitting on the sofa reading, half in, half out of the shadow. He is wearing a vest and shorts. I hold my breath and carry on walking. Has he seen me? Shall I stop and say hello?

'Hey – *h h h* hi,' he says.

I stop. I blush.

He puts down his book and shades his eyes. I look at the floor: the cold tiles, my bare feet, pink toenails. I painted them for the party last night.

'Hey,' he sits forward, pats the seat of the chair in front of him. 'Come here.' His voice is croaky. It's Dad's chair. It's caught in a stream of light, dust glittering the air. 'Come and tell me about yourself, talk to me.'

Talk to you? Tell you about myself?

I walk towards him. My body feels funny, too big. I sit on the chair.

'Sylvie,' he says.

He looks different in the light: his skin is smooth and thin with long lines to his cheeks and marks like spot scars. His bright eyes flick across my face, it makes my stomach turn. Big eyes with spidery veins: Sam says he looks like a frog; the thought of it makes me want to laugh. A frog – *croak croak croak.*

His hand rests on my leg.

'*La la – last,*' he strains, and I try not to look at him. What should

I do when he stutters? '*Last* night, you looked beautiful,' he says, and my mind races with images of wearing that dress, his look when I laughed. It's embarrassing. 'You left so early, what happened to you?'

I didn't leave; I just went to bed. I was tired and everyone was being weird. Dad had that spaced-out look, as if there were nothing behind his eyes.

'It was a good night. Did you enjoy it?' he asks. He is circling his finger lightly on my knee; it tickles. 'It looked like you were having *f f f* …'

Fun. Do I say it for him? Show him his stammer doesn't matter? It doesn't embarrass me like it might other people.

'*Fun*,' he says finally, his face strained, as if the word hurts.

The circle runs the other way, slowly, a roughness on his finger catching my skin. 'I thought of you this morning,' he says. 'And when I opened the *va va va va* – doors to my van, there you were. You were sitting on the belvedere and I wanted to come over, but you were busy playing with your friend and I didn't want *to to to to* …' He stops, pauses, tries again. '*Disturb* you,' he says.

I look down. He thought I was playing. I wasn't playing.

The circle gets bigger.

His knee is a tarnished colour from the sun, gingery tight hairs like webs.

'You are shy,' he says. 'I can see that. Fragile.'

I am not shy.

His fingers are now around mine, edging their way in, curling. It sends weird feelings through me, like when Peter tickled my skin.

'Sylvie,' he says. 'Look at me. Look at my face.'

I look at him and my body feels cold.

'Then I meet you,' he smiles.

There's a noise, a noise in the kitchen. I jump up. He looks at me and his eyes twinkle. I straighten my shorts; my legs are sweaty. Someone is coming. 'I have to go,' I say, and turn away. I leave the room and go outside.

I walk straight to the gate and the sunbathing ledge and I sit in the heat. I can't breathe. I hug my knees. My mind is blank. What happened?

I look out at the view, shading my eyes. My mind has stopped. I'm pushing it to think about what happened: he touched my leg; he said things; he thought of me when he woke up this morning; he wanted to come over and talk to me.

I stretch out my legs. He touched me: the feel of his finger on my skin; what did it feel like? Was it nice? Was it tingly?

I put my head back and close my eyes. The sun is too bright; it burns.

I wait.

I walk over to the belvedere, looking towards the house, my feet falling heavily on the gravel. I wonder if he is still in the living room.

I stand on the belvedere. I take a packet of cigarettes from my pocket and light one. Smoking, I wonder what he would do if he saw me here, if he would come over and tell me that I'm beautiful.

I sit like this for a while, watching the ants make a trail from their ant house, looking out at the view and listening for the Italian boys as they pass on their motorbikes. I don't know how long I'll have to wait. I look towards the house. I could be upstairs with Josie as she reads in our room, I could be talking to Alanka on the bed, I could be listening to Soma as she recites the shopping list in Italian. But I don't want to do any of those things. I silently count, *one two three*, and watch the numbers form in my mind.

My stomach does a flip when I see him.

His hands are in his pockets, there's a book in the crook of his arm. He looks over at me but he doesn't wave. He acts as if he hasn't seen me, walking away from the house and up the drive.

I slowly leave the belvedere. Calvin Klein is sunbathing his furry tummy on the gravel. I squat to talk to him. I talk about silly things, about the ants and the gravel and the dust it leaves on your fingers, and the way the sun feels when it touches your face. I ask Calvin if he gets hot in his hairy suit. 'What do you think, Calvin?' I ask him.

Jeet hovers at the top of the drive. He stands and looks around, leaning down, picking something up, throwing it to the side of the road. Then he comes back. He must see me sitting here, but I pretend I haven't noticed him, until he is standing right above me, his feet beside my knee.

'Hello,' he says.

I look up.

'Come here, I want to show you something.'

I get up and let him lead me to the belvedere. He takes off his hat. He puts it on the wall, his cigarettes, his book. 'Here,' he says, leaning over the wall. He pulls back a branch heavy with plums. 'Have you tried one of these?'

He squeezes it between his fingers and the plum splits, juice running down his arm. 'Try a bit,' he says, and tears it, holding it out to me. I take it gently in my mouth. It is ripe and sweet. I can feel his eyes on me as I chew. He eats the rest, leaning forward to spit the stone over the wall. '*Theeey They* are good. The fruit is very good here, it must be fertile earth,' he says. He takes a handkerchief from his pocket and wipes his hands.

He stares at me, smiling as if he knows something, as if it's a secret, looking at me in this way. It makes me feel uncomfortable. I should say something, but I'm too scared of sounding silly. I want to sit on the wall, but my arms and legs are too heavy to move.

'There's something special about you, Sylvie,' he says.

Special.

'When I'm with you I feel different, listen to me,' he says. 'My *s s s stammer—*' he tuts, laughs to himself. 'My stammer is *almost* gone. Can you hear it?'

I can hear it; it is better. Perhaps that means he feels

comfortable when he's with me, I hope he does. He squints at me and leans his head on a column, watching me for what seems like ages. I look down at my hands.

'I'll tell you a funny story,' he says finally. 'I used to eat a lot of fruit in India, even though we were warned against it – you know, Delhi Belly. But I love fruit. It's my favourite, particularly tomatoes, all different types, currants, pears, cherries. So I'd eat all this fruit, but I never got ill. My friends used to call me an Indian – *You have the head of an Englishman and the soul of an Indian*. Anyway, I was in Delhi and a man was selling tomatoes on the side of the road and I buy a bag, pay him, leave and walk away, and the next thing I turn around and there he is, he's not only following me but blatantly masturbating.' I blush. I try not to laugh. 'I keep looking around. I'm amused. What does this man want? I remember his face, a sly cocked smile. What on earth was going on in that mind of his? Anyway, the next time I look, he walks straight into a tree.' He laughs. I laugh with him. 'Listen to me, to how easily the words come,' he claps his hands. 'This is a gift – it doesn't happen with everyone Sylvie, it is *sssp ssp special*,' he says. He holds both my hands, squeezes them.

'Anyway. The poor man, he was so embarrassed he picked himself up and rushed off in the other direction, his *lungi* flapping between his legs. What do you think?' he looks at me. 'Do you think that's funny?'

I nod.

He sighs. 'And you know what?' He looks out at the view. 'There is peace here. Something special. I like it here. I like it that I've met you,' he looks at me. 'And what is all this talk? It is pointless. A poet once said that love is when the sentence needn't be completed and it's understood, do you believe that?'

I shrug, embarrassed. I don't know.

'What do I think of love?' He sits on the wall, pulls me to sit with him. 'I think love is a tragedy,' he says. 'Two people meet, they desire each other, they find each other attractive and *POW* suddenly they move in together, start to tell each other their wildest secrets, late nights smoking cigarettes, making love. And the next thing she is wanting his babies, crying – *Why can't you commit to me, bond with me, bind me?* It's bullshit. I had that once and I don't want it again.'

His grip loosens on my hands. I want to pull away, wipe my sweaty palms on my shorts. He looks out at the view. 'What was it that Joyce said? Love is unnatural, that it can't repeat itself, the soul can never become virgin again. You love once and you are drowned. What is there for us? What is left for us?' He looks at me. 'But who's to say that he is right?' He strokes my cheek. 'Everything has been so stale, so safe, and then something happens.'

A wind comes up from the trees. It circles me and is caught in my hair, blowing fine strands into my mouth. I search my face with my fingers.

'*Ssh*,' he whispers. 'Don't worry. Look how beautiful it is.'

I look to the hills and the breeze touches my face.

'I know about lust,' he says. 'And maybe this is lust. I know about lust… and… I know about love,' His face softens. He leans towards me. 'And I know that I am in love with you.' He whispers it.

I stare at him.

'And you, Sylvie, are in love with me.'

What?

'Hey,' he says. 'You look afraid. Come here.' He hugs me.

Did he say he loves me?

'You have to trust me, Sylvie. I am not going to hurt you.' He pulls me tighter. 'You are shaking,' he laughs. 'You are shaking because you love me. Here, feel my heart.' He puts my hand to his heart. 'Feel how much my heart beats, Sylvie. It is beating for you. I am nervous as well. This is what you do to me. You make me shake, do you see? Oh, my sweet one.' He pulls me to him again, his heart fluttering against my chest. 'I want to spend time with you, Sylvie.'

I can see a lizard on the wall behind him, still and suspended.

'What do you think? Would you like that?'

If I reach out maybe I can touch it; would it run away from me?

'Hey, Sylvie, you'd like that wouldn't you?' He holds me to face him. 'Hey?' I look at him, his wrinkly face, shrivelled like an old plum. 'Hey?'

I nod.

He laughs. 'Oh,' he sighs, hugging me again. 'God, I love this love, whatever it is.'

I can hardly breathe.

He hugs me. He doesn't let go. I can't see the house, I can't see whether anyone is there, Sam, Max, Josie. I don't want them to see me. I don't understand what he is saying to me. I don't understand about love. How can he love me? He doesn't know me.

'Let's not move too quickly,' he says, pulling away. 'Let's not be greedy.'

I take a quick glance over my shoulder. There is no-one there.

'Let's treasure it, every moment,' he says. 'Come on, you should go back to the house, people might wonder where you are.'

I get to my feet. I step back. I feel dizzy. I cling onto the wall for balance. He doesn't notice, he's too busy looking around him, for his hat, his cigarettes, and I'm just left standing. Should I leave? I want to be back at the house, in the kitchen, in Dad's room. I want to be safe.

'I'm going to go,' I say quietly, and realize they are the first words I've said.

'OK, darling.' But he doesn't look at me. Is it over already?

I turn. My legs feel wobbly. I step off the belvedere, carefully placing my feet on the gravel. I walk back to the house. Maybe he is watching me. I wonder what I look like from behind. I want to check that my shorts aren't baggy, making my bum look big: Sam filmed me the other day and called me elephant arse. I carefully check them at my waist. What would he be thinking? About me, and the back of my head, my legs, my back, my hair?

I glance over my shoulder, but he isn't looking. He's facing the view, a cigarette in his hand, as if he is thinking about something else. I feel as if I want to cry, but I don't think it's sadness.

Inside the house, I stop. He told me he loves me. A feeling rushes through me and I run up the stairs.

Josie is in our room. She's lying on her bed. I slam the door behind me. My breathing is broken, shaky. I stop and think for a moment. Did that really happen?

'Oh my God,' I say into my hand. I sit down, lie down, sit up, get up. I don't know what to do. Josie stares at me. I don't know whether it is love or excitement, I don't think it can be love – how can it be?

'Josie,' I say from behind my hand. I can't keep it in. I'm giggling, laughing. She's looking at me as if I'm completely mad. 'That man,' I say, pointing to the door, 'he just told me he loves me.'

She sits up: 'What man?'

I'm laughing because I can't believe it. I want to climb a mountain, ride a camel, jump off a cliff. I can do anything there is so much of it. I jump up and down, dance around the room.

'Sylvie,' she says, 'what man?'

I grab her hands, linking them in mine, spinning her around. '*Jeet*,' I scream.

'What?' she says.

'*Jeet*, that man, outside,' I say.

I'm spinning her around. She pulls me to stop. She grips my hands and looks at me. 'You're joking,' she says. 'You're lying.'

'I'm not lying,' I shout. 'It's true. He just told me outside, on the belvedere. He said he's in love with me, and I'm in love with him. I was shaking. And I don't know if I'm in love but I just had this mad feeling. Whether that's love or whatever it is, I don't know. But he told me I was special, he told me I was beautiful.' I rush to the mirror. He thinks I'm beautiful. I look at myself and see the whites of my eyes, my lips, my bright hair against brown skin, and I think maybe I am beautiful. I am beautiful.

I see Josie staring at me.

I turn around and grip her hands, my smile so wide I feel as if my cheeks might break. I notice her frown. 'Josie,' I say. 'You mustn't tell a soul, no-one, not Sam or Max, you promise. Don't tell anyone about this, OK?'

'But Sylvie,' she says. 'He's... he's really old.'

'Do you promise?' I say. 'On your mum's life for ever and ever.'

She nods, looks at me sideways, unsure of me. 'I promise,' she says.

Shit. What's the time? I jump and look at the wall, forgetting that there's no clock; I'm at my uncle's. It's almost dark. My arm is dead, pins and needles in my legs. I must have been sitting here for ages. What was I thinking? Maybe I was staring into space, or at that patch of rotten carpet below the plant that I keep over-watering. I stretch my arms above my head, my portfolio. My portfolio. It's just as I left it this afternoon, leaning against the wall. I push myself forward and kick it – what a total fucking waste of time.

What's the point? What is the point in coming here? Why do I expose myself to it? Show these people my work and open myself to criticism. I should set up my own exhibitions: there are plenty of small galleries. Why do I put myself in the same position every time, asking to be rejected?

I'm pacing the room. I feel foolish, coming all this way, screwing up my relationship, and for what? So that that ugly vole can look at me over her glasses and tell me my photographs are too big. Too big? What does she know? She's probably a frustrated photographer, all her creativity wound into a tight little ball.

I pick up my phone and check for messages, nothing.

Now look at me. I'm pining after some stupid man who can't even respond to a text message. Where's his courtesy? I thought we were friends.

I stand at the balcony doors, my face against the window, wondering why I'm here.

Dad.

Sinking, slowly, I curl onto the floor. It makes me feel sick to think about it, sick, slow and sad. I'm such a coward. I want to see him, but I'm not even able to phone him. To phone Sam to find out what's happening.

I wonder what Sam wants to tell me: that Dad is ready to see me; he has missed me, and he thinks of me every day? Not likely. I know that he's been living alone since Alanka left him: maybe he's changed, he's woken up, he wants to pick up the pieces of his life. Or perhaps he's ill and dying. 'Don't barge in there, Sylvie,' Sam will say. He won't be thinking of me. Always protecting our father, and for what? I wonder if Sam has seen him. Would he tell Dad I'm here? 'Sylvie wants to see you, at last, after all these years. She loves you, forgives you.' But do I forgive him? You wouldn't forgive a friend for doing what he did. No, that's not the point: you wouldn't forgive a father.

But why am I really here?

Max could be with me. We could be watching the world from the darkness, almost like watching a film. Things are slower here, unreal. We could make a nest, snug and warm, and stock up with supplies of wine, fruit and cheese, easy food. We could stay like this for days and no-one would know. It would be our secret. Just once. Not more than that. Once would be enough.

Last time we met, there were no photographs. We spent the afternoon drinking in a pub in Brixton. Van Morrison and Pink Floyd on the jukebox, Dire Straits' 'Telegraph Road', we sang along to all the old classics. Cosy in a corner, catching each other's eyes when our knees touched. I was in London for work. I called him that morning: he wanted to see me. What do we talk about? Nothing much, but time between us seems to pass in a haze. There's a comfort there, that clarity.

He started telling me about his girlfriend, Louise. He'd never spoken about her before. He told me that she was good for him.

She kept his bad side at bay, and I asked – *Is that all she gives you?* I was only teasing, but he looked at me and held my gaze. *Why?* he asked. *Are you offering me more?*

Had I thought of him in that way? It's hard to say. I'm never good at identifying these things. But what he proposed seemed funny to me, unreal. I don't know if it was because of our shared childhoods – that month in Italy – but I found it hard to detach the image of him as an over-excitable teenager from what I saw then, sitting opposite me in that pub: his lankiness having found space to settle, his large square knees, a part of his masculinity, not awkward and bony like they were back then. His ginger hair faded, a contrast to his dark eyes. His fingers were damaged, like his arms, tobacco yellow and dented nails, they looked like claws, and I suddenly found myself imagining what it would feel like to be held by him.

We spent the night together. We left the pub and it was dark outside. He knew of a gig; had been on the phone to his friends. 'You're coming with me,' he said.

'No I'm not.' I stopped and frowned, focused on him.

'You fucking are,' he said, and grabbed my hand, pulling me through the streets.

'If you think I'm coming with you, you've got another thought coming,' I was saying. 'You're a bully, let me go.'

'Shut up,' he said. 'Shut up and sit down,' and we were suddenly in a cab.

The gig was in a church, a series of dark caverns lit by candlelight, where everyone seemed to know his name. I slipped and swayed, drinking some more, until he led me into a corner, blocked me with his leg, his shoulder, and I looked up at him, his face in shadow, and I thought: this is it, he's going to kiss me. But he didn't, instead he slipped his finger into my mouth – it was big and dry – and left something behind, passing me a bottle of water to help me swallow.

Would once be enough? Or is there something more? Once I

got a taste, could I say no? Would I become a liar, unfaithful, deceitful: such frightening words, words I equate with my father, not me, not my world.

We danced that night, the two of us. I wasn't aware of anyone else. We danced and we held each other's hands, arms, hips, moving together, my head on his chest, it felt like paradise. I didn't notice the band pack up, his friends leave, the venue empty around us. When there was no-one left, he led me away. He drugged me and took me to his bed. But he wouldn't make love to me. He wouldn't even kiss me. He held my hand and traced my fingers along his arms. His scars looked different, softer, faded. But watching his face as I touched him made something stir inside, as if that was all we needed at that moment; any more would have blown it apart, ended it all before it had even started. I analysed his tattoos, two tiny spiders on either inside wrist, a snake curled up his upper arm, a dragon on his calf. I looked so closely at his skin that I saw every mark. I asked him to tell me the stories. We lay together until daylight and talked about his travels, the places he had been.

Jack was on the sofa reading when I got home. I stood in the doorway, stretched my arms above my head and yawned. 'It was a hard job,' I said, and he looked at me, his eyes lingering a little longer than normal, as if he knew something.

We never talked about it. I couldn't tell him and he never asked, but things changed after that day. Jack looked different. Was it then that the magic went away? Perhaps life *is* simple: it's Max that I want, not Jack. Jack is wrong, Max is right – maybe it's just taken me this long to realize that. Max led the way, he put the pill in my mouth, he took me back to his flat. Things were much easier before that. All I was doing was photographing him.

And here I am, kneeling on the floor, my mobile poised, his name on the screen. I could phone him. He might not have got my text. It's OK to phone, isn't it?

I hold my finger over the call button. Perhaps I've fallen in love, maybe that's it. It's got nothing to do with my dad or Jeet. It's about Max, I'll tell him now. We'll meet. I take a deep breath: don't be a coward, don't run away, you always do. I press call; I press it. He'll be happy to hear from me, won't he? It's been about a month. The phone rings.

The messaging service clicks in.

The clash of music, his dark voice telling me he'll get back to me soon.

What do I say?

A big black bird drops onto the balcony. It gives me a fright. I get to my knees, clutching the phone to my chest and peer out to see the pigeon still unruffled on its nest. The black bird struts a few steps, it flickers its eyes at me before flying off. I sit down again, remembering the phone in my hand. I put it to my ear, darkness, dead, it must still be recording and all he'll hear is emptiness.

I had a feather in my book. I stuck a beautiful feather in one of the pages, it was a baby bird's feather – Deeva told me – and I always wondered how the baby might have died. I found it on the side of the road: it could have fallen trying to fly, it could have been killed by a car, swooped on by a cat, squashed by a wild boar. I wanted to ask Deeva, but it upset me too much. It never crossed my mind that perhaps the bird just lost a feather, it may not have died.

I walk into the bedroom and turn on the light. Taking my book out of my bag, I flick through the pages. A squashed spider, a splatter of blood where I'd killed a mosquito, there's even a small cluster of ants: Max and Sam had singed their tiny bodies with a lighter.

I flick to the back of the book and find the photograph of me and Josie sitting beneath the magic tree. It was the tree where Deeva did her spells. This was the first photograph Jeet took of me, sensing my disappointment with Dad, and with that simple perception, he got me. With the clunk of the shutter, I was his.

Max is sitting on the gravel with a moped engine between his legs. Sam is kicking a football around, and Josie is making a flower necklace. I'm painting the house, with a wash of yellow watercolour for the walls, green for the shutters and Dad's balcony doors, only the pages of my book are getting wrinkly because they aren't thick like proper watercolour paper.

I'm also trying to paint the cat: he's sitting on the top of Jeet's van with his paws stretched out as if he's airing his armpits.

'That definitely does not look like a cat,' Sam says over my shoulder.

'Oh, shut up.' I pull the book towards me.

I continue painting, squinting at the house, sizing up the plant pot with my pencil like my art teacher taught me, when Jeet comes outside. I quickly lean down to rinse my paintbrush as he goes to his van, opens the back door and climbs in.

'There he is,' Josie points, grinning.

Max walks over to us. There's grease and oil all over his hands and sleeves.

'He's in the Monster Mobile,' she says.

'Who, that weirdo guy?' Max asks.

Jeet comes out of the van with a bag. Maybe it's his camera. He doesn't look over at me; he doesn't wave.

'Yeah,' says Josie. 'I reckon he's *really* weird. You won't believe what he did the other day,' she says, half looking at me. I stare at her. 'He was in his van and he was eating raw meat.' I look back at my painting.

'*Nah,*' Max says.

'He was. It was long strips of raw meat and it smelt. I could smell it from outside.'

'Yeah, right,' I say. 'It was probably just that ham they all eat here, cured ham.'

'Prosciutto,' says Sam.

'Prosciutto,' I say.

'Well, whatever. But I still think he's weird. What do *you* reckon Sylvie?' Josie asks. 'Do you reckon he's the Florence Monster?'

'No,' I laugh. 'Of course he's not the Florence Monster.'

'But he could be.'

'How could he be?' I look over at the van. 'The Florence Monster is Italian anyway. He's English isn't he – look at his numberplate.'

'English schminglish – it's not hard to learn a language, have a disguise.'

I pause. No, he's definitely English. And anyway, he's a photographer: he can't be a serial killer. 'Don't be stupid,' I say.

'*I* know,' Max says. 'He could be the subject of our next film. We'll question him, ask him what he was doing the morning of the sighting. Try to catch him out.'

'Yeah, we could follow him, see what he gets up to after dark,' says Sam.

'You can't do that,' I exclaim.

'Why not?'

'I don't know, you just can't. You can't treat someone like a murderer.'

'But what if he is?' Max says. 'What if we actually find something out? Our names in the papers: four English teenagers save the day by catching the serial killer.'

'We might even get a reward,' Josie shouts. 'We'd better get a move on. Catch him while he's here.'

'What do you mean?' I look at her.

'He's leaving tonight.'

'No he's not.'

'Yes he is.'

'He's not,' I say. 'He's staying here to be the photographer for the book, he's going to photograph me, Dad told me.'

'Then why did I overhear him talking to Paritosh in the kitchen, getting directions for driving away from here? Towards the coast, where he's staying with his girlfriend or something.'

His girlfriend?

'That's what I heard,' she leans towards me, her hands on her hips.

I shrug as if I don't care, and go back to my painting.

His girlfriend, he has a girlfriend. A tall woman called Uta who Parameshvar fancied, I remember Soma and Paritosh talking about it. Maybe they're not together any more: maybe they've split up.

There are quick steps across the gravel. I look up. Soma is rushing towards us, her skirt flapping and her hair wild around her face. '*You!*' she shouts, rattling a tin. We all look at each other. 'I want to speak with you. *You!*' She is pointing at Sam. He backs away until he hits the wall. 'Don't run away from me,' she says, and walks right up to him shaking the tin; it's the household kitty. 'Your father may let you roam around like you are an adult, but adults don't steal unless they are criminals. Eh? Are you a criminal?'

His cheeks have gone red. He shakes his head.

'Eh?' she says. 'I saw you snooping around, you stupid. You are a criminal. No-one else in this house would steal their own money. Every day I go to the market and buy fresh vegetables so I can put food on the table for you to eat and all you do to thank me is steal my money.' She thrusts the tin into his hands. 'You will pay back every last lire by the end of the day or you,' she prods his chest, 'will be the cook from now on.' And with this she storms off.

I rush over to Sam. 'What was that about?' I ask. 'What was she talking about?'

He's sitting on the wall, his eyes scanning the ground. He suddenly seems small, fragile.

'Sam, what happened?'

He looks up, 'I don't know,' he says.

'*Wicked*,' Max is pacing the floor, laughing. 'She was well angry. That was brilliant, mate.' He goes to slap his friend's hand, but Sam turns away. 'Come on, did you see her face? That was fucking hilarious.'

'What was it?' I ask, ignoring Max. 'Did you steal the money?'

'No,' Sam shakes his head.

'Yes you fucking did!' Max stops dead.

'Did *you* steal the money?' I ask, turning to Max.

'No,' he shouts. '*He* did.'

'*I didn't*,' Sam says, looking at him.

'Sam,' Max raises an eyebrow, 'you fucking did, are you going gaga?'

'*I didn't*,' he says and rushes towards the house throwing the tin into a bush.

Josie gets up to follow him and then stops. 'Should I go after him?' she asks.

I shrug, walking past Max, who is still laughing, shaking his head. '*Eejit*,' I say.

'*What?*' Max follows me. 'What was that for? I didn't do anything wrong.'

'I bet you made him do it.' I pick the tin up from the bush and brush off the dust. The glint of Parameshvar's eye, his hand out in a wave.

'Bollocks,' he says, and starts to walk back to his moped.

'My brother doesn't steal,' I say, following him. 'There's no way he'd do that without you encouraging him.'

'*Oi*,' Max turns around. He points his finger at me, poking my chest. 'You don't know me,' he says. 'You don't know whether I steal or not, you don't know nothing.'

I walk back to the belvedere, trying to keep calm. I lean down to pick up my book.

'I don't steal, all right? I may do other things, but I don't steal,' Max shouts after me. 'Stealing is for losers,' he says.

'Well, why is Sam stealing then?' I say, turning around. 'He's not a loser.'

'I dunno,' he shrugs. 'Why are you asking me?' He sits on the ground and starts fiddling with the engine.

I stand for a moment. I look at Josie, who shrugs at me, and then back at Max.

'Well, if he did it, then where's the money?' I walk towards him. 'We need to put it back in the tin, we have to give it back to Soma, before she tells Dad.'

Max doesn't say anything.

'You must know where it is, tell me.'

He looks up at me. 'Where do you think it is?' he says.

'I don't know,' I laugh. 'How am I supposed to know? I didn't even know it was stolen.'

Max frowns in the sunlight. 'What about that book he bought you? Didn't you wonder how he got the money?'

The book? What book? I look down. My lovely Florentine book. I peel it away from my chest. 'This?' I ask.

'*Duh*,' he says, as if I'm stupid. 'What did you think, he miraculously magicked the money out of thin air? You probably think he's just like all these other fucking hippies with their stupid appearing acts. There's no such thing as *magic*, Sylvie,' he says, and scrambles to his feet, walking away.

'Oh,' I say, looking down at the book.

'I don't understand,' Josie says from behind me.

'This book,' I say.

'What about it?' she asks.

'Sam bought it for me.'

'Really?' Josie sighs. 'That's amazing. He's so sweet. I wish I had a brother like him.'

I look towards the house. Sam bought me this book? He stole money to buy me this book. 'What am I going to do?' I say.

I go to Sam's room, but he's not there. I go to my room and sit on the bed. Perhaps I should admit to it, tell Soma that Sam stole the money, say that he bought me the book and she can have it if she wants. I open the front page – but I've already written my name in it, stuck a tarot card next to a sketch of Dad, painted the house. I flick through the pages, blank and ready to be filled. I was so happy when I got it.

I go to the study.

I hang around Dad while he talks to Paritosh. There is a stack of loose paper on his desk that keeps flapping in the wind from the fan; I try to weigh it down by placing a box of cigarettes on top, a stapler. When Paritosh has gone, I say: 'Hari.'

He looks at me. I need to tell him: I hope it doesn't make him angry. 'You see this book,' I say.

'What's that?'

'This one,' I say, holding it out to him. Of course he doesn't know about it: he didn't buy it for me.

'That's a nice book.'

'I know,' I say. 'I love it,' and I stroke its cover.

Dad goes back to his work.

'Dad,' I say. 'I mean, Hari.'

Dad smiles as though he thinks I'm funny. 'Yes, lovey?'

'Can I ask you something?'

'Yes.'

'You see this book,' I take a deep breath, 'well, Sam bought it for me with money he stole from the kitty and Soma is really angry and says that he has to pay the money back by the end of the day and I don't know how he's going to do it because he spent it all on this book, and it was for me. He bought it for me, which means it is stolen, and perhaps I should give the book back, or give it to Soma to say sorry.' My other hand is behind my back and my fingers are squeezed tightly together.

Dad smiles. 'Hey,' he says, and holds out his hand. 'Let me see that.' I pass him the book and he holds it in both hands, flicking through the pages. 'You've drawn in it already,' he says.

'I know,' I reply. 'I love it.' I say it louder this time.

'I can see that.' He raises his eyebrows. He looks amused. He passes the book back to me, half stands and digs into his pocket. He fingers through the notes. 'There is a very simple solution to this problem,' he says, and holds them out to me. 'Go and give this to your brother to give back to Soma or she'll have him spend the rest of his holiday washing dishes.'

'*Oh my God*,' I say, looking at all the little notes in my hand – lire, there are thousands of them. 'Thanks so much Dad.' I throw my arms around his neck.

'That's all right.' He laughs. 'You see. Is it such a terrible problem?'

'No,' I say, shaking my head.

Sam is sitting at the top of the drive. He is squatting on the ground and playing with stones.

'What are you doing?' I ask, as I come up from behind him.

'Killing ants,' he says.

I squat beside him and watch him for a while. Every time he squashes an ant the others in the trail stop and twitch around it, trying to lift its little body and take it with them.

I put my book down on the ground and Sam looks at it.

'Thanks for getting me the book,' I say. 'Max told me.'

He shrugs.

'I was thinking maybe I should give it back, because you bought it with stolen money, but I've already drawn in it,' I say. I open it and show him the sketch I did of Dad, 'Look,' I say. 'Do you think it looks like him?'

Sam tilts his head at it, squinting to get a good view. He nods, 'Yeah, it's alright,' he says. He catches my eye, and quickly looks away.

I reach into my pocket and pull the wedge of cash out. '*Ta da,*' I say, waving it under his nose.

'Where'd you get that?'

'Dad gave it to me,' I laugh. 'I just went up to the office and explained what happened and he reached into his pocket and gave me the money. He said you should give it to Soma or she might make you wash dishes for the rest of the holiday.'

'Dad just gave it to you?'

'Yeah,' I say, laughing. He's so cool.

Sam frowns. 'Wasn't he annoyed I'd stolen it?'

I shake my head. 'No, not at all.'

'He didn't even want to see me about it?'

'No,' I say. 'Isn't he brilliant?'

'Yeah, brilliant,' he says, sarcastically.

I don't see Jeet the whole day. Whenever I'm in the kitchen, he isn't there. Whenever I'm hanging around in the courtyard, I can't see him anywhere. I don't know where he's gone. Sam gives the money back to Soma and she really embarrasses him by hugging him; he says she smells of spaghetti. I told him he's silly – that spaghetti doesn't have a smell. I told him it must be the tomatoes or the basil. It makes us both laugh. I'm secretly pleased that he bought me the book and I really love it again. I even write a story about it. It's called 'Stolen Dreams'. But I'm sitting on the belvedere and as I write I keep looking up with every noise that comes from the house. I want to know why Jeet is leaving. He told me he wanted to spend time with me.

I see him at supper, but he doesn't appear to notice me. He talks to Nim about something serious, and every time he looks at me he skims me with his eyes as if I'm no different to anyone else.

Later, after dinner, I'm in the kitchen helping wash up when he comes in and gives Deeva a hum hug. I stand by the sink and wait until the humming has stopped and then I turn around. They are still hugging, but Jeet opens his eyes and winks at me and I bite my lip to try to stop myself from smiling.

'Hey,' he says when they have finished. He touches the end of my nose. 'It has been amazing meeting you my special one.' What does he mean? He stops at the doorway and slips on his shoes, walks outside.

'Where is he going?' I ask Deeva.

'Continuing his travels I suppose.'

I stand at the window and watch as he climbs into his van. How could he just go? He closes the door, switches on the interior light. Is that it? What if I never see him again? The thought makes me heavy and sad, as if I want to go to bed and cover my head in a duvet.

He unwinds the window and puts a cigarette in his mouth, turns on the engine. I head upstairs.

Dad and Alanka are sitting on the bed. I walk to the balcony doors and look outside. The van is still in the drive, the engine rumbling. I hold my book to my chest. I wish I'd kept something of his to put in it. The van starts to roll, backwards at first as he turns it around. When he passes beneath the window I can just about see his face, and a long white cigarette hanging from his mouth. I watch the back of the van as it goes up the drive and turns onto the road. I try to listen out in case he beeps around the corners, but all I can hear is the crickets.

I sit on the bed, but I don't stay long. I ask Dad if he'll do my tarot reading, but he says he's too tired. I hardly talk: I don't know what to say, so after a while I leave. From the corridor I can hear

Sam, Max and Josie in the living room watching MTV. I don't want to go downstairs. Deeva and Peter are in the kitchen, and it suddenly upsets me, as if everyone is having more fun than me, and whether I want to or not I can't join in.

I go to my bedroom and turn on the light. There's something on my pillow: a big red tomato. I think it must be a joke, Sam and Max being stupid, but closer I notice a piece of paper.

Sylvie, Sylvie Sylvie I read. I touch my neck.

I have had to go away tonight. I didn't want to go so soon, to break up this connection that we have. But I will be back, and very soon. I loved meeting you — your tenderness, your serious face, I have watched you from afar today. You concentrate when you eat, the little crease in your forehead, your teeth. You have beautiful teeth Sylvie, white and strong. I want to spend time with you. I want to show you ways of not being so serious. I would like to call you Leela, it means play. If you were a disciple, I think that is the name that Parameshvar would give you. Perhaps we could share a secret name. Leela, do you like it? I think you could wear it like an angel.

But I want you to do something for me. When you have finished reading this note, I want you to sit down in your bed and dig your beautiful teeth deep into the flesh of this tomato. I want you to take big mouthfuls and let the juice drip down your face, onto your T-shirt. I don't want you to worry about the mess that you make. And I want you to think of me as you eat it and I will be thinking of you as I make my lonely drive through the night. But above all else I want you to enjoy it.

Love knows only giving, and remember what I said. Remember you are Leela. Remember that I love you.

Jeet.

Leela Leela Leela. He wants to call me Leela.

I look at the letter again. He said *love*. He said I have beautiful teeth, he watched me as I ate. I look at his handwriting. He wrote this letter to me, his long thin writing, the way he loops his Ls. And then I look at the tomato. Why does he want me to eat a tomato?

I sit on the edge of the bed and put it to my nose, sniffing it, it smells sweet. I put it to my mouth. The thought of eating it makes me laugh. He says make a mess; let it drip down your face. I take a big bite and have to slurp to stop dribbling. I take another, and the juice runs down my chin, it tickles. I wipe it with the back of my hand, wet tomato juice on my skin. I concentrate on imagining Jeet in his van, driving down the winding roads, thinking of me sitting here eating a tomato. And then I think of Josie. What if she had come into the room before me? What if she had read the letter and found the tomato? What would she have thought?

Deeva sighs as she puts her head back on the sun lounger, closes her eyes. '*Porco dio,*' she says, rubbing her forehead. 'This life.'

I sit up and put my book on the floor, pulling my tummy in as I lean forward. Deeva stares towards the swimming pool, shading her eyes, watching the people as they sunbathe and swim. She sighs again.

'Are you all right?' I ask. I look down and check that I haven't got a tummy roll.

'Bloody life,' she says, changing position as if she is uncomfortable, readjusting her bikini. She wipes the sweat from between her boobs.

'What's wrong?' I ask. It was her idea to come here, but she's hardly said anything since we arrived.

She blows out through her nose. 'What's wrong, what's wrong,' she repeats to herself.

A tall man with skin the colour of chocolate slows as he walks past us. He looks down at Deeva. She shades her eyes. He is wearing tiny red swimming trunks and his legs shine like wax.

She watches him as he walks away. She sighs again, picking up each boob from beneath her bikini top, trying to make them look perky, but when she lets them go they just splay out like soft silky cushions.

'I don't know what it is Sylvie,' she looks at me. 'Perhaps it is just love.'

'With Peter?' I ask, sitting closer. I want to know what it feels like, what love is like.

She laughs. 'God, no,' she says. 'Not with Peter.'

She looks into the distance. Sam and Max are doing bombs into the pool and Josie is watching. She's wearing her school swimming costume, the elastic fraying around her legs. I look down at my bikini. It's Alanka's. It's designed by an Italian and does up at the front with a little gold clasp.

Deeva sits up, slips her feet into her flip-flops and rubs cream into her thighs.

'Not Peter,' she says again. 'I could never love Peter.'

'Why not?' I ask, thinking of them in her room: the candlelight, his naked body on the bed waiting for her.

'I don't know,' she sighs, and looks away again, frowning towards the sun.

She twists her hair into a bun and ties it at the back of her head. 'If you go on changing your lover you become neurotic, mad,' she shuffles her bottom backwards on the lounger. 'There are all these sounds, all these different vibrations, different ways of doing things – this man likes honey on his bread, this man does his teeth before he makes love to you, this man smells of coffee.' She looks at me. 'I am afraid that I will become addicted to change, you know?'

'Then why don't you stay with Peter?'

'Because it is not love.'

She flaps her hand beneath the lounger to find her sunglasses.

'Then, what is it?' I ask.

She sighs, slipping them on. 'It is accidental. It is two people. They are lonely, their needs are met, they call it love.'

'So, it may be love?'

'It is not love,' she says. 'You fall in love with a man because you like his butt, you like the way he moves, you like his eyebrows, no?' she laughs. 'But that is not love.'

I frown.

The chocolate man walks past us again and Deeva looks up at him. He must have been around the pool about three times. Maybe he likes her. He looks at her, and she waves her hand at him as though she is not interested. 'Nice thick eyebrows,' she says to herself.

'Who him?' I ask, watching him as he slowly walks away, a slight swing in his hips.

'No!' she whacks my leg. 'Not him.'

'Oh,' I laugh.

She looks at him sideways. 'Men in general,' she says. 'They have these big bushy eyebrows and we women think, look at him, he is strong, he has this – what's the word? Sexual fertility? But that is not going to help him stay in your life, be around for all the years that you want him to stay when you have his child, you see?' She flips onto her side to face me.

I turn towards her, the sun beating hard on my back.

'Eyebrows are a bit of an unimportant part of a person, no?' she says, laughing.

'Yeah, I guess,' I say. What are Jeet's eyebrows like? I'm losing the image of his face already and he's only been gone a couple of days.

'But love,' she says. 'Love is something else. It comes from here,' she taps her chest and her boobs wobble.

Love.

'I love your father,' she says, looking away from me.

You love my…

There's shouting from the swimming pool and I look around to see Max's head emerge from the water, his arms flailing. Sam is laughing at him. People around them are swearing.

Deeva sits up and tuts: 'These boys, they will get us thrown out. We are not guests at the hotel, you might have to tell them to shush.' She lies back down again. 'What was I saying?'

'My father,' I say. You said you loved him.

'Yes,' she says, thoughtfully. 'Your father.'

'But what about Peter?' I ask again. What about Alanka?

'I love your father, but it doesn't mean that we should be together. You know – love exists outside of ourselves, it is every-where, in the sky, in the land under our feet. I could pick up a rock and I could do it with love. It is in me, it doesn't have to mean sex. It doesn't have to mean fucking and living together: that never worked between me and Hari, he was always looking elsewhere and I would get very jealous – we had terrible fights. He was like a father to me, yes, he was: I wouldn't do anything without asking him first. It was like a trap, it wasn't healthy. Peter makes me feel like a woman, your father made me feel like a child.'

I close my eyes, a scorching red. The heat, it makes my head pound.

'And now he has his new child.'

I open my eyes and look at her.

'He has small fragile Alanka,' she says.

The dark-skinned man walks over again and says something as he passes. Deeva shades her eyes and says something back. He stops and smiles, looking at her body, up and down, like Jeet did with me. He glances at me. I shift my weight onto my side, leaning my head on my hand and flicking the edge of my towel over the cover of my book so he thinks I'm Italian. When the man talks he sounds like a film star. Deeva sits up and crosses her ankles, pointing her toes to make her legs look longer. He says something and she waves her hand at him. She turns on her side. He hovers a moment, a half-smile, before walking away.

'So when you have your baby, will Peter be like the father?' I ask. Josie and I were talking about it the other day.

'Peter as father?' she says. 'I don't think so.'

I told Josie I thought he would. I thought they loved each other. I thought that's what happens when you have sex all the time. My mum says it's chemical.

'Because you don't love him?' I ask.

'Oh, I do love him,' she says, letting her head fall to the side. 'I just don't *love* him.'

'Oh,' I say.

The man has stopped walking past. He has settled himself beside two women at the other side of the pool.

'How come?' I ask.

'Oh, I don't know.' She sits up. 'Oh, listen to my nonsense. You know, whatever. I am having fun. He is a good lover and that is all I really want from him. I don't want love right now. Not after Glenn. I need some fun, yes?' She looks over at the chocolate coloured man. He is kissing one of the women's hands. She turns her body away from him. 'It's funny, for a time I worked in the local vegetable shop and I would watch the people as they came in, I would watch the couples, and you know what's interesting? Women are always dominant in a relationship, whatever it looks like from the outside. They are always in control. Even with Glenn. He might use his hand to get his way, but I had my ways as well. I would always win, and often he didn't even know it.'

'But Glenn used to hit you,' I say.

'Yes, and lots of people are not nice.'

'But Peter is nice.'

She stops and thinks for a minute. 'Yes, but Peter is young. He doesn't want a child. Who would want a child in their lives that wasn't even theirs?' She fiddles with the gap in the chair. 'I sometimes wonder if your father would want another child,' she says.

My father, another child?

'But he can't, can he?' she says.

'Why not?' I ask.

'You know,' she turns to me. 'He has been castrated, had the snip.' She cuts the air with her fingers.

'What do you mean, castrated?' I ask. 'Doesn't that mean—'

'Not castrated, no. I mean, you know, his tubes where the sperm swim, he has had them snipped so he can't get anyone pregnant. A great way of having contraception, but not so great if he ever wants a child.'

My face reddens. I didn't know that. 'Why did he do that?' I ask.

'He didn't want any more kids? Made the mistake once, twice, didn't want to do it again?' she shrugs. 'I don't know, you should ask him. Probably to stop little Haris from popping up all over the world.'

It gets so hot that every single part of my skin is sweating and I just can't get comfortable. I sit up. 'I'm going for a swim,' I say.

Sam and Max are sitting at the pool bar drinking Coke. I walk towards the pool, discreetly pulling my bikini out of my bum, hoping that no-one is watching. I sit on the edge of the pool and slowly lower myself in. The coldness of the water runs up my skin, rushing to my head and cooling it off like ice. I swim, wetting my hair and my face. It relaxes me. It felt weird up there talking about those things.

I watch as Deeva lies flat, her body splayed out like a whale, a dark fuzz of hair crawling down from her bikini bottoms. Josie reads her book, and Sam and Max bounce and fidget at the pool bar. Max is wearing a T-shirt even though he just got out of the pool. He says it's to stop himself from burning, but I know that's not the only reason. Max looks at me. I catch his eye and he immediately looks away. I pull myself out of the pool. Jeet says I'm beautiful, Alanka says I look good in her bikini. I walk more slowly than before, my head up and my chest out, maybe other people can see it as well, maybe even that dark-coloured man with the waxy legs.

'That Max boy,' Deeva says as I dry myself. 'He likes you.'

'No he doesn't,' I say, blushing, laying my towel back down.

'He does, I can tell. Believe me, I know about these things. He couldn't keep his eyes off you when you walked back from the pool. He definitely likes you.'

'He doesn't.' I hug my legs, scratching an old mosquito bite on my ankle. Max likes me? Does he also think I'm beautiful? I lie down on my back. Sometimes I notice him look at me in a certain way; sometimes he laughs at my jokes. Maybe he does like me. Little drops of water shine against my skin. I think of that girl in my favourite picture, her strips of wet hair and spots on her swimsuit like diamonds. 'He wouldn't ever fancy me,' I say, and close my eyes.

'*Agh*, that is so cute,' Deeva whacks me. 'Maybe we can have a romance in the house – no-one is interested in Peter and me. Young love is far more exciting.'

I run through the living room, picking up my skirt so I don't trip over, the fast drumbeat fading as my feet hit the cold stone tiles of the hall. I close the living-room door. It's dark. I can hear my breathing. I fumble for the light switch, tracing my hands along the wall. The sound of Nim's laughter carries through the house.

I throw myself onto the loo, my skirt bunched in my lap, my head falling forward, laughing. It's so much fun. The music had me running around the table, faster and faster; I felt light, like rushing water. I hurry to finish. I don't want Paritosh and Nim to leave, to switch off the stereo, to turn their backs on the evening and go to bed. At the basin I look at myself in the mirror. I look so brown in this light, almost black: there's redness in my cheeks, sweat glistening on my upper lip, my white T-shirt that keeps slipping from my shoulder. I smile at myself. I wonder what I look like when I dance? I sway my hips and arms to imaginary music, the beat in my head. I flick my hair. I want to look like Nim. I want to look free.

I rush back through the living room, past Sam and Max watching TV.

Nim and Paritosh are still in the kitchen. Nim is pinning her hair back, sweat shining on her chest, patches on the silk beneath her arms. When she sees me she beams. Paritosh moves towards her and grabs her waist. He pulls her to him until their bodies are touching. She laughs, throwing back her head, curving her spine, her hair uncurling, her hands on the floor and the ends of her hair touching the ground. Her back makes a perfect arc. The drumbeat quickens, and suddenly they are both on me, their sticky hands, the wet of Paritosh's naked skin. They are pulling me outside, the hard gravel piercing my bare feet.

'Did you see the moon? It is a perfect crescent.' Nim squeezes my hand and pulls me to the belvedere. 'Look how clear the sky is, look at the stars.'

We lean against the wall and reach into the night, the moon slicing the sky. 'Wow,' I say, my eyes stretching in the darkness.

'It's winking,' Nim laughs.

'Hmm,' Paritosh looks up. 'What do you say, two weeks until the full moon? Strange things might happen,' he says, and howls like a wolf.

'Oh, Toshy,' she laughs. 'You make me want to scream.'

But I'm just mesmerized by the sky, the sliver of a moon and the bright glittery stars. I've never seen anything so pretty.

'*Ahh*, come here,' Nim pulls me to her chest, letting me snuggle against the silkiness of her dress. 'Sometimes you can see shooting stars,' she says. 'And when you see one you must make a wish. My wishes always come true.'

I look up at her. What would I wish for?

'You like to hug, don't you?' Her face is so close; the warm smell of cigarettes on her breath. I nod. It feels comfortable here.

'Oh, this song,' Nim pulls away. 'Can you hear it?' She sways around the belvedere. 'It reminds me of India, of the beat of the monsoon rains, listen.' She is smiling so much that her teeth are shining, the whites of her eyes. She grabs my hands and pulls me around the belvedere. 'Listen to the beat. Let yourself go. Trust me. Come on,' she repeats it, *Let yourself go*, like a mantra, as she spins me around. I loosen my arms and let her hold me, support my body, as we spin. I close my eyes, my head falling back. When I open them again, her face glistens from light to dark, the air circles me, the blur of colours as I try to see the house. Which side is it? Where am I? Where will I stop?

When she slows, my mind takes time to catch up. When she stops I nearly fall over. Paritosh catches me, and holds me to his chest, his sweat cold in the night air. I catch my breath, as my eyes adjust, my cheek wet against his bare skin.

'Come on,' Nim pulls me towards the house.

She and Paritosh loop arms around the courtyard, as Josie stands in the kitchen doorway, watching. She is a shadow against the light of the house. I can see her leg moving, twitching to the beat. I rush up to her, grab both her arms and drag her into the kitchen, skipping and jumping around the table, laughing.

She laughs with me.

'*Woohoo*,' I scream. The drumbeats carrying me, faster and faster. 'Come on,' I call as I pull her around the table, just as Nim did to me.

Josie laughs, her hips moving jerkily, not quite catching the beat. 'Loosen up,' I call. But she just thinks it's funny.

I stop and clap my hands, try to catch my breath. 'Where are the boys?' I ask. 'Let's harass them.'

They are lying on the sofa in the living room.

'Come on,' I call from the doorway. 'Get up lazybones.'

Josie joins me. 'Come on, come dance.'

They look at each other.

We rush over and grab their arms, laughing, pulling them up, leading them into the kitchen. My hand gripping Max's, his sweaty scratchy palms.

Sam does silly dancing. He's swaying his arms, pretending to have long floppy hair, his disciple piss-take. Josie claps her hands and laughs. I move my hips towards Max. I'm watching him, trying to get him to look at me, willing him with my eyes, but he moves awkwardly, his head down as he concentrates on the floor. He tries to sit down. Sam does bunny hops around the room, which makes Max laugh.

I pull him to standing. 'Come on,' I say. 'Come on Max.'

He looks down at me.

I slowly, firmly, drive him to the back of the room with my hips, moving them in the same way I saw Nim move with Paritosh. I stare at him, trying to catch his eyes, my hands on either side of his arms, not touching, just encouraging, slowly encouraging until we are up against the wall, and there is nowhere for him to go. I push my hips against his. His smell, rich and sharp, the feel of his leg between mine. He holds my gaze. Something in his eyes sparkles.

I hook my fingers inside the top of his gloves and with one movement I rip them off his arms, pulling them all the way off his fingers. Naked, palms outstretched, thick raised pleats are scattered against his milky white skin, scratches, bruises, clots of blood. It looks terrible. I look up at his face. I can see what you do to yourself.

He grapples at me, tries to grab the gloves.

My heart is beating fast. You do this. You cut yourself.

The music continues.

He grabs my arm and yanks it, pushing me to face the room, my back to him, his arm deep in my stomach making me exhale, a wheezing sound. And with his other hand he grabs the gloves, ripping them from me. Sam and Josie stand still. Max shoves me hard, and I fall against the sink, almost to the floor as he lurches around the table and out of the kitchen.

I get to my feet, wipe the hair from my face.

'*What?*' I say, as Sam and Josie stare. Josie looks at her feet. 'It was only a joke,' I say. Sam switches off the stereo. Silence. Crickets. My heart: it feels fragile and flighty in my chest.

'What?' I ask again.

'That was cruel.' Sam shakes his head. 'You shouldn't have done that.'

'I didn't mean it,' I laugh.

Josie twists towards Sam.

'What?' I say again. 'What's the big deal?'

'You know what the big deal is,' Sam says. 'That wasn't good.' He pauses. 'That was bad.' And with that he leaves the room.

I lean against the table and scratch my leg with my foot. 'That was bad,' I repeat with a little laugh.

Josie doesn't say anything.

I blow air up my nose, '*Woah*, it's hot,' I say.

'Yeah,' Josie says, feebly flapping her T-shirt. She looks towards the door.

'I don't know what all the fuss is about, it was only a joke,' I say.

Josie shrugs, she won't look at me.

'Shall we watch some telly?' I say quickly.

She pauses.

'Come on, let's watch MTV.' I move towards the door.

'I don't know,' she says.

I stop. I don't turn around.

'I don't know if I want to,' she says. 'I might go upstairs.'

'OK,' I say, and carry on walking.

Jeet has been away for four days. He hasn't phoned. I wonder if he is coming back. Every time I ask Dad he tells me he doesn't know. It doesn't bother him that I'm interested. He doesn't look at me strangely. He hasn't wondered why I want him to come back, that it's not just because I'm being photographed for *Alpha Child*. Now I'm walking with Deeva and I'm thinking that she might know.

It's early evening. The sun is low and still hot so we've found ways of staying in the shade of the big pines that stretch on either side of the road like monster Christmas trees. Deeva wanted to get away from the house, she says the communal way of life is too much. She calls it suffocation. I was also happy to leave. Sam, Max and Josie are playing football in the drive, and I don't like football.

We stop at a *taverna*. Deeva has a fizzy water and I have a pear juice and we talk about her spells.

'Hey,' she says. 'You know what we can do? We can find some laurel. Soma has run out of bay leaves and I want some to do my incantations. Bay leaves are for success, if you put them on your palms you might become a famous artist.'

I look at my hands.

'Now where did I see the trees? Come quickly, before it gets dark.'

As we walk, the image of a branch comes into my mind, but it's a branch covered in blood as there's a girl lying naked on the ground and the branch is sticking out of her bits. I look around. We are heading up the hill, away from the house. It is getting dark.

Deeva hums as she walks, and traces her hand against the feathery trees. The light is fading quickly. I wonder whether we should turn back. I've been thinking about Max, about what happened yesterday.

There's a rumbling sensation beneath my feet, my flip-flops on the concrete. A vibration.

'A car,' Deeva takes my hand. We step to the side of the road. It's difficult to see it at first as there are no lights, just a shadow moving slowly towards us. As it passes, I see a man. He looks at us, but he doesn't wave. A chill. I hug my arms to my chest. It's cold. I'm only wearing a bikini and a pair of shorts.

We start to walk again. 'Deeva,' I say. 'What do you think of the Florence Monster?'

'What do you mean, what do I think?'

'Does it scare you?' I ask.

'Not really,' she says. 'He likes the young girls, he is not interested in someone like me.'

'Girls? Young girls?'

'Yes, they are teenagers. It is only the women he cuts up, not the man. He is a heterosexual obviously,' she laughs. 'He doesn't like to play with a man's penis. But who blames him?'

If I stare straight ahead, I can't see the dark gaps between the trees, the thick branches, the dark knotted foliage.

'I don't know,' Deeva continues. 'These men, they are inadequate: they think that if they are intimate with a young girl they get their energy and it makes them feel young. They are perverts. We don't need to know how their brains work.'

The image of the girl and the branch floats around in my mind. I close my eyes.

'Deeva,' I say, running to catch up with her. 'You know some people cut themselves, cut their arms?'

'Eh?' she looks at me.

'Not by accident, but on purpose, you know, with knives, something sharp.'

'Mmm, yes? I suppose so,' she says. Her face is becoming hazy in the near darkness.

'Why do you think they do it?'

'Pah,' she says. 'I don't know. They are mad? Why would you want to do such a thing?'

'I don't know,' I say. 'Maybe because they are sad.'

'Perhaps,' she says. 'But it's a very weird thing to do. If I hurt, I go to my room and punch some pillows, it is much better.'

I shrug and carry on walking. My flip-flops are rubbing against the inside of my toes.

'Ssh,' Deeva stops. 'Listen. Can you hear the water?'

I stop. Quiet. Stillness. The light trickle of water.

'A stream,' she says, and hurries towards the sound. The space she leaves between us is dark, almost too dark to see. I follow her.

'Deeva,' I say. 'I think maybe we should turn around.'

She doesn't hear me or doesn't listen, as she is kneeling at the side of the road, splashing water on her face. 'Oh, it is delicious,' she says and grabs my wrist. 'Here, drink some, it will revive you, give you energy.' I cup the water in my hands. It is cold. It chills my insides.

'Come on,' Deeva waves at me. 'I'm sure we are nearly there, at the top of the hill, it is a farmer's land, there are lots of herbs.'

I grab hold of her arm and walk close, *One Two, One Two*, if I say it in my mind it stops the thoughts from flooding in. I look at the sky – the dark blue sky, the tall black trees like puppets dancing in the breeze. It must be darker down here than anywhere else in the world.

Deeva's humming turns to Italian words, beautiful flowing words.

'What are you singing?' I ask.

'It is a romantic song,' she says, and sways her arms. 'I am not old enough to love you, I am not old enough to be alone with you, and I shouldn't have anything to say to you because you know much more than I do...'

I listen. *I'm not old enough to love you*. It's as if she's singing about me.

'What is it my *amore*?' she grabs my hand and swings it as she walks. 'Come on and sing. It will take your mind off the darkness.' But she's singing in Italian and I don't know the words.

'Are we nearly there?' I ask.

'Yes, my chicken,' she says and picks up her pace. But I can't see where we are going. It seems as though the road leads nowhere.

'*Amore Amore Amore*,' Deeva shouts to the sky and it echoes all around. There's a crashing, a sudden sound high up in the trees. I gasp and grab Deeva. The treetops are shattered by the screeching of birds, then a rustling that falls like a stone. There's something closer, nearer our feet. We stop. Broken breathing, my heart beating, and then it calms to nothing, just silence, dead silence.

'Come on,' she says, and heads off without me.

She has stopped singing. I want to keep talking so I can't hear my feet on the ground, so small and unimportant. 'But what if the Monster was here,' I say. 'Doesn't the thought scare you?'

She laughs: 'It is not here my *bambina*. Honestly, you are thinking black and unnecessary thoughts.'

Soon we can see the end of the darkness. There is a clearing; the trees have stopped. We run to the top of the hill where the land becomes flat. The expanse of sky, the moon. We stop. My heart beats so loudly that I can barely hear Deeva when she says: 'I knew it was here.'

The moon lights up the fields, corn fields, bales of hay like large black wheels.

'Here,' she says, tracing her hand against a tree at the side of the road. 'I know where to go, wait here.' The sweet smell of herbs fills the air. She rushes into the field, towards the darkness of the wood until I can barely see her. 'Deeva,' I call. But I'm too scared to follow.

I stand completely still, my eyes dead ahead to the darkness of the wood. I don't think I even blink.

I've never been afraid of the dark. Alone in my bedroom at home, I would lie on my back and wait for my eyes to adapt and I would look at all the shapes that the darkness made. Sometimes my clothes looked like animals, sometimes the streetlights reflected on the ceiling like a shimmery ghost, sometimes they made the shape of a dog. I called him Angus. Other times little cars drove across the ceiling like Dinky toys. On quiet nights, I would get out of bed and stand at the top of the stairs and I would hear Mum, on the phone or singing along to music, the sound of her voice soothing me. I was never afraid. But it feels different here; here I suddenly feel very alone.

When Deeva returns she has taken off her T-shirt, the laurel branches wrapped inside. She is wearing just her bra.

We run. It's easier downhill. Deeva is calling as she runs, screaming as if it's a release. I open my mouth but no noise comes out. I just want to get home.

'Hey, you are scared,' Deeva reaches for me. 'What should you do when you are scared?'

I don't know.

'You should think of calming thoughts, things that make you happy. I think of my Buddha statue at home, my bath, my baby.'

All I can think about is middle-aged men, greying hair, werewolves.

We turn a corner and the road seems to go on for ever: there is no shape, beginning or end, just a fuzz of darkness framed by black with nowhere to rest your eyes. I don't know whether there is anyone behind us, following us, because all I can hear is my heavy quick breath and my heart. But suddenly there's a different sound, the sound of voices. 'Ssh,' I say, and pull Deeva to stop. 'What's that?'

'What?' she stills. 'What?' she says again, as if she too is scared. It is so dark her face is black and it frightens me.

'Voices,' I say.

There's movement at the end of the road.

'There are people,' says Deeva. 'Don't worry, my Sylvie, there are other people in this world but you and me.'

It's a man, a man's voice. I follow Deeva as she walks towards him. My mind is blank.

'It's someone at the spring,' Deeva says. 'They are filling up with water.'

Closer I can see that there are two people: a man and a child. The child disappears. The shadow of a car... a van.

'Hey,' says Deeva. 'Isn't that...?'

I squint again, walk a little quicker. I stop. Tall, thin, the bend of his shoulder. Is it Jeet? Is he back?

'Hey,' Deeva calls out and waves.

Even when we're up close, I can't see his face, just a dark blurry figure against the road. It's only his voice that I recognize.

'*H H H Hey* guys,' he says.

As they hug, Jeet and Deeva's shadows merge.

I climb into the back of the van and there's a girl sitting in the front seat. She is small and blonde. She doesn't turn to look at me. Jeet calls her Bria. I don't know where she came from. Deeva squeezes beside her. As Jeet drives, I slip and slide on a bench, trying to make out the things that are in the dark, the bed, the cooker, the washbasin.

It's not far to the house, much closer than I imagined. Jeet drives down the drive, the darkness lit up by his headlights and the glow from the kitchen windows. Peter stands at the doorway and Deeva jumps out before we have parked. Bria follows her and runs towards the belvedere. It's as if she has been here before.

I don't know how to open the door, so I have to wait for Jeet. He turns off the engine and twists around in his seat. '*H H H How* have you been my Leela?' he asks, and the name makes me blush.

Bria is on the belvedere, she is sitting on the wall, and there beside her is another girl, she is dark-haired, she is dressed in white.

'There are some people I'd like you to meet,' he says.

Anya has dark silky hair and it is so long it nearly touches the seat where she is sitting. I had a good look when I sat down for supper. She also has very bright green eyes. Alanka says it is unusual for someone with such dark skin to have such green eyes. She says they are amazing, almost the colour of emeralds. She thinks Anya is beautiful. She says that when she sits opposite her, she finds it hard not to look at her. I wonder whether she thinks she is more beautiful than me.

Anya is Italian, but she speaks with an American accent. She says that she doesn't have a nationality, because she was born a disciple and disciples don't belong to one country. Bria was born in Holland, but she doesn't consider herself to be Dutch.

'Where are you from then?' I ask. They must belong somewhere.

'We come from Parameshvar,' Anya says. 'We are his children.'

When Anya talks, Nim shakes her head as if she can't believe it, agreeing with everything that she says, and she occasionally puts her hand on Paritosh's shoulder or my dad's knee and says, 'Wow, this kid is amazing.'

Anya seems to know everything. Her mum is a therapist and does workshops on lovemaking. She travels the world to perform in front of millions of people. I can see Max and Sam sniggering at the idea of her mum performing lovemaking, but I don't think she actually has sex on stage. Anya travels to lots of exotic places with her. She says she wants to be a therapist, and at every workshop she takes notes. Anya is fourteen but she seems more grown-up. She talks a lot and uses words like 'release' and 'ego' and 'aloneness'.

Anya *is* really pretty. She has the kind of face that you want to stare at for hours, the kind you see in magazines. Her eyelashes are so long and dark that it looks as though she is wearing mascara, and her lips are a lovely cherry colour. She reminds me of the girl I saw in one of Dad's photography books, with her brushed hair and clean plimsolls, standing between two boys, unsure which one she should choose.

When she stands up from the table, she puts her hand on her hips and curves her body towards the person she is talking to, and the person she talks to most over supper is my dad. When my dad laughs, Anya laughs, and when he looks at her she moves closer to him until her body is touching his arm. She's wearing a loose white shirt that has no buttons and is tied in a knot around her ribs. You can see her tummy, and sometimes you can see her boobs. She's chewing bubble gum even though we are about to eat supper: she makes clicking noises when she chews and then she blows sticky big bubbles that make my dad laugh when they pop right next to his ear.

I'm trying not to look at her, but every time I look away my eyes drift back to where she's standing with her hips against my dad's arm and her boobs almost touching his face.

But then Dad isn't sitting where he normally sits, because that's where Bria is sitting. Nobody seems to talk to Bria. She is small and thin and spends most of her time gazing at nothing and twisting her hair around her finger. Before supper, I saw her with Jeet and she was clinging onto him, holding onto his side while he tried to lay the table. It reminded me of how I sometimes feel with Dad: a sense that if you let go you may never get a hug again. It made me wonder whether Jeet is Bria's father.

Bria fiddles. If she's not fiddling with her hair, she's tearing up pieces of paper, making patterns out of her napkin, unrolling the little wax matches that fall out of their flip-top box. All around her is a mess of torn up and broken things. When Anya nudges her to stop, Bria scrunches her eyes so tightly it's as if she doesn't want to exist. There's something strange about Bria. Josie thinks she's an albino. I didn't know that humans could be albino; I've only ever seen an albino rabbit: white and silky with watery pink eyes.

While we're still eating supper, Anya twists her body past Dad and walks towards the belvedere. She walks slowly, as if she is dreaming, tracing her hand through the air. I watch her as Soma brings out the pudding, and spoons a big portion of stewed fruit onto my plate. Anya is leaning against the wall and gazing at the landscape. I keep my eye on her as I quickly eat my pudding. She walks to the table on the belvedere and picks up the video camera. I eye Sam. He is looking at his empty plate and at the dish of fruit to see if there is enough for another helping. 'Look,' I say. He glances towards the belvedere and thumps Max's arm, jumping to his feet and rushing over.

Anya has the camera to her face.

Sam and Max stand behind her, kicking their feet.

'Go on.' I'm there beside them. 'Say something.'

'Hey, what's that?' it's Bria. A tilt of American. I look around.

'A video camera.' Josie's there too. 'What do you think it is?' she says.

'I know what it is,' Bria says, reddening.

Anya gives it to Bria, who handles it carefully. Then she does this really funny thing. She holds it to her face but instead of looking through the viewfinder she looks through the lens. Josie laughs.

'Not like that,' I reach for it. 'Like this,' I say, showing her.

'I know how to use it,' Bria says.

'Give it here or it'll break,' says Sam. He takes it from her, clutching it and sitting at the table, far away from the girls as they settle themselves on the belvedere wall.

'It's pretty, isn't it?' I move closer to Anya, who is looking at the view, the little sparkles of houses in the dark. 'That's the road that goes into Florence. We sometimes go down there on our mopeds. You can have a go on one if you like.' She flinches. She doesn't look at me. 'Maybe you have a moped already,' I say.

'No,' she sighs. 'We don't need them where we live. We're right by the sea.'

'Really?' I say. 'Right next to it?' I'd love to live by the sea. I wish Dad would take us there, even just for a day.

'Yeah,' she says. 'Literally, like two minutes up the road. We're on the beach all the time.'

'Wow. No wonder you're so brown.'

She looks at me, at my arms and legs, and I wonder if I'm pale in comparison.

'You go quite a nice colour,' she says. 'A sort of goldeny colour. Not like me. I'm olive.' I look at Josie all splodgy, and Bria with her pale skin and eyes, and I wish I was more like Anya.

Anya goes into her bag and pulls out a packet of cigarettes. They are Merit, the same brand that Jeet smokes. She takes one and lights it.

'Can I have one?' I lean in closer.

'Sure.' She offers me the packet. When I put the cigarette to my lips she strikes a match for me.

'Oh, you've got a packet of those.' Josie steps towards us. 'I love wax matches. They're so funny. I've been collecting them.'

'Right,' says Anya. She looks at Bria and they both laugh. I laugh as well.

'Huh,' I say, taking a drag from my cigarette. 'Wax matches. *Everyone* uses them here. They're not that special.'

Josie turns a dark crimson.

Anya offers her packet of cigarettes around: to Sam and Max sitting at the table fiddling with the video camera, Max takes one but Sam says no; to Josie, who stumbles over her words, 'I smoke don't,' she says, and this time when Anya laughs Josie laughs as well. Josie backs away from us, sitting with the boys, her eyes flicking from girls to ground.

Anya takes a drag of her cigarette. 'So,' she says, 'what do you do with that thing?' She waves at the video camera.

'We make videos,' I say.

'About the Florence Monster,' Sam says.

'A monster, *woah*,' Anya laughs. She passes her cigarette to Bria, who puffs on it quietly.

'Have you heard of him?' Josie asks.

Anya looks at Bria and they both laugh. 'The Florence what?'

'The Florence Monster,' Josie says. 'He's been killing for years, young couples who have sex up in the hills.'

'Oh, yeah,' Anya nods. 'We've known about that for ages. It's all fabrication. Probably some anal husband killing his wife and blaming it on a monster.'

'Yeah,' I laugh. 'That's what I reckon.'

'Anyway, what's the big deal, there are far sicker things happening in this world, like war, starvation.' She flicks her hair and Bria nods, agreeing.

'So,' Anya says, taking the cigarette back from Bria. 'Are you making a video about him?'

No-one says anything. I look at Sam. 'Yeah,' he says quietly.

'Sounds fascinating,' she says. 'Maybe we could be the star victims. What do you think Bria, do I look dead?' She imitates a dead person. Sam and Max frown at her, and I laugh. I always thought the film was a stupid idea.

There's movement back at the house. Soma is clearing up and everyone else is chatting. Jeet leans back in his chair and looks over at us. I wonder whether he's pleased to see us all getting along.

When I look at Bria, I notice a clump of hair fall from her hands, small fine slivers like silvery fish. She puts her hand back to her head and continues to twist. She sees me watching, so I drop my eyes to the ground. Anya's feet are dark and dusty, her toenails painted a rich dark purple.

'So,' I say. 'Are you on holiday?'

Anya looks at me sideways. 'Holiday?' she laughs. 'We're always on holiday.'

'Always?' I ask, surprised. I clear my throat. 'I mean, really? What about school?'

'We don't go to school,' she says. 'I left school about a year ago, Bria left about three years ago. Didn't you Bria.'

Bria nods and continues to twist.

'It was Bria who got me here,' says Anya. She holds out her hand to her friend who comes to her, snuggles against her chest. 'If it wasn't for Bria, I'd still be killing myself in India. I hated it.' They lean together on the wall. Bria whispers something to Anya, and they both laugh. I look at Sam. He looks up at me, catches my eye.

'I wish I didn't have to go to school,' I say. Sam looks away. 'I hate it as well.'

Anya's eyes twinkle, her skin soft and smooth. 'If the house was burning down, would you get out of the fire?' she asks.

'Yes,' I nod. I feel Sam watching me.

'Well then,' she shrugs.

I sit and think for a moment. Maybe it is that easy. Maybe I can just leave. Mum isn't at home anyway. It's not as if she's there watching over us every day.

'I *am* going to leave,' I say, sitting up straight. 'I'm going to live here with my dad. Go to Italian school, learn Italian.' I say it quickly, hoping that Sam won't hear me. He doesn't look up.

'So, your dad's Harideva, right?' Anya asks.

'Yes,' I nod.

'He's the one writing the book about kids? He's cool,' she says. 'He's a cool dad, you're lucky.'

I look at the ground, he *is* a cool dad: he's not an idiot like Sam says.

'Are you going to be models for the book?' I ask Anya.

'I guess so,' she says. 'Jeet's always getting us into weird shit. I just go along with whatever he tells me.'

'I'm going to be a model as well,' I say.

'Oh yeah?'

'Yeah, I'm going to be the main model.'

'Oh, are you?' Anya scans me, up and down. I shift my weight, placing my hand on my hip. 'And you?' She turns to Josie. 'Are you a model?'

Josie shakes her head.

'No, just me,' I say. 'They only wanted me.'

Josie stands up.

'Yeah,' Anya laughs. 'Jeet takes his photography very seriously.'

Josie hovers for a moment, before straightening her shorts and walking away. She appears odd, awkward. She continues to walk, off the belvedere and towards the house. I don't call after her.

'Is she your friend?' Anya whispers.

'Yeah, sort of,' I say.

Anya and Bria laugh.

I sit back and gaze towards the table as Soma and Nim tidy up. Jeet gets up and walks towards Dad and they stand together, Dad's arm around his waist as they talk. Dad eventually follows Jeet into the house.

'Look,' Bria points towards them.

Anya smiles and nods. 'Can you guess what they're doing?' she asks me.

I shrug.

'The book isn't the only reason Jeet's here,' she says.

I blush hot – does she know? Has he told her about us?

'Shall we tell her?' Anya asks Bria.

Bria shrugs, nods her head.

'What? Tell me what?' I ask, my heartbeat quickening.

'There's something else going on between Jeet and your dad,' Anya says. 'It's a little thing called a truth drug,' she nudges Bria.

Bria takes a small box out of her pocket and tips the contents onto her palm. There are five little capsules, filled with a browny white powder.

I stand up. 'What's the truth drug?' I ask.

'It's a very special thing,' says Anya. 'Some people call it the love drug because it makes you feel all light in your heart, light and lusty. But we think it's really the truth drug. You can stay up all night telling each other things you never even knew you felt. And when you touch, it sends shivers all the way through your body. It's way out.' Anya picks one up between her fingers.

'But isn't it bad for you?' I ask.

'No,' Anya says. 'It's only ground nutmeg, it's totally harmless. You should try it. It's amazing. It's totally out of this world.'

Sam and Max are standing behind Bria, staring at the little capsules in her hand.

'Fucking hell,' Max says.

About three years ago, I convinced myself that Jack was in love with someone else. There was no evidence for it, only a glimpse of an idea that, once grasped, I turned over in my mind, looking at it from different angles, fuelling it to grow. But it wasn't completely unfounded. They were friends at university, a world I had nothing to do with. No, it was more than that: Jack had mentioned that she might have fallen in love with him. Her name was Tamsin. He told me he didn't feel the same way, even that their relationship had become awkward, but I started to understand it differently. In my mind, they were destined to be together. It was only a matter of time.

He kept in contact with her through mutual friends. We would occasionally hear about her: a renovation course she was doing, a job in a stately home. Jack in architectural reclamation – the perfect match. I found photographs of her in his private boxes. I studied them: her long wavy hair, her creamy skin and soft fleshy body. She was graceful, comfortable with her womanliness; I saw her as everything I wasn't. I started to think about her as I thought Jack might, noticing her roundness, her plump lips, the way her face glittered in the sunlight. It was like getting there first, preparing myself for the inevitable.

I knew I had to tell him. I knew that part of the problem was that I kept it to myself, allowing it to grow and expand every time I thought about it. I would close my eyes and say it in my mind: 'Are you in love with Tamsin?' Trying to find a time and place when I could confront him. Only the more I practised it, the more it became my reality: 'You *are* in love with Tamsin.'

One evening, we were invited out. It was a university friend's birthday and I knew she would be there. Jack and I arrived early, sitting together on one side of the table, someone else on the other side of Jack. That way Tamsin would have to sit next to me, or opposite us where I could capture the secret glances, a long and lingering gaze. But by the time she arrived, the person beside Jack had got up and she had slipped into his place.

She was dressed casually, a shapely skirt and blouse, a warm and sensual angora cardigan; her hair fell naturally down her back. She was more beautiful than I remembered from the photographs.

The night started off OK, but I soon became aware of my silence, my inability to join in. I'm drinking too much wine; my stomach feels tight; I don't want to eat. The banter gets louder, laughter all around, but none of it is with me. Everyone smokes, my head spins. He is talking to her and there is no-one talking to me. If I press myself into his arm, will he notice me? Will he stop and look over, reassure me? How can I be so weak, so needy? This isn't me.

She is laughing, she is throwing her head back and laughing. I get up from the table, push past the seats and run outside. It is cold. I stop and close my eyes, hold my head in my hands. How can I be doing this, when I know it's not real, I know I'm imagining it; I even know why.

'Hey, Sylvie, what is it?' It's Jack. He's behind me.

I'm breathing into my hands. I left the restaurant, in front of everyone, so dramatically. I can never go back there again. What will they think of me?

'Sylvie,' he grabs my arm. 'What is it? Sylvie look at me.'

'I can't,' I murmur. 'I can't.'

'You can't what? You can't look at me?'

'I can't,' I say.

'Why can't you look at me?'

'I can't,' I say again, crying. 'I can't go on like this. I can't do it. I can't feel like this any more.' I turn around and cry it out to him, *I can't I can't*.

'What?' he asks. 'Feel what?'

Can I say it? Can I tell him?

'What, Sylvie?' he clings to me. 'What's happened to you, what is it?'

What's happened? You've seen it. You've sensed that there's something wrong. I am no longer the girl you met, the girl you fell in love with. How can I be? I'm not strong; I'm not independent like I was before. I'm small, fragile and needy. How can you love me? I'm fucking everything up. I'm destroying everything.

'I want to go home,' I say.

'OK,' he says. 'It's OK.' And he turns around to head back inside. He holds his hand out to me.

'I can't come in. I can't say goodbye.'

'But your coat.'

'You can get it.'

'*God!*' he says.

'What is it?' I gasp. 'Why are you annoyed? What's wrong?' It is so cold I am shaking.

'What do you mean what's wrong?' he says. 'What's wrong with you?' he shouts. 'We're out with our friends and you run away like that, what happened?' I grapple for him and he comes back to me.

I cry into his shoulder. 'It's terrible – what I've done, terrible.'

'What?' He's looking at me, pulling me to face him. His eyes, his face. 'What's happened?'

I'm crying. How am I going to tell him?

'What?' he grabs me. Angry, his breath like steam. 'Have you met someone else, is that it?'

I look at him, shocked. 'What?'

'You've been acting weird.' He's away from me, he's dropped my arms. 'I knew there was something.' He's pacing. 'I'm such an idiot, why didn't I see it? You've met someone, you've fallen in love with someone else, that's it.'

I stand still. I'm in love with someone else? 'No I'm not.' Suddenly I'm laughing. How can he think that?

'But you've been so distant and then there's this thing, what is it?'

I take a deep breath, looking at him. His pained eyes, he looks angry, hurt – he doesn't know.

I have to say those words, however mad they may be, I have to say it: 'Are you in love with Tamsin?' But the minute they leave my mouth it seems impossible.

He looks at me. He stands back and looks at me, his mouth slowly curving into a smile. He's smiling. He thinks I'm joking. He starts to laugh and I curl into my arms against the wall, curling up and crawling into myself, away from him, the restaurant, the world. Where can I go, how can I get away from here? He's grabbing my arms, trying to bring me back, just snippets from him saying: 'Sylvie, What is this? You think I'm in love? Tamsin? You can't be serious.' And I'm curling and crying and I can't get away from him.

But what if I am serious? What if it is the most serious thing I have ever had to say?

'Come on, come here, hug me.' He holds me tightly in his arms.

And really I know, I know somewhere deep down, I know that the thing that would say it in so few words is that I'm not deserving of him. I don't deserve his love.

We went home. We didn't go back to the restaurant. Jack got my coat and he helped me home, and he didn't ask me to explain, although I really needed to talk.

Back at the flat it was quiet and cold. He made tea while I climbed into bed and clutched the duvet to me. I was shaking. I was breathing into my hands and saying – I'll tell him all about my dad, all about Jeet and my dad and all about Dad loving everyone else more than me.

He got into bed and his legs were warm. He passed me my tea and it felt hot in my hands. He looked at me and his eyes welled with tears and he told me he loved me, he told me he loved me more than anyone he'd ever loved and that he could never love anyone else. And then he listed all the reasons he loves me.

He told me he always wanted to be with me. He told me I should always talk to him, whatever I felt, however mad it may seem. And I looked at his face, his simple open smile.

My dad directs Anya and Bria to sit on the belvedere wall and look out at the view while Jeet leans against a wooden column with his camera. I think he is doing a close-up shot as he is using a really big lens. Dad wants Anya and Bria to look as though they're laughing, so he tells them a silly joke, but they stare at him vacantly. Then he makes farty noises, and Anya scrunches up her nose and waves the air as if the sounds smell.

Alanka and Nim sit on the wall and watch. Anya is wearing one of Alanka's dresses, it's purple with buttons at the front; it's not as pretty as the one I wore to the party. Bria is wearing stripy trousers and a cut-off T-shirt, with leather necklaces around her neck as though she's a member of A-Ha.

When Jeet takes the pictures, he leans against the wall, kneels on the ground, or stands with his legs astride, and he sometimes uses a tripod. To get their attention, he tells Anya and Bria that they are beautiful: 'That's right, That's right, just there, yes, good,' he says.

I sit and watch, wondering when it will be my turn. I'm sitting with my feet up on the wall, leaning against a column. I'm wearing one of Alanka's skirts, it is green and has flowers on it and I have to be careful to tuck it between my legs so that my knickers don't show.

My dad told me that most of the photography should be finished by the end of the day. He says he knows how I will be photographed: mine will be a beauty shot taken in front of the house; he wants me to look pensive, he says, and the printed picture will be layered with a photograph of some trees. He says it's a special technique. He says I'll look like a child of the earth.

Jeet slings his cameras across his body and waves to everyone to follow him to the orchard. Anya and Bria are still sitting on the wall, and Dad has to call them about three times before they follow him. I'm already at the gate by the time they get there.

'Dad,' I say as he passes. I say it quietly so no-one else can hear. 'When is it going to be my turn?'

'Later my sweets,' he says. 'Soon, don't worry.'

But I'm not worried, I want to say.

I hold open the gate as everyone walks past and I watch as they weave their way through the allotment: Dad, followed by Jeet, Alanka in her long skirt rushing to catch up with them, Nim slowing to talk to Anya and Bria as they whisper and giggle at the back. I slowly follow, picking flowers as I go and smelling them, wondering whether Dad will come and get me if I go into the house, if he'll tell me when it's my turn. At one point Anya looks back at me and whispers something to Bria that makes her laugh.

I stand and watch as Jeet directs the girls. Anya is sitting against a tree and Bria is fiddling with her necklaces. Dad is watching with his arms crossed. I go over to him and quietly ask if I can listen to music in his bedroom.

I sit on the floor and go through his tapes: there's Joan Armatrading, Joni Mitchell and Phil Collins. I put on a Phil Collins tape and the first song fills the room – 'In the Air Tonight'. I sit cross-legged in front of the mirror and pout at myself, looking at my face from different angles, spinning around and glancing over my shoulder. I need to work out my best side; I wonder which is Marilyn Monroe's best side. I smile at myself but it looks odd. I laugh but it seems fake. When Dad makes me laugh, I look natural.

The music continues: 'This must be love'. I lie on the floor and count the different coloured weaves in the carpet.

I hear laughing and clapping. I turn down the music and look outside. Nim is shouting excitedly, and I think perhaps they have finished. Maybe it's my turn.

I wait and watch until Anya and Bria rush through the gate into the courtyard. They pose to each other, Anya with her hand on her hip, her silky hair hanging around her face and a flash of her white teeth. Alanka follows and they all stand at the table beneath the weeping tree.

Soma puts two large jugs of lemonade on the table.

'*Dad*,' I call from the balcony when I see him.

He looks up.

I beckon to him: 'Is it my turn?'

He strains at me as if he can't hear.

'*My turn*,' I say, leaning over the railings.

'*Ah*,' he says, and looks back at everyone helping themselves to lemonade. His face crumples into a sorry: 'All finished now, lovey,' he says. 'We've done enough now, we've got what we want. We'll use you again on something else, I promise.'

Done enough? I look over at the group and notice Anya looking at me.

It's OK – I think. I'll go outside and join in, have a glass of lemonade. But outside, I stop by the door. There's lots of chatter, Dad showing Polaroids to the girls. No-one looks around. I don't mind – I think. I'll be used for something else, there'll be other books. But my body feels heavy, as though there are weights in my pockets, and I feel like I might cry. Jeet looks over at me and smiles, but he doesn't ask me to join them. I'd feel OK if he said: *Come over here*, loud enough for everyone to hear, and poured me a glass of lemonade.

I walk towards the allotment, letting the gate swing closed

behind me as I go down the steps, dodging the lines of vegetables before sitting beneath the magic tree. I won't cry.

I should have known it would all be a lie. That Dad didn't mean what he said. Why does he keep on doing that? Promising me things that don't come true. Who wants to have a stupid picture taken anyway? I don't care; I don't want to be photographed for the book, there'll be other things, like Dad said, there'll be something else.

I lean my head back on the tree and try to feel its magic. Deeva says if you make a wish here it'll come true. One day she was worried about her baby, she was worried it might be dead, so she sat beneath the tree and said in her mind – *Please let my baby give me a sign that it is alive.* And after a while she felt a flutter. She took a deep breath and waited, and there it was again. She told me that at that moment an image of a little boy popped into her mind and she called him Angelo, just like Angel.

I close my eyes and think of that song again: 'This Must be Love'. What should I wish for? *Love.* But I don't know what love is.

I hear a noise. I look up to see Josie. She is squatting and picking wild flowers.

'Josie,' I call her over. I'm pleased to see her. 'What are you doing?'

'I thought I might make a bracelet,' she says.

'That sounds nice.'

She stands, the flowers in one hand and her book in the other.

'What are you reading?' I ask.

She looks at the book. 'I just finished it,' she says.

'What was it about?'

She walks towards me. 'Oh nothing, nothing really.'

'What do you mean "nothing"?' I say. 'It can't be about nothing.'

'Well, obviously,' she says and we both laugh.

'Go on then,' I pat the ground beside me. I want her to sit down. 'What's it about?'

'Well,' she says. 'There's this girl. She's called Jane, she's an orphan, but she has this dog called Frankie, and he looks after her. And all these terrible things happen like she loses him and he nearly... but,' she looks at me. 'I shouldn't say any more.'

'Why not?'

'Because you might want to read it,' she says, and passes me the book. It has a picture of a girl on the front; she is smiling and kneeling beside a dog. 'We've got another two weeks of the holiday left,' she says. 'You have to do something with your time.'

Another two weeks: I wonder if she's bored; if she wants to go home.

Something falls out of her pocket. I pick it up. It's a lighter. 'Where'd you get this?'

'Just found it,' she says.

I frown at her. 'What do you want a lighter for? Are you collecting them?'

She shrugs. 'Not really,' she says. 'I just liked the colour that's all.'

It's a purple lighter; I think it belongs to Jeet. I slip it into my pocket.

Josie squints at the view, the flowers shimmering in the light. 'I was sitting down here earlier,' she says. 'And those girls came down. That man was photographing them and it all looked a bit pervy.'

'What do you mean?'

'You know, two young girls sitting in a field, that weird man. It just felt a bit odd.'

I pull a piece of grass out of the ground and split it in half with my nail.

'They were shitty models anyway,' she says.

'In what way?'

'I don't know, that girl, the dark one, she was acting really spoilt.

She wouldn't do what your dad asked her to do, she kept yawning and telling them to hurry up and I reckon your dad was getting really annoyed.'

'Really?' I shift around so I'm facing her.

'Yeah,' she says. 'She wasn't a good model, whatever anyone says.'

'Why, what else did she do?'

Josie laughs. 'It was really funny,' she says. 'Your dad asked them to pretend to meditate. And she sits there and she closes her eyes and she doesn't hold her hands in the right way—'

'What, like this?' I ask, holding my thumb and forefinger together. I know how to do it.

'Yeah,' she laughs. 'It's easy enough, isn't it?'

'And Bria,' I say. 'Could she do it?'

'Oh, Bria,' she says. 'She's just weird.'

'In what way?'

'She reminds me of an alien,' she says, and it makes me laugh.

We sit in silence for a while. I shift back and lean against the tree, close my eyes. I would have been a much better model if only I'd had a chance to be photographed.

'Can I tell you a secret?' Josie leans towards me.

'What?'

'Earlier today I could hear them talking. They were talking about sex.'

'So?' I laugh. Sex, so what? 'What were they saying?'

'Well, they were talking about it like they did it all the time, all these different positions.'

'Like what?'

'I don't know, like weird stuff. They were saying all these men's names and talking about their… you know, their willies,' she giggles. 'Apparently this friend of theirs had sex with her dad or something.'

'Her dad?' I'm shocked. 'She can't have, you must have heard it wrong.'

'Honestly,' she nods. 'Seriously – and they were talking about Jeet.'

'What about him?' I flush red.

'I don't know, I couldn't really hear, but they said his name and then they were talking about oral sex.'

'Oral sex?'

'Yeah.'

'With Jeet?'

She looks at me, shrugs. 'I don't know, maybe.'

I look away. I don't believe her. He wouldn't do that. She's making it up. 'You're making it up,' I say, half looking at her.

'I'm not.' She shakes her head.

'Well, so what,' I say. 'You don't know what they were saying really.' I tug at a flower, smell it.

'I just think it's weird,' she says. 'They're talking like it's what they do all the time, like they're prostitutes or something. There's something strange about them, something not right.'

I shrug. 'They're just different,' I say. 'You know, children of the commune, they all have sex really young – it's no big deal.'

Josie looks at me. She looks serious.

'What?' I say.

She shrugs. 'It was more than that,' she says.

'What?' I ask.

'I don't know,' she says. 'There's just something not right.'

Josie makes her bracelet with lots of little flowers, and I flick the lighter on and off, watching the flame. An image of Jeet comes into my mind. He is lying on the bed and Anya and Bria are unzipping his trousers, stroking his underpants and taking out his willy. I try to imagine what an erection looks like. I've only ever seen one before. It was a photograph of Dad. I was going through his drawers, years ago in Hampstead, when I found pictures of him and Deeva naked. Dad's willy was lying on his tummy, it looked like an enormous slug, and another one showed a close-up of Deeva's fanny, a big bush of black hair. I remember once sitting on Dad's lap. I was undoing the buttons of his shirt one by one. I was telling him something. What was I saying? Sometimes daughters have sex with their dads. But I can't have said that. How would he have reacted? Why would I say a thing like that?

'Come on,' I say to Josie. 'Let's get a drink.'

I never said that to my dad. It's what Anya and Bria's friend did. It's got nothing to do with me.

'Come on,' I say again.

As we are getting to our feet, Jeet walks towards us through the allotment. He's holding his camera. I stop and put my hand on Josie's.

'What?' She looks at me.

'Oh, nothing,' I continue to get up, straightening my skirt.

'*H H H Hey*,' he says as he gets closer.

'Oh no,' Josie whispers and tugs my arm.

'Don't get up,' he says. 'You look beautiful sitting there. It reminds me of a painting – a Manet.' He holds up his camera. 'Sit down,' he says as he kneels in the grass. Josie looks at me. 'Go on, both of you,' he says. 'I need both of you for this one, the light is perfect.'

I sit down and arrange my skirt over my knees. Josie carefully sits beside me.

'Perfect,' he says, and I try to let my head relax back on the tree trunk. 'The light is beautiful. Wow. That's really beautiful. Your hair's a beautiful auburn, Josie. Look over there,' he directs her. 'And, Sylvie. ' I look at him. 'That's right. You look at the camera, that's perfect. Perfect.' I stare into the lens thinking – *Perfect*, did he say that to Anya and Bria?

'I wish you could see what I can see,' he says.

What does he see?

Josie nudges me and I ignore her.

Closer, he tells us to look at each other. He wants us to look straight into each other's eyes and laugh. I do as he says. I look at Josie: her eyes are flickering, her mouth strained in a smile; she looks nervous. '*Bejeesus,*' I whisper and she looks at the ground. '*Look up,*' I say, and she looks at me. She laughs just as he takes the picture.

Jeet continues to take photographs. Everything he asks of me, I do: when he tells me to laugh, I think of funny things; when he tells me to look dreamy, I gaze into the distance; when he tells me to look serious, I think of things that make me sad. As he takes pictures he tells us we are beautiful, he says we are great models. He says this three times.

When he has finished, he kneels in the grass and starts to unwind the film. 'I think I've got it,' he says. 'I've captured something.'

Captured what?

I watch as he unwinds the film. He took pictures of me. Something in me skips. Dad says they have what they need for the book, but Jeet took pictures of me. I want to fling my arms around his neck and kiss him on the cheek, say thank you.

I glance at Josie. I wish she wasn't here.

He kneels as if he is about to stand. He'll get up and leave, but I don't want him to go. I think of bravery, of Alanka saying I should make the first move. I take a deep breath and get to my feet.

'Where are you going?' Josie asks from behind me. She tugs at my skirt.

I ignore her, and walk towards him.

I sit in the grass and my hand touches his as I ask to see his camera. I don't look at Josie. I don't care if she's watching.

'I've never seen one like that before,' I say carefully. He looks surprised. He passes me the camera and I can feel him watching me as I hold it in my hands.

'Do you like photography?' he asks.

I look at him: his dark face, his warm milky eyes. 'Yes, I do.'

'Would you like to take some pictures?'

My heart is beating so fast that I hope he doesn't hear my words shaking when I say: 'You'll have to teach me how.'

He puts his arm around my shoulder and kisses my forehead and says into my hair so that Josie can't hear, 'I would love to do that Leela, I would love to teach you how.'

I went back to the gallery to see the angel-like children, and it stirred something in me. I felt an urgency to leave, to run across town and get back to the flat to start sketching out a painting. I haven't had such a powerful urge to paint in years. I bought a bottle of wine on the way and now I'm here, sitting on the floor, my legs outstretched around sheets of paper as I'm drawing the image of Bria with a clarity I didn't have before, as if somehow I might be able to save her. I still have art materials at home: an old easel, a palette, a selection of brushes. I put them away; perhaps I was saving them for this day. I'm listening to one of my uncle's CDs – it's turned up loud and I'm singing the words, words I haven't heard since I was at school.

I sit back and look around me. I've brought warmth to this place. A plate and a mug left on the floor, cushions in the corner, magazines covering the sofa. The doors are open and cool air fills the room, the music spilling outside. I take a gulp of wine and refill my glass.

It's strange this feeling, a sort of possession. I've depicted her standing at the top of the drive in Italy. It was early morning, the air was damp and cold, and she was hovering beneath the sunless sky. She was floating like a ghost, gauzy and opalescent. I didn't approach her to ask how she got there. I just closed the door of Jeet's van and turned away towards the house. It was the night of the boys and the drugs – I wasn't myself – I could easily have imagined it. I look at my sketch. I've got it this time, it's not just my niece Isabelle, there's something more, something tangible.

I congratulate myself; take another sip of wine.

I thought I saw her once in London. She was standing at a bus stop on Kentish Town Road. It was raining and she was wearing a green waterproof, too big, as if it belonged to someone else. I was on the other side of the street, on my way home from school. I didn't stop, just slowed to look more closely. It was a couple of years after the holiday; she would have been sixteen. I shook my head; it's not her. What would she be doing here on a busy London street, when she could be in Italy, playing by the sea, or India in the monsoon rain? And then I noticed her bare feet: her small pale ankles and her feet, dirty and fragile. The bus came and blocked my view, and when it left she was gone. I wondered where she was going, whether she had a home.

I had a home: I had a mother who loved me, a brother, friends, a school. I now have Jack, a job, a beautiful home in the country.

I finish my glass of wine, pour myself some more, get up and swing my arms around: perfect – my very own dance floor.

What was I doing at sixteen? Skiving lessons, hanging out with friends, sneaking drinks from parents' drink cabinets, dancing around the living room, to Michael Jackson, Luther Vandross, Loose Ends. Or maybe we'd argue, scream at each other until we made ourselves cry. But we were teenage girls. Isn't that what they do, get drunk and cry?

I reach for my glass, sip at it in front of the mirror. I want a cigarette. I want to smoke. Take me back to that time: sneaking fags out of the window, writing romantic notes to fantasy boys, imagining what our husbands might look like – thinking: What if I passed him on the street and didn't know? We had so much freedom: we were at the beginning of our lives. We should have been happy.

I look down at my hand where my engagement ring should be.

I go to the bedroom, find the pouch where I left it. Slip on the ring. 'I love you Jack,' I say, and kiss my finger.

'Jack,' I'm lying on the floor, the empty bottle of wine and glass beside me. 'Talk to me… Tell me you love me… Tell me you'll always be there for me, tell me.'

'Sylvie, you're whispering.'

'I'm not whispering,' I whisper, laughing.

'Are you drunk?'

'No.'

When I open my eyes, the room is unsteady.

'I just want to tell you things,' I say. 'Silly things, nothing really.' There are blotches in front of my eyes; it makes it hard to see. 'Things that have been in my mind, so many different things, and… I'm sorry.'

'Why are you sorry?'

I'm silent.

'Sylvie, why are you sorry?'

'For being such an idiot,' I say.

He's quiet. He doesn't say anything.

'I think about it every day,' I say. 'I do, think. Always,' I start to cry. 'I mean it.'

'OK,' he says. 'But I'm tired. Can we talk about this ano—'

'I love you,' I say.

He doesn't answer.

'I love you, I want to be with you, I do.'

No answer.

'Sing to me, make me feel better.' I put my free arm into the air; let it hang.

'What do you want me to sing?'

'Something happy; something about how you won't leave me.' I try to remember the tune. 'Something romantic,' I say. 'Something you used to sing.'

He clears his throat. 'Not now,' he says.

'Why?'

He sighs: 'Because it's late.'

My arm collapses beside me.

'I'm going to go now,' he says.

I sit up. The room sways: 'Where are you going?'

'I'm going back to bed. You woke me up, Sylvie.'

'But Jack,' I say.

'What?'

'If you ever leave me, can I come too?'

Silence.

'Jack?'

'Sylvie, call me back when you're sober, OK?'

I hang up the phone and stagger to my feet. I step on something, something sharp. I pick it up. My ring. It sparkles in my hand. I took it off while I was talking to him. I wanted to wear it again, but something made me take it off.

I'm on the belvedere taking photographs, looking at my feet, the varying shades of stone tile, the textures of the brick wall, the jagged cracks, the moss, the ants. I want to make a photomontage. Calvin Klein mews at me and I sit next to him and tell him I'm going to be a photographer. 'Just you wait,' I say. 'I'm going to be the most famous photographer in the world.' Calvin looks up at me. I take a picture of his fluffy fat cheeks.

I'm ignoring Josie, Sam and Max because they're mad. They've made a list of all the reasons Jeet is the Florence Monster: he's a werewolf, he eats raw meat, he drives a camper van and sleeps with two girls in the back. He has a girlfriend but no-one knows where she is. '*And* he has long nails,' Josie shouts.

Max wants to interview him. He wants to catch him out and call the police on him. But I've got much more important things to do.

I slip away when they're not looking. I go into the house, stand at the living-room door, listening. Jeet is in the kitchen.

There's a big spider lit up in the sunlight. It's caught between the window frame and the wall. It's shivering in its web. Maybe I could photograph it, impress Jeet if he walks through the door and sees me.

I take a photograph, and then another.

I hear a cough. It's him, but he doesn't come.

I wait. I hear a noise somewhere else in the house, so I take a deep breath and walk into the kitchen.

'Hi,' I say.

He's at the cooker. He turns around. 'Hi.'

'I took some photographs,' I say.

'I know,' he holds his hand out for the camera. I pass it to him. 'There's one left, lucky,' he says, and takes a picture of me before I have a chance to look into the lens or smile. I blush. 'Natural,' he says, and starts to unwind the film. 'Your expression. That's what I like to see,' his eyes narrow, 'unexpected beauty. It's like being a fly on the wall – not the easiest thing to do, as people are so bloody self-conscious. What was it someone said? Beauty without expression is boring. Something Emerson – that was it. He wrote about nature.' He taps his head. 'I have a book in my van. But I suppose you don't know about that.' He looks at me and I blush, thinking of Deeva's song: *I don't have anything to say to you because you know more than I do.*

'Hey. How do you fancy helping me develop some pictures? We can develop yours if you want.'

'*Wow, really?*' I gasp. 'I mean, yes, I'd like that.'

Jeet says we have to wait for the temperature to cool before we can start developing. That means waiting until it's dark. I go to Dad and Alanka's room where Alanka is ironing. I jump on the bed.

'Lanks,' I say. 'Have you ever developed your own photographs?'

'No,' she says. 'But your father has, he used to have his own darkroom.'

'What's a darkroom?'

'It's the place where you develop pictures, it has to be totally black or else it doesn't work. Ask your father.'

'But if it's totally black, how are you supposed to see?'

She giggles as if I'm silly. 'You are sweet. You are a questioner,' she says as she pushes the iron into the creases of Dad's underpants.

We sit down for supper at the big table beneath the weeping tree. Soma has made risotto, which is normally my favourite, but when she puts it on the table the smell makes me feel sick. I keep thinking about the darkroom. Jeet is sitting opposite me; I'm trying not to look at him. The sun has gone down and soon it will be dark and he will have to go into his darkroom. I don't know what is going to happen in there.

After supper I help tidy up by taking everything from the table into the kitchen where I look at the washing-up rota. Even though it's not my turn, I ask Nim if I can take her place tonight. She frowns at me – 'Why *bambina*? Why would you want to do that?' I don't want to tell her that I'm trying to keep busy, so I don't have to go into Jeet's darkroom.

I think about hiding in my room, playing ping-pong with the boys, but then I think about my pictures of Calvin and the ants and Max with his head cut off and I wonder what photographs look like as they develop.

Jeet is in his van. He's lying on his bed: I can see his bare feet sticking out of the back. I hang around outside the house and smoke a cigarette.

'What are you doing?' It's Anya. She and Bria are hanging out of the living-room window.

'Nothing,' I say, 'just having a fag.'

Anya comes outside. Bria follows her. 'I like your T-shirt,' she says.

'Thanks.'

'Do you like mine?' she asks. It is pink and slips off one shoulder.

'Yes,' I say.

'You're not wearing a bra,' she says, and touches one of my breasts. 'I can see your boobies.'

I flush red and look down.

'You've got nice boobies,' she says. 'Hasn't she, Bria?'

Bria giggles.

I cross my arms so they can't see.

'I don't wear bras,' Anya says. 'I like them to be free and easy, bouncing around.' She jumps up and down and her boobs jiggle. 'Is that what you like?' she looks at me slyly. 'Or maybe you just want someone to notice you. Are you waiting for Jeet?' she whispers.

'No,' I say surprised.

'What do you reckon, Bria?' she asks. 'What do you think Sylvie's doing?'

Bria moves closer to me, sucking a strand of her hair.

'I think you like him,' Anya says.

'No, I don't,' I say.

'Then why are you standing outside his van?'

'He's going to show me how to develop photos,' I say.

'Develop photos,' she laughs. 'Did you hear that, Bria?'

'What's wrong with that?' I ask.

Anya sticks her tongue out, the tip of it touching her top lip. 'I just thought you might want to know something,' she says. 'Something that might concern you. You might thank us if I told you.'

'What?' I ask.

Anya steps towards me. 'Jeet, he's—'

'Hey girls,' Jeet's head emerges from the back of the van. 'What are you doing?' He swings out, his feet on the gravel.

'Nothing,' Anya steps away from me.

He walks over. 'Sylvie, you want to do some developing?'

I look at Anya, who narrows her eyes. What did she want to say?

'Come on,' he holds out his hand. 'Don't look so scared. I'm not a monster.'

It smells in his van: a sort of eggy smell, like farts.

Jeet tells me to sit down.

I sit on the edge of the bed. The light is on and his equipment is on the side. There are trays and bottles, and a long piece of cord hangs from the ceiling with what looks like negatives pinned to it.

'Is this your darkroom?' I ask quietly.

'I suppose you could call it that,' he says, leaning over the driver's seat and sticking something to the window. Looking around, I notice there are thick silver pads blocking out the light. I wonder whether they are sound proof.

Jeet silently moves around the van, looking at negatives, pouring liquid into trays, and I stare at a piece of gravel outside. It is bigger than the other pieces, and shines white in the dull light. Anya wanted to tell me something, as if she were warning me. The gravel is outside, while I am in. I could step down and my foot would be on it.

Jeet moves past me and closes the doors with a clunk. The air feels close. The smell. It hurts my throat when I breathe.

'You'll get used to it,' he says.

He sits beside me on the bed, our knees touching. He shows me a sheet of paper covered with black-and-white boxes, pictures in each. 'Here,' he says. 'This is called a contact sheet.'

I expect to see photographs of Calvin, a spider, a headless Max in front of the house, but instead there's Anya and Bria, and there – there's me and Josie sitting beneath the tree. Some have blue squares around them; others have big black ticks.

'There, this one,' he says, pointing to one of me staring at the camera. 'This is the one I like.' And he looks at me in that way that makes me feel nervous. 'You look sort of,' he pauses, twists his mouth. 'You look sad.'

I look sad.

'Do you see it?' he asks.

I look at the photograph. My eyes are big, but my mouth is small and tight. I think I look scared.

When he stands up I join him. I notice another contact sheet: the spider, the ants. 'Are those mine?' I ask.

'Yes,' he laughs. 'They're cute. Maybe you want to develop one of the cat?' He's laughing at me again, so I put the contact sheet down, face down so he can't see.

The space is so small that Jeet keeps on touching me. Every time he goes to get something, he holds my arms and moves me. His grip is firm; sometimes it hurts. He presses past me to get to the light. He switches it off and everything goes black.

I can't see.

There's not even an outline, or a shadow.

My head buzzes and I feel dizzy.

There's a whirring somewhere, a distant laugh, music coming from the house. Jeet sighs. I want to put out my hand, but I don't want to touch him, so I stand totally still. I don't move. My ears stretch to the sounds. I can hear the wheeze in his chest. His croak.

'Where the fuck is it?' he says suddenly. It makes me jump.

What would happen if he tried to kill me? Would they hear me scream?

Light: a red light suddenly glows.

His face.

There are long shadows under his eyes, a crease in his forehead, exaggerated from the top of his brow. It's a vein pulsing, almost like a scar.

The room glows red and I'm trying to focus, looking around at the small and cluttered space that seemed massive in the dark. My heart is fluttering. My hands are wet with sweat. I hope he doesn't ask me to hold anything.

'OK,' he says. 'Look, here, we can start with the girls.'

He moves out of the way so I can see.

A small light has lit up an image on a board. It looks weird. It is a close-up of Anya and Bria, but their eyes and teeth are black, their skin white.

'Here,' he says. 'It is up to you how big you want the image, how small. You see here.' The wheel moves the projector up and down. 'And then you focus.'

I nod, trying to show him that I understand.

He turns off the light and places a piece of paper on the board. 'Shall we say twelve seconds?'

I nod again.

He turns the projector light back on and the picture illuminates on the paper. 'One elephant, Two elephant, Three elephant,' he says and it makes me smile. 'Five elephant, six elephant, seven elephant…' he looks at me as though he wants me to join in. 'Ten elephant, eleven elephant, twelve elephant.' We say it together: my voice sounds small.

He switches off the light. 'OK,' he says, putting the paper into one of the trays. 'Now watch,' he says, as he tips the tray and gently swishes the liquid. 'Watch what happens.'

And then I see something – a darkening, a shape appearing. It's so faint it looks almost like a ghost, or a pattern, like lace, and then another shape: the trees and there is the side of Anya's face and her teeth, white, and her nose and her eye, big, dark and bright, and slowly the image of Anya and Bria appears.

'Wow,' I find myself saying. 'That's mad.'

'Isn't it,' Jeet says. 'You think it's ready? You think that's it?' He slops the liquid around some more. 'Sometimes you've got to be quick,' he says, and he whisks it out and dips it in another tray, before leaving it in the third.

I grin at him.

'You liked that, huh?'

'Yes,' I say. I want to do it again.

'OK,' he says. 'Now it's your turn.'

He lights a cigarette and the smoke mixes with the smell of chemicals and I realize I haven't thought about the smell for a while. He asks me to choose which picture I want and says I have to do it all by myself, make the image appear without his help.

But what if I get it wrong?

He tells me the projector light exposes the image: leave it on too long and the image will be too dark, too short and it will be too pale.

'So which picture do you want?' he asks.

I look at the contact sheet and I want to choose one of me, but I choose one of Anya and Bria instead. It's the one of them meditating.

'Come on,' he says, the cigarette hanging from his mouth. 'Don't be shy, why not choose one of the beautiful ones,' and he winks at me. 'Like this one.'

He thinks the ones of me are more beautiful. It's the one he said was his favourite.

'But what if I get it wrong?'

He laughs. 'So, it doesn't matter if you get the girls wrong? Do I sense a hint of jealousy?'

'No,' I say. 'I'm not jealous.'

He looks at me, and suddenly he looks different: his eyes lost in their sockets, the shadows growing as he moves. He looms above me. I step back. Is he angry? Did I say something wrong?

He clears his throat and goes back to the negatives. 'Come on,' he says. 'You need to concentrate.'

I take a deep breath. My hands are shaking.

I position the negative as carefully as I can. Before I put down the paper, I look at the image on the board. It's me and Josie sitting beneath the tree, it's me looking at the camera: I look strange, my eyes dark and sunken, my mouth like a slash. I position it so that it's straight and Jeet leans over me, smoking, clearing his throat. He doesn't tell me what to do but he guides my hand to move the wheel.

We have it in place, I think it's in focus, and I look over my shoulder. I look at him as if to ask how many elephants and he says: 'What do you think?'

'I don't know,' I say.

'Think about it, think about the light in the last picture.'

I can't remember the light in the last picture, only that it was probably brighter because the photo was taken earlier in the day, so maybe you need more exposure to stop it from being too light.

'Ten?' I ask.

He cocks his head and says: 'Give it a go.'

I carefully reach for the paper and he stops my hand just in time, and without a word he guides it to the light and presses my finger against the button to turn it off, and my heart is beating fast and I'm so afraid of making another mistake. The light is off, so I place the paper under the image, and I look over my shoulder and say: 'Is it in the right place?' and he nods and I take a deep breath and switch the light back on, and 'One elephant,' I look at him. 'Two elephant.' He doesn't say it with me. 'Three elephant.' I'm staring at the image, my finger ready to turn off the light. 'Four elephant. Five elephant. Six elephant, seven elephant, eight elephant, nine elephant...'

'And,' he says.

'*Ten elephant.*'

We say it together and a fluttery feeling rushes through me as I take the tweezers from him and slowly pick up the corner of the paper and place it in the tray. Looking at him again and acknowledging his nod, I swirl the liquid around and the image starts to emerge. The first thing I see is Josie's hand: it is bigger than I thought it would be, it is gripping something. As the image starts to emerge, I see that she is gripping onto me; she is holding my hand.

Then I see her shoulder and the side of her face, her skin and eyes filling in, and then there's me. My eyes are the first to appear, they're looking directly at me. I didn't realize that he has made the image bigger. You can see my eyes and you can see my face and I look different to how I think I look. I look older. Do I look sad?

'Beautiful,' he says, as he leans over me. His hot skin sticks to mine.

But then the image starts to darken. It gets darker and darker, my eyes filling in, my mouth, my hair and then my body, as if I'm melting, disappearing.

'What's happening?' I grapple for it. I've ruined it. I look terrible.

'Shit,' he snaps 'Quick, pull it out.'

I use my fingers.

'Not like that.' He pushes past me and gets the corner of the photograph with his tweezers, pulling it out of the mixture. He looks at it. It's horrible, ruined. He laughs. 'Oh dear,' he says.

I look up at him. Is he angry?

He touches my nose and says: 'We'll just have to do it again.'

Do it again?

'Fewer elephants this time, eh?'

I must get it right this time. I must get it right.

I soon get the hang of it and develop a few more pictures, and there's one close-up photograph that I didn't realize he'd taken. I'm playing with a lighter, and Josie is beside me with a string of flowers in her hands.

All the while he smokes and tells me my photographs are perfect, that I'm a natural and I have a good eye.

He wants to develop a few more before packing up his equipment, so I sit on the bed and watch him. His long red body like a shadow. Sometimes he talks to himself, sometimes he whistles. He pins the pictures up as he goes.

I wonder how long we've been here. I look around and remember as if for the first time that the house is outside, and the belvedere, the table where we all had supper. It feels like a different world, days away, somewhere else.

I try to listen to see if I can hear anything, but there is no sound. I wonder if anyone can hear us.

What time is it? Has everyone gone to bed? I sit up. Sam and Josie, they'll be worried. What about Dad?

'Just one more,' he says, as if he's reading my mind.

Once he has counted the last elephants and put the paper in the tray, I stand beside him, the skin of our arms just touching. He holds his cigarette to his lips as he watches the photograph develop. I wait with him as an image appears: a nose and a mouth, eyes. It's a woman, she has long dark hair; her mouth is open, as if it's curled around a word, her lips turned up at the edges, her eyes smiling. She is leaning towards the camera with her arm out-stretched. Uta. It must be Uta. He is watching as her image develops. I quickly look away.

When Jeet opens the van doors, a cool breeze hits me and I'm surprised by how clean the air smells. I look at the house. Only a few lights are on. Dad's is one of them: he's still awake.

'What time is it?' I ask as Jeet closes the van doors. He seems illuminated, brighter out here in the moonlight.

'I guess it's late,' he says.

There's a light, something glowing from the belvedere. Anya and Bria are sitting on the floor, a candle between them. They are looking at us.

'Oh, look,' I gasp. 'Their beds, they must be tired.'

'Oh, they're all right. They're good girls,' he says, and walks towards them.

I watch as Bria rushes to him and he puts his arm around her. Her body fits into him like a jigsaw. He strokes her face, saying something that makes her nod. I wish I could hear what he says. Anya leans back on her hands and watches them. I wonder how long they've been waiting, why they didn't come and knock on the door.

I go into the kitchen and turn on the light. The brightness hurts my eyes. I take a glass out of the cupboard, open the fridge door. I feel dizzy, strange.

'It's a beautiful night.' I hear his voice from behind me. 'Let's sit outside for a while,' he says. 'The girls are tired. They've gone to bed.'

I let him lead me.

Outside, he takes my hand and I try to tread quietly as we pass the van. A light glows through the open back doors, but I can't hear talking. What are they doing in there? Are they watching us?

We sit opposite each other, our legs on either side of the wall. He shuffles me to sit close to him, guiding my legs so they fall across his thighs. I'm so close to him that I'm level with his chest, his body a blur. I'm too close to look at his face. I close my eyes to the breeze. It twirls around us and swooshes through the trees. It's calming.

'Look, look up at the sky.' He guides me with his face to the pattern of stars, like silver jewels. If you stare at them long enough you can see them die. 'When I was a child my mother told me there were nymphs up there – the Gods hung them as stars in the sky,' he says. I open my face to them. Does that mean that the nymphs die, just like the stars? 'Sometimes I sleep under the open sky. It is so good for you, so nourishing to be a part of nature. You fall asleep with darkness and you wake with light, you don't know what time it is. It doesn't matter.' He looks at me, his face distant, blurry. 'I'd like to sleep beneath the stars with you,' he says, 'somewhere else, away from here, somewhere up in the hills. Waking up with the elements – it's one of the best things in this world.' I'm watching the way he speaks. It's as if his mouth moves out of time with his words.

I jump to a sound: a thump in the allotment, as if something has been knocked over, a scrambling and a sudden rush through the bushes.

'Ssh,' he says. "'*Be not afeard: the isle is full of noises. Sounds and sweet airs, that give delight and hurt not.*'"

I look up at him and a cool breeze prickles my skin. It makes me shiver.

'Come here,' he says. 'You're cold.' He lifts me and pulls me closer, guiding me so that my head is on his chest and his arms are looped around my back. I close my eyes. I can hear his breath grate inside his chest. It's a funny sound, as if there's something trapped in there. My eyes are closed, my body moving with his, up and down.

He shifts, his bristle against my forehead. I open my eyes. I can see his mouth. Is he trying to say something? But his lips are on my face, my eye, my cheek. I can see them and they look big and wide up close. I close my eyes again.

He is trying to kiss me.

My head feels heavy as I tilt my mouth towards his. Our lips touch, gently, touching, as his tongue tries to ease its way in. I let him. I lean into him. My hands linked in my lap. We're kissing.

I fall away. I roll my head onto his shoulder. I laugh, thinking about the nymphs, his mother, and I say, 'If my mother could see me now.'

He laughs with me and hugs me, and says, 'If my mother could see *me* now.'

I don't let myself think that my dad could be watching, standing on his balcony smoking and looking at the stars.

We kissed.

I open my eyes to the dark rolling landscape, and everything buzzes, ziggedy lines, a distance, as if my mind is somewhere else.

We kissed.

We sit. My face against his chest, his arms around my back, the *beat beat beat* of his heart, and he holds me, he holds me.

'Look,' he says suddenly. 'A shooting star.'

'Where?' I pull away even though I could have stayed like that for ever. I look up at the sky, and the glistening stars wink at me, but there is no shooting star.

'Watch a while,' he says. 'They are so quick, they're gone in a second.'

I watch. I smile, my body relaxed. I dream. What would I ask for? *Please let me see one. Please make this night perfect for me.*

But there is no shooting star.

I look down at my hands, twisted in my lap.

Jeet is looking at me. He's looking at me.

'Leela,' he says, and the name surprises me. 'You are my Leela.' His hand guides my face. He strokes my cheek. Is he smiling?

'I want to tell you something,' he says, his strange moving mouth. He sighs. I listen. What does he want to say?

'I would like to make love to you,' he says.

I look down.

Make love.

'I would like to make love to you, but the girls are in my van, not tonight. It's not the right time, but it will be.'

I nod. I look at my hands, so small and distant in this light.

I squint. I try to shake my head, say it over in my mind: He wants to make love to me. Make love? But I feel numb – the words don't mean anything. Make love, that's sex. Have sex. But you're not supposed to do that until you're sixteen. I told my friends I wanted to wait, for that special person.

I look towards the house. I squint towards the balcony, Dad's room. Is the light still on? Is he there? I wonder where Josie is. Whether she's awake, or asleep on her mattress on the floor, her silent breathing, her arms slung above her head. I'm shaking. I'm cold. I yawn to show him that I'm tired.

'What do you think of that?' he searches my face as if he wants to read me. 'Am I being too forward? I'm *im im im im*pulsive, I'm sorry. I don't want to push you.'

'No,' I'm shaking my head. You are not pushing me.

'OK,' he sighs, then laughs, he kisses my hand. 'It is just this, you know, this beautiful place, being with you. It makes me happy.' He grips my hands.

I try to smile but my teeth are chattering.

'Oh, look at you, come on, you are cold. I'm getting carried away. We need to get you to bed.'

I nod, relieved.

I follow him into the house. We are holding hands. The van light is off and I can see the faint outline of a leg hanging over the edge of the bed, a mattress on the floor, and I wonder which girl shares his bed.

I follow him into the kitchen. He turns on the light. He sits on the edge of the table and puts his arms around my waist and pulls me to him. We hug. He groans as he pulls me tighter. This time I keep my eyes open. He wants to make love to me. He wants to have sex. I look down his back, the stray hairs, the thin skin a sickly colour in this light. He is not my special person.

He edges his face to mine again, and this time I'm standing taller than him as his lips touch mine and it's rougher than before and my eyes are open and I see his teeth and his wide lips, his eyes closed, as he gropes for me, his mouth moving roughly, moving, his tongue forcing its way, and it is dry, his grating breath, the smell of him sharp, he didn't smell like this before. I try to pull away, but my teeth knock against his. He groans as he kisses me. His hands are under my skirt and they are holding my buttocks, one in each hand, and he is pushing his fingers into my flesh so my body rolls into him, taller than him so he has to stretch his neck to reach me and I feel his fingers escape beneath the edge of my knickers. I pull away. I have to pull away.

He hugs me again. My legs are between his and his bristle scratches my skin. He groans and I feel something twitch in his trousers. I know what it is. I keep my eyes open.

An image of something comes into my mind. A woman is sitting with her legs open and her vagina is covered in shaving foam. It was a film at Dad's, years ago in London. I don't know why it was on, but Dad was there, and Sam, watching this woman, shaving herself with a razor. I stopped in the doorway and wondered – why is she doing that? She was saying something like: *My boyfriend likes it when I shave myself, when my pussy is as smooth as a baby's.* And I stood there and wondered: Why would her boyfriend want her to do that?

Jeet won't let me go. He's still holding me.

I look at the floor. I try to think of ways to pull away. I look down, and there, scuttling towards us, is a small black creature. I gasp. 'Look,' I point. 'What is it?'

It's heading for my feet, my bare feet in their flip-flops.

'Shit,' he jumps away from me. 'It's a scorpion, don't move.'

I stand completely still and watch as Jeet circles it. The scorpion freezes. Jeet carefully kneels on the ground and places a bowl over it. He catches it and, using a piece of card under the bowl, he carries it outside and releases it.

Jeet kisses me gently on the nose and he lets me go. He tells me not to worry about the scorpion. It's gone, he says, it won't come back. My body feels light, as if it is not my own.

I slowly walk up the stairs, tracing my hand along the uneven surface of the wall. Dad's light is on. I can see it slip beneath his door. I stop in the corridor. I stop and it's almost as if I sway: can I go to him? I walk lightly, trying not to make a noise. I listen. I can hear my heart, but there is also a low murmur: he is talking. I knock on the door. He calls me in, as if he knows I'm here.

The light is dull: it glows orange from the bedside lamp. Dad is cross-legged on the bed. He is still dressed. Soft music flows through the room, like a forest, there's water trickling and the sound of birds. Alanka pulls herself up, props her head on the pillow. Her eyes look big, almost wild.

'Hey,' Dad says. 'What's been going on in the world of my daughter? Come and talk to us.'

I sit on the edge of the bed and he reaches out to me, he grips my hand, squeezes it. 'How is my beautiful girl?'

'OK,' I say.

He looks strange, his eyes darker, stretched, a sparkle that makes him look different from normal, as though there's someone else inside.

'You know what, Lanks?' he says. 'This girl here, my daughter,' he strokes the naked flesh on my leg. 'She is the only person in this world who really knows me. She knows me better than anyone.'

I look at him. Does he mean that? Alanka grins and purrs, rubbing her cheek against his shoulder like a cat. The only person in the world? More than Mum and Sam, more than Alanka?

'We have a special bond, you and I,' he says. 'It's like we know what the other is feeling, it's more than just a father-daughter thing.'

I nod, but does that mean...? The air feels thick and fuzzy. There's something strange. I look down. Shall I tell him? 'I was outside,' I say. 'I was with Jeet.'

'Jeet,' Dad smiles. 'I love that man. Do you know where I met him, Lanks?' He takes her hand. 'We met at the ashram and we immediately bonded. Do you ever get that? When you meet a person and you feel like you've made a friend for life, like falling in love? You know?'

She nods and smiles. She lies down again. She closes her eyes.

Like falling in love.

There's silence. No noise, but the soft waves of music. I trace my fingers on the bedspread. Dad hums.

'We were sitting outside,' I say, looking up at him. 'Jeet saw a shooting star.'

'Isn't it beautiful here?' Dad says. 'I bet you never want to go home.'

I touch my neck. I squint at him. It's as if my eyes aren't working: everything seems blurry, distant, my dad, Alanka, this room. Never go home. I rub my eyes.

'We were just talking,' Dad says, 'about life, about love.'

'I was going to bed,' I say.

'Oh, stay,' he touches my leg. 'I'm enjoying talking to you – talk to us.'

I sit and watch as his head drops and he closes his eyes. I sit and wait but he doesn't say anything. His body rocks. Alanka lies back as if she is asleep. She strokes the bedspread. 'It feels wonderful,' she says. 'Like cold water trickling over naked skin.' She reaches out for Dad's hand. He strokes it, leans over and whispers something. She giggles quietly, whispers back. They kiss, longer than normal.

I look away. I want to go to bed. I yawn and stretch my arms over my head.

Dad glances up at me as if he's surprised that I am still here.

When I kiss him goodnight he squeezes me so tightly that my bones pop. When I kiss Alanka she tells me my lips feel like silk.

There's no sound as I turn around and walk out of the room, except for the soft flutes and waterfalls.

I'm standing in front of the back view of a seated nude, and her proportions are monstrous: her back about twenty foot long, her flesh bulging to the edges of the canvas, the side of her face squashed as if it's pressed against glass. I'm transfixed. This is where large works work. If nothing else, the presence and physicality of the paint gives it reason to exist. Not like a one-dimensional photograph that needs to be blown up in order to be noticed.

I move around to look at it from another angle. I squint and stand on tiptoe to see the application of paint. This is perfect.

When I was at school I loved painting portraits. They were often of myself through necessity: a melancholy teenager, an emancipated body, large head and sad eyes. I always started with the eye: I'd spend a whole day on the pupil, slowly working the paint outwards to include the eye socket, the eyelid and under eye with its spectrum of bruise-coloured shades. I spent weeks, months on one image.

My art tutors told me I was talented. They told me I should go to life-drawing classes, art school, be a representative of oil painting when everyone else was obsessed with conceptualism. But photography crept in. I became fascinated with the randomness of capturing the perfect image through the click of a button, the interesting patterns on a body: a pleat in an earlobe, a curly mole on the dip of a collarbone, the texture of old skin.

But why photography over painting? I sometimes wonder whether I was seduced by the image of the photographer. I would lie in bed and imagine walking across a field with a large camera in my hand, another slung over my shoulder, dragging a tripod through the grass, just as Jeet did that day in my dad's garden. But Jack tells me it's a detached art, always once removed, the profession of a voyeur. He sees it as deceitful: capturing a moment of time and making it permanent by its very existence. Trapped in a photograph, a particular time, a time you don't want to think about. What if I did only choose photography because of Jeet? What if I'm struggling in this career because of him? I don't like that thought.

But I approach it differently: I like to know my subjects, have a relationship with them, bond with them. I'm not content with a snapshot, catching people unawares. I like my subjects to sit for me a number of times. I like to capture that sacred relationship between artist and model. I approach it with more depth, more meaning, more soul; just as I might a painting.

If I hadn't chosen photography, could I have painted something like this? A work so bold hung in one of the country's leading galleries? Would I be painting and lecturing and travelling the world? Or would I, like now, be one of the undiscovered? Having to make my money by other means.

I don't hate photographing weddings, but I don't like it either. I'm fed up with being a witness to other people's happiness. I want my own.

I go to the café and order a pot of peppermint tea. Just hot water, no milk. I could get a sandwich, but I don't want the bread. Something healthier: some soup, a salad. I gaze at the cakes: a large slice of chocolate sponge sits beside lemon tart and a wedge of carrot cake. I pull my eyes away, pay for my tea and sit down. I stare at the thin green liquid, too hot to drink. A woman at the counter reaches for a slice of carrot cake. I find myself watching her. She's tall in her pencil skirt and jacket, with long slim legs, neat feet and elegant court shoes. She sits down and opens her paper, delicately putting a forkful of cake into her mouth. She reads and chews. She's not thinking about the cake, about the indulgence, the fat and sugar, the calories, the way it might block her arteries. It's carrot cake, for God's sake, it's made of vegetables. I get up and take a slice. It's delicious, sweet and moist, and sticks to the roof of my mouth. I pick at it, until there is nothing left. I discreetly finish every crumb. Indulgence – it's good sometimes. If Jack were here, he'd be proud of me.

I stand outside the gallery, dial Jack's number. I'm happy to hear his voice.

'You're not drunk are you?' he laughs.

'No, I'm not drunk.' I hug myself to the railings, my back to the street. We both pause. He doesn't say anything to fill the silence.

'I've wanted to call all morning,' I say. 'But I've had my head full – of portraiture, photography, the wedding this Friday. I've been looking at paintings, wondering if I'm in the right profession.'

'Oh,' he says. 'Having one of those days.'

'Hmm, one of those days,' I repeat. 'But, I was thinking. I chose photography all that time ago. I abandoned my drawing and painting and because of what, because of some stupid man—'

'What man?'

I stop. Could I do it? Tell him here and now, out here on the street. That man – my father's friend – who made me fall in love with him, who seduced me and then... 'You know,' I say. 'That man in Italy.'

'Oh,' he laughs. 'The old one, the one you fancied.'

I pause. 'Yes,' I say. 'The one I fancied.'

There's silence. How do I even begin?

If I push the phone to my ear, perhaps I'll hear the sound of his boots on the gravel path, the seagulls crying over the canal. I jump to the sound of a siren behind me, car horns beeping as an ambulance tries to get through the traffic.

'Anyway,' I say. 'You know how people, certain people, they can have an impact on your life and you don't realize it. Well, I'm wondering if that happened to me, with that man.'

'But he introduced you to photography—'

'But that's not all he did.' The blood rushes to my face.

He doesn't say anything. Did he hear me?

I clear my throat. 'I'd just like to get back into painting again – there's something more collaborative about it, more truthful.'

'That can only be a good thing.'

'I'd like to come home,' I say suddenly. 'I don't want to do a wedding this weekend. Do you think I can tell them I'm ill, I've come down with some awful infection, I can't walk?'

'You've got gangrenous hands and you can't hold a camera.'

'Yeah,' I laugh. 'Oh, Jack,' I say, hugging the phone. 'I wish you could come here and do it for me.'

'Yeah, right,' he laughs. 'I'd end up taking photos of the panel doors and the cornices.'

'But at least you'd be here.'

He pauses. 'You didn't want me there before.'

'I know,' I say.

We're silent; neither of us says anything. I sense he wants to go, but I don't want him to. There's something I want to say: 'I'm sorry.'

'Not this again,' he laughs.

'No, seriously,' I say. 'There are things I need to talk to you about, serious things.'

'Like what?'

Things you won't want to hear, things that will affect your view of me, things that might make you hate me. 'I can't talk about it now. I'll come home. I'll do the wedding and come home.' I hear my heart. 'I love you,' I say.

He pauses. I hold my breath: please say it back to me, please. I cross my fingers behind my back.

'I love you too,' he says, and I drop my head.

'I'd better go,' I say.

'Sylvie.'

'Yes?' I look up.

'What about your dad?'

What about my dad?

I get back to the flat and stand on the balcony, a photograph in my hand. It's me at the beach; I was there with Jeet. It was the day I slept in his van for the first time. I used to love this photograph – I had it on my wall for years. I liked the sadness in it, the vulnerability, because those were the things he said he loved about me. I hold the photograph over the side of the balcony. I could drop it. Let it be carried through the air and land somewhere on the street, trampled on, footmarks across my face, or I could rip it into tiny pieces, smaller and smaller until they are like confetti.

'What happened to you last night?' It's Josie.

I open my eyes. The room is light.

I've been drifting, thinking of the moonlight, my head on his chest, his heart. All those words he said, making love, happiness.

'Nothing.' I turn over to face her. 'Jeet showed me how to develop photographs.'

His face glowing red, the long dark circles.

'Really?' Josie asks. 'Where?'

'In his van.'

'In his van? You developed photographs in his van? What, all night?'

'No, not all night,' I say. 'I was in there for a bit, and then I went to see Dad. He was in his room.' I turn onto my back and look at the ceiling. Jeet told me I was beautiful. He said he wanted to make love to me. How did I respond? Did I look worried, scared? Did I act like a child?

'Why are you lying?' she asks.

'I'm not lying.' I look at her.

'Yes, you are,' she says. She gets out of bed. She stands over me.

'No, I'm not.'

'You are!' she shouts.

'How do you know?'

She ignores me, pulling on her shorts, her T-shirt. She picks her cardigan off the floor and a collection of matchboxes and multi-coloured lighters falls from its creases.

'What's that?' I ask, leaning down and picking one up. 'Have you been stealing?'

'No,' she says, reddening.

'I knew you were up to something weird, why have you got so many lighters?'

'No reason,' she says.

'You *were* collecting them, weren't you? Stealing them from people. Why would you want to collect lighters?'

'Well, at least it's not as bad as collecting dead things,' she says.

'What's that supposed to mean?'

'All the things that you're interested in are dead. Lighters give fire, they give life.'

'They also burn and scald,' I say.

She grabs her things and goes to leave the room. She turns around at the door. 'You're being so selfish,' she says, her voice is shaking. 'I can't believe how selfish you are. You don't care about anyone but yourself. You don't care about me. You just leave me on my own and I have to find things to do, I have to hang around with Sam and Max and they don't always want me there. You're cruel. You're just like your dad.'

'Josie,' I say. I get to my knees. 'What do you mean?'

'It is true,' she says. She's crying. 'And you know what? I don't want to hang out with you all the time either, so you'd better leave me alone. I don't even know if you are my friend any more.' And with that she leaves the room, slamming the door behind her.

I look at the floor, and then at the mirror on the wardrobe. I am kneeling in my vest and knickers, my skin is brown, dark against the white of my underwear. My heart is beating. She said I was like Dad – the thought tugs me sharply. She doesn't know my dad. No-one does, not like me. I get to my feet. I move closer to the mirror. I look into my eyes: clear and bright. I'm fine. There's nothing wrong with me. I'm glad she's fed up with me; I'm fed up with her, too. I don't care if she doesn't want to be my friend any more. Good riddance.

Downstairs, I check Jeet's van. He's there. It makes my stomach turn. I can't go out there, not yet.

I go into the kitchen.

Deeva is making coffee. She is leaning against the counter rubbing her face; her eyes look bleary. '*Mi dispiace tanto,*' she yawns. 'I cannot even speak English before I have had my coffee.'

I want to tell her about last night, about the kiss, about Jeet telling me he wants to have sex with me, but I'm frightened to. Peter comes into the kitchen, holds his hand on her stomach and rubs his face against her neck. He whispers something, loud enough for me to hear – he says: 'I keep on thinking about last night.' She turns to him and slings her arms around his neck, kissing him on the mouth. I can see their tongues.

I stand at the window. Jeet's foot is sticking out of the van. Be brave. Be grown-up.

I slowly count to ten.

I try to be quiet when I step onto the gravel. I swing my head around the van door. 'Morning,' I say.

He smiles when he sees me. He's lying across his bed, reading.

'Hey,' he says, and crawls out of the van, his bare feet on the ground. He holds his hands on either side of my hips. 'How are you, my Leela?'

'I'm OK,' I say. 'I had a nice sleep.'

I want to say things – tell him how I feel. I don't want to be quiet any more.

'Good.' His eyes twinkle. 'Hey, when I woke up this morning I felt happy.' He smiles at me. 'Happier than I've felt in months. You did that to me Leela, you made an old man happy.'

I smile. I can't stop smiling. I want to tell him: *I felt happy as well, you make me happy too* – I'm saying it over and over, I'm opening my mouth—

'Hey guys.' I jump and turn around. 'What are you guys doing?' It's Anya. She's leaning against the van door, Bria behind her, her head on Anya's shoulder. I step back. Jeet still has his hands on my hips. I step back some more.

'We've been making braids,' Anya says. 'What do you think?' She turns around to show me her hair. A long French plait twists down her back like a snake.

I look up at Jeet and then back at her. 'It looks nice,' I say.

'I can do one for you if you like,' she says, and fingers my hair. 'You've got pretty hair.'

'Or maybe you'd like one of these,' Bria holds out her arm. There's a brightly coloured bracelet, it's a friendship bracelet, on her wrist.

'You can have one like Bria's,' says Anya. 'Or,' she says, holding her wrist out to me, 'you can have one like mine.' Her wrist is thin and brown. The bracelet is a tight weave of yellow and orange. 'I'll make you one,' she says. 'What's your favourite colour?'

Jeet is back in his van, facing away from us, looking for something. I feel unsure, uncertain. I grip hold of the end of the bed.

'You must have a favourite colour,' she says.

I shrug. I want to say green, but there is something about the way Anya is looking at me that makes me say, 'Yellow.'

'Hey,' she says. 'That's my favourite colour, isn't that freaky? Maybe I'll make you a friendship bracelet just like mine,' she says, and flashes her teeth at me in a pretend smile.

Jeet returns, sitting on the edge of the bed, fiddling with something metal in his hands. 'Right, girls,' he says. 'I have work to do, why don't you go and do your hair or make jewellery or something?'

I look at Anya. I don't want to make bracelets with her. I'd much rather stay here with him.

'OK Daddy,' Anya says, and suddenly swings herself to sit on his lap. He laughs, grabbing hold of her hips so she doesn't fall. Bria clings onto the van door. 'Jeet,' Anya fingers the neck of his T-shirt. 'Have you told Sylvie about our trip tomorrow?'

Trip?

She is sitting sideways on his lap, her long brown legs swinging and her arm around his neck as he continues to fix the machinery in his hands.

'Jeet,' she says, jiggling up and down.

He grabs hold of her. 'Careful,' he says. 'You'll fall.'

'Well, tell me,' she whines. 'Have you told Sylvie about our trip tomorrow?'

'No, I haven't,' he says.

What trip?

'To the sea,' she looks at me.

The sea.

'Bria and I are going home tomorrow, thank God,' she rolls her eyes. 'And Jeet is taking us, and we thought maybe you'd like to come with us and have a trip to the sea. What do you think, Jeet, is that a good idea?' She digs her fingers into his armpits, tickling him.

'OK, OK,' Jeet says, laughing.

'Well, do you?' She jiggles again. 'Do you think it's a good idea that Sylvie should come with us to the sea?'

He looks at me. His blue eyes. '*I I I If* she *w w w wants*—'

'Come on stutterer,' Anya laughs, and pinches him.

He smiles. '*W W Wants* to,' he says. 'Perhaps she doesn't want to.'

'Do you want to?' Anya asks me.

I shrug, looking at Jeet. His head is down. He doesn't look at me. Does he want me to go? I shrug again. 'I guess,' I say.

'Great, it'll be so exciting.' Anya flings both arms around Jeet's neck. She puts her head on his shoulder and for a minute I think she whispers something.

I run up the stairs two at a time towards Dad's room. Will he let me go? Do I tell him the girls invited me? He's more likely to say yes if I do.

Max comes out of his and Sam's room. His chest is bare. When he sees me, he struggles to pull his T-shirt over his head. Shadows: I see the shadows along his arms. He tucks his T-shirt into his shorts and straightens the arms to his wrists. I stop in front of him. 'Why not show your arms?' I say boldly. 'No-one would mind.' He looks down at me. 'It's nothing to be ashamed of.' I try to pass him, but he takes a step towards me, the air between us close.

'Why don't you stop hanging around with that creep?' he says. He looks down at me. I feel his leg as it lightly touches mine. I blush.

Sam comes out of their room and Max steps away. I push past them.

'All right?' Sam says. 'Hey, what's the hurry?'

I ignore him. I don't turn around.

'Hey, Sylvie,' he says, just as I reach Dad's room. 'We're going to interview that weirdo. We're going to nail the bastard.'

I want to tell him that Jeet is busy; he's fixing his van. I want to tell him he's not a bastard, but instead I stand with my back to them until I know they have gone. Then I knock on Dad's door. No-one answers, so I knock again. I open the door. The room is tidy, the bed is made, but there is no-one there. I have a flash of last night, the dull orangey light, it seemed like a dream. I close the door, walk back down the corridor and climb the stairs to the study.

'Your dad's been gone all morning,' Paritosh tells me.

'Where?' I ask.

'I don't know. I guess he and Lanks left early. I haven't seen them.'

I frown. Where have they gone?

When I get downstairs, Sam, Max and Josie are standing around

Jeet's van. A hot tight feeling fills me. I should just ignore them; show Josie I don't care. But they are interviewing him. I stand behind them.

Jeet is kneeling in the gravel, trying to change a tyre. He keeps stopping and mopping his forehead with his hanky.

Josie is talking into a make-up brush, and Sam is filming. Max is beside me; I won't look at him. I lean against the van door.

'So,' she says in her pretend grown-up voice. 'What brings you to this area of Italy?' Jeet is trying to unscrew the wheel. He grunts as he turns the spanner, the thin muscles working beneath his skin. 'Excuse me,' she says waving the make-up brush at him. 'We need the answers to these questions for our documentary *A Month in Italy.*'

I cringe. If she could hear herself. It's so embarrassing.

'OK,' Jeet sighs sitting back. '*W W What* What brings me here? Um – its beauty?' he says.

Josie takes a step forward. 'So, nothing else?'

'Nothing else,' he says, and goes back to his wheel.

'Right.' Josie clears her throat. 'So, are you on your own, or do you have a travelling companion?'

With some effort, Jeet manages to loosen the nut, and then the others, one by one. Max is twitching beside me. I glance at him. He doesn't look at me.

Jeet grunts as he works, sweat collecting on his upper lip and in his hair. He ignores Josie's question. She looks at Sam to ask for help; he nudges her to carry on. 'Do you—'

'A travelling companion,' he laughs. 'What's that?'

'I mean,' she laughs, blushing. 'Um, you know, someone to travel with, a friend?'

'Do I look like I have a travelling companion?'

'What about Anya and Bria?'

'Anya and Bria,' Jeet says. '*H H He*y, what's-your-name,' he calls to Max. 'Can you give me a hand?'

Max mumbles something before he throws himself on the ground beside Jeet, helping him pull the wheel from under the van.

'OK,' says Josie. 'Was there someone else travelling with you?'

'Yes,' Jeet says. 'I was with my friend, Uta.'

Josie winks at Sam. I lean against the van with my arms crossed. Uta – but he called her a friend.

Jeet tells Max to carry the wheel to the back of the van. Max lumbers off, and Jeet follows him.

'And where is Uta now?' Josie calls after him.

'Uta,' Jeet says from the back of the van, 'Uta is somewhere in Umbria.'

Umbria?

Jeet directs Max to put the new tyre on the ground. Max squats down with it and rolls up his sleeves. I can see his scars. He glances up at me for a moment: is he trying to prove something?

'That's enough now,' Jeet says. 'I can do it from here.'

'Thanks for the thanks, man,' Max mumbles. I move away when he comes to stand beside me.

'What's she doing in Umbria?' Josie asks, as Jeet sits back on his heels. He fumbles around for a lighter. Josie takes one out of her pocket, offers it to him.

'I don't know. Probably screaming her head off at some poor helpless soul.'

Screaming her head off? Why? What's wrong with her?

He smokes his cigarette slowly, thoughtfully. 'What else?' he says. 'What else do you want to know?'

'But, why is she not with you?' Josie asks.

He looks at her, laughs. 'Why is the sky blue?' he says.

That got her. She glances around, anxiously.

'I know,' she says suddenly. 'Where were you last year at the time of the full moon?'

I grab my forehead.

'Where was I last year at the time of the full moon?' he repeats.

'I don't know, Kerala or somewhere. What relevance does that have?'

'I mean—' she says.

'OK guys,' Jeet interrupts her. 'You mainly want to know *sss sta sta* standard stuff right? The life of someone like me, what I do with my time?' Josie nods carefully. 'I'll tell you a story. I was told it years ago by Parameshvar and it is about a Chinese Taoist and a tree.' He kneels forwards and starts to fix the new tyre to his van. 'The Taoist is travelling with his disciples when they come to a forest. There are lots of carpenters working, building a *pa pa pal* – a grand palace, and all the trees have been cut, except for one big ugly tree. The Taoist asks why have they not cut this tree? They reply that the tree is useless as it has too many knots to make furniture or fuel. The Taoist laughs and turns to his disciples and says, 'Take a lesson from these carpenters. Be like this tree, be useless and you will survive in this world.' Jeet screws the last nut and hits the tyre. He sits back. 'Some people think this is impractical, but life is to enjoy. It is to grow. It is not to be a utility, a commodity. What am I about?' he says. 'Very *sim sim* simple things. I just like to hang around, enjoy the small details with no particular place to go except perhaps the grocery shop for food, the tobacconist for cigarettes. I just exist,' he says.

'Oh,' says Josie. She clears her throat. 'So, how long are you staying in Italy?'

'I don't know.' He gets to his feet. He narrows his eyes.

'Don't you ever want to go home?' she asks.

'You know what?' he says. 'I've just about had enough now. It's too hot for this interrogation.' And he peels his vest over his head. He turns and Josie gasps. She flaps her arms at Sam to continue filming. Jeet bundles his vest in his hand and walks to the back of the van. We all stare. There, on his back, is a large dark mark about the size of a pancake, stretching right across his skin.

Look, Josie mimes.

'It's a birthmark,' I say, as I head upstairs. Josie follows me.

'Weird birthmark,' she says. 'Why don't you just admit it. You're in love with a man who is a werewolf.'

'No I'm not,' I say. 'I'm not in love.'

'You are,' she says. 'Just admit it. Go on. *Grr*,' she makes a growling noise and laughs from behind me.

'Stop following me,' I say, as I get to the top of the stairs.

'*You're in love. You're in love,*' she chants.

'Stop it!' I shout, turning around.

'*Sylvie's in love with a grrr monster werewolf.*'

'Fucking shut up!' I shout. 'What are you doing? Leave me alone. I thought you didn't want to be my friend.'

She looks up at me. She stops. She looks at me. 'If that's what you want,' she says.

'Just leave me alone,' I shout, and rush down the corridor to Dad's room, where I throw myself onto his empty bed.

I wait for Dad, but he doesn't come back. I think about the saying: a watched phone never rings, so I go back to my room to get my book, and then sit on his bed flicking through the pages, looking at all the things I've found since arriving here three weeks ago. In a week, we'll be going home. I look around the room. I want something of Dad's. I want something to take with me. I see a coin on the chest. I slip it into my pocket. I open the drawer beside the bed: his collection of watches, a pen, a hanky. I pick out the hanky. The creases crusted together. I put it to my nose. It smells of him, his sweetness like vanilla. I wonder if he'll notice it's gone.

The sun starts to sink and I stand at the balcony doors and watch as Anya and Bria help to lay the table for supper. Dad should be home by now. I watch Jeet as he casually walks towards the girls, their quiet talk, murmurings. There seem to be secrets between them, things I don't know.

After supper I ask Deeva if she's seen Dad. 'I don't know where he is,' I say.

'Oh, honey,' she hugs me. 'Didn't he tell you? He's gone to a retreat with Alanka. She needed to talk. Perhaps they have stayed over.'

'Oh,' I say. He's gone to a retreat. I might have wanted to go with them. 'It's just that…' I say, but Deeva is already gone. I wanted to tell her about the trip tomorrow. I want to tell someone.

Jeet says we should leave early, before the sun is up, so that we have the whole day at the beach. He says the journey might take a couple of hours. He's going to wake me up with a cup of tea in my room. I go to bed before Josie. I don't tell her that I'm going away tomorrow. She, Sam and Max are the only people I don't want to tell.

I wake up and the room is dark. There's movement in the corridor. A quiet *knock knock*. Jeet opens the door and stands in the darkness. Josie is still asleep. I get out of bed. I am wearing only knickers and a vest. He passes me a cup of tea. 'Get ready and we'll go,' he says. I search for his face.

I quietly sip my tea, sitting on the edge of the bed. My legs are cold. Perhaps I won't go. I'll stay here and wait for Dad to get home.

I put my bikini on beneath my clothes. I slip my feet into my flip-flops. I stop and look at Josie. I can't see whether her eyes are open or closed.

I open the door and close it gently behind me.

Downstairs, the kitchen light is on. Soma is there, a cup of steaming herbal tea. 'Hello,' she says. 'You are awake early.'

'I'm going away,' I say. 'I'm going to the seaside.'

'You will love the seaside,' she says.

'I am going with Jeet,' I say. 'Will you tell my dad when he comes back? Will you tell him I'm with Jeet?'

She takes my hands, presses them together and says, 'Of course I will my *bambina*. You will have fun with Jeet.'

Anya's favourite pop star is Madonna. She calls herself a Madonna freak. We're listening to 'Holiday' on the van stereo and Anya and Bria are singing and trying to dance in the back. Every time the van goes around a corner or lurches to a stop they fall over and laugh.

I'm sitting next to Jeet. I watch as his leg moves up and down as he puts his foot on the clutch, as he squints through the rear-view mirror, as he gently eases the gear stick to change gear.

Anya hugs the back of my seat and shouts the lyrics. She tugs on my shoulders and tells me to sing, and I show her that I am, but the music is too loud for her to hear that no words are coming out.

I watch as the light quickly fills the sky, and the hills turn to busy streets with their advertising boards on either side, and I think: we've been in Italy nearly three weeks and I've barely left the house: the furthest I've travelled is to the hotel swimming pool up the road.

Jeet stops to get cigarettes and I hear Anya and Bria whispering in the back. I don't look around.

'Sylvie,' I hear a voice. It's not Anya. I turn around and Bria is sitting on the bed and she's holding something out to me. 'We made you this,' she says, and she passes me a friendship bracelet. It is red and black, not the colours Anya said she'd make for me.

'Thanks,' I say.

'Here, shall I put it on for you?' She secures the bracelet around my wrist.

'Do you like it?' Anya asks, kneeling beside her.

'Yes,' I say.

'Now you have to make a pact,' she says. 'A truth pact.'

I nod.

'Anything I ask, you have to tell me the truth.'

I look into her eyes, her emerald eyes. They can ask me questions. I've got nothing to hide.

Jeet pulls himself into the van. Anya tells him, 'We gave Sylvie a friendship bracelet, which makes her our friend.'

Jeet turns on the engine. 'That's great, girls,' he says, and he puts the van in reverse.

Jeet manages to persuade Anya to let him change the tape, and Joan Armatrading fills the van. I close my eyes and feel the breeze from the open window. When I open them again we are passing a huge swathe of sunflowers, their heads nodding towards the sun. I touch my friendship bracelet and smile to myself.

Soon the road cuts through a forest of trees. Giant feathery trees that block out the sun and seem to go on for ever.

'Not long now,' Jeet says touching my knee.

The girls are asleep in the back: Anya with her legs twisted and one arm hanging over the side of the bed, Bria curled up in a triangle of space beside her. Bria has her thumb in her mouth. They look like children when they sleep.

The van rattles and lurches as Jeet sweeps it off the main road and takes a dirt track. The track is narrow and unstable as we bounce over rocks and boulders. The breeze has dropped and the heat and the sound of crickets fill the stillness.

We pass people walking barefooted on the side of the road, towels draped over their shoulders, and I think they must be going to the beach. At one point Jeet reverses to pull over to let a car pass, our tyres skidding off the track. The woman in the car waves at us and blows a kiss to Jeet.

On the road again, Jeet slows to talk to two people.

'Hey, beloved,' the woman says. She isn't Italian. She is dressed in a long white dress that is so thin you can see her knickers, and she has orange socks beneath her open-toe sandals. 'Hey, you brought them home,' she says, looking into the back of the van.

Anya and Bria have woken up, stretching and rubbing their eyes.

'The kids have been asking after them, they'll be so happy to see them. *Hi*,' she says, her lips spread in a smile.

'Hi,' Anya and Bria chant from the back.

'Hey, Jeet,' the woman says. 'Are you staying?'

'That depends on what *you you you you're offer offer*ing,' Jeet says, and I try not to look at him.

'What was that?' the woman squints through the van window.

'Oh, nothing,' he waves at her. He pushes his foot on the accelerator and pulls away. I can't tell whether his face is red because he's hot or embarrassed; I can hear the woman laughing.

This commune is really different to Dad's: it's lots of small houses and feels a bit like a school as there are signs everywhere: one of them says '*Smoker's triangle*', in front of a collection of benches; while another says '*No ping-pong during meditation*'.

Anya and Bria run off towards the main house, while I hang back with Jeet.

Everyone seems to know him. As we walk, people stop to hug him. Jeet talks to a man in silky pink trousers that balloon in the breeze. He looks down at me and says: 'Where did you find this one?'

Jeet puts his arm around me. 'This is Hari's daughter, her name is Leela.'

Anya and Bria rush out of the house with a group of kids dressed in colourful clothes. 'Come and meet our friend,' they call as they circle me. 'This is Sylvie,' Anya says. The kids look at me, moving in close. They don't smile.

'Are you coming down to the beach?' Anya tugs at my hand.

'Hey, you go down,' Jeet calls. 'I'll be there in a minute.' I look at him and then at the kids. I don't want to go without him. 'Go on, I won't be long,' he says.

I follow the kids down a long sandy path that's covered in stones and pine needles. They all run, most of them with bare feet. I try to keep up but the pine needles get into my flip-flops and prick my skin. The beach is really stony. Boulders and pebbles stretch right down to the sea. You can hardly see the sand there are so many.

The kids fling off their clothes and run into the water. Anya is wearing a bikini, but some of the girls only wear knickers. They run around and do cartwheels, letting the boys push them as they fall over as if they don't care that their boobs are showing.

Anya doesn't call me into the water and I'm afraid that my feet will hurt on the stones, so I sit on a rock and watch. It is hot here, but I don't want to take off my clothes. I wish Jeet was here.

'Hey.'

I turn around and he's walking towards me. 'What are you doing? Don't you want to swim?'

'Maybe later,' I say.

He pulls his vest over his head and slips off his shorts, sitting beside me. He is wearing a small pair of black swimming trunks. 'You haven't taken off your dress, come on,' he says. He traces his finger along my leg. 'There's no reason to be shy. We're all friends here. You're a funny one. Caught in yourself, eh?'

I sit up and stretch my dress over my head. I lay it in my lap and hug my knees.

'You're sweet,' he says. 'You're so shy.' He looks out towards the sea to all the girls whooping and chasing the boys.

He sits up and clears a space, throwing the stones towards the trees. He lays down his towel and lies on his side, propped on his elbow. I continue to sit on the rock, looking out to sea.

'Hey,' he reaches for me. 'Come and lie down.'

I sit on the towel. I lie back on the ground, the sun above me. I shade my eyes. I look up at him looking down at me.

'What am I going to do with you?' he says, stroking my face. 'What goes on in that pretty little head? I want to climb in and live in there for a while.'

The idea makes me laugh.

'That's better,' he says, and leans over me, his head blocking the light. 'I want to kiss you.' He moves closer. 'Your lips look very beautiful, sensual.' He touches them with his finger and then his lips. I try to close my eyes, but I am too afraid that Anya or Bria might see.

When he opens his eyes, they look sunken, his face misshapen. 'I hope you're not afraid of me,' he says.

The kids rush out of the water, running towards us, laughing and shouting as they fall over the rocks. They stand before us, their wet bodies glistening in the sun.

'Are you in love?' a girl asks. Another says: 'Do you love her?' I sit up and hug my legs. I look at Jeet, who is squinting at them. He kicks his foot and a shower of sand sprays them. They back off, running away and laughing.

'Why did they ask that?' I say.

'I don't know.' He rolls onto his side. 'Perhaps they sense something.'

I wonder what it is that they sense.

Anya runs towards us: her long brown legs, and her wet hair slapping against her back. 'Come on,' she calls. 'Come into the water.'

'Go on,' Jeet says. 'I'll wait here.'

I get to my feet and Anya grabs my hand, dragging me towards the sea. But I can't keep up. I don't want to trip on a rock, for it to cut me or twist my feet.

She lets go of me, running towards the water and diving in, while I stumble across the stones, my arms outstretched. I think about Jeet watching me, seeing how stupid I look beside these children who are all so free.

The water is cold. I am shivering it is so cold. Anya is beckoning to me, she's calling me to dive in, jump in like she did, but I'm too scared. I'm a scaredy cat. I'm scared of everything. *You have to do it. You have to do it,* I say to myself again and again and I try to think of warm things like being under the duvet in my bed back at home, sitting in front of the fire, listening to Nina Simone, my mum singing along to all the words. And in I dive, and the cold rushes through me. I hold my breath. I swim breaststroke as quickly as I can, pushing through the cold current, singing the words to all the songs I can think of over and over again. And very soon my blood starts to warm.

I can't see the ground beneath me. I don't want to put my feet down, so I carry on swimming until I am close to Anya and Bria. They are treading water. I look back at the shore, at Jeet, small like a doll, the kids, playing mostly in the shallows.

'You made it,' Anya calls. 'I thought you couldn't swim.'

'I can swim.' I try to catch my breath.

'Can you dive under?' Anya flips forward, her head under the water and her bottom in the air. She appears again, sleek and silky like a seal.

'Yes,' I say, treading water.

'Go on then,' she says.

I turn away, ignoring her.

Anya jumps onto Bria, crossing her legs behind her back, holding her tightly around the neck. Bria laughs. I start to swim away.

'So, do you love him?' Anya calls after me.

'What?' I stop; turn around.

'Jeet, do you love him?' she says, her face in shadow.

I don't answer.

Anya and Bria move towards me, still attached, like a two-headed monster.

'Did you have sex with him?' Anya asks.

'No.' I back away.

'I don't believe you,' she says, disconnecting from Bria.

'Well, I didn't,' I reply. She is swimming towards me. The water is deep. I am not a good swimmer.

Closer, her face is wet, her hair slicked back like oil. She looks different, harder.

'You have to tell me the truth,' she says.

'I am.' My heart is beating fast. I'm finding it hard to catch my breath. I glance towards the shore; it seems so far away.

'When you were in his van, the other night, we heard you.'

I ignore her. I start to swim away, towards the beach.

'Tell me,' she says, catching up with me. 'Or you have to take that bracelet off.'

'I am telling you,' I insist. There's a lump in my throat. *Don't cry. Don't cry.*

'Tell me.' She grabs a clump of my hair. She pulls it really hard. '*Tell me,*' she says again.

'Get off,' I shout, and tears sting my eyes.

She grabs hold of my arms, pinches and twists my flesh. '*Tell me,*' she shouts.

'I am telling you. I didn't have sex with him. I'm a virgin,' I shout. I pull away from her.

She stops, looks over at Bria, and laughs. 'You're a virgin?' she says. And I'm sobbing and trying to catch my breath, trying to keep afloat and I know I have to pull myself together and I can't let them see me like this, not anyone, not Jeet, and I swim away from her and she calls after me. She calls: 'For your information, Bria is in love with Jeet, so you'd better lay off him, OK?'

'No I'm not,' I hear a small voice.

'*You are,*' I hear Anya say.

I look around as I swim and I see Bria's head, her light-coloured hair and her strange eyes, pink from the sting of the water, and she looks like an angel hovering there, a odd mutant angel.

'*Virgin,*' Anya shouts. 'Just in case you're wondering, you're not my friend.'

I take lots of deep breaths as I walk along the beach. Jeet is sunbathing. I lie down and close my eyes, streams of tears tickling my cheeks.

'Hey,' he leans over me. 'What is this?' He wipes my face. 'Ssh,' he says, and I feel his lips on my eyes, one by one. 'Why are you crying, my sweet one?'

I don't want to tell him. I don't want to hear the sound of the kids, screaming and laughing. I don't want to look up and see Anya and Bria dunking each other's heads under the water, gasping for breath, still breathing. I don't want to be here, so I turn to him and say: 'Do you think we could go somewhere else?' and he looks down at me and smiles.

He traces his finger along the centre of my tummy, right down to my navel, it makes a fluttering feeling, and he says: 'Of course we can. We can go wherever you want.' As we leave, I look behind me and see Anya watching. I don't see Bria. I wonder where she is, where she might possibly hide.

Jeet takes me to another beach a short way down the coast and we spend the day sunbathing and swimming and he takes photos of me in my bikini. There are other people around, families and couples, and I wonder what they think when they look at us.

I watch the sun as it moves across the sky and soon Jeet is leaning over me, a shadow across my body, and he is saying: 'I'm starving. I need to eat. Shall we go?' And I realize that I haven't had any breakfast or lunch and that I too am really hungry.

We walk back to the van and I feel hot and sticky, a sheet of sand covering the whole of my body. It scratches my thighs as I sit down. In the van I look at myself in the mirror: my hair is a mat of white curls and my cheeks sparkle with sand.

We listen to Joan Armatrading: 'Somebody Who Loves You'. I listen to the lyrics and look over at Jeet and I wonder whether I love him, I wonder whether he loves me, and I wonder how many other people he loves.

Jeet takes me to a restaurant about an hour away. It feels as though it's in someone's garden. There are lots of tables with plastic tablecloths beneath twisting vines and trees that glow with lanterns.

As we sit down, a large group of people arrives and sits at a long table on the other side of the restaurant. Jeet smokes and watches them, but I can't see anything because my back is to the restaurant. All I can see is Jeet and the rough stone wall behind him.

A waitress comes over, places a candle between us and tells us in Italian what is on the menu. Jeet asks me whether I want rabbit or veal: I say veal because it sounds like a vegetable and I definitely don't want to eat a rabbit.

Our food takes ages to arrive. I watch Jeet as he smokes and drinks red wine. Every time his glass is empty he pours himself another.

'The Italians,' he says, 'they are such a funny race, so exuberant and sociable.'

I twist around and try to get a glimpse of who he is talking about, but all I can see are children running around.

'Their family is everything,' he says. 'Family and food, a simple life.' He sighs. 'But they are a narrow-minded race. I don't know how much longer I can stay in this country.'

I turn back to him. I squeeze my fingers in my lap and rehearse what I want to say. 'Might you go back to England?' I ask finally. There, I said it.

'England?' he says. He looks at me sideways, takes another drag of his cigarette, staring at me while the smoke swirls past his eyes. 'Am I going back to England?' he asks. 'Why would you want to know that, I wonder?' He is smiling at me like he thinks it's funny.

'I don't know.' My voice sounds small. 'I just wondered.' I shrug and look down at my hands.

'Come on,' he reaches forward. 'I'm teasing you, it's just that you look so serious,' he says. 'I don't know whether I'll go back; I'm not sure I have anything to go back to. I can only really think from tomorrow. I'll take you back to your dad's and then I'll decide.' He leans towards me. 'I won't stay for any other reason but for you,' he says, and picks up a strand of my hair, lets it fall. 'Normally I would have left by now, off somewhere else, meeting new people, but I find you interesting, so I'll stay a little longer.'

Interesting. But what if I stop being interesting?

He sits back again. 'I don't know,' he says. 'Maybe I'll do some work for Deeva's book on magic. I'll have to try and find Uta at some point, she'll probably need rescuing.'

I look down at the cigarettes on the table. I push them around. Uta.

'Is she still your girlfriend?' I ask quietly.

He smiles at me. 'My girlfriend?' he says, laughing. 'Well, she is a girl – well, I suppose more a woman – and she is my friend, so I guess she is a girlfriend. We are friends, companions, she relies on me even though she treats me like shit sometimes. She likes me to save her, but there are lots of people in this world that I try to save.'

'Like Bria?' I say.

He sloshes more wine into his glass and waves at the waitress. He gestures for some bread. He takes a sip of wine. 'Uta is a good person, she has a good heart, she is just very fiery. Sometimes I wonder whether I am cut out for that kind of thing. I don't like confrontation, it makes me anxious, you know, but then I keep on going back for more. Maybe it's the passion. She is like an Italian, all fire and no substance.' He smiles at the waitress who places a basket of bread on the table. He watches her as she walks away.

He lights another cigarette.

'But what about Bria?' I ask again. There's a whining in my ear: a mosquito, I wave my hand to get rid of it.

'What about her?' he sits back, his eyes narrowing.

'Anya said—'

'—don't listen to those girls. They play games. They see your pretty little head and they get jealous, they want to stir trouble. I'm surprised they have been so nice to you, they are normally like cats.' He follows the mosquito with his eyes. 'Honestly, my love,' he says, placing his cigarette in the ashtray. 'You don't need to worry about things like that; they are insignificant, like little irritating fleas.' He claps his hands together to catch it. '*Got ya.*' He looks at its splattered body in his palm. I catch a glimpse of blood; I wonder whether it's his or mine. He wipes it on a handkerchief.

Our food finally arrives: a thin slab of pale meat and a bowl of beans and nothing else, while Jeet has a plate of dark meat on the bone. He picks up a joint and tears at it with his teeth.

I pick at my meat with my knife and fork.

'Is it good?' Jeet leans over and opens his mouth for me to give him some. '*Mmm*, perfectly tender,' he says, chewing. 'Just as baby cow should be.'

I look down at my plate: baby cow? I try to swallow, but my throat feels tight. I'm a vegetarian: I don't want to eat a baby cow.

I can't finish my food. I take small mouthfuls to pretend, but Jeet keeps looking at me, watching as I chew. I feel sick; my stomach feels tight and small. Jeet finishes his rabbit and asks if he can eat mine. I pass him my plate.

When he has finished, he empties the bottle of wine into his glass, takes one more slug and asks the waitress for the bill.

'How long will it take to get home?' I ask. Suddenly I want to be there, away from here.

Jeet looks at me, and laughs. 'We won't be going home tonight,' he says.

I look at him. But where will we go?

'Does that bother you?' he asks, a smile on his face.

'No,' I shake my head. 'It's just...' I'm thinking about my dad, about the fact he doesn't know I'm here. 'Where will we go?'

'Listen darling,' he says. 'Look at me. I'm drunk. I can't drive much further than a clearing somewhere. We'll stay in the van, all right?'

Sleeping in his van, in a clearing. But I don't want to. I want to go home.

Jeet pays the bill and pushes back his chair. As we leave I look at the family sitting at the long table. It's a big family, mothers, fathers, grandparents and children. They are laughing and talking loudly, they seem like nice people. I want one of them to notice me, see me as I walk away with this man who is so much older than me. Old enough to be my dad.

Jeet puts his arm around me. 'You've got to learn to relax my Leela. Relaxation is the key to a happy little bunny,' he says, and I think about that poor rabbit who died and is now being digested in his stomach.

As we drive, the night breeze feels clean and sharp through the open window, the smell of ripe pine and herbs, the furious spark of crickets. It's cold, my skin is prickly, but I don't know how to close the window. I pull my towel over my shoulders and watch, mesmerized as the moths glow in the headlamps. When they hit the front of the van do they die? Or are they sucked beneath to flutter in the air that is left behind? Jeet drives fast down a winding road. We are entering a forest; we are surrounded by trees. Jeet is driving so fast that I have to grip the door handle to stop myself from being thrown around.

It's a while before we pull over, and we don't pass any cars. Jeet is silent as we come off the road.

We drive through a path cut out between the trees; branches lit up in the headlights, rushing towards us before scratching the windscreen. I find myself jumping at the sound they make on the glass.

We stop. Jeet turns off the engine and the headlights, and for a moment we are in total darkness. The air is still. There is no sound. I can no longer hear the crickets.

Jeet switches on the van light and climbs into the back, arranging the bed. He draws the curtains. 'We'll make it comfortable,' he says. 'You shall be comfortable in my humble abode.' And I'm thinking: Anya and Bria, they stayed with him, they trusted him. Bria is in love with him. *I will be all right. I will be all right.* But my fingers are squeezed tightly together, and I keep thinking of Josie, Sam and Max. Dad and Alanka wondering where I am. Will Dad be angry with me?

Jeet opens the back door, climbs outside and lights a cigarette. He smokes and looks around, while I sit in the front. 'It's almost a full moon,' he says.

It is almost a full moon.

'But the forest is so dense and dark, you can't see a thing.'

I don't want to look. I don't want to move.

I have an image of a man running through a forest, it is the man who turned into a werewolf in *American Werewolf in London*. He was being chased. Who was chasing him? Was it a dream? Dad let me watch it and it scared me so much I couldn't sleep.

'Come on,' he says from outside the back of the van. 'Let's get you into bed, you must be tired.'

I slip off my flip-flops; my feet are still covered with sand. I'm still wearing my bikini. I try to wipe away the sand, but it sticks to me.

'You'll want a clean towel,' he says as he rummages around in the back, his cigarette hanging from his mouth. He comes around the side of the van, opens the door. 'Here,' he says, and guides me to hold his shoulder as he lifts my feet one by one and wipes away the sand, it scratches as it clings to my skin. 'I'll get you something to wear,' he says, and reaches for a shirt. 'Put this on,' and he leaves me on my own. I slip off my clothes, my dress and my bikini top, and quickly push my arms into his shirt, not looking into the darkness and all the things that could be watching me.

I climb over the back of the seat and lie down in the corner of the bed. I cover myself with the sheet and think: I have to let go of thoughts of Dad, of Josie, Max and Sam, the Florence Monster. I have to lie down and close my eyes and think about nice things to help me sleep. I don't have to kiss him. I don't have to do anything with him.

He crawls in beside me. He leans on his elbow and looks down at me, he strokes the hair from my face. 'Are you all right?' he asks.

I look up at him, his face in half-light, the dark circles beneath his eyes, and I nod, I say: 'Yes.'

'Good,' he kisses the tip of my nose. 'Can I see a smile?' he says. 'I'm not such a bad person, am I?'

'No.' I shake my head.

'That's better,' he says. 'Now close your eyes.' He lays his hand over my eyes, blocking out the light. 'You look so beautiful, so peaceful. I wish I could capture this moment, remember it in my mind when we are apart. Maybe we could run away, be together always. What do you think?'

I open my eyes, I look at him. I search his face.

'Ssh,' he says. 'Ssh,' he repeats. 'I love you,' he says it softly, the smell of wine on his breath, the smell of rabbit, meat. I pull away. 'I love you,' he says again. And he strokes my hair, he looks at my face, he looks at me, and he says: 'Everything about you. You're a special person, Leela. You're a serious person, your sadness, there is something vulnerable there – I can see it. I think that's what has captured me about you, Leela, it's your vulnerability,' and I'm looking at him and he softens in this light. He thinks I'm vulnerable. He sees it. I close my eyes. 'I love you,' he whispers. 'It's easy with you, your ease, to talk, to listen,' he says, and I flinch as his hand touches my face again, and then his lips, my mouth limp as he eases his way in. 'I love you, I love you, I love you,' and I let him kiss me.

I hear a noise, somewhere out there in the dark. I jump. I pull away, my eyes stretched open. 'What was that?' I ask: images of monsters and men, guns and knives. They could be everywhere, all around us in the dark shadows between the trees.

He lifts the curtain and looks outside. 'It's nothing.'

He strokes my face again. 'Don't worry,' he whispers. 'You are like the sky. You see clouds come and go, stars, and the sky remains the same. You are like the sky, you are not corrupted, you are free by your very nature, *ssh.*' He pulls me towards him and I want to tell him that I am scared, that I want him to hold me, protect me, let me sleep in his arms, but all I can do is let him kiss me, his hand moving under the duvet, my skin beneath his shirt, my breasts, his hands either side of my hips as he pulls me towards him. His kisses become firmer. He slips on top of me, easing my legs apart, his sharp hipbones cutting into my thighs. He groans, he pushes his body into me. I'm carried along with him. I could ask him to stop but I don't know how.

His breathing quickens as he reaches down and curls his fingers inside my bikini bottoms, pulling them down. Am I holding my breath? He reaches down to his shorts; he struggles with them. I open my eyes. I try to shake myself awake. His back, his stray hairs, his thin skin, the birthmark: *I don't want this. I don't want this. I'm not ready for it.* He rummages around under the covers, adjusting himself, jerky movements. I'm biting my lip, I'm biting so hard it might bleed, and suddenly he stops. His head is face down on the pillow, a quick rhythmic movement beneath the covers, his quick breath, he groans, but it's a different kind of groan.

'Shit,' he says, and he falls off me. He lies beside me. '*Shit Shit Shit.*'

'What's wrong?' I try to touch him. He jolts away. 'What?' I say. What have I done?

'*What What What?*' he mimics me.

I lie on my back, looking at the air as it pulsates around me.

'Just give me a minute,' he says and he turns over.

Tears start to well up in my eyes. I wipe them away. I can't do this. I can't cry.

He lies totally still. 'Come on, you bastard,' he says, and his body judders, a quick vibration. What's he doing? He turns over again, leans on his elbow, looks at me. 'Maybe I have to see you, maybe that's it,' he says, and he looms over me and tries to kiss me again, his eyes open, watching me. But I pull away.

'What is it?' he asks, annoyed. 'What are you doing?'

'I don't understand,' I say, and I can't help myself, I'm crying.

'Oh for God's sake,' he says. 'Don't cry, Don't cry. Look, it just happens sometimes, it's got nothing to do with you, it's just my bastard body, it doesn't always do what I want it to do. It happens to everyone. It's not a big deal. Here,' he reaches for my hand and puts it under the cover and he places it there, a warmth, a slight hardness, I hold it lightly in my hand, it flops.

'Not like that,' he says harshly, and he takes my hand and guides it up and down. 'Your hand is like a glove. Not like that, like this,' and he shows me how to hold it and he guides my hand rhythmically up and down, the skin loosening and tightening as it starts to grow. 'That's it,' he says. His head falls back: '*Yes*,' he groans, and his eyes are closed and it grows bigger and harder in my hand. I carry on like this for a while, up and down, and I wonder how long I have to do it, when he suddenly grabs me. He pins both my hands behind my head. I let out a squeal as he gets on top of me, his weight pinning me down. He pushes his hips into me, my legs apart, he pushes into me, it hurts – I want to scream, I want to tell him to stop. I catch a glimpse of his face, he is looking over my head, he is biting his lip. '*Fuck!*' he shouts and his body slumps. He is heavy, I can't breathe. Did it happen? Did he do it? '*Fuck Fuck Fuck!*' He rolls off me again. 'I'm sorry,' he kicks the end of the van. 'Fuck,' he says again and reaches up to turn off the light. We are in darkness.

I lie here listening to his breathing, listening as it slows and steadies. He turns onto his side, and sleeps while I lie here, the sheet pulled tightly around my neck, my legs pinned straight, wondering how to get my bikini bottoms back on. I don't want to wake him. I lie like this for what seems like ages, looking into the darkness, trying to find somewhere to rest my eyes, something to focus on, a bead of light, a lighter shade, but I can't see anything. Soon, his breath quietens. I can't hear anything. Just silence. Would I know if there was something out there in the darkness?

I am relieved when I open my eyes that it is light and that I have slept. I didn't think I would. A dull blue light escapes from the sides of the curtains. It is daylight. I lie still. Jeet is on his back beside me. His eyes closed, a gentle wheeze as he breathes with his mouth open. I look at the roof. Last night: what happened? He tried to have sex with me but it didn't work. His thingy was soft. Was it because of me? Was it because he could sense that I was nervous, that I didn't want it? Or was it because I held it like a glove? Should I have been doing more? Maybe I should tell him, ask him to show me how it's done. Maybe I should tell him I'm a virgin and I've never done anything like that before.

He twitches, rubs his nose and opens his eyes.

'Hi,' I say, lying on my side. His eyes are swollen. I smile at him.

He looks at me and then away. He doesn't say anything; he doesn't smile.

He clears his throat. He coughs. Is he thinking about last night? He coughs so hard that it forces him to sit up. His body retches. I put my arm out to him, but I don't touch him. He finds a cigarette, lights it and kicks open the back door. He stands and looks around as he smokes, and then he walks away.

We drive back to the house and Jeet hardly says a word. He just follows the road and fiddles with the car stereo, playing music I don't know. Sometimes he sings and taps his thumb on the steering wheel, but he doesn't look at me, he doesn't touch my knee and ask if I'm all right.

I catch sight of myself in the wing mirror. My face is burnt from the sun, a red stripe across my nose and cheeks, and my eyes are bloodshot. What will people think when I get back? What will Dad say?

We've been driving a while and I start to recognize places that we passed on the way: a narrow street where the van nearly got stuck, a stripy church, a vegetable market. Jeet stops at a shop. He returns with two bottles of water; he passes one to me. It is cold. I hold it to my face and it feels so refreshing that I almost cry.

Soon we are climbing the long winding road that leads to the house, Jeet pushing the horn as we go around corners. We are nearly there and I'm running through excuses in my mind: We ran out of petrol. We stayed at the commune. We broke down on the way and we couldn't get back. Or do I tell Dad the truth, that Jeet drank too much red wine and we slept in his van in a forest with no-one else around? Do I tell Dad that his friend tried to have sex with me?

I try to get Jeet to look at me. I try to see whether he is annoyed. I don't want him to be annoyed with me.

At the top of the drive Jeet switches off the engine.

He turns to me, his eyes soft. He says, 'Hey,' and he opens his arms and I fall into them. He hugs me and I press my face to his chest and I hold back the tears and he kisses the top of my head. 'I'm sorry,' he says. 'I'm sorry for being an idiot, will you forgive me?'

I breathe into his vest, the sharp smell of his sweat, and I say, 'Yes.'

When we pull into the drive, I look up at the house and it appears different, something strange. Most of the shutters are closed, as if everyone is still in bed. Deeva's is the only window that is open, her white curtains billowing in the breeze. Perhaps Dad hasn't returned home from the retreat – I hadn't even thought of that. I leave Jeet in his van as I walk to the kitchen. Soma is there, sitting at the table and drinking fruity tea, just as she was when I left. She gasps when she sees me. 'My *bambina*,' she's on her feet, her arms outstretched, hugging me. 'My darling,' she looks at me, her eyes seem distant. 'A terrible thing has happened,' she says, and I freeze. 'Your father, he is in his room, you go to him.'

My father.

'Just go,' she says, and she looks as if she might cry.

I run up the stairs two at a time. He is hurt, he is injured, is he dead?

I run down the corridor to his bedroom. The door is closed and I hear crying, a woman crying, wailing – *No. No. No.*

Alanka.

I burst through the door.

It is dark, a thin light escaping through the shutters.

A figure sits on the bed. It is Dad. He is alive. A woman lies in the bed; he is stroking her hair. Alanka moves out of the shadows. I take a step forward. I squint towards the woman in the bed, the woman Dad is comforting. She is sobbing. It is Deeva. Alanka comes to me. She takes my hand. Dad looks at me and then away.

Alanka leads me into the corridor. 'It's Deeva,' she whispers. 'She has had a miscarriage.'

'A what?' I look at her and then towards the bedroom; the sound of Deeva's crying fading into my dad's soft chords.

'A miscarriage, she has lost her baby. Her baby is dead.'

'Her baby is dead?'

Alanka won't let me see Deeva. She won't let me sit with them. I beg her. I ask her again and again whether I can just sit on the edge of the bed, I won't say a word. I'm crying. But she won't let me. She backs away, opening the door, her hand on the doorknob, saying Deeva doesn't want anyone there; she only wants to be with her and Dad, no-one else, not even Peter. 'But maybe she wants me there, I am her friend,' I say.

Alanka goes back into the bedroom, closing the door behind her, and Deeva's cries fade. I can no longer hear the sound of Dad's soothing voice. I don't need to think about him stroking her head, his nice words, I don't need to hear them.

I go downstairs, open the shutters in the living room, and sit on the sofa, watching the patterns the light makes in the dust. I think about Jeet outside in his van. I think about what he said about us going away together. I think about leaving school, home. I think about my dad up there in his room and I think about Deeva with her dead baby inside her, and the tears start rolling.

Josie's head pops up past the window. She is in the room. 'Sylvie,' she shouts. She rushes towards me, she skids, trips and lands at my feet. 'Oh my God,' she says. 'What happened to you?'

I cry and laugh at the same time. 'Are you all right?' I ask, helping her up.

'No, are you all right?' she says. She sits on the sofa next to me. 'I'm so sorry – about being horrible to you – I didn't think you'd just disappear like that, go off and not tell us where you were. I saw his van. What did he do to you? Did he hurt you?'

'He didn't do anything to me,' I say.

'Ssh,' she says. 'Calm down, calm down,' as if she's saying it to herself. 'Now look at me,' she says. I look at her. 'What happened. Why are you crying?'

'Deeva,' I answer. 'She lost her baby. Her baby's dead.' And it makes me cry again.

'Oh,' she looks surprised. 'Didn't…' she waves outside. 'But what about him? Where have you been? Didn't he do something to you?'

'No.' I shake my head.

'But you didn't come back. Soma told us you'd gone to the seaside. Why didn't you tell us where you were going?'

'Because… I don't know,' I say, all my excuses gone.

'But he didn't hurt you?'

I shake my head again.

She looks at me. She looks at what I'm wearing, my dress all dirty and the sand in my hair, and she wipes something from my chest. 'Thank God for that,' she says. 'You wouldn't believe what's been going on in our minds – murder, rape, torture. Either Jeet murders you or the Florence Monster murders both of you, cuts off your genitals, hangs them up in his front room, rotting in the heat, the smell – pooh,' she waves the air in front of her nose. 'And it would all be my fault. I would never forgive myself. I don't really think you're not my friend. I didn't mean it.'

I laugh, take her hands. 'It's OK,' I say. 'I know.'

She pauses, looks outside. 'Where did you sleep?'

'In his van.'

'You slept in his van?'

I nod.

'With Anya and Bria?'

'No.'

'No?' she shouts. 'And nothing happened? I don't believe you,' she says.

'Ssh,' I try to keep her voice down. 'Nothing happened OK?' I whisper. 'He's not the Florence Monster. I wish you'd realize that: he's not a monster, he's just a normal man. He's a nice man, he was nice to me.'

'Something happened, didn't it?'

I pause. I look down.

'What was it, tell me.'

I dust sand from my toes.

'You have to tell me, Sylvie.'

'We kissed,' I mumble.

'You kissed?'

'Yes.'

Sam and Max rush past the window looking in. They must have seen the van. I grab Josie and whisper: 'You mustn't say a word, not to Sam, Max, anyone.'

Josie looks behind her as they rush in.

'Where've you been?' Sam looks angry.

I laugh, wiping the tears from my face. 'Nowhere,' I say.

'What do you mean, nowhere?' Sam asks. 'Why did you just go off like that? Why didn't you tell us? Why did you just leave, and with him?' he gestures outside.

'We just left early,' I say. 'I told Soma, I knew she would tell you.'

'But you didn't come back. All night.'

'*I know*,' I say, annoyed. 'I'm sorry. I should have phoned but I forgot the number. We slept in the commune,' I lie. 'Jeet ran out of petrol and we slept in the commune, me in one of the bunk beds with the kids. It was fine. We had fun. We went swimming in the sea.'

Sam frowns at me. I don't look at Josie.

'I don't believe you,' Sam says.

'Well, you can believe what you like.' I jump up and rush outside. As I pass Max, he pushes into me, my shoulder knocking into his chest. I look up at him and our eyes meet.

I get to the belvedere. I'm shaking. It's OK, I say to myself. They're just being stupid, they're immature, I can't expect them to understand. I look out to the view and take a deep breath. It's OK. I'll still be able to see him. I'll just have to sneak around, go to his van when they're not looking. He loves me, I love him – we'll be together whatever happens, no-one will stop us.

I hear the sound of gravel beneath feet: I look around. Sam is striding towards me. 'What the fuck are you doing – are you mad?'

'What?' I back away.

'You fucking kissed him. What's wrong with you? He's a perve, a sicko. He's a fucking nonce.'

'What? – *Ssh*,' I grab him. 'What did Josie say? I can't believe she told you.'

His face is red, he's glancing around, at Jeet's van, at the house, at me.

'Honestly, Sam. Please, don't do anything. What did she say?'

'Why does it matter what she said?'

'Because she's lying,' I say. 'I didn't kiss him. He tried to kiss me and I said no, honestly. Please Sam, believe me. Honestly.'

'Don't talk shit Sylvie. Josie told me and I believe her, you kissed. It's disgusting, you're fucking mad.' He jumps from foot to foot. 'I'm going to smash his fucking windows, I'm going to get him.'

'Sam,' I grab him. 'What's happened to you? Why are you so angry?'

He looks at me. 'Why am I so angry? Why do you think?'

'I don't know, I don't know what the problem is – it's Max, he's made you weird, stealing things, threatening people. You're never normally like this.'

He pauses, looks at me for a minute. He frowns.

'Honestly,' I say. 'You've changed since you've met him, since you've been here.'

He looks at me, his bloodshot eyes. He stares at me.

'It's like you're crashing around and causing trouble and it's all because of him isn't it, it's not you. He's just horrible—' He starts to shake his head. 'I don't know why you're—'

'Don't!' he shouts holding up his hand. I stop talking. 'Don't bullshit me,' he says slowly. 'It's got nothing to do with Max. Look at what's happening. It's right in front of your eyes. Look. Be honest.'

'I am looking,' I say. 'I *am* being honest.'

'Then tell me what happened.'

'Nothing happened!' I shout.

'Don't lie.' He suddenly laughs. 'I can't believe you're so blatantly lying like this.'

'I'm not lying.'

'You are lying,' he says in my face.

'*I'm not lying.*' I stamp my feet.

'You are, Sylvie,' he says. 'Just admit it. You fucking kissed him.

He told you a load of shit, he wangled his nasty way into your head and you kissed him.'

I look at him. I can't say anything.

'Don't be a liar,' he shakes his head. 'Don't be like Dad.'

I burst into tears. I fall onto the wall. I clutch my arms to my chest. I cry, while he just stands there watching me.

He sighs. 'Come on, Sylvie,' he sits beside me. 'Don't cry.'

'I'm not a liar,' I say. 'Why is everyone ganging up on me? You, Josie, Max – you're all horrible to me and I haven't done anything wrong.'

'We're not ganging up on you,' he says. He touches my hand. 'It's just I've been watching this happen, we all have. He's a creep—'

'Please don't do anything, don't tell Mum, don't tell anyone.' I'm sobbing.

'Listen,' he grips my arms. 'Look at me.'

'Please don't. She'll kill me, she won't understand. Please.'

I look at him. He looks back at me.

'Please Sam, please. I won't see him again. I won't spend any time with him, I promise, please don't tell anyone.'

He sighs. 'I won't tell anyone,' he says. 'I'll let it go, but only on one condition.'

I hold his gaze.

'That you don't see him any more. You don't go to his van, you don't go anywhere near him. You spend the rest of the holiday with us.'

I look towards the house. Josie pops her head around the front door, sees me and disappears again.

'I mean it, Sylvie,' he says.

'OK,' I laugh lightly. 'I don't want to see him again anyway. He makes me feel weird. He's old – he's as old as Dad,' I say, and knock into Sam.

Sam raises his eyebrows. 'I know he is,' he says, and puts his arms around me.

I sit on the belvedere with my book, digging in my Biro, drawing dark knotted patterns while smoking cigarettes. From here I can see Jeet's van. He hasn't come out for a while. I wonder whether he is asleep. I can also see Dad's balcony, so I can catch him the moment he opens his shutters. I feel weird, sort of buzzy, as if all I want to do is smoke. I'm trying not to think about Jeet. I'm really trying, but my eyes keep wandering to his van. I want to see him, but I don't want to see him, I want to be near him, but I don't. Sam says I shouldn't talk to him: *I don't want to see him. I don't want to see him. I don't want to see him.*

I tear the paper with the pressure of my pen. I try to fix it by pushing in from the back. When I look up again Dad's balcony doors are open, the shutters flat against the walls. I jump up. Maybe Dad will help me. Maybe I can talk to him – tell him what happened. Maybe he'll listen to me, or maybe he'll read my tarot cards.

As I walk towards the house, Dad comes out of his room and stands on the balcony. He looks at his watch. He has a dark patch of sweat or tears down the front of his shirt.

I run up the stairs, along the corridor, through his open door. Alanka is making the bed. Deeva is no longer there. The room smells funny: it smells of bodies, of sweat. I wonder whether a miscarriage has a smell.

I sit on the bed. Alanka sips from a glass of water. She looks at Dad.

'Is Deeva OK?' I ask; the thought of her makes me sad.

'Yes,' she whispers. 'She has gone to bed, she has gone to Peter.' Alanka sits beside me. 'She is still very sensitive,' she says.

'How did it happen?' I ask. How can a baby die?

'Too much sex,' Dad says, coming in from the balcony. 'They were at it like bloody rabbits.'

I gasp. 'Really?'

'Hari,' Alanka says. '*Ssh.* Nobody knows what causes a miscarriage. It is the body rejecting the baby for some reason, I don't know why.'

'Oh, come on Lanks, she didn't want that baby,' Dad says. 'She's far too selfish.'

But Deeva did want her baby. I know she did.

'You women always want what you can't have,' he says, and I look at Alanka. She traces her fine fingers along the patterns of the bedspread. 'Anyway,' Dad puts his heavy hand on my head, 'what happened to you last night?'

I flush red.

'You were with Jeet,' he says.

I look at him.

'Don't think I haven't noticed what's been going on between you.'

I suddenly feel hot.

'Don't embarrass her,' Alanka says. 'It is only attraction, all men will find her attractive.'

'Not in this way,' Dad says.

'Leave her alone,' Alanka touches my knee. 'It is not so bad.'

'Oh, it's not bad,' Dad says. 'How can love be bad?'

The word burns me.

I watch as he walks to the balcony, leans out, lights a cigarette.

'You look sad,' Alanka says.

I look at her and nod, sudden tears making my vision blurry.

She guides my head to her lap, strokes my hair. 'Look at what you have done,' she says to Dad. 'You have upset her.'

'Oh, I haven't upset her.'

I push myself up, rub my eyes. I want to say something, but I can't find the words.

'I haven't upset my precious daughter, have I?' he asks, looking at me.

'No,' I shake my head. 'You haven't upset me.'

'Then why are you crying?' Alanka strokes the tears from my face.

'I don't know,' I say. 'I don't know why I'm crying.'

'What's upsetting you?'

I pause. I shake my head.

'Come on darling.'

'It's just... Jeet,' I say carefully.

'What's he been up to?' Dad stands above me.

'I don't know. Nothing,' I shake my head again.

'Come on, I bet he's been up to something.'

I look up at him. Can I tell him? 'It's just weird,' I say. 'He's really nice to me but then... he expects things. I really like him, but–' I pause. 'He scares me.'

'He scares you?' his eyebrow raised.

I nod. There, I said it.

'Because he loves you?' Dad asks. 'You should not be afraid of love.'

'I'm not,' I say, looking at him. 'I'm not afraid of... It's not about love – it's that... he... he always wants to kiss me.'

Dad and Alanka laugh. Why are they laughing?

'He wants to kiss you?' Dad says. 'What man wouldn't?' He walks back to the balcony, scans the courtyard.

'Oh, it's so sweet,' Alanka grips my hand. 'Your first experience of it, and with someone like him. It is good.'

I look at her, 'But,' I say, 'isn't it wrong?'

'Wrong?'

'He's... so old,' I say.

Dad laughs from the balcony. 'He's only as old as me. What are you saying, that your dad's old?'

'No,' I say quickly. That's not what I'm saying.

'You can't be too old to love. Everyone has feelings, however old they are.'

'Come on,' Alanka tries to hug me. 'You are so melodramatic.

You have to learn to relax about men, you'll waste far too much energy worrying every time a man pays you a compliment.'

'But –' I swallow hard. They don't understand. 'But – I slept in his bed and… he tried to have sex with me.'

Dad stops, his back to me as he looks out from the balcony. I see his shoulders rise; his fingers twitch. He glances back at me. I must be bright red, as my heart is pounding in my ears. Alanka is staring up at him, her eyes wide. What have I said?

Dad leans out. He doesn't say anything. It's as if he's looking for someone. He whistles and waves. I look at Alanka, but she won't look at me.

He walks back in, slips on his shoes. He puts his hands in his pockets, glances at his reflection in the mirror, flicks the hair from his eyes. He stops and waits. He looks towards the door.

Sweat trickles down my sides. I want to wipe it away, but I'm afraid to move. I want to say something, but I don't know what to say.

There's a knock at the door.

'Come in,' Dad calls. The door opens and Jeet walks in. My stomach turns. He glances at me, his eyes wide. Dad grips his arm. 'Come and sit down,' he says. He guides Jeet to the bed, where he sits on the edge. I can see only the back of him.

'How are you, my friend?' Dad stands above him.

'*Goo Goo Goo Goo Good*,' Jeet says, and clears his throat.

Dad puts his hand on Jeet's shoulder: Jeet flinches.

'It's all right,' Dad laughs. He turns around and walks the other way. Alanka grips my hand, squeezes it.

'We have known one another a long time,' Dad says. 'You are a friend, a good friend. I consider you one of my closest.' He turns to Jeet. 'Do you consider me a good friend?'

'Yes.' Jeet nods.

'Good. I trust you Jeet – I want you to know that. I trust you. I would trust you with my life.'

Jeet nods again, his leg jiggling.

'Do you think I trust you with my daughter?'

I stare at my hands.

'Look at her,' Dad says.

I slowly look up.

Jeet turns his head towards me, his eyes settle on my collarbone.

'Look at her face, how young she is.'

Jeet's eyes meet mine; he quickly looks away.

'Do you know how precious she is to me?' Dad asks.

'Yes.' Jeet nods.

'Good.' Dad closes his eyes. 'Now take her hand,' he says. Jeet looks at me questioning: I want to shrug, to tell him I don't know. 'Have you got her hand?'

Jeet tentatively reaches for me. 'Yes,' he says. It is damp and cold.

'Now take her away,' he says.

I look at Dad.

'Go on.'

I look at Alanka; she smiles. *Go on*, she mimes.

I look at Jeet. He stands, he reaches out to me. I take his hands and Dad steps back to give us room. I stop for a minute, between Dad and Jeet, Alanka still sitting on the bed, I stop and I look at Dad's feet, a slice of brown flesh between his trousers and his slip-on shoes.

'Thank you,' Jeet says, as he leads me out of the room.

In the corridor he stops. 'Are you all right?' he asks me.

I stare up at him. Am I all right? I'm shaking. My whole body is shaking.

Newly weds, Eddie and Julia slip away from the dance floor. I grip onto my camera and move out of the way of the hordes of people heading for the music. I've finished. Now I can go home.

'Oh, Sylvie,' it's Diane. She looks hot and flustered. 'You've done a wonderful job, darling. I can't wait to see the pictures. Hope you got that fabulous move of Eddie's. And, you know,' she leans towards me, 'it wasn't even rehearsed.'

'It was very good,' I say.

'Now, you must have a glass of champagne. A piece of cake?'

'No, thank you, I—' but she's already gone to the bar.

I watch the clusters of guests huddled in the alcoves. It's not the easiest place to take pictures: there's no natural light, no windows to let in the bright sunny weather outside. People push past me. I cling onto my camera and back up against the wall. I'll have a quick drink to be polite and then I'll order a cab.

Diane returns with a large goblet of champagne and a wedge of cake. 'I'm sorry, darling,' she says. 'There were no flutes left. Now you'll stay won't you? I'll introduce you to people.' I force a smile and take a sip from my drink while she looks around.

'Julia,' Diane grabs her daughter.

Julia smiles at me, her toothy smile; I hope I got some pictures with her mouth shut. 'The wine is running out,' she whispers to her mother.

'Oh, OK, just give me a minute. Julia, sweetie, be kind and

introduce Sylvie to your friends.' She rushes off.

'I'm OK, really,' I tell Julia, who looks up at me awkwardly. 'I'll finish this and then I'll go, I'm very tired. But *you* must be exhausted. Have you had a lovely day?'

Julia's face relaxes. 'Amazing,' she says. 'Better than I could have imagined. Now that the speeches are over, I intend to get very pissed and embarrass myself.'

I laugh. 'Good on you,' I say. She looks around, takes a sip of champagne. 'It was a beautiful ceremony,' I add. It was. There was something about her and Eddie, an intimacy that you don't always see between people. 'Listen, don't worry about me, I'm fine. You've got people to talk to. I'll be going soon.'

'Thank you,' she says and takes my hand. 'Thanks for such a great job, and remember what I said – are you going to go home? Talk to him?'

I shrug, 'Yes.'

'Good, because he sounds like a lovely man.' She kisses me on the cheek and swooshes away, lifting her train as she goes.

I lean against the wall, fingering my mobile in my pocket. I like Julia. We chatted at the hairdresser. Her hair in curlers, she was waiting for it to set and kept asking me questions. It took her mind off things, she said. I told her about Jack, about my uncertainty – I didn't tell her the whole story. But she nodded as I spoke and said she and Eddie hadn't always been sure. They even separated soon after they got engaged; she had an affair before she realized how much she loved him. She told me never to have an affair – 'Have sex with someone else and it kills something. It took me and Eddie ages to connect again. He was so angry with me. I was worried it would never be the same.' She asked me where my ring was. I lied. I said it was at the jeweller's being mended, one of the diamonds had fallen out. She looked at me. 'Whatever you do, don't have sex with someone else,' she said.

I shook my head. 'I wouldn't do that,' I said. 'Not to Jack.'

'You look like you deserve that drink.' I glance behind me. It's the tall pink man I photographed on the street, a bright and vibrant flamingo next to his penguin friends. He has a light yellow stain on his lapel. He looks down. 'Pavlova,' he says. 'Fucking whipped cream,' and he rubs it with his thumb.

'So, tell me,' he says, leaning against the wall. 'Is it hilarious seeing all these couples squeezed into their best, relying on you to make them look beautiful?'

I cock my head. 'It's interesting,' I reply. 'I've just got to get a good picture, that's why I'm here.'

'Are you up to the job?' he raises an eyebrow.

'I should hope so.'

He takes a sip of wine, looking at me all the while. 'Are you married?'

'No,' I say.

'I didn't think so.'

I frown. 'How does a married person look any different to an unmarried person?'

'Subtle things,' he says. 'I just know.'

I shift my position and face him. He has a soft face, if a little over tanned. Curly long eyelashes.

'No, tell me, I'm interested. What is it about me that says I'm not married?'

'There's a sparkle in your eye,' he says, and purses his lips. Is he gay?

'What about you?' I ask. 'Are you married?'

'What do you think?'

I look down, his shiny white shoes, 'No,' I decide.

'I was,' he says. 'You might have felt differently if you'd met me six months ago.'

'Did you divorce?'

'Yes,' he says.

'I'm sorry.'

'Don't be.' He raises his glass. 'Getting married was probably the worst mistake of my long and eventful life.'

A woman slings her arm over his shoulder, which hoists up her dress, almost exposing a breast. It's the feather woman – she was wearing a beautiful ivory feather shawl, which is no longer on her shoulders, revealing instead her mottled chubby arms.

'James,' she sloshes her glass of red wine towards him.

'Lucy, darling,' he says. 'Watch the Paul Smith.'

'Bloody hell!' She lurches. 'I've been arguing with that Molly Moo, what's her face, over that fucking reading. She thinks it's charming that they had a Nick Cave, but honestly. That girl has already got her little claws into him, bringing that Goth into their ceremony. She should be shot.'

'Darling,' James sighs. 'Keep your voice down, we're surrounded by her family.'

'Fuck those alcoholics,' she says, almost falling over as she turns to look around. 'Give me a fag, Jay.'

'This is Lucy,' James says, taking a packet of cigarettes from his pocket. 'She's had a little too much to drink, haven't you darling.' He offers me a cigarette. I hesitate. The idea suddenly appeals. Would one hurt? Lucy blows smoke at me. 'No thanks,' I shake my head.

He lights his own. 'This is—' he says, gesturing to me.

'Sylvie.' I hold out my hand.

'Ah, the lady with the camera,' Lucy says. 'Now, did you manage to get shots of those two together without knocking off one of their heads? I don't know what he was thinking choosing to marry such a short arse.'

'Oh, for God's sake Lucy, will you shut up,' James hisses. 'Sylvie might be a friend of the bride.'

'I only met her today,' I say.

'Oh, she hasn't got any friends,' snipes Lucy. 'These are all Eddie's Oxford chums.'

'Yes, Lucy, but you're forgetting that he met Julia at Oxford.'

'Oh, whatever,' she waves her hand at him. 'I'm just going to have to say no from now on. When I get an invitation I'm going to RSVP saying *No Thanking You* – not interested in your lies and your stupid games, your idiotic... tradition. It won't last between them,' she says. 'She's a midget and he's a giant, how the fuck do they have sex?' James lets out a loud sharp laugh and I take a gulp of champagne. 'I don't know,' she continues. 'I don't know why people bother. Marriage is for losers...' Julia walks past. I press myself against the wall. 'It's the most unchallenging thing that humans ever invented.' She sways towards James. He puts his arm around her.

'You might have gathered that we both belong to the anti-marriage club,' he says.

'Huh,' she exclaims. 'Have you heard his story? Guess how long this lovely boy's marriage lasted.'

I shrug. 'I don't know. A year, two years?'

'Two fucking weeks,' she says.

I look at him. 'Really?'

'Oh, don't tell me you're one of the naive ones,' she jeers. 'One of those silly girls who thinks she'll be saved by marriage. Waiting for the day when her little boyfriend gets on one knee.' Her face is close, her eye make-up smudged, lipstick on her teeth. I back away. Her breath smells.

'Yes, two weeks,' James chuckles. 'It just didn't work. We were in love, we got married, and then everything went flat. We shouldn't have done it.'

'But two weeks,' I say. 'It's not very long—'

'No-one should do it,' Lucy slurs.

'Not everyone is the same,' I object.

'That's what you think,' she says. 'I guarantee that if you get married, you will divorce within the year.'

Something in me rises. She's starting to piss me off.

'I promise. Here,' she says, going into her bag, getting out her wallet and passing me her card. 'Take my number, call me when it happens. I'm going to write a book about it, it's called *Dying to Get Up the Aisle*, it's the biggest waste of time this society has ever invented.'

'That's your opinion.' I scrunch her card in my fist.

'Are you married?' she looks at me.

'What do you think?' James challenges her.

She squints; looks at me up and down. 'No,' she says.

He laughs. 'Why not?'

'Because she's too trim, she cares too much about her appearance. She's too independent.'

'That's bollocks,' I laugh. 'You don't know what you're talking about.'

'I know exactly what I'm talking about missy,' she waves her finger at me. 'We're on this earth to be alone. I can see who you are. You may think you're perfect but you're kidding yourself. You'll wake up one day and you will have lost your life, all those missed opportunities—'

'Oh for God's sake,' I'm suddenly angry. 'You don't know me, you don't know anything about my life.'

'*Oh*, pickle,' she says.

'Whatever.' I clutch onto my camera and push past her.

Outside on the street, I lean against the railings. My heart is beating fast. I feel sick. What was that about? Why did I react to a bitter old drunk? I hold my head. Why do I care anyway?

A man comes out and lights a cigarette.

'Excuse me,' I say. 'Do you have any spare?'

He smiles and passes one to me, strikes a match. I look at the cigarette in my hand. I shake my head. 'It's OK,' I say. 'I'll just hold it for a while.'

'*Ah*,' he laughs. 'Giving up are you?'

No, I'm not giving up – I think, as I lean against the railings. I haven't even started.

I take a sip of champagne. I swill what's left in the base of my glass. I should go. I should go home. I should go back to the flat, phone Sam, find out about Dad. I should see him, tell him about Jack, ask him to give me away, and then I should go home.

I take my mobile out of my pocket and dial Jack's number. The phone rings, it rings and rings. Where is he? The answer machine kicks in. I clear my throat. 'Jack,' I say. 'It's me,' I pause. 'I just wanted to talk to you. I'm at the wedding, talking to some horrible people,' I laugh. 'I'm missing you. I'm – can you call me when you get this.'

I hang up. I lean against the railings, look out towards the Thames. I *could* live in the country. It's so beautiful there. I could give it a try. If it doesn't work we can come back, or maybe move away, maybe live somewhere else for a while. Spain, Amsterdam, Italy...

My phone rings.

'Hi,' I say, relieved.

'Hi.'

'Are you all right?' I ask.

'Yes,' a dark voice. 'I got your text, my phone's been off—' It's not Jack: a deeper voice; a tilt of something else.

My stomach turns. 'Who is this?'

'Sorry,' he laughs.

'Max,' I say, and curl into myself.

'Your number,' he says. 'It came up on my phone – maybe Wednesday – did you call? I've been away, in Abergavenny with some kids on a field trip. You didn't leave a message.'

'No,' I say. 'I mean, yes, I did call,' I say. 'I called because I'm here, in London. Are you back?' My phone beeps, a call waiting.

'Yes, I'm back. Are you still here?'

'Yes.' *Beep.*

'Where are you?'

'In town.'

'Working?'

'Yes, but it's finished.' I'm pacing, up and down. The beeping stops. 'Where are you?'

'I'm out and about. I could… come into town.'

'Could you?' I feel as if I've stopped breathing.

'Do you want to meet, have a drink?'

I look down at the cigarette; twiddle it between my fingers. 'Yeah,' I say.

I hang up the phone and breathe out. I'm smiling. I skip and ask a passer-by for a light. I take a deep drag. It goes straight to my head. I feel dizzy. My phone beeps and vibrates in my hand, a voice message, it says. I don't listen to it. I rush back into the venue and ask the receptionist to order me a cab. I'll go home, drop off my equipment. I switch off my phone and push it to the bottom of my bag.

Deeva doesn't come down to dinner. I want to go up to her room to see how she is, but Nim tells me we should leave her alone: 'Aloneness is important at this time,' she says. I watch as Soma fills a plate with food and quietly takes it upstairs.

No-one says much over dinner. It is so quiet that everyone seems to whisper: Can you pass me the salt? *Namaste*, the vino, the water. At one point Paritosh sighs loudly and tells some jokes, but his jokes are really bad and no-one laughs. Peter sits at the end of the table and stares at his food. I wonder what he's thinking. Throughout the entire meal, I try not to look at Jeet even though he's sitting right opposite me.

When everyone has finished, I help clear up. It's my turn to wash up and Nim's turn to dry. We load up the dishes and I fill the sink with hot soapy water. I can hear as people come into the kitchen to bring more plates and glasses, the clink of china and a low murmur, while Nim solemnly dries.

Soma flicks through the music tapes on the windowsill and slips one into the cassette player. Music fills the kitchen: urgent drumbeats and cymbals. She turns it up loud. Nim starts swaying. Paritosh comes up from behind her and grabs her hips, and soon their bodies make strange shapes around the room.

Soma stands and watches. Nim rushes up to her, her cheeks shining. 'Do you think she would be pleased to see us dancing?' She clings hold of Soma's hands.

The kitchen table is moved to clear the floor, and Paritosh grabs my hand, pulling me towards him, spinning me around and making me dance. He shouts and chants while I try to keep up with the quick beat of the drums.

The music gets faster and I pound my feet on the ground, my body loose, my head rolling, my hair over my face. The heat is rising, my heart beating so fast that I find it hard to breathe. The room seems to spin. And then I stop. Jeet is standing in the doorway, leaning against the wall. He is smoking; his eyes are narrow behind the swirls of smoke. He is watching me. Just like he did at the party. He is watching me.

I dance, I dance. I sway my body, my head, my hips. I dance towards him. I catch his eyes and he watches me, following me, and just as I get close I move away. His eyes are boring into me. He is making me feel alive. I move towards him again, I roll my hips, I say to him, 'Come on, come and dance.' I will him, but he just watches, a glint in his eye and a smile so slight that it might not even be there. I fling myself around the room, my arms flailing, my limbs loose. I feel light. I feel alive.

When I turn back to Jeet I see something else: an image against the darkness of outside. I jump. I stop. There's a white face: a ghost at the window. I scream. The image disappears. Everyone stops and looks around.

'A ghost, a ghost,' I shout.

Jeet walks to the window. He leans out.

I rush to be beside him.

There is nothing there.

'I swear I saw it,' I say. 'It was a ghost, it was there and then gone, a white face.'

I hear laughter in the living room.

Sam, Max and Josie are on the sofa. Sam and Max have their heads buried in cushions, they are laughing. They stop when they see me, holding their breath, their shiny faces, tears reddening their eyes. Then they point at me and the laughter explodes again. There is a sheet draped over Max's thigh.

Josie sits between them. Her face is solemn. 'They took that drug,' she says. 'They tried to scare you.'

The air feels cold. I wipe the sweat from my face. 'Why did you do that?' I ask. But they're still laughing, not able to answer me.

I kneel at their feet. 'What does it feel like?' I ask.

Their eyes look strange, just like Dad's did that night. As though the sockets are stretched; large black pupils like marbles.

'Fucking wicked,' Max says.

He takes two capsules out of his pocket, holds them out to me. I look at Sam: he is gazing at me; his face open, like a child's.

'*I'm* not going to do it,' Josie says. 'You don't know what might be in it.'

I look down at the capsules. I hear a door close. I look around and see Jeet walking outside. He is laughing to himself; someone must have made him laugh. I look at Sam and Max, like innocence. I take a capsule and pop it in my mouth.

I check my watch as the cab turns into Shaftesbury Avenue: 8.20p.m. I'm twenty minutes late. I ruffle my hair, rub coloured lipsalve into my lips; take a deep breath. Why am I so nervous?

The pub is smoky and busy, the fug and chatter hitting me as I open the door.

I see Max immediately, and my heart jumps. He is standing at the head of the bar: a mop of ginger hair, pale pinky skin, a black T-shirt. He has short sleeves; his spidery tattoos crawl down his arms. He looks as though he is reading, but by the time I have pushed through the crowd, a man has his arm around him.

'Max,' I say.

He looks at me, a glazed expression, before his face breaks into a smile. 'Sylvie,' he opens his arms.

Max is surrounded by people he knows: excited urgent banter, jokes and anecdotes, pints that get finished in one movement. I had images of us sitting in a quiet corner, somewhere to talk. I fidget, lean over the bar and try to order a drink. I fiddle with Max's packet of rolling tobacco. I had a cigarette at the wedding. But it was only one. Can I control myself and not have another? Does it really matter?

'What are you doing?' Max exclaims. 'Don't get yourself a drink. Johnny, get the girl a drink, and another for me.' The barman leans forward and asks me what I want.

'A glass of white wine.'

'Make that a large one,' Max shouts.

By the time my glass arrives, I have already made myself a cigarette.

Max and a blond-haired man are in an embrace, the blond man telling him something urgent, Max listening intently between laughs. He doesn't seem to notice me, standing at the bar, talking to no-one. I look around the pub, it's an arty crowd: pork pie hats and skinny trousers, cross-chatting between tables.

I reach around in my bag. My phone. I pull it out and turn it on. Three missed calls: all of them from Jack. I think about calling him. I think about standing outside the pub and telling him I'm having a drink with a friend. I press the message key: I'll text him instead.

'So, how are you?' Max is standing above me. I drop the phone back into my bag.

'All right,' I say. His eyes are bloodshot, his eyelids heavy. He takes a swig from his pint glass. 'It's good to see you.' I have to shout above the noise.

'Have you got enough to drink?'

I look down at my half-drunk glass of wine.

'Drink up,' he says, waving at the barman. 'I'll get you another one.'

We stay like this for some time. Moving with the crowd. We're trying to talk, nothing much, but Max is constantly being interrupted, and I'm wondering why I bothered to come. I could be sitting in the flat sorting out my negatives, listening to music, sketching. I could be getting ready to go home. But soon, after a couple of refills and a couple more cigarettes, I find myself chatting to his friends, answering their questions and laughing at their jokes.

'Come on,' Max holds my waist. 'I've had enough of these people.' He takes my hand and leads me to the back of the pub, to a door marked PRIVATE. The noise escapes behind the closed door, replaced by soft music, candlelight and small tables, intimate couples huddled together, and a group of men drinking champagne. I sit down at a corner seat. Max sits opposite me. I relax.

We sit. He has his hands behind his head, looking at me. I sit forward. I feel drunk, tipsy.

'I was having a strange time,' I say. 'At the wedding. I wanted to leave and then you phoned, as if you sensed it. Funny isn't it?'

'I guess,' he says.

'I wanted to see you.' I fiddle with a box of matches. 'If just to say hello. I thought you might feel... weird about me.'

'Why?'

'I don't know. It's just that the last time we met all that stuff happened and we haven't spoken about it. I was going to call, but... I didn't. I guess I've been busy.'

'Don't worry about it,' he says. 'It's all cool.'

He takes a drag from his cigarette, scans the room.

I lean towards him. 'Oh, Max. My life is so strange at the moment. Things are weird, with Jack, with work. I don't know what I'm doing.'

He looks at me. I want him to put his arm around me, but he doesn't. He looks at me and a smile creeps across his face. He glances around. 'I know what'll cheer you up,' he says, and takes a small white envelope out of his wallet.

It takes me a moment to realize what it is. 'You can't do that here, people will see.'

Max ignores me, chopping two thick lines of white powder onto the table. He leans forward, and in a swoop one of them escapes up his nose. He passes me the rolled-up note. 'Nobody cares,' he says, holding his nose.

I look at him for a moment, his heavy eyes, his pale skin. Do I want this?

'Go on,' he says. 'Before someone else asks for it.'

I lean forward with the tip of the note inside my nose.

I sit back. I laugh. He laughs with me.

Max gets more drinks. I've lost track of how many I've had. I make another cigarette. When he returns, I move my chair closer to his.

'Do you remember,' I say. 'That summer in Italy – the night we took ecstasy?'

He nods, takes a sip of beer. 'Yes, I remember,' he says.

***

I'm sitting in the corner of the room where the spider lives. If I had Jeet's camera I would *click click click*, but I haven't got Jeet's camera, so I'm humming instead, stroking the hem of my skirt, which feels silky, the tiles beneath my feet cold like chilled cream. I am tracing patterns with my toes and drowning in the sounds, the music in the kitchen and the shuffling and laughing of the boys. I am sitting in the corner of the room and I don't know whether I am sitting on the spider. When I light my cigarette the flame glows bright. I can see the paper burn.

***

I lean closer to Max. I touch his hand. 'Do you remember what it felt like?'

He looks at me sideways. He shrugs, 'Kind of,' he says.

'You must remember. It felt unreal,' I say. 'I remember feeling happier than I thought I could ever feel.'

***

Outside on the belvedere, my arms prickle cold, the air caressing my skin, the lights from the luminous hills sparking at me. I laugh and roll into Max, who stretches his arms around me and pulls me close. I feel so safe here against his chest, the blackness, his smell and warmth. I want to lie beside him, tell him things.

***

'I love Jack, I do,' I say. 'But there's something about him that I can't grasp. Something that just stops me from being totally relaxed, you know? On the face of it, we have everything: a nice house, a loving relationship, respect, we get on, you know, I find him attractive. But there is this thing, you know, and I don't know what it is.' Max is rolling a cigarette and watching me as I speak. 'I mean, I love him. I do. But sometimes I wonder whether he's just not interesting enough for me, edgy enough. I wonder whether because I had that weird time with my dad, that I will always only ever fall for people who are a bit of trouble, you know? Maybe I'm kidding myself thinking I can be normal, find a normal guy.'

'Why, what happened with your dad?' Max asks.

I stop. I look at him. 'You know,' I say. 'All that stuff that summer,' I pause. 'He provoked things, encouraged things to happen. You knew that, didn't you?'

He pulls a face at me, shrugs.

'No,' I shake my head. 'It was more than that, he fucking pimped me.' I've never said it like that. My heart is beating fast, I feel shaky. I look at Max. I wait for a response, but his face is blank. I take a deep breath, try to calm myself, but I feel speedy, out of control. I laugh. 'Oh, listen to me, caught back there. I should get on with my life. I should be happy with what I have. I've got a lot – look at me, I'm healthy, I'm attractive, I'm good at what I do, people like me, Jack loves me, I've got family, I've...'

Max listens, he occasionally rolls another cigarette, passes it to me or smokes it himself, and he gets us another round of drinks, puts another two lines on the table and then, in a moment of silence, he stands up and says. 'Come on, let's go.'

We sit together in the cab. Max's face changes from grey to orange as we rumble down busy streets. I look at him. I lean into him. He doesn't ask me if I want to go home. I don't ask where we are going.

We trundle across the river. Twisted roads turn to thoroughfares. We turn into an estate.

We climb the stairs in silence.

The flat smells damp. The air feels cold. The dull coloured walls and the broken lino. The light in the kitchen burns my eyes. Max takes a half-drunk bottle of wine from the fridge. I sit down. There are dirty pans on the stove, teabags on the table.

'What about you?' I ask, fingering the wine glass. 'How is your life?'

He looks at me. He shrugs. 'What kind of question's that?'

***

MTV is on but the television hurts my eyes. I prefer to put my head on his chest, feel the soft cotton of his T-shirt against my cheek. I don't know where Sam is; we lost him ages ago. Our fingers are knotted together; every time I move my fingers, he moves his with me: we've been staring at them for ages. It's been making us laugh. Earlier, I was lying on his bed and he wanted to change his shorts – they felt scratchy, he said. He was moving and talking and I was listening, but not listening. The sheets felt cool and slippery beneath my skin, like grass after it rains. I wanted him to kiss me: I should have asked him to. Now he's talking again; he's telling me about his mum and how she died. She had cancer. It started in her breast and then spread around her body. All her hair fell out, she had to wear wigs to the shops, and then one day she could no longer walk. The night before she died she let Max crawl into her bed and watch telly till way after his bedtime.

I look at Max, his soft face, his baby skin, and I want to tell him something. I want to tell him that I love him.

'You told me about your mother,' I say.

'Did I?' he looks surprised.

'Yes,' I say. 'You told me about her dying. I never knew you could be so open, so soft.'

'It must have been the drugs,' he laughs.

'It wasn't the drugs,' I reach my hand out to him, but he doesn't take it.

'What about you?' he says. 'What happened to you?'

'What do you mean?'

'That night. What happened to you?'

I was alone in the living room. 'You left me,' I say.

'We didn't leave you.'

***

The house is quiet. It's the first time that I've noticed that there is no-one around. I wonder what time it is. It must be late. I stand up, go to the window. There are no lights on in Jeet's van; he must be asleep. Would he mind if I knocked on his door and said hello?

I tiptoe to his van. I knock on the door. He doesn't answer. I try again.

The door slowly opens and his face looks bleary, his eyes swollen. He doesn't smile. Is he annoyed with me?

'I just wanted to say hello,' I say, and then, 'I took the truth drug.'

He opens the door some more and I climb in. I lie beside him in the bed. It is dark. My head feels as if there are a million buzzing bees inside. I want to say things to take the sound away. 'It was funny,' I say. 'We danced and we spun around and the music felt so cosy, and everything that you touch it's soft and nice and...'

'Like this,' he says, and traces his finger along my arm.

'Mmm,' I laugh as shivers run up and down my body.

'And this,' he says, as he lifts my T-shirt and kisses my tummy button. 'Does that feel nice?' he asks.

'Yes,' I breathe in, a flutter of butterflies.

'And this,' he says, as he kisses my stomach, his lips moving down. I close my eyes.

***

Max holds his hand out to me. I take it and follow him into the bedroom. He doesn't turn on the light. He leads me to the end of the bed where he kisses me. He undoes the buttons of my blouse, slowly. I look at him, the shadow of his face in the dull light. He kisses my breasts through my bra. I hold onto his head. He undoes my jeans, tracing his fingers around the rim of my knickers. He pushes me onto the bed.

***

It's funny, but Jeet is kissing me and I feel as if I'm not really here. As if I'm not beneath him, my lips to his, his tongue in my mouth. It's as if I'm watching it all happen below me, as if he can't touch me. It's weird. I could stay like this a while, closing my eyes, feeling the fumble of his hands, my clothes scrunch beneath me, his quick rasping breath. But then he climbs on top of me, and his hips stab my thighs like knives. My eyes are open and the shadow of his head, his neck; he bites. I suddenly want him to stop. I don't want to be here any more.

He whispers, things I can't hear: things to himself or to me as he grips hold of my knickers and pulls them down my legs.

***

Max is kissing me, softly, his mouth hot and wet. He is holding me, his large hands. I am moving with him, into him, I am releasing. He kisses me as if he is hungry for me.

'I've got you,' he says into my skin. 'I've got you.'

I open my eyes. I can see the contours of his back, the grey of his skin, his shaped hairless arms. I touch his arms, searching, a small ridge beneath my finger, hardly discernible. I try not to think of it, of the scars and how they might have disappeared; that maybe time heals. Jack heals me: a sudden thought, and an image of him standing at the end of a jetty reaching out to me. The sea is black, I don't know what's down there, but he takes my hand. He promises. I close my eyes and we jump. But the moment we hit water, I lose him. I plunge into darkness, silence, and suddenly everything stops. Will I make it?

I try to see Max's face, but it is deep in my skin, he won't look into my eyes.

Jack is shouting at me as I burst through the surface, his face beaming, water sliding across his skin. I reach out for him. He loops my legs around his waist, kisses me. We were in New Zealand, the year we met. I was so in love with him.

Max's skin is different, his smell sharper, more ripe, no fuzz of hair at the back of his neck. He kisses me roughly; he's not gentle like Jack.

'Wait,' I say, pushing him away. 'I'm not protected.'

He jumps out of bed and moves in and out of the light. He rummages through a drawer, rattles a packet and swears as he throws it into the bin. 'None left,' he says.

A sudden relief.

He makes a grunting sound as he grabs both of my thighs and pulls me to him, his body between my legs, his mouth on mine. 'Don't worry,' he breathes.

'What?'

'I said don't worry.'

'What do you mean?' I pull away.

'I've done this plenty of times before, I'm a professional.' He holds his penis and gently eases it inside me.

I gasp as he groans. He's slow at first and I'm thinking – This has got to stop. But I'm being carried along, carried by his rhythm. I close my eyes. It's dark, the smell, the heat, the feel of the sheets beneath me. Nylon sheets.

And there he is, there's Jeet: he's ramming hard and fast, so fast that I can hardly breathe, he's panting like a dog. I can't see him because my eyes are closed, but I can hear him: '*Fucking you, fucking you, I'm fucking you,*' he repeats, over and over. It burns, it hurts, I'm crying. I didn't stop it. I wanted it to stop, but I didn't.

I open my eyes, cold, senseless. I grasp both of Max's arms. '*Don't.*' I must whisper it. He doesn't hear me. His broad body looms; his pressure. I want him off me. '*No,*' I breathe. '*No,*' I say louder and try to push him away. He looks down at me. 'Please stop.' I twist my body away from him. I shuffle to the wall, grip hold of the covers. 'I'm sorry,' I say.

'What?' He kneels before me. 'What's wrong?'

'Nothing.'

'What? What did I do?'

'It's nothing, really. Don't worry. I just can't.' I want him to go away.

'For fuck's sake, Sylvie,' he says. 'What the fuck is wrong with you?'

'Nothing's wrong, I just can't do it, that's all. I've got a boy-friend, you've got a girlfriend.' I suddenly shout: 'What's the big deal?'

'For fuck's sake,' he rips himself away from me, switches on the light. He wraps a towel around his waist. He goes to leave and then swings back at me. 'You haven't changed, have you? You've got the whole fucking world running around you. Take a look at yourself. You're not the only person in this world, Sylvie.' And he leaves the room.

I lie on my side looking at the wall, the yellow stained paint. I start to cry.

Jeet didn't use a condom. He didn't even ask me, not that I would have known what to say if he had. He just did it, hard and fast so he wouldn't lose his erection, hard and fast for his own satisfaction while I lay there too frightened to move, to make a noise. When he came he made a sound like a woman, a desperate little squeal.

'I made you some tea.' I stir in bed, the unfamiliar sound of buses on the street outside. I turn over and open my eyes.

Max stands in the morning light, a cup of tea in his hand. 'I didn't know if you take sugar.'

I sit up and rub my face. My head hurts.

He sits beside me while I sip my tea. The blinds flap at the open window, it looks like a sunny day.

'Do you want some toast?' he asks.

When I get dressed I notice a picture of him and a girl on the mantle shelf. They're in a restaurant and he's looking at her, his eyes softened by what he sees. She has a nice face, open, approachable, trusting.

I eat my toast in the living room, perched on the edge of a sofa, its holes covered with throws.

'I'm thinking of moving,' Max says. 'Louise wants us to get a flat together, she's found a place. I wasn't sure at first, but it's closer to my work, it might be good to give it a go.'

'Why not?' I say.

We are silent for a while. I want to finish my toast, get a move on, go home.

'How's your photography?' he asks.

I shrug. 'It's all right,' I say.

'Your pictures? If you want to photograph any more of the kids, I'm sure they'd sit for you. I could ask them.'

I smile at him. 'That's kind,' I say. 'Maybe.' But it suddenly feels distant. Everything feels weightless. 'I don't know.' I get to my feet. I carry my plate and cup through to the kitchen. 'To be honest, I'm not sure it's really me. I keep on having ideas and I'm starting to visualize them more as paintings, it's like a kind of shift, maybe I should listen to it.' I turn to face him.

'You were always good at painting,' he says.

'Yeah, I suppose I was.'

As I get ready to leave, Max hugs me goodbye. 'I'm sorry about last night,' he says.

'No, I'm sorry,' I say.

'I didn't mean… you know.'

'It's OK,' I say. 'Really.'

I take my bag and follow him to the front door. In the hallway I notice something on the bookshelf in amongst the line of videos – big black writing: *A Month in Italy*.

'The video,' I say.

'What video?'

I take it off the shelf. 'I didn't know you had this.'

'Yeah,' he laughs. 'I've had it for years.'

I look at it, amazed. The video.

'I haven't even watched it,' he says. 'I can't because the bloody thing's Betamax. You should give it to Sam. He'd know what to do with it.'

I grip hold of it. *A Month in Italy*. I can't believe it. Here in my hands.

'Although I'm not desperate to be transported back there again, it's embarrassing,' he laughs.

I look up at him. 'Why is it embarrassing?'

'You know, kids' stuff. It seems so long ago now. It's almost like another life.'

I turn the cassette over in my hands: it was a long time ago; it's almost like another life. Another life.

I wake up in a pool of sweat, my T-shirt twisted around my body, the sheets a damp tangle at the end of the bed. I sit up. Josie's bed is empty beside me. What happened? Last night: I tiptoed past the boys asleep in the living room, the crackle of MTV. I ran a bath. I couldn't get the water hot enough. I was shivering. An image of a girl comes into my mind. Did I see someone at the end of the drive? Bria. She looked like a ghost, what was she doing there? A different kind of heat rises in me, this one is hot and sticky and close. I feel as if I might be sick.

My legs ache as I get dressed. There are faint yellow bruises at the top of my thighs.

Outside, Sam, Max and Josie are on the belvedere. Josie is talking, while Sam and Max lean back lazily in their chairs. I hug my cardigan to my chest and hurry past Jeet's van.

'Hiya,' Josie calls when she sees me. 'How are you feeling?'

'OK,' I say. I hover beside her; there aren't enough chairs.

'Here,' she pats her lap. 'You can sit here if you want.'

I curl onto her, keeping my body close.

Sam is fiddling with the video camera. 'We're trying to think of an idea for a film,' he says. 'The Florence Monster has died.'

'What do you mean?' I ask.

'It's finished. We've worn it out – it's boring,' he says.

'Oh.' I look out at the hills.

Max yawns, waves at us. 'I reckon we should wait till we're at the airport. We could do an *Airplane!* spoof, you know, crazy people in airports, crashed aeroplanes.'

The airport. It's almost time to go home.

Jeet comes out of the house. He stops and talks to Deeva, puts his arms around her and I watch as they hug. He holds both of her hands and looks down at her, says something that makes her laugh. She holds her head to his chest and strokes his stomach. I look away.

I get up and walk towards the view. I lean on the wall. I look out. The landscape looks different: flatter, duller.

'You were funny last night.' It's Josie, standing beside me.

I don't look at her.

'Are you OK?'

'Feel a bit sick,' I say.

'I knew you would, that stuff isn't good for you, whatever your dad says.'

A tear rolls down my nose and falls onto my hand. I rub my face. I can feel Josie's fingers on my back, as light as leaves.

'We're going to have some fun these last days, I'll make sure of it,' she says. 'We'll make picnics and go to the lake. We won't be afraid of the Florence Monster, scorpions, spiders or anything. It'll be fun,' she says, as I stand beside her, silently crying.

'You know,' she whispers, looking back towards the house. 'You could always ask your dad to tell him to leave.'

I look at her.

'He'll do it for you if you ask him.'

I shake my head. You don't know, I think. You don't know what he did.

'Go on, don't be silly. He's your dad,' she says.

I don't get a chance to talk to Dad for most of the day. He is working in the morning and he's only briefly at lunch. I watch as he closes his balcony shutters and I wait for him and Alanka to wake up from their siesta, but he doesn't re-emerge for what seems like hours. I walk up the stairs and to the end of the corridor. I hang around his closed door, listening, trying to hear for any noise. When there's nothing, I walk back towards my room. I try again and again, every ten minutes or so. I even count the seconds. And at last I hear the bedcovers rustling and when I knock he calls: 'Come in.'

I open the door and the room is dark and shadowy. 'What is it?' Dad says.

'I want to ask you something.'

I can't see his face, just his large arm and the mound of his body beneath the dark sheets. 'What is it?' he asks, his voice sounds sleepy.

I take a deep breath. 'It's Jeet,' I say. And in one breath I tell him: 'I don't want him here. I wondered if you might ask him to leave.'

He shifts in bed, sits up so I can see the shadow of his face. 'Why?' he asks.

'Because…' I pause. 'Because he is making me unhappy.'

I hear a groan as Alanka rolls over in bed. Dad sighs and says something, muffled, as he lies back down again. I can no longer see his face.

'What, Dad?' I stand forward, stretching towards him so I might be able to hear.

'I'll talk to you later,' he murmurs. 'I need to sleep.'

My head drops. I go to leave. Why? I think. Why won't you help me? I stop before I get to the door. 'Why won't you help me?' I say. The sheet rustles, he clears his throat. I don't know whether he hears me.

'What did he say?' Josie asks when I get outside.

I shrug.

'Did he say no?'

'No, he didn't say no.'

'But he didn't say yes either?'

I shrug again.

'*I'll* tell him to leave,' she says.

I'm too tired to say no.

Sam comes up from behind her. He is biting his nails, tearing at the skin. 'What's going on?' he asks.

'Sylvie wants Jeet to leave,' Josie replies. 'And she asked your dad, but he won't tell him to.'

'I'll fucking tell him,' Sam spits.

'No,' I say. I can see Jeet at his van. 'I'll tell him. I'll tell him to go.'

I go over. Sam and Josie stay on the belvedere. They don't watch.

Jeet is inside his van. The bed is stripped; he is taking the pillowcases off the pillows. I remember the blood: stains of it down my legs. I wonder if it was all over his sheets.

'Hello there,' he says when he sees me. 'I was wondering when you might come over. Have you been avoiding me?'

My heart is beating wildly.

I don't think about it. Sam says it's best not to. He told me just to say the first thing that comes into my head. 'I want you to leave,' I say quietly.

He looks at me, narrows his eyes.

'I want you to leave.' My voice gets louder. 'I want you to leave by the morning. When I wake up I don't want you to be here.'

'Hey,' his face softens. 'Come here, let's talk about this.' He pats the bed.

'No,' I say, my voice is shaking. 'I'm going to go now, I'm going to turn around and go back into the house and I never want to see you again.'

His face changes. 'All right, all right,' he puts his hands up to me. 'You want me to leave, well it just so happens that I'm going anyway,' he waves at his bags. He's packed his bags. 'I beat you to it, lovely. I'm going tonight. Uta called a couple of days ago, she's apologized, she wants to talk. I'm going to meet her and take her home, we're going back to London. Sorry I didn't tell you.'

My face is burning.

'Travelling is not just seeing the new, it is also leaving things behind,' he says, and turns his back to me.

I leave. I walk away. I hate him. I stride into the house. I climb the stairs two at a time. I slam the bedroom door. I sit on the edge of the bed. Uta phoned him and he didn't tell me. He is leaving. I hate him. I am shaking. I am so angry I want to kill him.

Josie comes to see if I am all right. I tell her I want to be left alone, and when she closes the door I cry. I bury my head in the bedclothes and I cry.

All I can see is her face, her long brown hair, her arms opening to him, him kissing her and them driving around Italy together, up and down the hills, laughing and listening to Joan Armatrading.

I stay in my bedroom until the light starts to fade. At one point I think I sleep. Josie knocks on the door and tells me it's time for supper. I tell her I don't want to eat.

I creep out of the room. I wander around the house. Everyone is outside sitting at the table. I wonder whether he has left yet, if he has gone. I don't want to go into Dad's room, so I let myself into Deeva's and watch from the window. He is there. He is sitting next to Nim and he is chatting, he seems happy, relaxed. It makes me sad. Dad sits at the head of the table, Alanka beside him, she is giggling at something Dad has said. Deeva is laughing, her head on Peter's chest. Nim helps Soma serve the food. I watch as it becomes dark and the candles flicker, and I wonder what happened to the magic, if it ever was really there.

I wait until the table is cleared and people go back into the house. I wait and I watch as Jeet organizes his van, his body lit up through the open doors. I listen as he says goodbye. Nim calls from the house, Yogi slaps his back. I see Dad approach him. I see him put his arm around him and give him a hug and I suddenly feel as if I made a mistake. I suddenly don't want him to go, my heart aches and I don't want him to go. I told him I never wanted to see him again, how can I be so cruel? It's not even true.

I rush out of the room. I jump down the stairs and run out of the house. He is standing at his van. My dad is there too, but I don't care. I fall into Jeet's arms sobbing into his chest. I am crying. He holds me. I am crying. I don't know how long my dad stands there. I don't care what he thinks. All I want is for Jeet to hold me and tell me that everything is going to be fine.

'Hey,' he says, kissing my head. 'You came back.'

I don't want to let go. I don't want to let go.

'What's wrong?' he says, trying to see my face.

I don't want to let go.

'Talk to me, Leela,' he coaxes, and the name fills me with warmth. I rub my eyes. I look at him. 'Look at that sweet little face,' he smiles.

He tells me to get into the van. 'We'll go for a drive, have a talk,' he says.

When we drive away, I look towards the house. I see Nim walking into the kitchen. I see Dad sitting at the living-room table. I see Josie standing by the TV. I see Sam, who is watching me.

Jeet drives up into the hills. He drives for some time. I don't care where he's taking me, my head is on the headrest and I'm letting the motion rock me. For some of the time I close my eyes.

We stop by the side of the road. Jeet turns the headlights off and it is dark. He lights a cigarette, his face shadowy in the match's glow.

'So, what am I supposed to think?' he asks. 'You oscillate from one place to the next, stay, go – stay, go. I said from the beginning I wasn't going to hurt you – but you, you make it difficult for me.'

'I'm sorry,' I say. I don't want him to be angry with me.

He reaches for my hand. 'Look,' he says. 'I have to go, but that doesn't mean the end. I will tell Uta about you. We will see each other again. She will like you, I know she will. I'll give you my number, and when you are ready, perhaps I will take you away – from home, from school, from all those things you despise.'

I look at him. Despise? Do I despise home? I never said that.

'Come here.' He holds out his arms. I hug him. 'Come here, fragile one. Come here,' he whispers and he is kissing my skin, my neck, my cheek, my face. 'Come here you pretty little thing.' He tries to kiss my mouth.

I pull away. 'Don't,' I say.

'Don't?' he looks surprised. '*Don't, don't, don't,*' he mimics. He pushes his hands up my skirt.

'No,' I say more firmly. 'I don't want to do that.'

'You don't want to do that?' He backs away. That strange dark shadow, that hardness, as though there is nothing soft inside. 'Come on,' he says, grabbing my thigh.

'No,' I say again. I am shaking. I back into the corner. I don't want him to touch me.

'No?' He slams his hands on the steering wheel. It makes me jump. 'What is it with you?' he shouts. 'Are you so arrogant, so in control that you can determine when and how you can have me? Are you now rejecting me? Who the fuck do you think you are?' His face is strained. I don't recognize him. He is scaring me. 'You are no-one, you hear me? No-one.'

'Please take me back,' I cry. 'Please take me home.'

He looks at me, he reaches out, flicks the hem of my skirt. '*Y Y Y You*, I don't want you anyway. It was only a game. You're a fucking whore,' he shouts. 'You open your legs to me so readily. You believed all my talk. Well, it was all bullshit. Look at you playing the innocent, pretending to be this sweet little virgin. You're a fucking liar, a manipulator. I should have—'

307

'I'm not!' I shout, tears stinging my eyes. 'I'm not any of those things. I'm not rejecting you. I just don't know what to do. I don't know.'

He looks at me. He looks at me for a moment, and I think that maybe his face is softening, maybe he'll put his arm around me, tell me everything is OK again, take me home.

'Get out of my fucking van,' he shouts. He leans over me and opens the door. 'Get out,' he screams, and with one shove he pushes me onto the ground. I land with a thud, stones piercing my skin. He pulls the door closed and the van speeds away. I watch as dust explodes from beneath its wheels. I watch as the taillights disappear over the hill and all I'm left with is darkness.

Darkness, it's like a blanket. The silence vibrates. I don't want to look to either side of me, to see the trees, the black holes, so I keep my eyes down. I quietly get to my feet. I press my chest to try to muffle the beat of my heart, my breath. A sting, blood on my fingers, my skirt – it's Alanka's skirt. If I stand here a while, maybe the sounds will stop and I'll be able to move again. How long did we drive, how long did it take? I can't remember. He has to come back. He can't just leave me here.

There's a noise. Something there beside me: a twig, a crackle, what is it? I stand absolutely still. I try not to move, I try not to breathe. I can hear something, a snuffling, it is close, so close it could be near me, at my feet, is it breathing? Is it a pig or a boar? Or a man in the bushes, waiting on all fours. I keep my eyes straight ahead. If I stand totally still it might think I'm a tree. But then it might smell me. If I run it might chase me. A sound of leaves, movement in the trees but it's higher than before. I look up. The sky is dark blue. Where is the moon? My head buzzes with silence, the noise has gone. I slowly put one foot in front of the other.

I remember, I remember that the moon was big. It rose over the tree in the garden, over the hills as we drove. If I walk I will reach that moon, I'll find my way home. There are noises out here in the dark. Noises like animals, things hiding in the trees. What did Deeva tell me – there are boars and owls and deer, there aren't murderers, not here. If I think of good things, happy films I have seen, like *The Sound of Music*: sitting on the floor at home, next to the Christmas tree, eating mince pies; or *Grease*: Sam and me in the bath singing along to the soundtrack – Mum recorded the entire film onto cassette, and I know all the words. Maybe I should sing. Jeet will come back, he can't leave me here, no-one would leave someone here in the dark on the side of the road, far away from home. If a car comes, if a car comes, I will hide in the bushes, down in the ditch where no-one can see me. I'll be OK, I'll get home again, to London, to my friends, to see my mum.

I walk. I don't know where I'm going. I walk I walk. I walk faster – my breath with my steps – I count, one two three four five six seven eight. I break into a run. I no longer hear the sounds. I run and run. I can run all the way home, up and down the hills, up and down.

My ankle goes. I slip, my flip-flop bent around my foot. I stop. The pain. I rub it. Don't cry, don't cry.

I kneel. What do I do? What do I say? I don't know any more.

I reach down to the ground. I touch it first and then sit on the cold tarmac. I put my head in my hands and I close my eyes. I curl into a ball, so tight and so small that maybe no-one will see me.

I feel the ground vibrate well before I hear the noise of the engine. I put my hand down. I listen. Is it a van? Soon I can hear the high whine of a moped. I get to my feet and shade my eyes as the single light rises through the darkness. I'm not afraid. I hobble to the side of the road. I don't hide. Closer, I hear my name. 'Sylvie.'

He stops beside me, my brother stops. It doesn't surprise me. 'Are you OK?' he says, and it feels like a dream. He tells me to climb on. I hug him tightly, the warm smell of his T-shirt. I should have thought he'd come. The air is cool and soft; it chills the tears to my cheeks. I don't ask how he found me. I lean my head against his back and watch as the moon rolls high over every hill.

Back at the house there's an empty space where Jeet's van had stood. Josie meets me at the door and helps me up the stairs. Max stands in the doorway of the living room, he watches me. In the bathroom Josie cleans my cuts, rubs cream into my bruises. When she's finished she says: 'There, it's all over now.' In the bedroom, she tucks me between the sheets and quietly leaves me to sleep.

I can't stop crying. It's silly really, but I'm sitting on the floor in the middle of the living room and all I can think about is my baby. I'm hiding. I'm trying to screw my eyes closed, here in the darkness of my hands, because I don't want to see.

My baby. I open my eyes. I've never really thought of it like that, but that's what it was, it was my baby. I stare at the floor. I shake my head, a sudden calm. I see myself in a sunlit room. I'm holding a newborn in my arms, but I'm not young like I was – I'm older, as I am now. It is my niece Isabelle. I feel calm, as if it's right that she's there and I'm there with her.

But it wasn't right, was it? All that time ago. How could it have been? That's why I didn't tell my mum, my dad, my friends; only Sam and Josie knew, and Carol, Josie's mum, and Jeet, of course.

I was still living with Carol when I did the pregnancy test: Josie made me do it when I told her I was ill. I felt sick, strange, discon-nected when in a room full of people, heavy and inert as if the room was closing in on me and I had nowhere to go. I also hadn't had a period in three months. It was Sunday morning, early. I'd woken suddenly from dreams of motorbikes out of control, my body lying paralysed at the side of the road, the wheels skidding towards me, squashing me into the tarmac, burying me deep below concrete. I waited in the half-lit hallway outside Carol's bedroom as she slept. The door was open and the morning light filled the room with red. She was sleeping, facing me, her long plaits on the pillow.

And then she opened her eyes. When I told her what had happened, she talked to me in hushed tones. I sat on her bed and she made me tea and toast with strawberry jam, which was too sweet for me to eat. She took me to the clinic and promised not to tell my mum. She sat me in the kitchen with Josie and Sam. It was November, I remember because it was a week after my birthday, and it was dark outside even though we'd only just returned home from school. She told them what had happened. Josie played with a hair scrunchy, rubbing it between her fingers and over her knuckles; she didn't once look up. And I didn't look at Sam. I couldn't bear to. I didn't talk about it after that day, not when Carol asked me if I was all right, out of earshot of the chaos at dinner time or on a weekend once Mum was back and I'd call on Josie. I never thought to tell my mum. Sometimes when I was with her a feeling would hit me, a strange sadness that left me dizzy, but I never put it down to what had happened. I didn't let myself think about it; it was simple, really. But of course it wasn't simple: I've since read that the body remembers things. However hard you try to forget, it is imprinted in your cells.

I rub my face, wiping my nose on my sleeve. I never told my dad. Maybe I should have. I've blamed him for so long, and he doesn't even know. I should tell him what happened. It suddenly seems so clear to me.

'Sam,' I say when he picks up the phone. 'I've realized the problem.'

'Oh, hello stranger,' he says sarcastically.

'No, listen, I've realized why I haven't seen Dad.'

'Yes?'

I pause. I take a deep breath. 'I've realized,' I say, 'that I can't not forgive him when I don't know what I'm not forgiving him for.' I laugh. 'It's simple: I remember you saying to me years ago, on the belvedere in Italy – you were telling me I wasn't being honest with myself, well, I'm not being honest with myself now. It's the abortion isn't it? It's the pregnancy and then the abortion, and we never talked about it, did we? I didn't talk about it to anyone. It's as if I haven't let myself think about it, and I haven't let myself think that actually Dad doesn't know. I never told him, so I haven't even given him a chance to be a father to me, have I?'

Sam is silent, so I go on:

'I haven't told anyone. I thought it would just disappear, but how could something like that disappear?'

Silence again.

'Sam, are you there?'

'Yes, I'm here,' he says quietly.

'All that time – all that fucking time. I thought I could just let it go, walk away.'

I stood outside my school waiting for Jeet to come and get me, my suitcase packed and beside me. I believed he'd come. I believed everything he said to me. How could I have been so stupid?

'I can't walk away from something like that,' I say, almost to myself. 'It's more than half of my life.'

I saw Jeet only once in London. It was when I told him what had happened. He picked me up on Camden Road. I was wearing a miniskirt, but it was too short and kept riding up when I walked. I was so nervous when we got to his flat that I had to go to the toilet, but it wouldn't flush. We sat in the living room and I cried and told him I hated school, I hated life. He gave me some money. He told me I should go home and pack my bags and that he would take me away. He promised. I was sitting on the sofa. He was kneeling on the floor between my legs. He tried to kiss me, but all I could think about was what I'd left in his toilet.

'Sylvie.' It's Sam. 'I'm here, not there. I'm here. 'Listen to me.'

'What?'

'What's going on? You haven't phoned all week and you spill out all this. You've got to backtrack a little bit, sis. Where's all this come from?'

'I've just been doing some thinking.'

'About Dad?'

'Of course.'

'OK,' he pauses. 'But talking to him about this – think about it. What will it gain? Him knowing. How will it change things?'

'Change things?' I stop. 'I don't know – it'll just make things clear. We'll be able to start again, won't we?'

He doesn't say anything.

'Sam, why are you acting so weird?'

'I'm not acting weird,' he says. 'I just don't know what you'll gain from reliving the past. It's like a dirty great wound. I'd let it go, Sylvie.'

A wound. Is that how he sees it? But it's not a wound; it's a part of me, it's all I've known for years.

'I'm just not sure that it's Dad who needs to know about all of this,' he says.

I stop. I pause.

I hear a baby in the background. It's Tom, then Josie. 'I'm sorry,' I say. 'Josie needs you, you have to go—'

'Wait,' he says, putting his hand on the mouthpiece. He speaks to Josie. I hear her talk urgently, she says Jack's name, something else. There's something about her tone.

'What did she say?' I ask.

'Nothing, nothing,' Sam answers. 'It's all right. It's just Jack—'

'What about Jack?' A sudden panic.

'It's all right—'

'What's all right?'

'Nothing, don't worry, he just called, that's all. Last night. I wasn't going to say anything, but he was in a state, he couldn't sleep. He was convinced there was something wrong – something happening.'

'What do you mean, something happening?'

'Something happening to you,' he says. 'He thought you were with someone, you know, last night.'

I blush. 'Did he?'

Sam laughs. 'I told him he was being paranoid. But he said he'd been trying to phone you. Where were you last night?'

The blood rushes to my face, I close my eyes. Last night. 'Nowhere,' I say.

'Nowhere—'

'—I was doing a wedding, then I came back to the flat. It's fine. I'll call him. I should have called him earlier, it's all fine, really.'

I feel ill. What have I done?

Sam pauses.

I don't say anything. I try not to think of anything. I try to ignore my heart. I hope he can't hear that I'm shaking.

'How much does he know?' Sam asks finally.

A panic strikes through me. 'How much does he know?' I'm fighting thoughts of Max. I don't want him in my mind, nowhere, here, please. 'What do you mean?'

'Does Jack know about what happened with Jeet? Did you ever tell him?'

I pause. I look at my hands. Heaviness. 'No,' I say.

'Why not?' he asks carefully.

Why not? Loads of reasons. I had them. It meant nothing. I was a child. What good would it do him to know? It's the past; it's got nothing to do with now. Why didn't I tell him? 'I don't know,' I say.

'Well, think about it will you?'

Sam tells me he has to go, but I don't want him to. I like having him there at the other end of the phone, as I listen to the distant sound of their life – the echoes from the kitchen, chairs scraping, Josie singing to Tom, Isabelle coming in from the garden, her small voice, asking all the questions that are so important to her at her age, at just six years old.

'How is Dad?' I ask. 'Have you seen him?'

'I wanted to tell you,' he says. 'All these things I wanted to tell you about how I think he is, but I don't know any more. He's not well, but he doesn't want to admit it.'

'Not well?'

'It's like he's given up, maybe it's because he's been on his own all this time. It's like he's got nothing left, nothing to look forward to any more. Except for the inheritance of course,' he laughs. 'A load of sad fantastical bollocks.'

'But there's always us,' I say. 'Isn't there?'

'Just go and see him, we'll talk about it after that. Just see him.'

He wants to go. I don't want him to. 'The video,' I say suddenly.

'What?'

'The video – I've got it. The one from Italy – the one we made.'

'That summer?' He sounds excited.

'Yes, isn't it funny?'

'But, I thought—'

'I've got it,' I say. 'Here in my hands, but it's Betamax. Maybe you could convert it and we could watch it. How funny is that?'

'But how come you've got it? I thought it was—'

'Max,' I say. 'He had it all this time. He gave it to me.'

Sam is quiet.

'Maybe we could meet, maybe I could give it to you, I'd love to see you,' I say. 'Please meet me, later today. Tomorrow, before I see Dad.'

'OK,' he says.

We agree to meet the next morning in town, near Dad's hotel. On one condition, Sam says, that I see Dad and then I go home. He says nothing about Max.

I hang up the phone. I stand at the window and look out at the tranquil gardens: the blue sky, the bright sun, the birds are singing. I wonder what they're singing at home, if Jack can hear their songs. I feel heavy and sad. Will Jack understand? Will he forgive me? Do I tell him everything?

I pick the videocassette up from the floor. That summer,

encapsulated in a small piece of plastic. Sam says that Dad has given up. I clutch it to me, a sudden rush of hope. He's been living alone. He must be lonely. Maybe he wants someone; maybe he'll open up to me, let me look after him. I could leave. I could go to America. We could get to know each other, father and daughter. I stop, put my finger to the glass, I trace the letters of my name: perhaps he'll just listen.

I watch a pigeon swoop to the window box; one of the eggs has hatched. It puts its beak into the baby's mouth. It's the bigger pigeon. I hope it's the father.

I sit outside a café and wait for Sam. I'm drinking coffee, which is probably a bad idea as my stomach hurts, and I keep glancing at the time. Dad's hotel is just streets away and I wonder if he has had coffee here; if he has seen what I see now. It's a sunny morning, warm and bright. I shade my eyes. Sam's car swings into a parking space across the street, and seeing him calms me, but then Josie waves and I catch glimpses of Isabelle and Tom in the back, and it annoys me. Why did he have to bring the family? I never see him on his own, not any more. Then I remember it's Sunday. Isabelle squashes her face against the window and it makes me smile.

Sam gets out of the car and pulls on his jacket, while Josie carries Tom. Isabelle jumps down and stands at the curb, bright in her pretty pink dress. Josie is dressed in baggy trousers and a flowery shirt, her hair in a loosely fixed bun, curls falling around her face. She and Sam talk between them, and Josie suddenly looks angry. They are arguing about something. I sit forward – is it me? Am I asking too much of Sam, coming here today, helping me? But like a gust of wind they are suddenly laughing again and I remember what Max said – it is not always about me. Sam pulls Isabelle onto his shoulders, and then puts his arm around Josie as they wait to cross the road and I think how grown-up they look. Sam is dressed casually in jeans and flip-flops, a baseball cap. He suddenly looks like a man and I wonder when he grew up and why I've never noticed it before.

They cross the road. Sam lets Isabelle down and she runs to me. She snuggles against me and sings 'Aunty Sylvie, we're going to the Natural History Museum.'

'Are you?'

'After tea,' Josie trills. 'We're having a drink here first.'

Tom smiles and squeals when he sees me.

'He's changed,' I say.

'That's what happens to babies when you don't see them for months,' says Sam, and it hurts me. My throat constricts and tears well into my eyes. I rub my forehead and force a smile.

'Hey,' Sam throws his arm around me. 'I didn't mean it, stupid,' he kisses me, his stubble scratching my face. 'Silly thing, don't cry in front of the kids, they'll think you're weird.' It makes me laugh. I catch sight of Isabelle looking up at me, her stare intent. She looks away shyly.

'Are you all right?' Josie touches my arm.

'Come on, Sylve,' Sam says. 'It may surprise you. You may not feel a thing.'

I'm embarrassed as I sit down. I want to apologize and say, it's not just that that's making me cry.

We order drinks and sit in the sun. Isabelle excitedly asks questions about dinosaurs, while Josie breastfeeds Tom, and Sam tells me about his latest documentary. He is animated, happy. I feel for the videocassette in my bag, but I wait before I give it to him. I want to ask if it's important that he goes to the museum today, more important than seeing his dad, than accompanying me? I relax when he talks; I'd forgotten how funny he can be. He makes me feel better, and I want to tell him that I miss him. Perhaps they could all come and stay, take a trip out of London. And perhaps one day the two of us could go away, the way things used to be. I want to say lots of things to him.

We finish our drinks and Sam gets up to pay. 'Right gang, let's get rolling,' he messes up Isabelle's hair. 'The dinosaurs await us.'

I sit back and watch them as they get ready and I suddenly feel tired. I don't know whether I'll see Dad. Maybe I'll just go home. Josie strokes my hand: 'Do you want Sam to go with you?' she asks.

I look over at Sam, who hesitates and steps towards his wife; Isabelle clings onto his leg. 'But you're coming with us,' she says looking up at her dad. He strokes his daughter's face. She sucks her thumb and looks up at me; she doesn't smile.

'No, it's all right,' I say. Of course he has to go; how could I have imagined it otherwise? There are more important things in his life than this.

Josie kisses me goodbye and takes Isabelle's hand. Isabelle turns as she walks across the road, 'Love you,' she calls and I wave at her and tell her I love her too and it makes me cry again.

Sam hugs me. 'Come on Sylvie, you're stronger than this.'

'I'm not,' I say. 'I'm not strong.'

'What is it?' He holds both my hands and I look up at him, his soft eyes squinting in the light, fine creases catching the shadows.

'I'm scared,' I admit.

'It's your choice,' he says. 'Just tell yourself that. Nothing has to hurt, not if you've had enough of it. Not if you want to be happy.'

'I have had enough,' I say, and for the first time I think I mean it.

As I wave goodbye I realize I forgot to give Sam the video. I rush towards the car as it pulls away, calling out. But it's too late. The car turns the corner and then it's gone. I am left with the video, a sudden weight in my bag.

I arrange to meet my dad at his hotel. He's staying at the Connaught. Apparently the people who tracked him down about his inheritance are footing the bill.

He tells me to wait in the foyer. I take many deep breaths.

I watch as he walks slowly down the stairs. He is wearing black, black trousers and a black shirt, his body is big and heavy, his small light-footed steps. He hasn't seen me yet. He readjusts his waistband, squints around the room. I suddenly feel calm. 'Dad,' I wave.

'Hey, toots,' he says. 'You came to see your old dad.'

Closer, his face is red and puffy, broken veins in his cheeks. He seems weightless and fragile behind his eyes. He reminds me of his father, my grandfather, long dead. It makes me sad.

When he hugs me I can smell fresh alcohol.

'Shall we go for a walk?' I say.

'Oh, really?' he frowns.

'Yes, come on, I'd like some fresh air.'

We walk to Hyde Park. Dad walks slowly. I watch as the sweat creeps down his neck. He is telling me about the inheritance. They found him over the internet. Some distant relative had died, hadn't written a will, and they tracked him down as the next of kin. 'It's incredible really,' he says.

'Extraordinary,' I agree. I don't tell him it sounds like a scam.

At the park we walk to the fountain where Dad lowers himself onto a bench. He frowns at the thick grey sky. 'London,' he says. 'It's such a shit hole.'

It makes me laugh. I look into the distance and notice the way the light is caught in the water's glow.

He has age spots on his hands, dry and scaly skin. I wonder if he eats properly, how he copes on his own. He squints at me in the silence, knocks his hand against my leg. 'So, how's my beautiful daughter?' he asks.

I look at him. His eyes are distant. I'm not sure he really wants to know.

'I'm fine, good,' I say. 'I'm working, you know, doing my photography. I'm with this lovely guy. His name is Jack. I'm missing him. We're getting married—'

'Oh, yeah?' Dad half looks at me. 'Marriage, hey? I remember that one. It's the biggest waste of time and money ever invented.' He glances at me. 'I'm so much happier now I'm on my own.'

'Are you?' I ask. He gazes into the distance, chews his mouth as if he hasn't heard me. I don't tell him we wanted him there.

We sit for a while, quietly. His hands twitch. He rubs the sweat from the back of his neck. He seems uncomfortable, but I don't want us to go, not yet. 'A funny thing,' I say, reaching into my bag. 'I found this,' I pass him the videocassette.

'*A Month in Italy*,' he reads. 'What is it?'

'It's the video we made that summer we stayed with you. Remember? When we came with our friends.'

He looks at me blankly.

'I thought you might want to see it.'

'No,' he says. 'You don't want me to have it.'

I frown at him: 'It's OK,' I say.

'But what would I do with it? I've got no use for it, lovey.' He passes it back to me.

'But I thought you might want to see it, all the people who lived in the house.'

'Oh, the house.' He shakes his head. 'I don't want to see the house.'

I look at the cassette in my hands. I suddenly don't want it, a strange feeling, as if I need to get rid of it, give it away. Perhaps it's Dad who needs to have it, not Sam. There must be something in it that I want him to see.

'Take it, Dad,' I say, passing it back to him. 'You never know, you might find it funny.'

'Really?' he says, looking at it.

'Yes,' I nod. 'Send it back to me when you're done with it.'

He puts it on the bench beside him, twitches, 'Damn flies,' he says. I can't see any flies. He looks at his watch. 'You want to stay out here long?'

I shrug. 'We don't have to,' I say, 'if you don't want to.'

He sighs: 'Your dad's OK.' He shifts his weight. 'It's OK. I'm going to get this money and I'm going to set up a trust fund for you guys. It's a lot of money,' he says. 'This man was a billionaire and, remarkably, he never spent any of it. And then he goes and dies and the whole thing is coming to me,' he laughs. 'This sort of thing could only happen to me, eh? I knew it would happen one day. I knew I'd make it.' He looks into the distance, at nothing. 'I'm just going to stay here another week or so and it'll be sorted, they're doing it as quick as they can. I'm hoping to give you about half a million: you'll never have to work again. What do you think of that?'

'That's great, Dad.' I touch his hand, his rough skin. 'That's really generous.'

'You'll see,' he says. 'Your dad will come good in the end.'

We sit silently for a while. I watch as children play with a ball, a couple with their yapping dog. The dog jumps into the fountain, the children laugh. 'Look,' I say, pointing as the dog swims in circles trying to get out. Dad squints towards the light, he nods before looking back at his hands. I watch him and I wonder what he notices, whether he notices anything at all.

It starts to rain, fine drops like spray.

'This fucking country,' he says. 'What's with this stupid weather? We get extremities in California: sometimes we have the most amazing storms, but mostly it's sunny. And then there are the fogs; they come rolling in from the mountains and cover the whole town. It makes it impossible to leave. You can spend days in one place, disconnected from the rest of the world, not like this.'

'You left here a long time ago,' I say.

'It was the best thing I ever did.'

His fingers twitch, each finger touching his thumb as if he's drumming a beat. The skin on the back of his hands is so dry it's peeling. Closer, I realize the marks are not age spots, but blisters. I don't ask how he got them. I look at my own skin, it is soft and smooth, the beginnings of tiny lines like ripples in sand. I think about the wound: what Sam said, picking at it, not letting it heal. He said it didn't need to hurt. Didn't Dad say the same thing to me all those years ago?

'Look at the time,' Dad says, glancing at his watch. 'I've got to get back. An important phone call.'

He finds it difficult to get up. I help him. As we get to the path, I notice he isn't holding the cassette. I look behind me: it is still on the bench. I stop. I want to tell him to wait, but I don't. There is something about his face, the way his eyes scan the ground, the way his mind is somewhere else: I don't want him to leave it in his hotel room, on the plane, in the dustbin outside his house. I found it. It's mine to lose.

I don't go back to get it.

On the walk back to the hotel, we are silent. The rain stops and there is a break in the clouds, a stream of sunlight brightening the pavement. A puff of wind is caught in the trees, a light dust of raindrops. An elegant woman passes and smiles at me, and I wonder what she sees: is it a father and daughter taking a stroll, or perhaps it's just me she's responding to – perhaps I look happy.

We stand outside. He doesn't invite me in. I go to kiss him.

'Come and see me again, eh?' he says.

I notice his scarred eye. I hadn't thought to look. It is the same as it was, while the rest of his face has fallen.

I nod, but I don't say anything.

He pauses a minute. 'I'm... It—' his brow creases as he stares at the ground.

I suddenly feel his hands. It shocks me. His palms are large and warm, strong around mine. 'It was a hard time for me,' he says, a pleading look on his face.

I glance down, at his feet in front of mine: his slip-on shoes, stained and old, the white skin of his feet just visible, and I remember those shoes. It was a hard time for me.

'I know it was, Dad,' I say, and I feel the lightness as I kiss him goodbye.

ACKNOWLEDGEMENTS

I would like to thank everyone who has read my novel at its various stages – Jess, Nicko, Em, Ben, Sarah and Emily – but particularly Jane Rogers for her excellent guidance, my agent Judith Murray for her unfaltering belief in me, and my editors Tasja Dorkofikis and Charlotte Webb for the finishing touches. I would especially like to thank my mother, Jane, who has always been interested in my mad schemes and has dropped everything when I've needed her, my loving husband Nick, who makes it all possible, and Dora, of course, for arriving with impeccable timing.